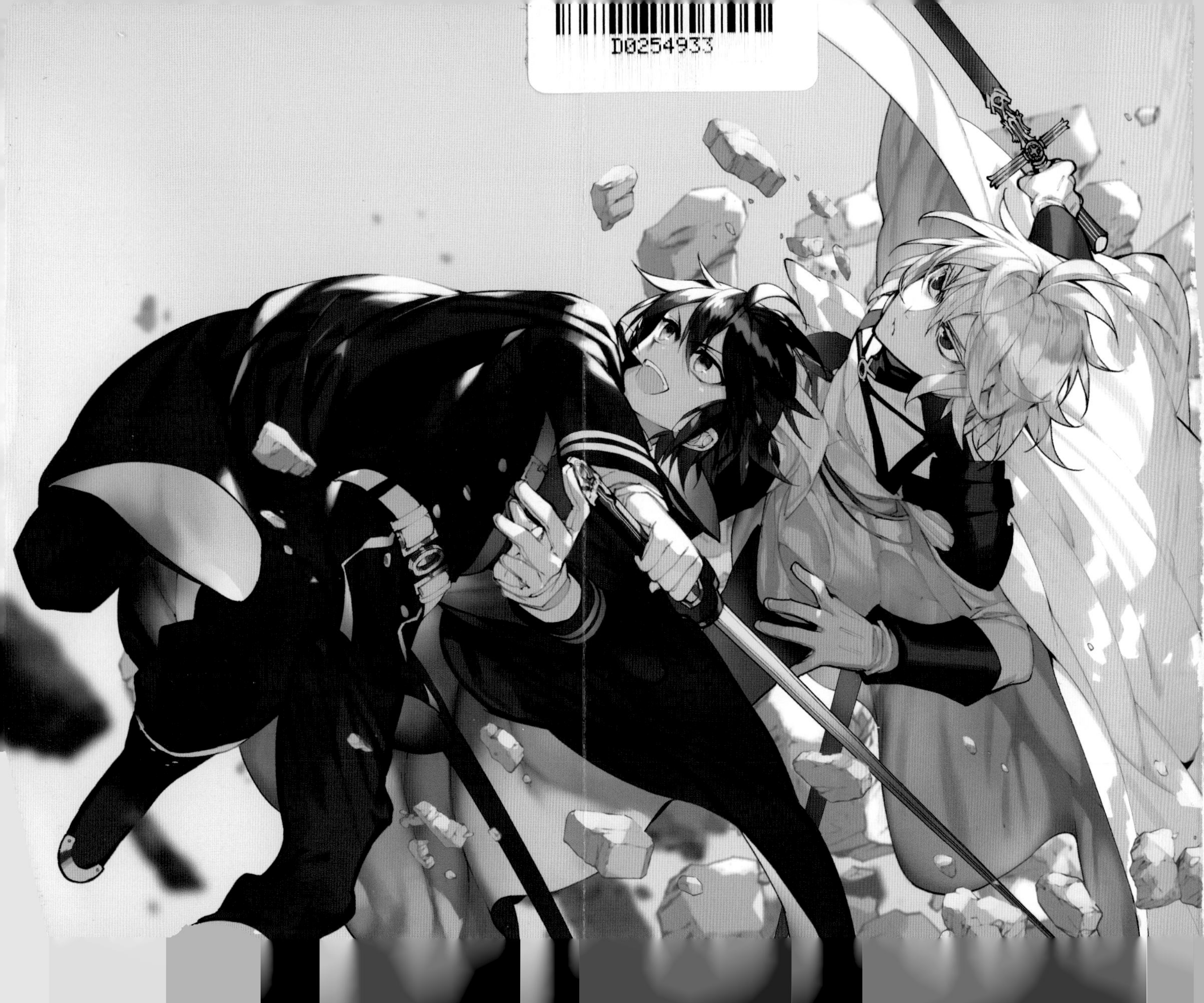

Seraph of the End

—VAMPIRE REIGN—

11

STORY BY **Takaya Kagami**
ART BY **Yamato Yamamoto**
STORYBOARDS BY **Daisuke Furuya**

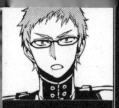

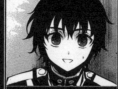

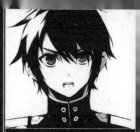

YUICHIRO HYAKUYA

A boy who escaped from the vampire capital, he has both great kindness and a great desire for revenge. Lone wolf. His Cursed Gear is Asuramaru, a katana.

YOICHI SAOTOME

Yuichiro's friend. His sister was killed by a vampire. His Cursed Gear is Gekkouin, a bow.

SHIHO KIMIZUKI

Yuichiro's friend. Smart but abrasive. His Cursed Gear is Kiseki-o, twin blades.

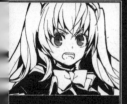

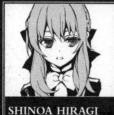

SHINOA HIRAGI

Guren's subordinate and Yuichiro's surveillance officer. Member of the illustrious Hiragi family. Her Cursed Gear is Shikama Doji, a scythe.

MITSUBA SANGU

An elite soldier who has been part of the Moon Demon Company since age 13. Bossy. Her Cursed Gear is Tenjiryu, a giant axe.

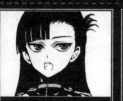

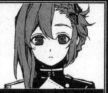

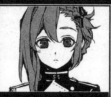

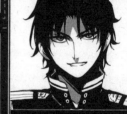

GUREN ICHINOSE

Lieutenant Colonel of the Moon Demon Company, a Vampire Extermination Unit. He recruited Yuichiro into the Japanese Imperial Demon Army. His Cursed Gear is Mahiru-no-yo, a katana.

SAYURI HANAYORI

A 2nd Lieutenant and Guren's subordinate. She's devoted to Guren.

SHIGURE YUKIMI

A 2nd Lieutenant and Guren's subordinate along with Sayuri. Very calm and collected.

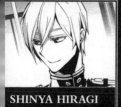

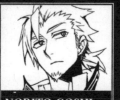

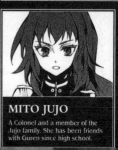

MITO JUJO

A Colonel and a member of the Jujo family. She has been friends with Guren since high school.

NORITO GOSHI

A Colonel and a member of the Goshi family. He has been friends with Guren since high school.

SHINYA HIRAGI

A Major General and an adopted member of the Hiragi Family. He was Mahiru Hiragi's fiancé.

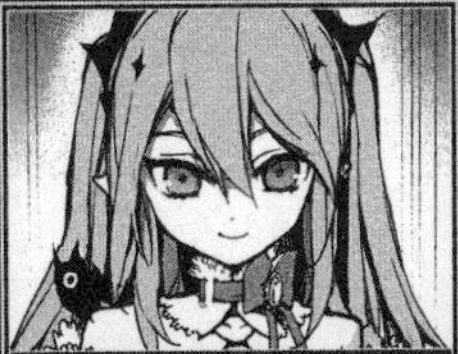

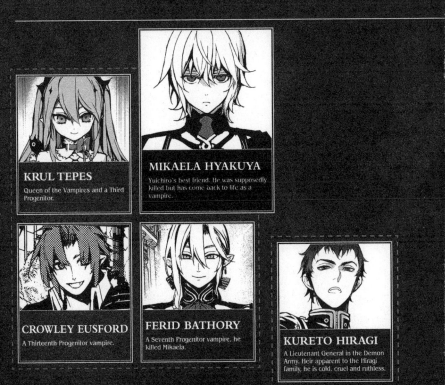

KRUL TEPES

Queen of the Vampires and a Third Progenitor.

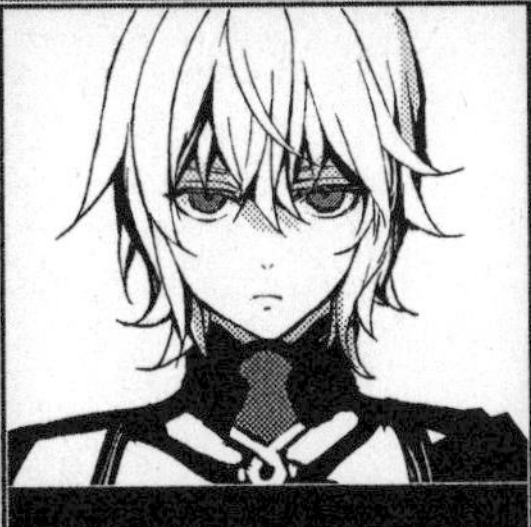

MIKAELA HYAKUYA

Yuichiro's best friend. He was supposedly killed but has come back to life as a vampire.

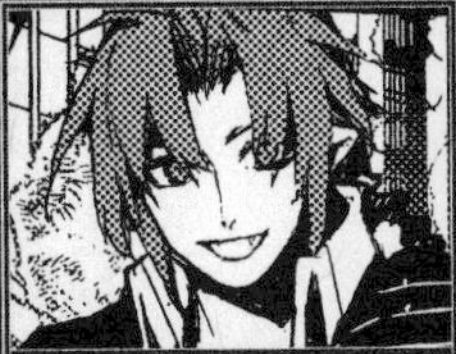

CROWLEY EUSFORD

A Thirteenth Progenitor vampire.

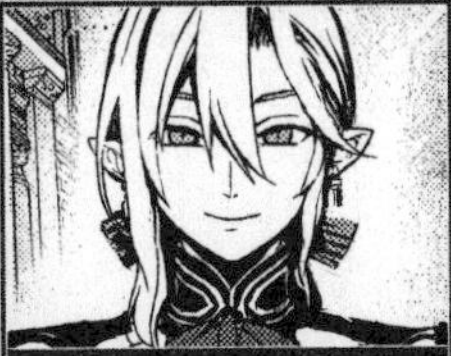

FERID BATHORY

A Seventh Progenitor vampire, he killed Mikaela.

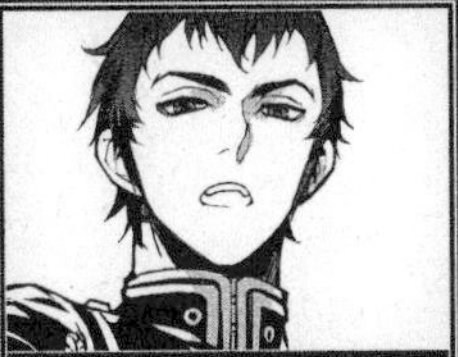

KURETO HIRAGI

A Lieutenant General in the Demon Army. Heir apparent to the Hiragi family, he is cold, cruel and ruthless.

STORY

A mysterious virus decimates the human population, and vampires claim dominion over the world. Yuichiro and his adopted family of orphans are kept as vampire fodder in an underground city until the day Mikaela, Yuichiro's best friend, plots an ill-fated escape for the orphans. Only Yuichiro survives and reaches the surface.

Four years later, Yuichiro enters into the Moon Demon Company, a Vampire Extermination Unit in the Japanese Imperial Demon Army, to enact his revenge. There he gains Asuramaru, a demon-possessed weapon capable of killing vampires. Along with his squad mates Yoichi, Shinoa, Kimizuki and Mitsuba, Yuichiro deploys to Shinjuku with orders to thwart a vampire attack.

In a battle against the vampires, Yuichiro discovers that not only is his friend Mikaela alive, but he also has been turned into a vampire. After, Yuichiro undergoes further training and not only grows stronger as a fighter, but also becomes much closer to his squad mates.

Under orders from Kureto, the Moon Demon Company attacks a vampire enclave in Nagoya, suffering massive casualties. Even Guren is captured! Shinya, Shinoa Squad and the remaining survivors fight their way out and stumble across Mikaela. Shinoa allows Mikaela to take Yu and escape. Finally reunited, Mikaela and Yu discuss what they need to do next, but both the Demon Army and the vampire forces appear to be up to something suspicious...

Seraph of the End
—VAMPIRE REIGN—

Seraph of the End
VAMPIRE REIGN

11

CONTENTS

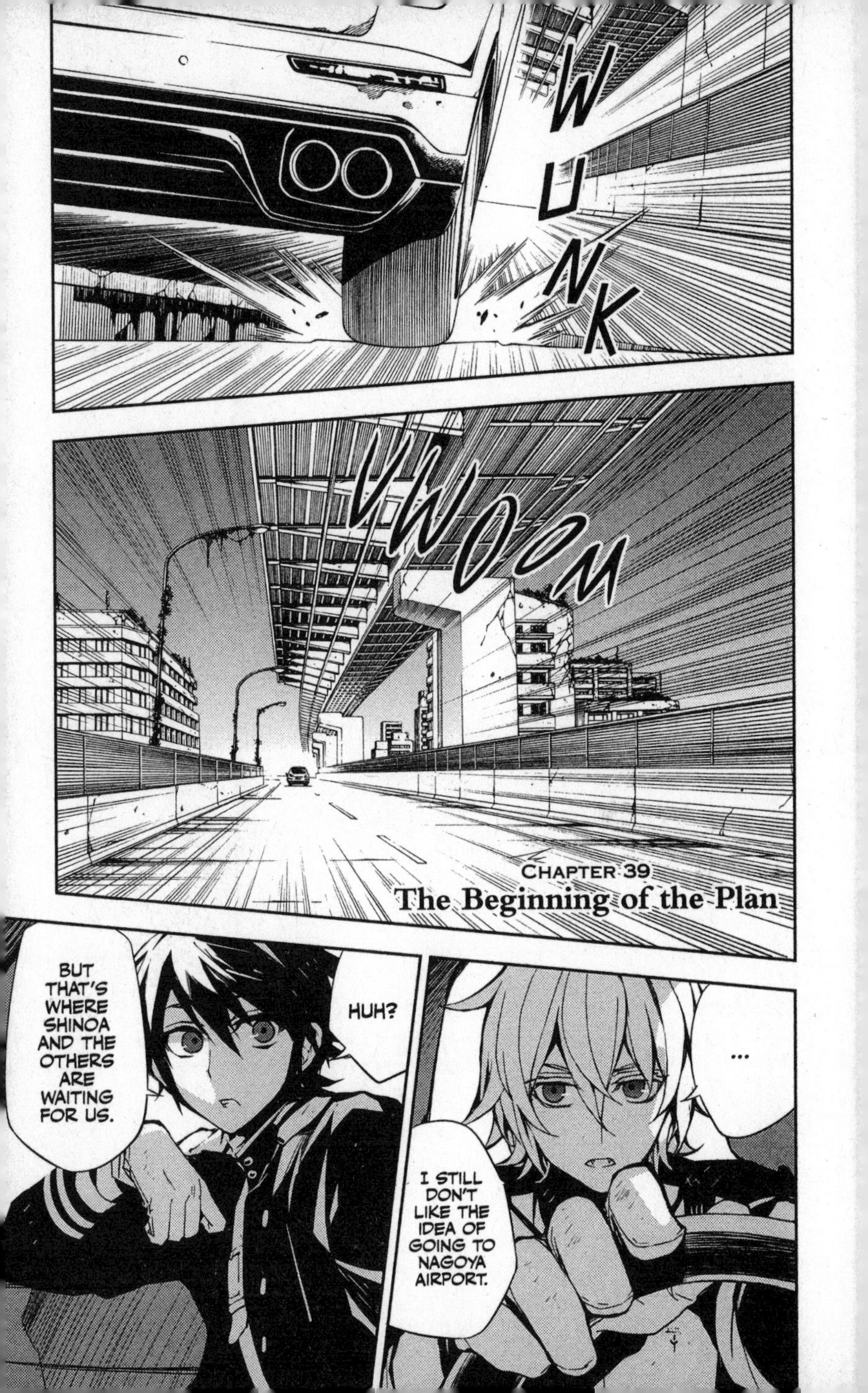
WUNK
VWOOM
CHAPTER 39
The Beginning of the Plan
...
I STILL DON'T LIKE THE IDEA OF GOING TO NAGOYA AIRPORT.
HUH?
BUT THAT'S WHERE SHINOA AND THE OTHERS ARE WAITING FOR US.

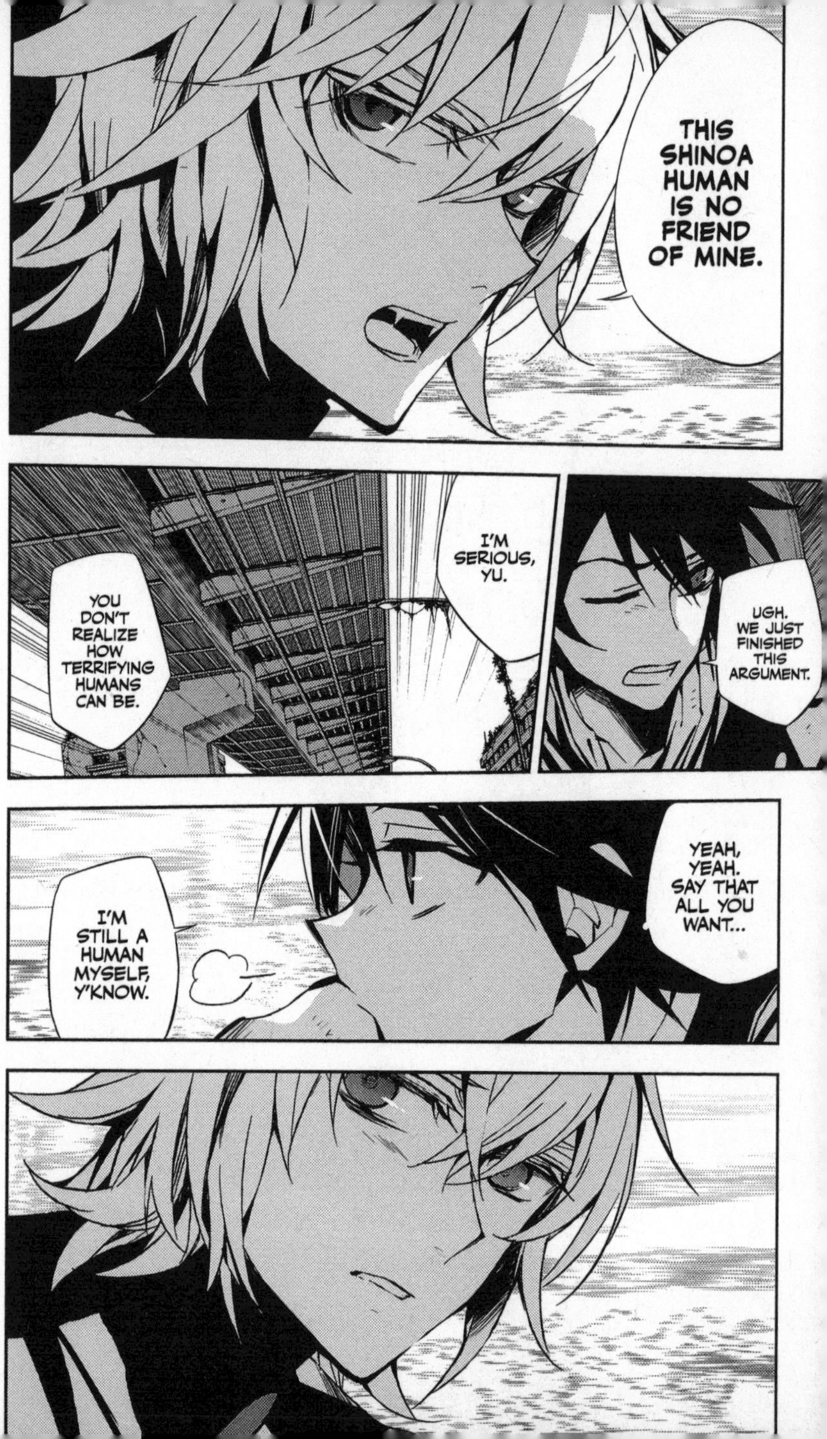
THIS SHINOA HUMAN IS NO FRIEND OF MINE.
UGH. WE JUST FINISHED THIS ARGUMENT.
I'M SERIOUS, YU.
YOU DON'T REALIZE HOW TERRIFYING HUMANS CAN BE.
YEAH, YEAH. SAY THAT ALL YOU WANT...
I'M STILL A HUMAN MYSELF, Y'KNOW.

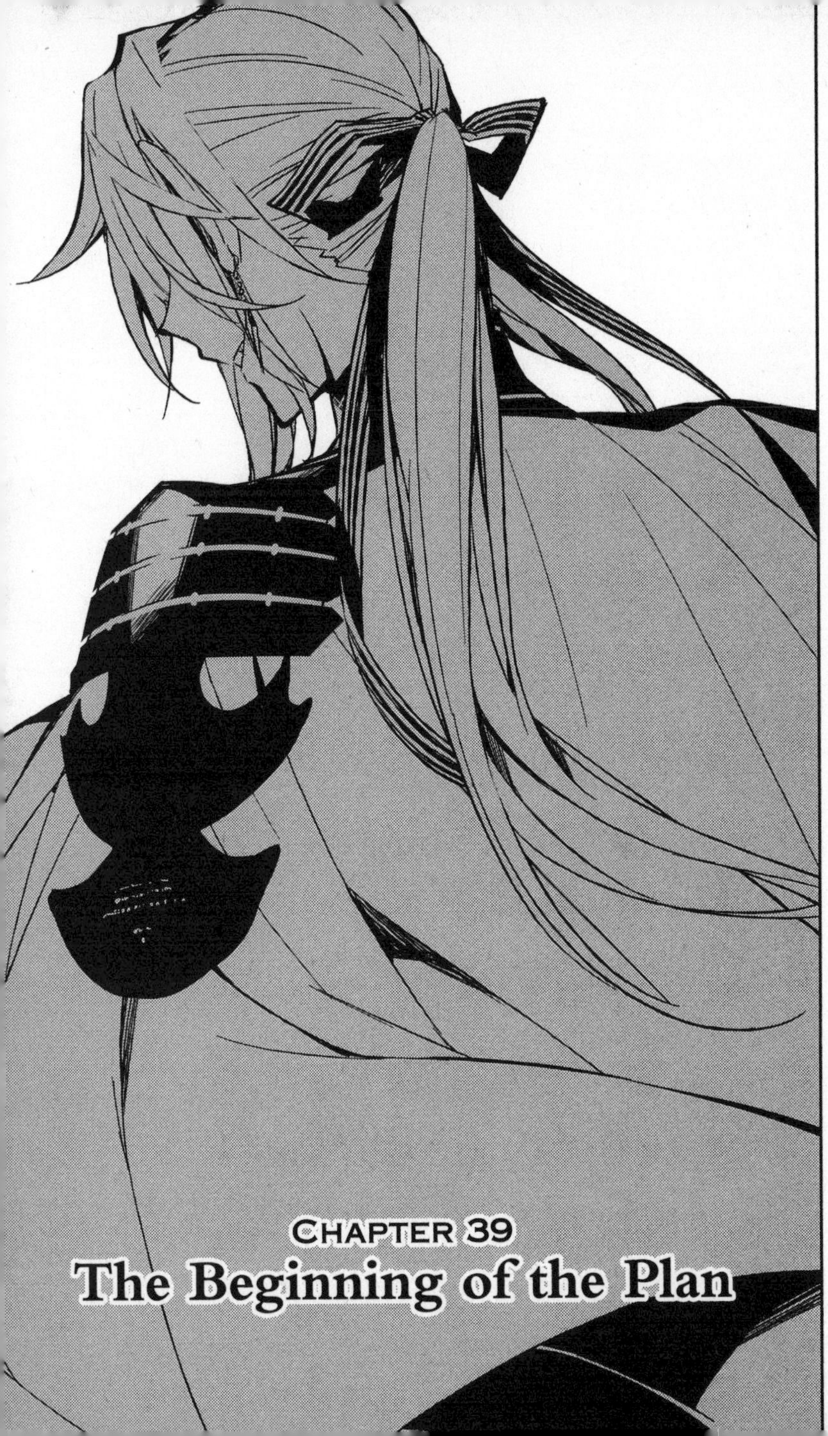

CHAPTER 39
The Beginning of the Plan

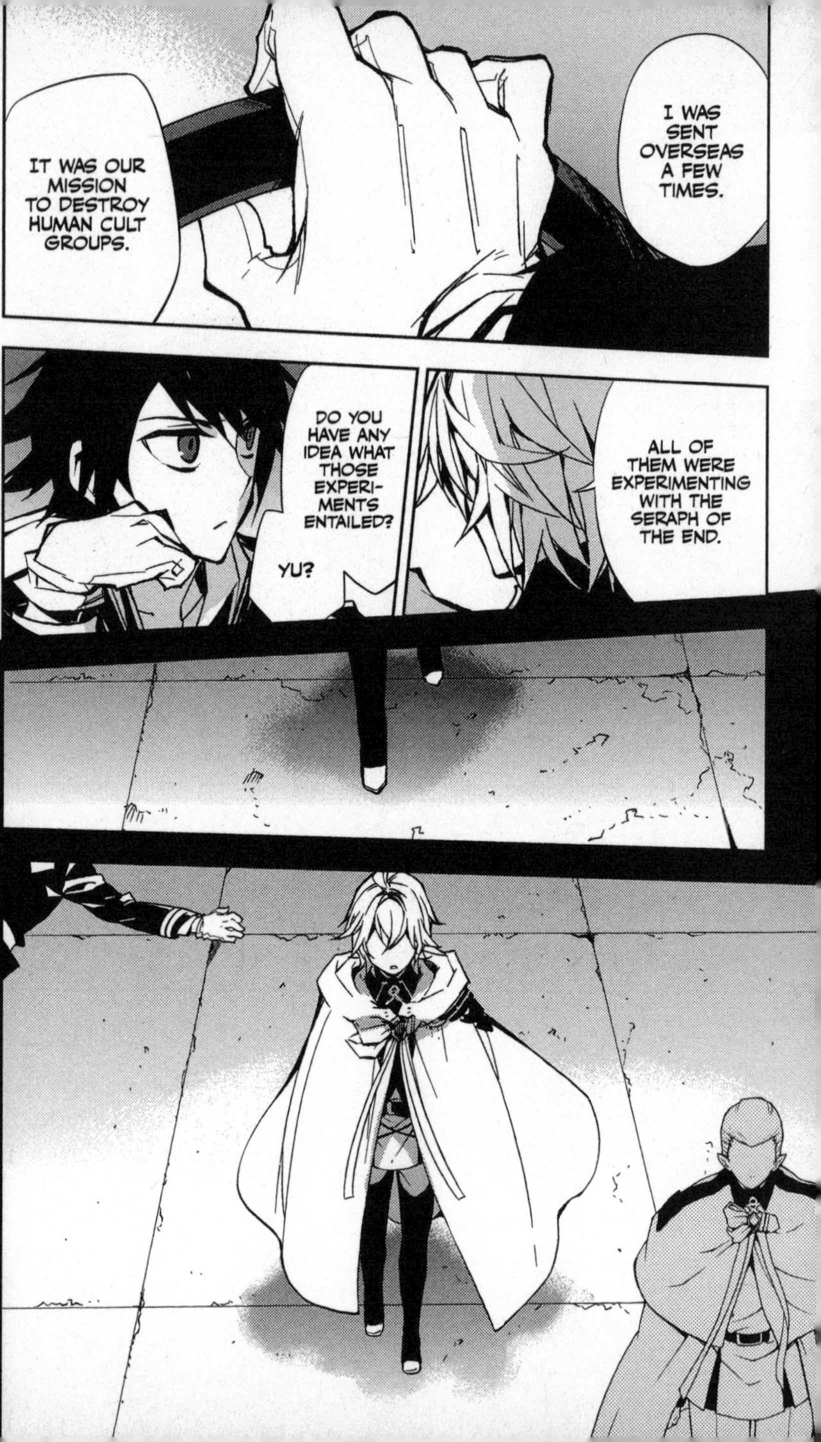
I WAS SENT OVERSEAS A FEW TIMES.
IT WAS OUR MISSION TO DESTROY HUMAN CULT GROUPS.
ALL OF THEM WERE EXPERIMENTING WITH THE SERAPH OF THE END.
DO YOU HAVE ANY IDEA WHAT THOSE EXPERI-MENTS ENTAILED?
YU?

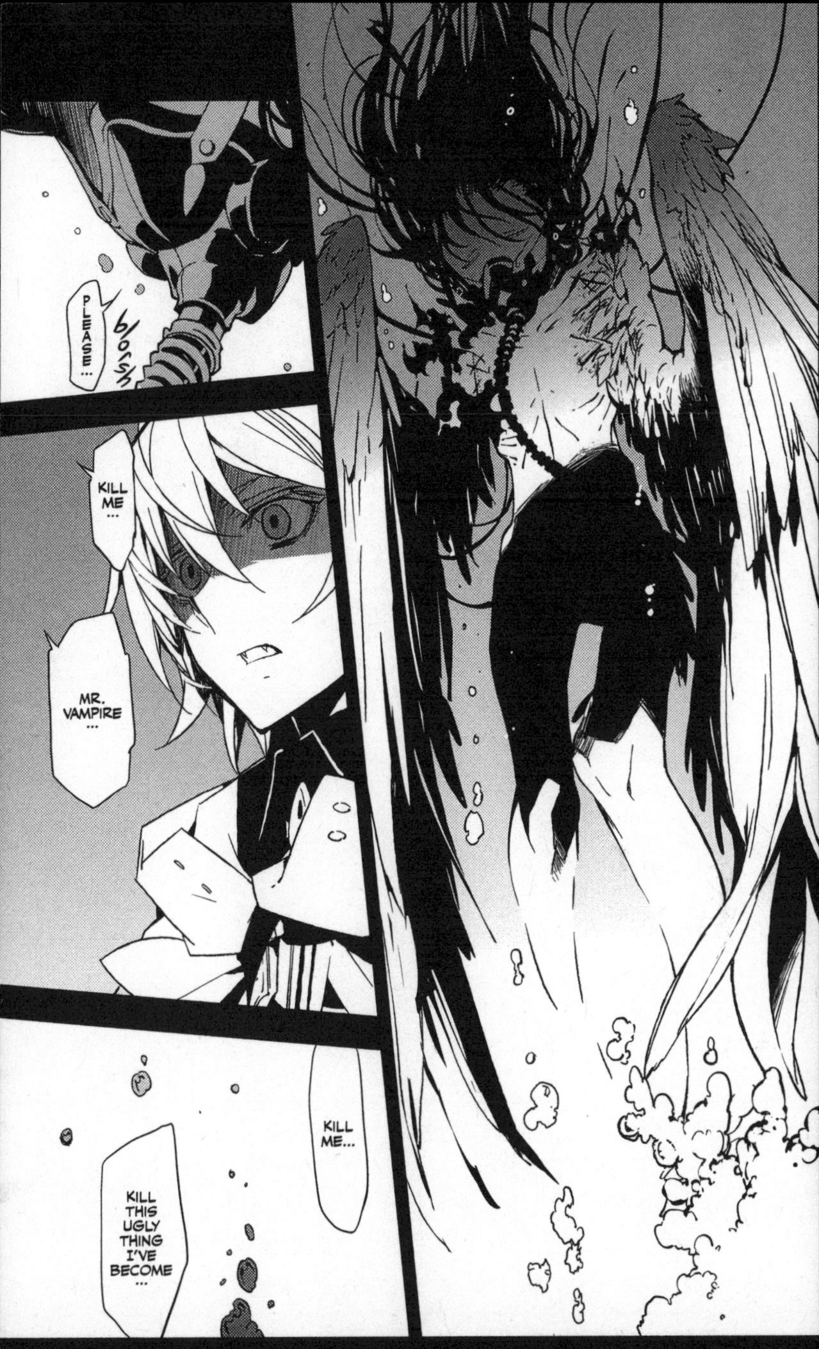
blorsh
PLEASE...
KILL ME...
MR. VAMPIRE...
KILL ME...
KILL THIS UGLY THING I'VE BECOME...

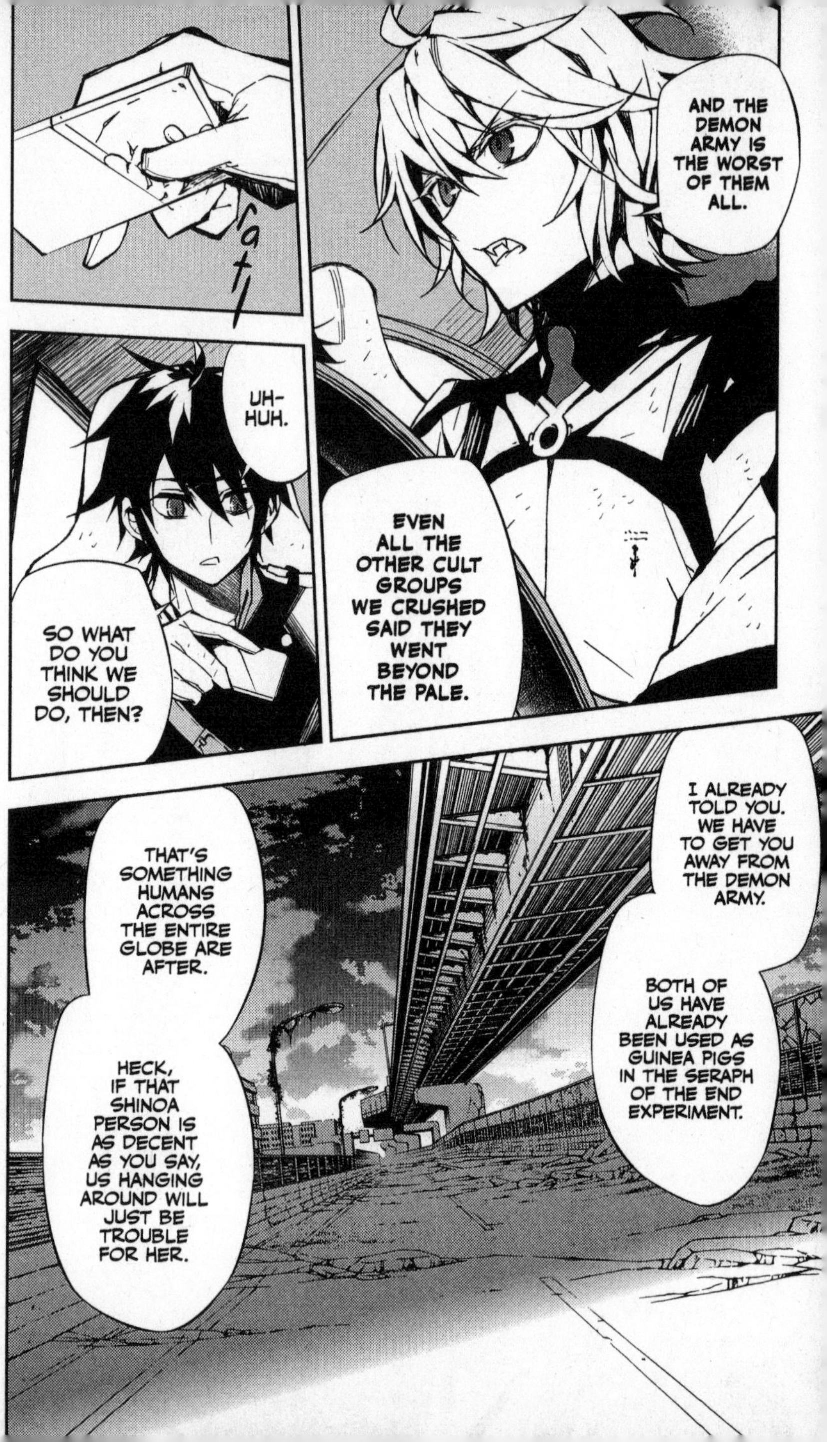
AND THE DEMON ARMY IS THE WORST OF THEM ALL.
EVEN ALL THE OTHER CULT GROUPS WE CRUSHED SAID THEY WENT BEYOND THE PALE.
UH-HUH.
SO WHAT DO YOU THINK WE SHOULD DO, THEN?
I ALREADY TOLD YOU. WE HAVE TO GET YOU AWAY FROM THE DEMON ARMY.
BOTH OF US HAVE ALREADY BEEN USED AS GUINEA PIGS IN THE SERAPH OF THE END EXPERIMENT.
THAT'S SOMETHING HUMANS ACROSS THE ENTIRE GLOBE ARE AFTER.
HECK, IF THAT SHINOA PERSON IS AS DECENT AS YOU SAY, US HANGING AROUND WILL JUST BE TROUBLE FOR HER.

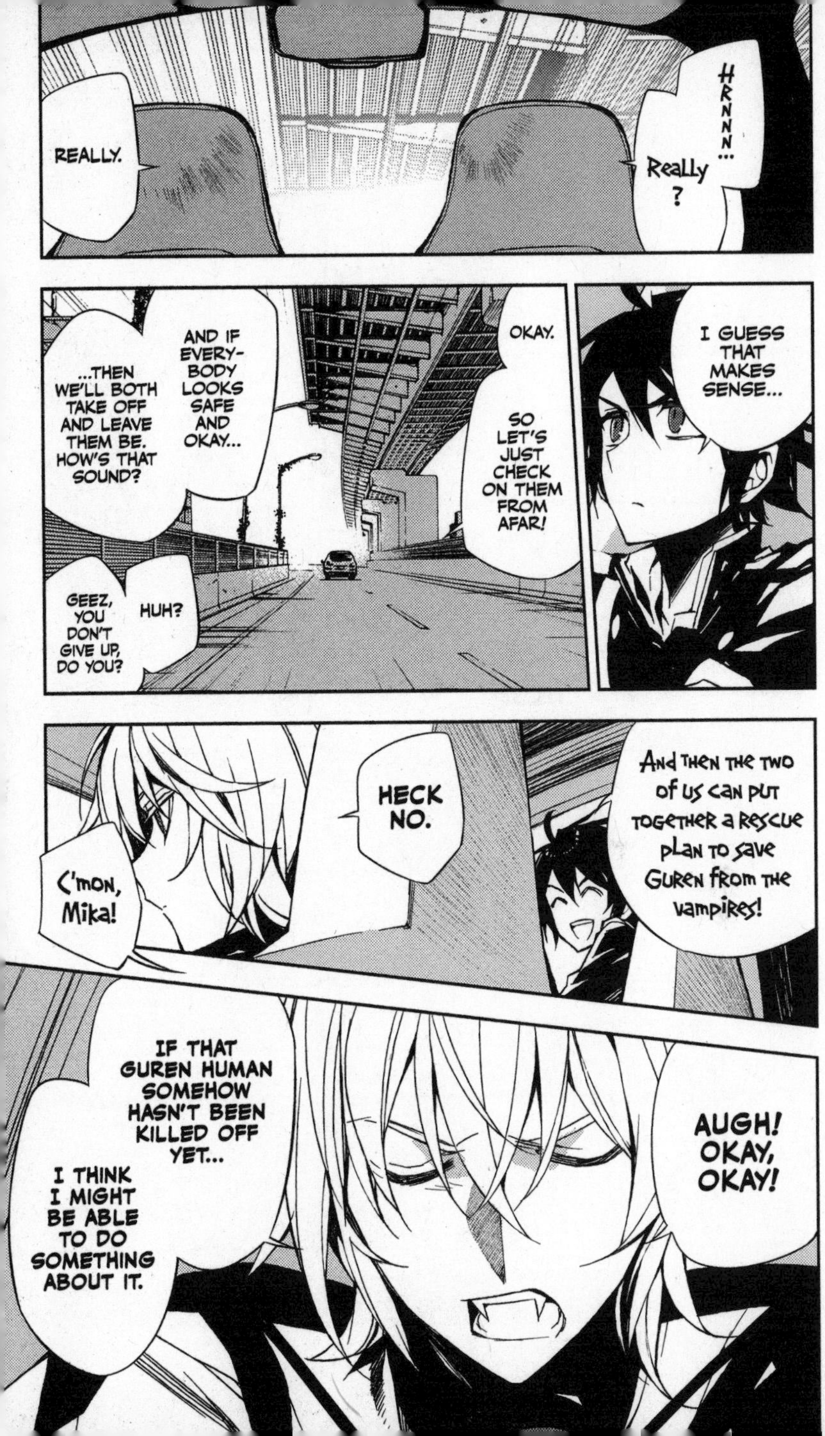
HRNNN... Really?
REALLY.
I GUESS THAT MAKES SENSE...
OKAY.
SO LET'S JUST CHECK ON THEM FROM AFAR!
AND IF EVERYBODY LOOKS SAFE AND OKAY...
...THEN WE'LL BOTH TAKE OFF AND LEAVE THEM BE. HOW'S THAT SOUND?
HUH?
GEEZ, YOU DON'T GIVE UP, DO YOU?
And then the two of us can put together a rescue plan to save Guren from the vampires!
HECK NO.
C'mon, Mika!
AUGH! OKAY, OKAY!
IF THAT GUREN HUMAN SOMEHOW HASN'T BEEN KILLED OFF YET...
I THINK I MIGHT BE ABLE TO DO SOMETHING ABOUT IT.

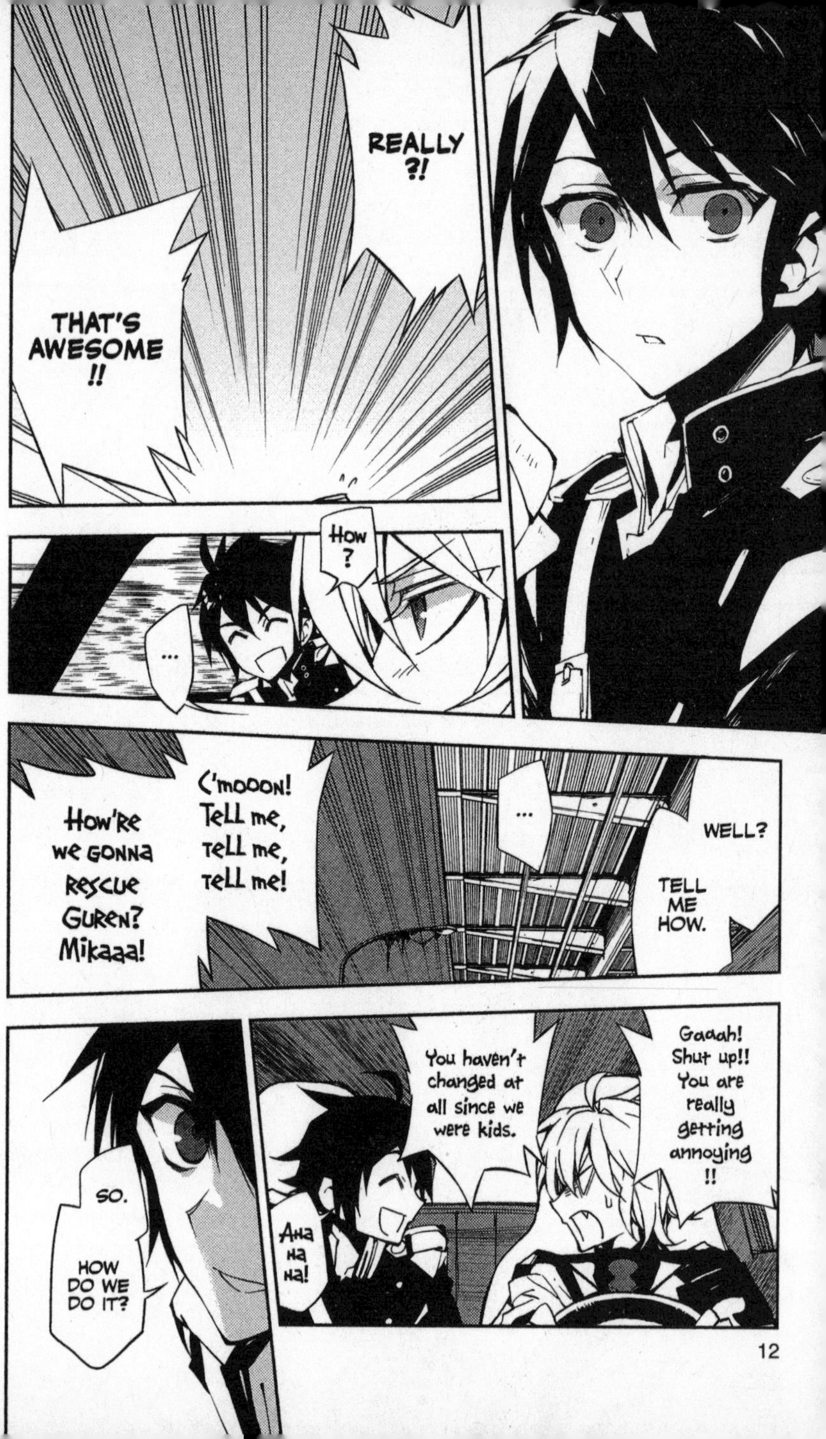
REALLY ?!
THAT'S AWESOME !!
How ?
...
WELL?
TELL ME HOW.
...
C'mooon! Tell me, tell me, tell me!
How're we gonna rescue Guren? Mikaaa!
Gaaah! Shut up!! You are really getting annoying !!
You haven't changed at all since we were kids.
Aha ha ha!
SO.
HOW DO WE DO IT?

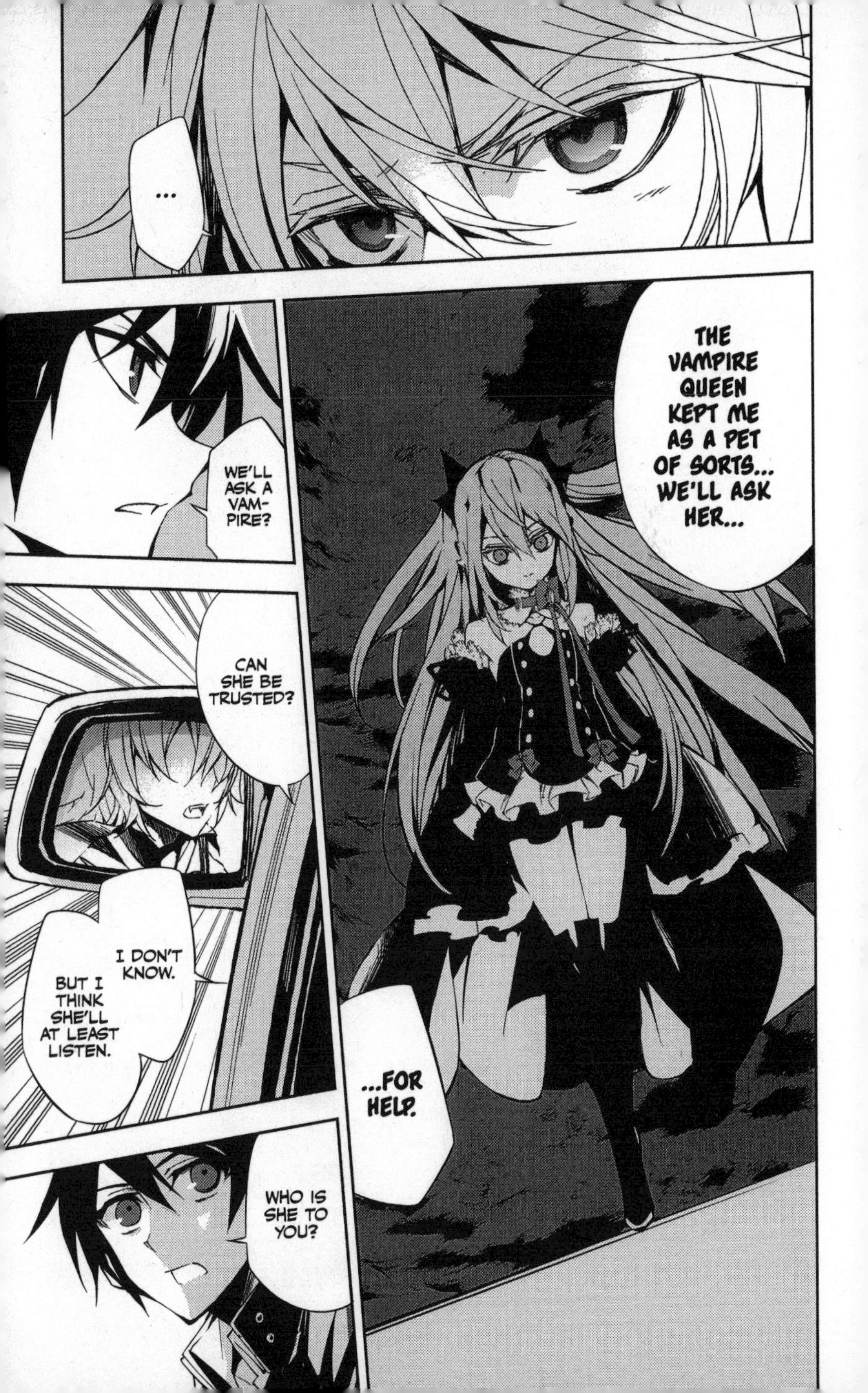
...
THE VAMPIRE QUEEN KEPT ME AS A PET OF SORTS... WE'LL ASK HER...
...FOR HELP.
WE'LL ASK A VAMPIRE?
CAN SHE BE TRUSTED?
I DON'T KNOW.
BUT I THINK SHE'LL AT LEAST LISTEN.
WHO IS SHE TO YOU?

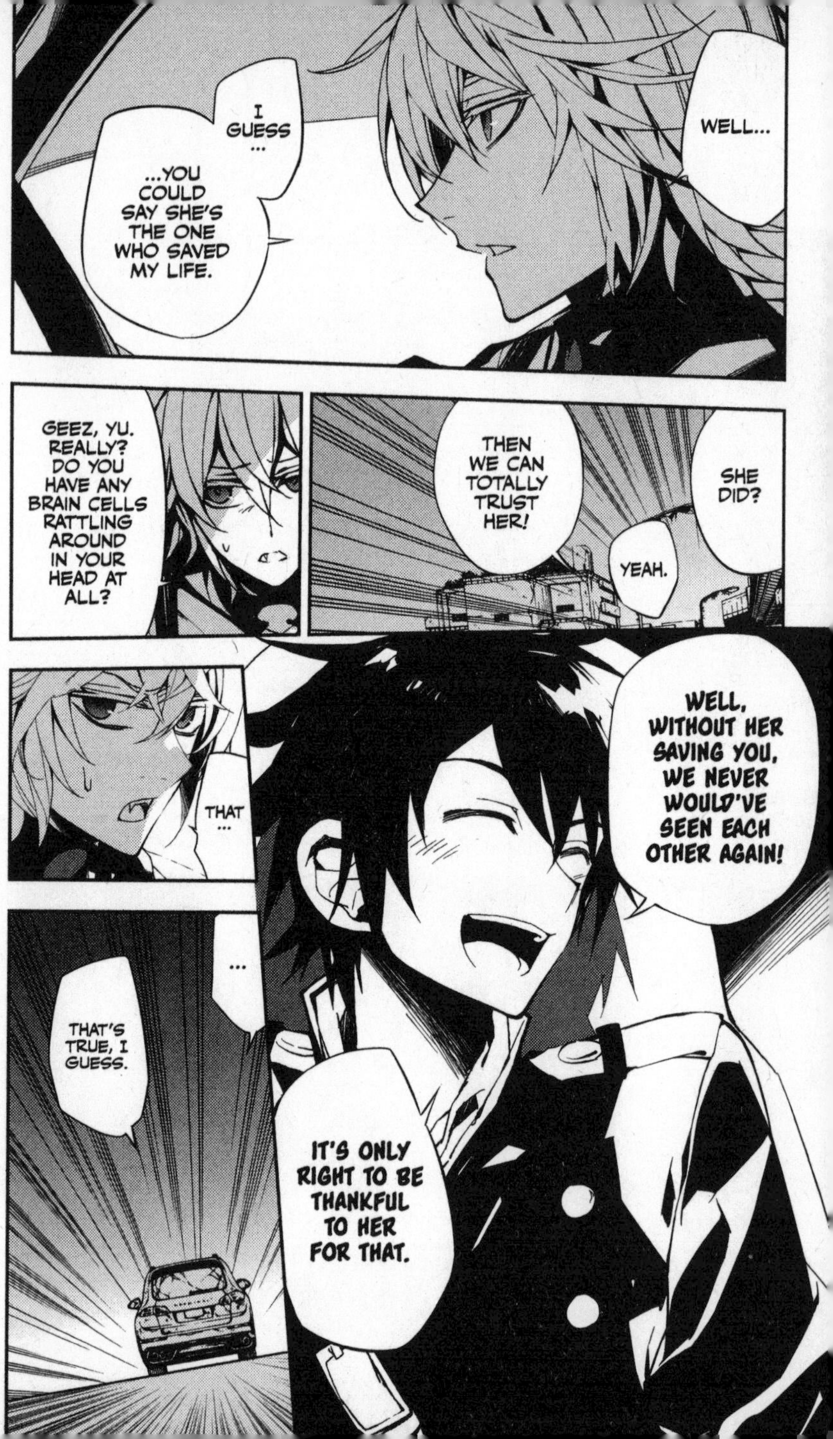
WELL...
I GUESS...
...YOU COULD SAY SHE'S THE ONE WHO SAVED MY LIFE.
SHE DID?
YEAH.
THEN WE CAN TOTALLY TRUST HER!
GEEZ, YU. REALLY? DO YOU HAVE ANY BRAIN CELLS RATTLING AROUND IN YOUR HEAD AT ALL?
WELL, WITHOUT HER SAVING YOU, WE NEVER WOULD'VE SEEN EACH OTHER AGAIN!
IT'S ONLY RIGHT TO BE THANKFUL TO HER FOR THAT.
THAT...
...
THAT'S TRUE, I GUESS.

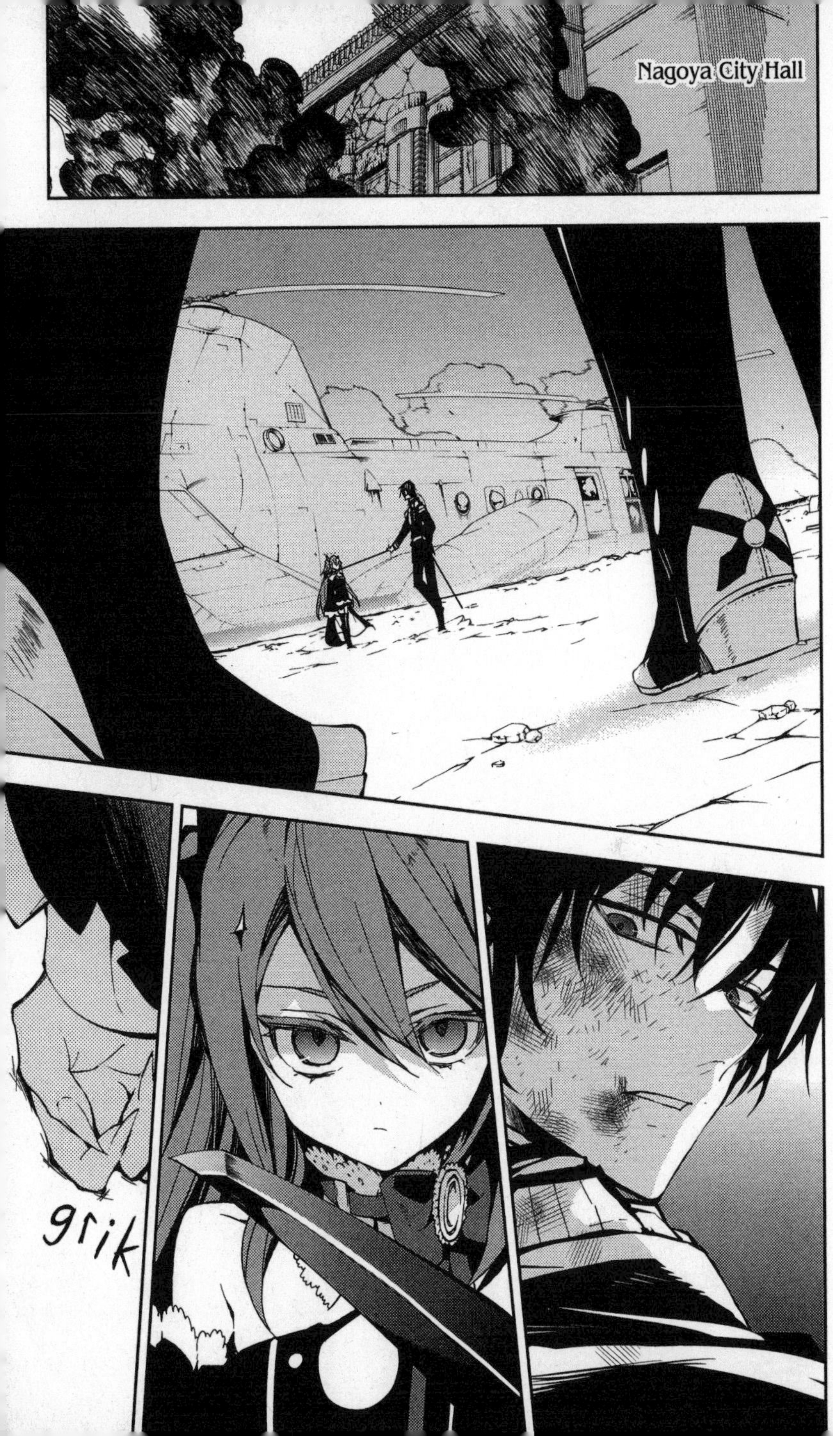
Nagoya City Hall
grik

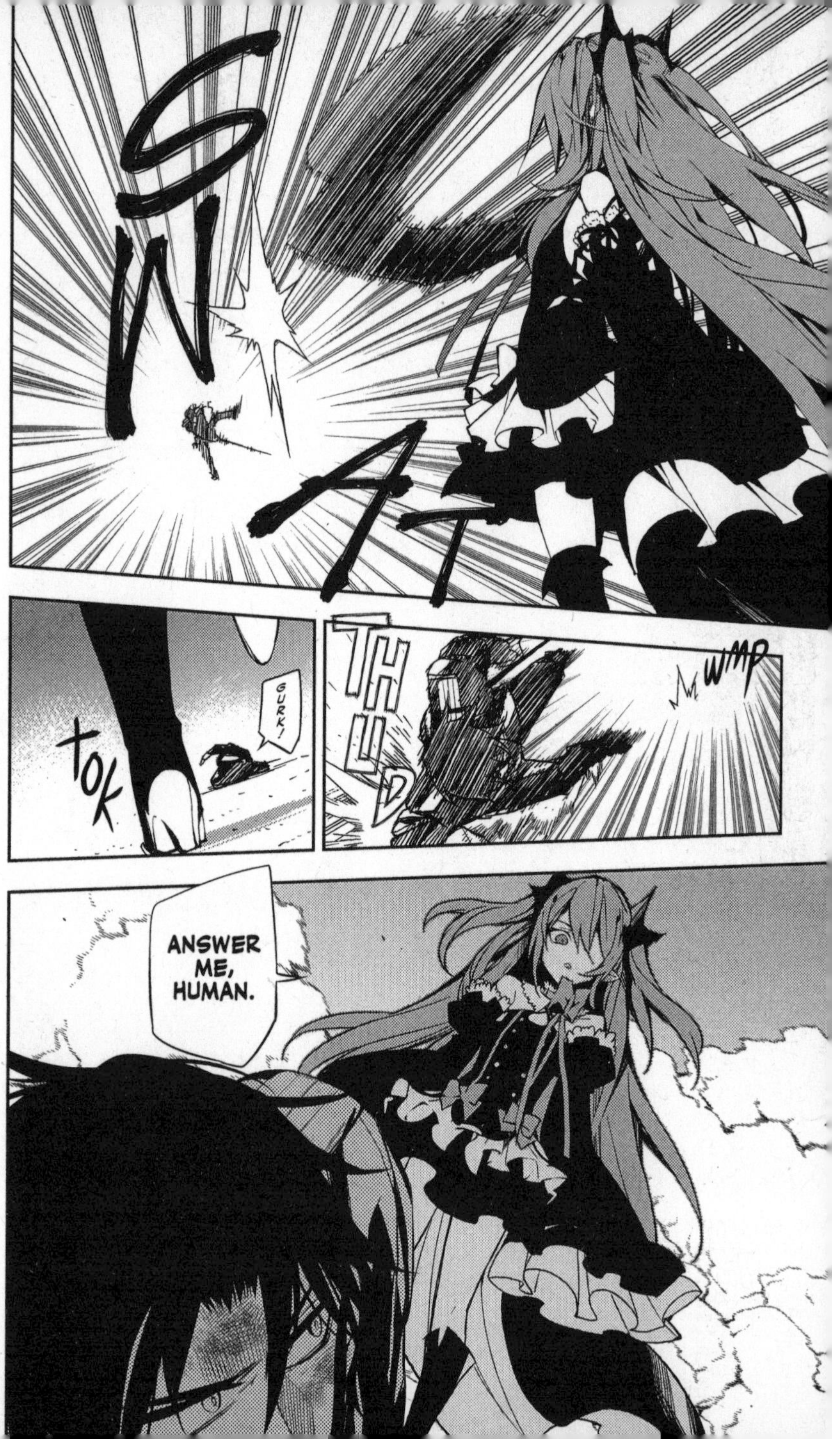
SNAT
THUD
WMP
GURK!
TOK
ANSWER ME, HUMAN.

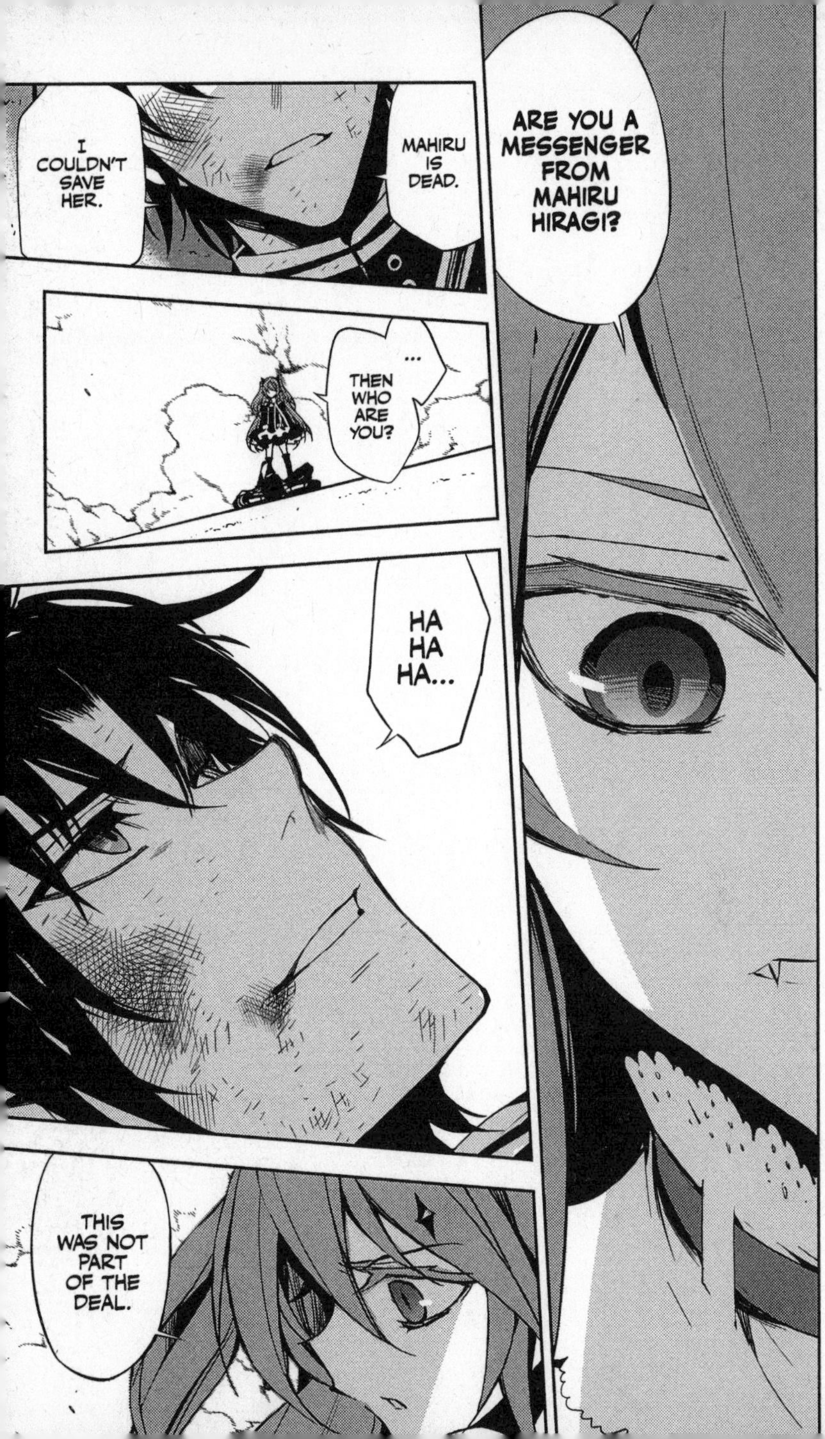
ARE YOU A MESSENGER FROM MAHIRU HIRAGI?
MAHIRU IS DEAD.
I COULDN'T SAVE HER.
... THEN WHO ARE YOU?
HA HA HA...
THIS WAS NOT PART OF THE DEAL.

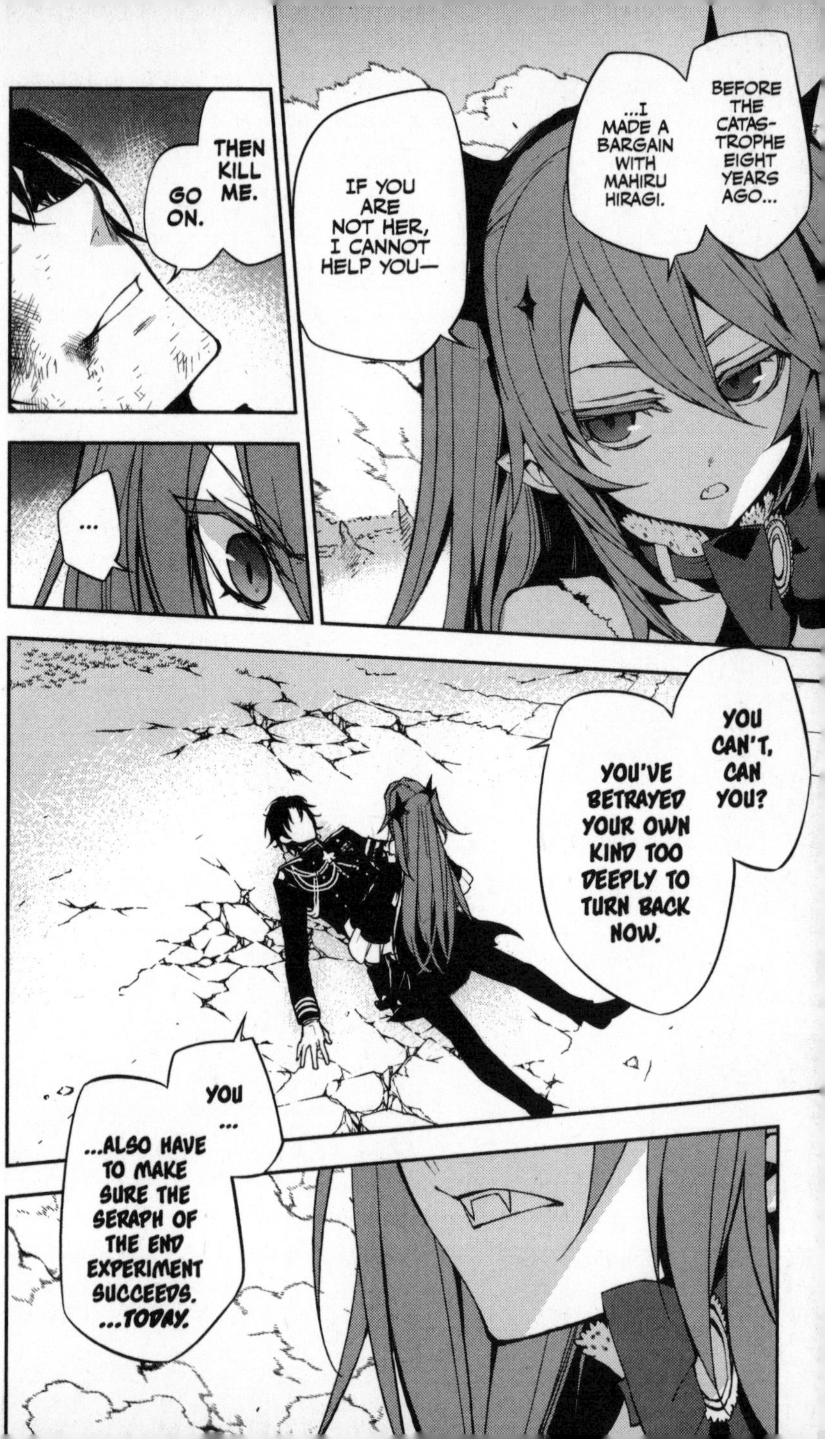
BEFORE THE CATASTROPHE EIGHT YEARS AGO...
...I MADE A BARGAIN WITH MAHIRU HIRAGI.
IF YOU ARE NOT HER, I CANNOT HELP YOU—
THEN KILL ME. GO ON.
...
YOU CAN'T, CAN YOU?
YOU'VE BETRAYED YOUR OWN KIND TOO DEEPLY TO TURN BACK NOW.
YOU...
...ALSO HAVE TO MAKE SURE THE SERAPH OF THE END EXPERIMENT SUCCEEDS. ...TODAY.

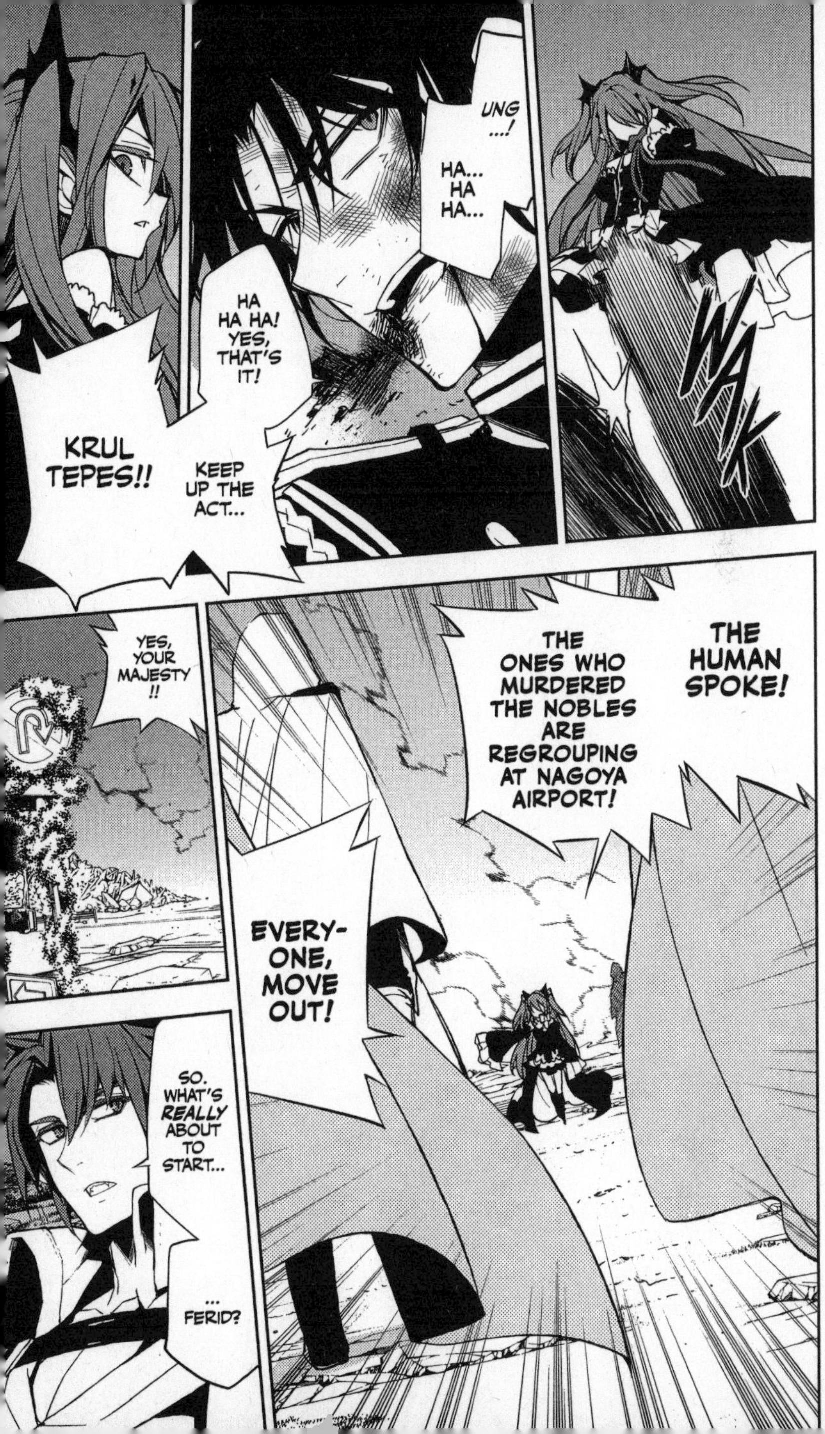
WAK
UNG...!
HA... HA HA...
HA HA HA! YES, THAT'S IT!
KEEP UP THE ACT...
KRUL TEPES!!
THE HUMAN SPOKE!
THE ONES WHO MURDERED THE NOBLES ARE REGROUPING AT NAGOYA AIRPORT!
EVERY-ONE, MOVE OUT!
YES, YOUR MAJESTY!!
SO. WHAT'S REALLY ABOUT TO START...
...FERID?

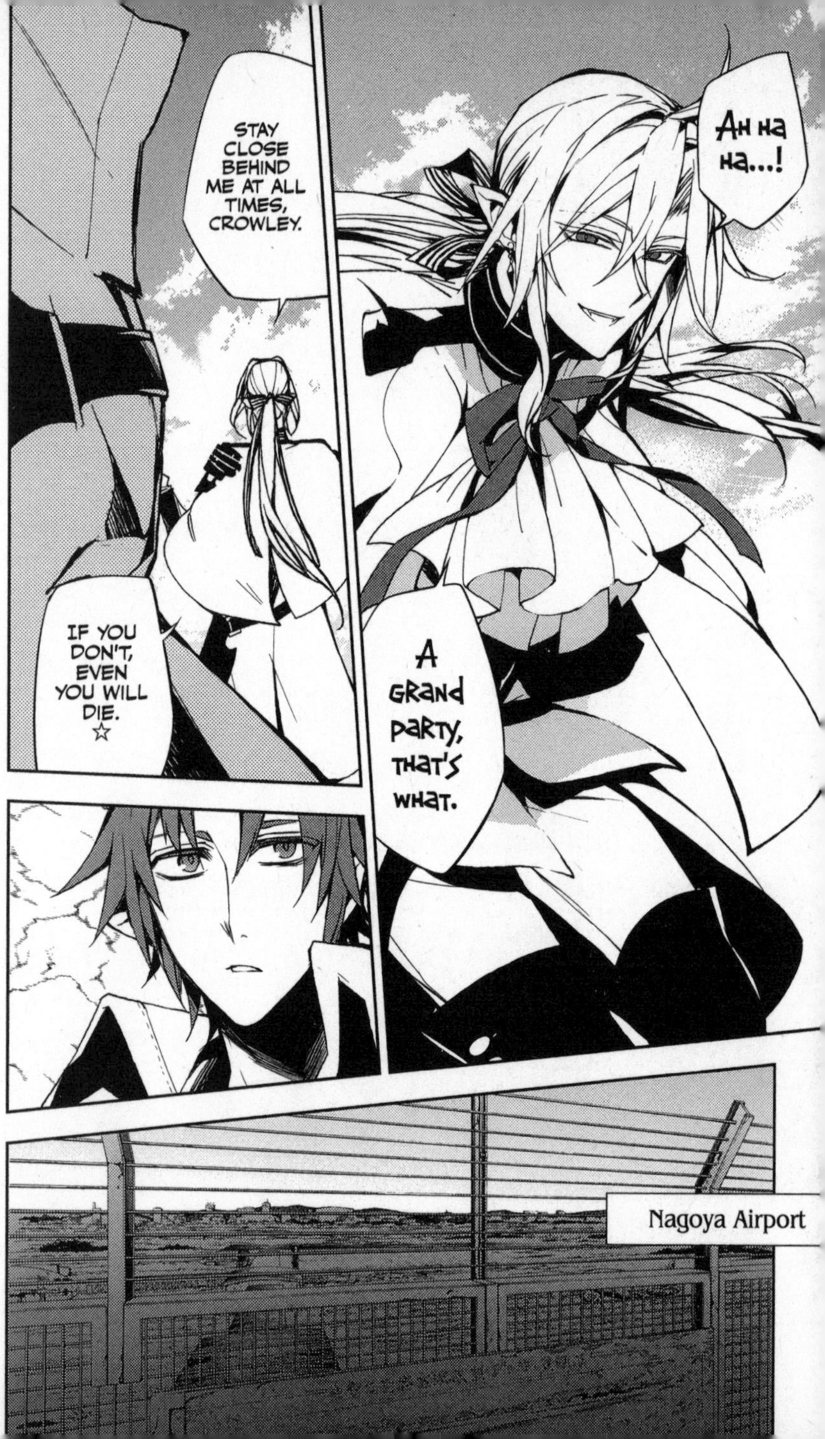
AH HA HA...!
A GRAND PARTY, THAT'S WHAT.
STAY CLOSE BEHIND ME AT ALL TIMES, CROWLEY.
IF YOU DON'T, EVEN YOU WILL DIE. ☆
Nagoya Airport

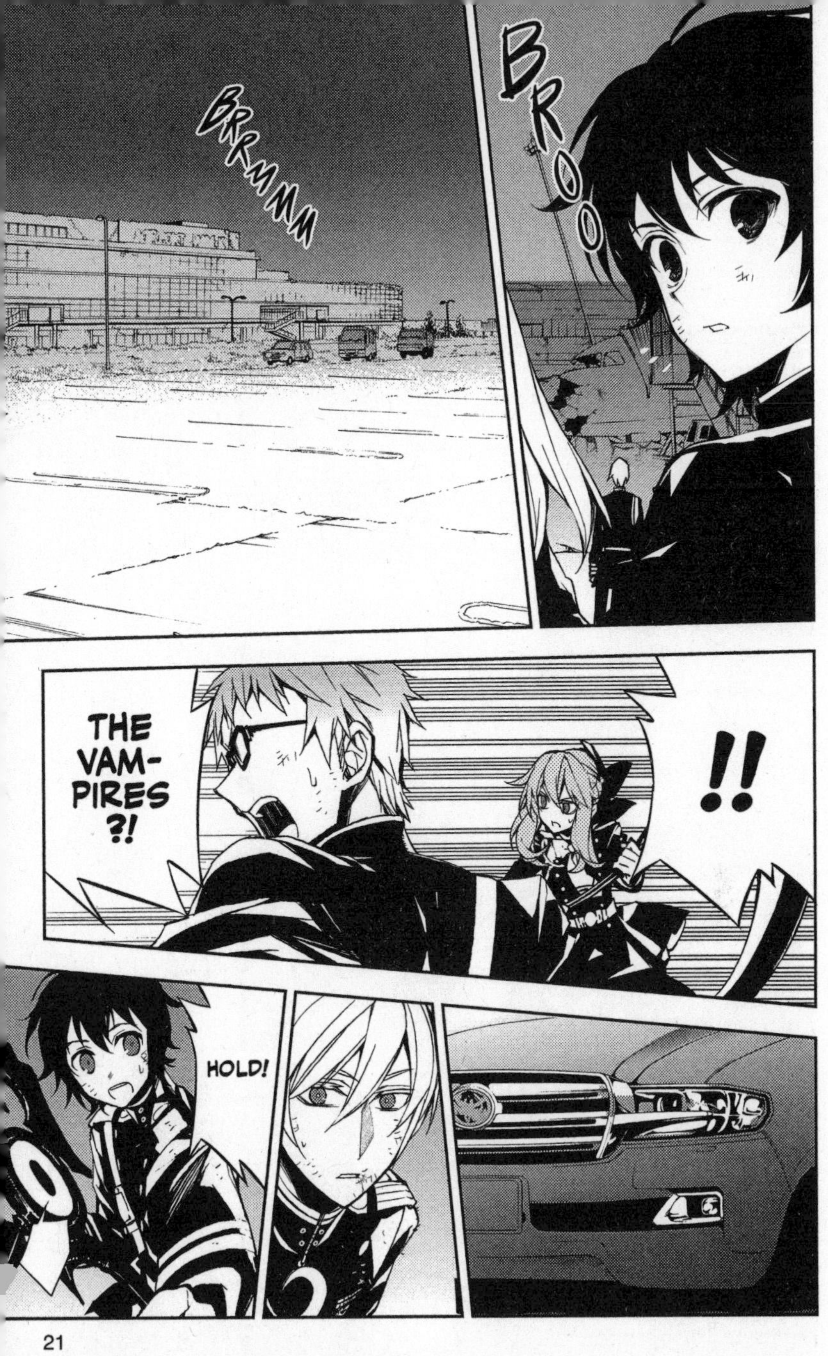
BROOO
BRRMMM
!!
THE VAM-PIRES?!
HOLD!

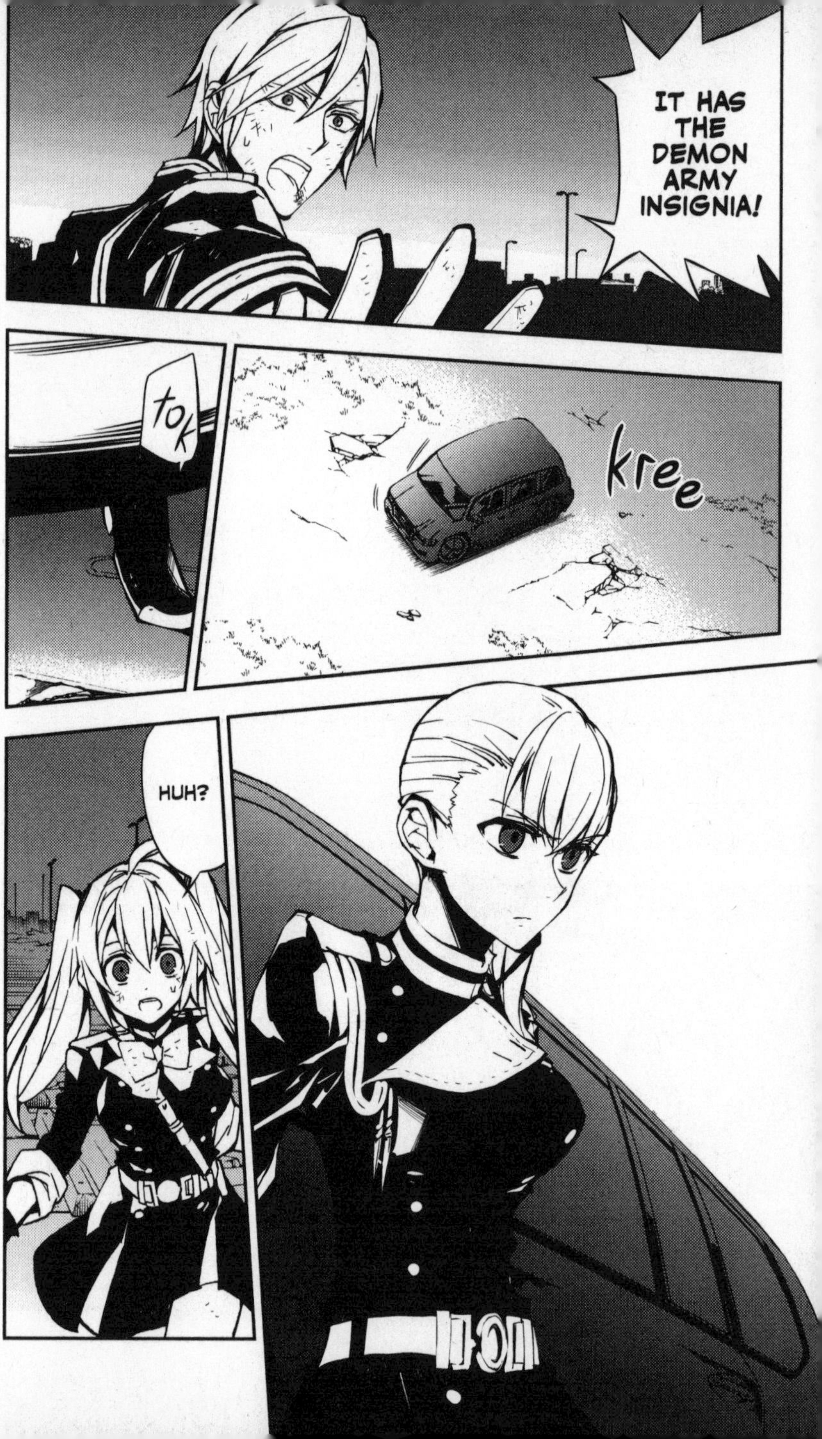
IT HAS THE DEMON ARMY INSIGNIA!
kree
tok
HUH?

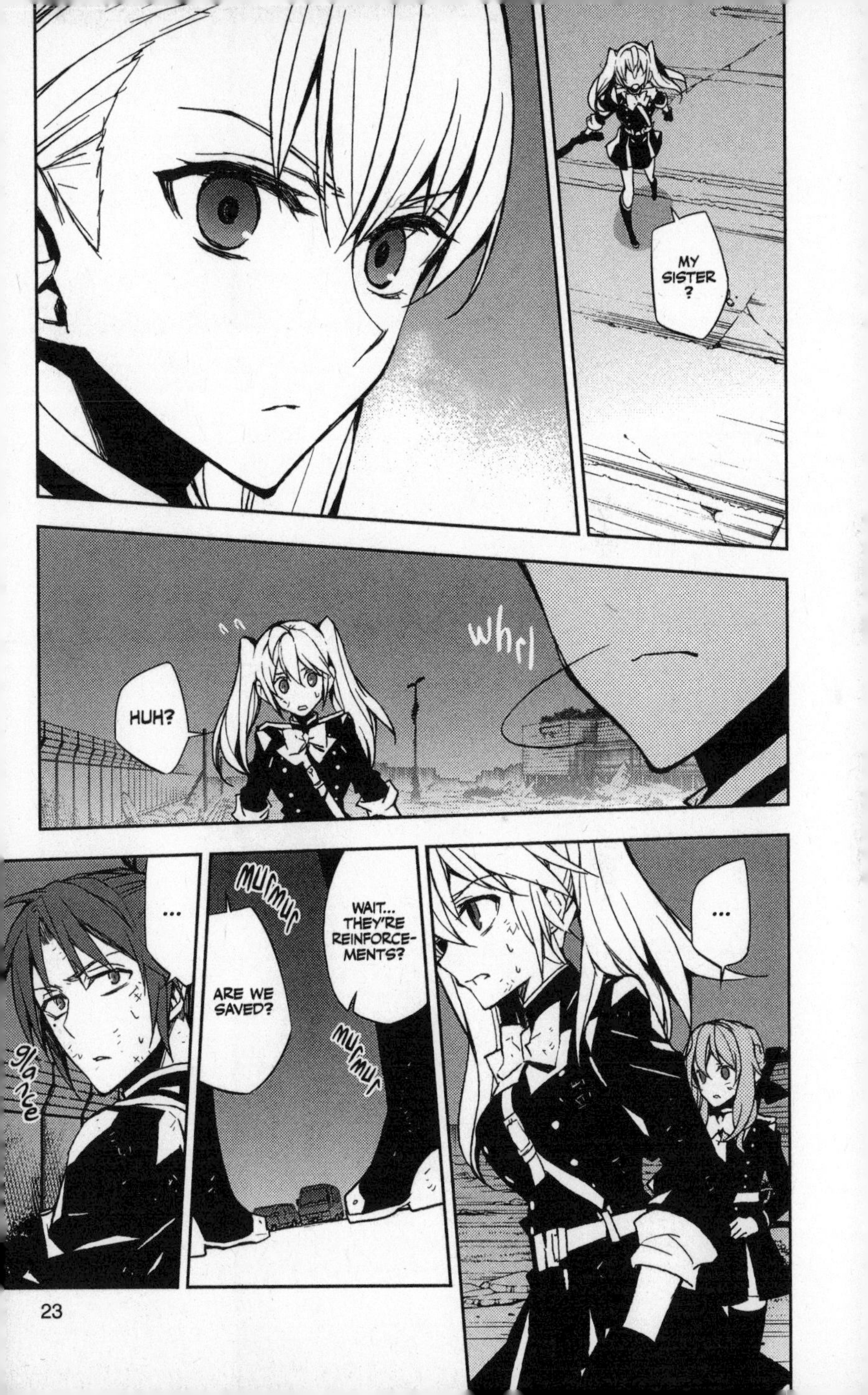
MY SISTER ?
whrl
HUH?
...
WAIT... THEY'RE REINFORCE-MENTS?
murmur
ARE WE SAVED?
murmur
...
glance

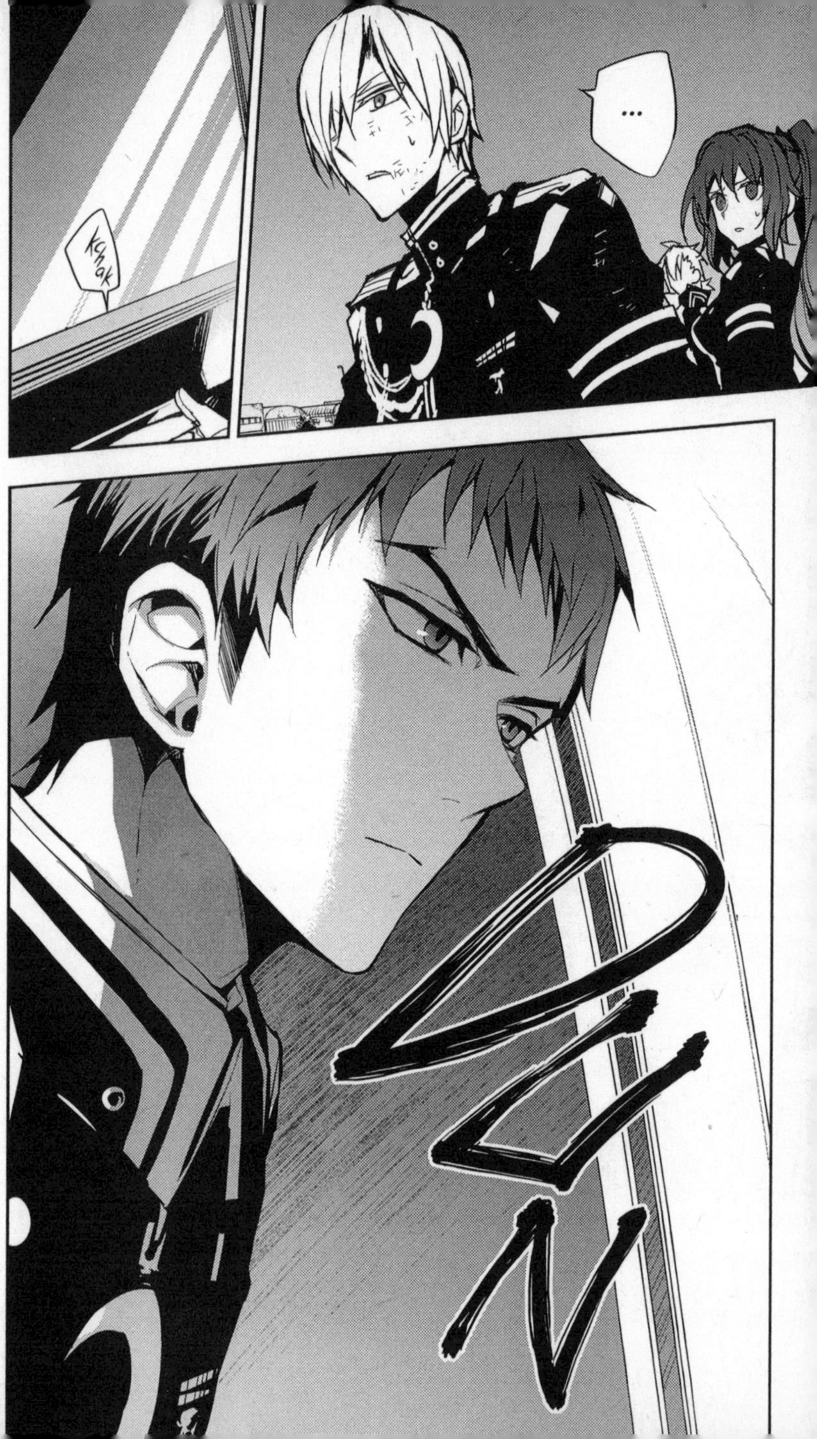
...
kchak

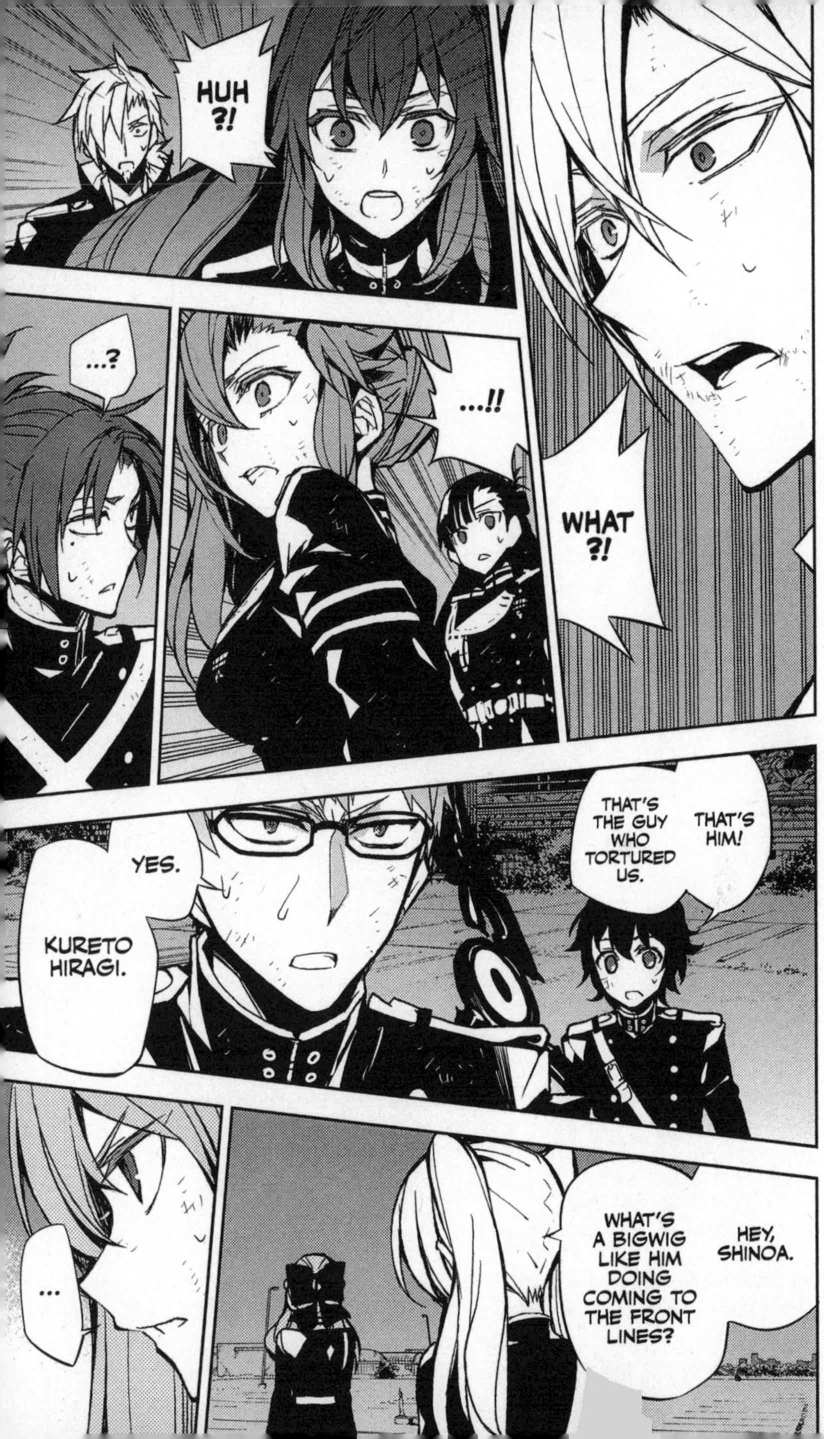
WHAT ?!
HUH ?!
...!!
...?
THAT'S HIM!
THAT'S THE GUY WHO TORTURED US.
YES.
KURETO HIRAGI.
HEY, SHINOA.
WHAT'S A BIGWIG LIKE HIM DOING COMING TO THE FRONT LINES?
...

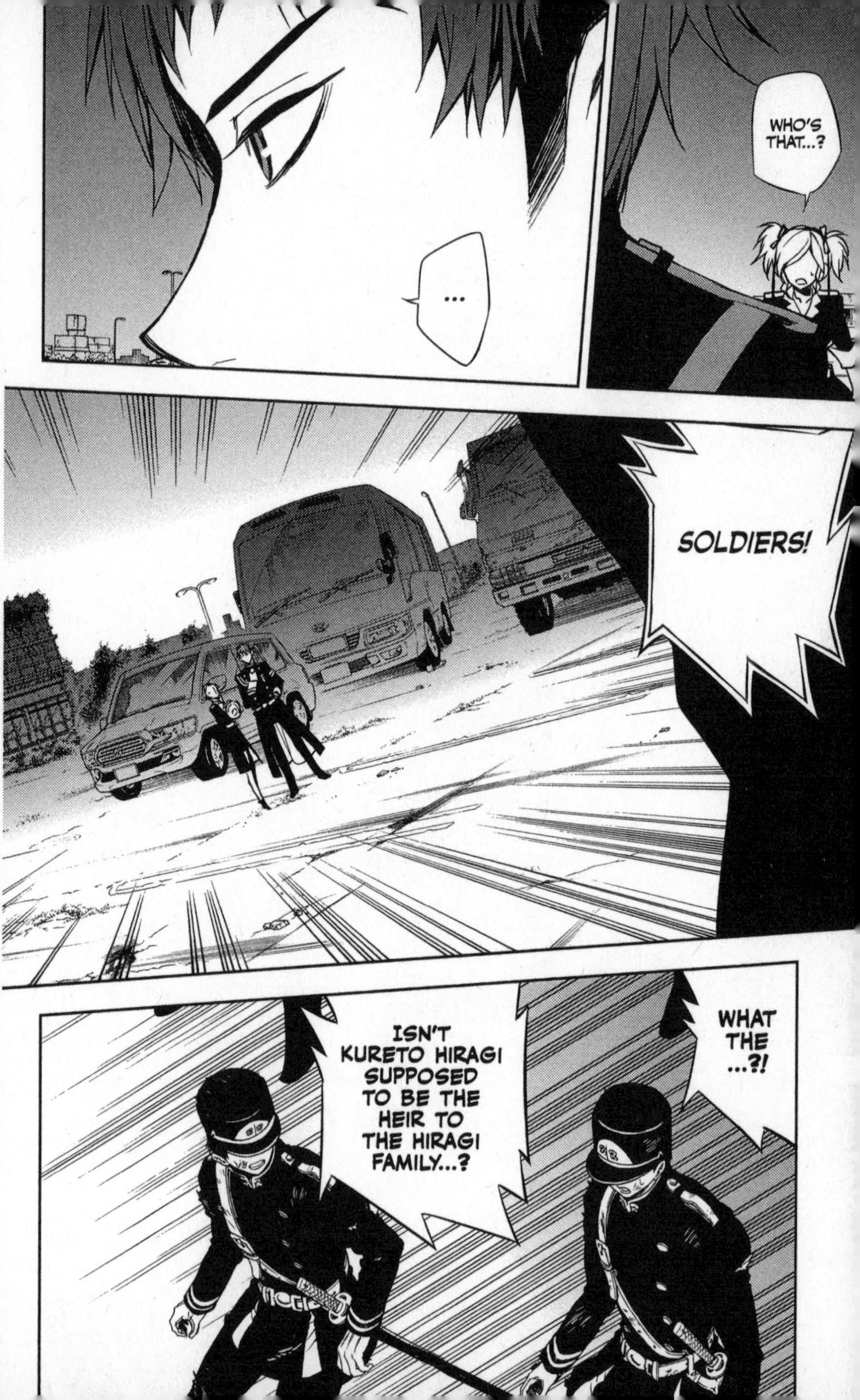
WHO'S THAT...?
...
SOLDIERS!
WHAT THE ...?!
ISN'T KURETO HIRAGI SUPPOSED TO BE THE HEIR TO THE HIRAGI FAMILY...?

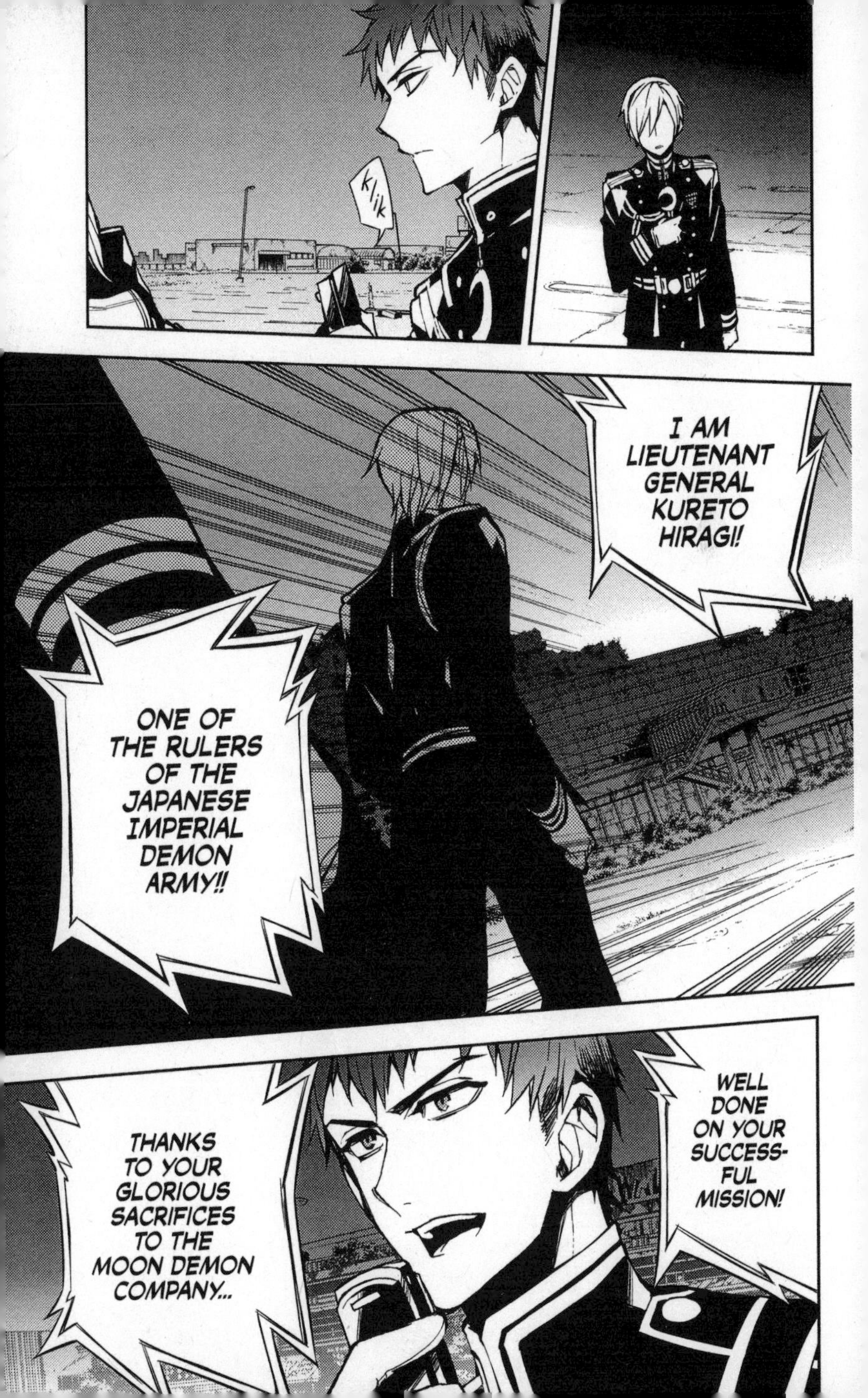
KLIK
I AM LIEUTENANT GENERAL KURETO HIRAGI!
ONE OF THE RULERS OF THE JAPANESE IMPERIAL DEMON ARMY!!
WELL DONE ON YOUR SUCCESS-FUL MISSION!
THANKS TO YOUR GLORIOUS SACRIFICES TO THE MOON DEMON COMPANY...

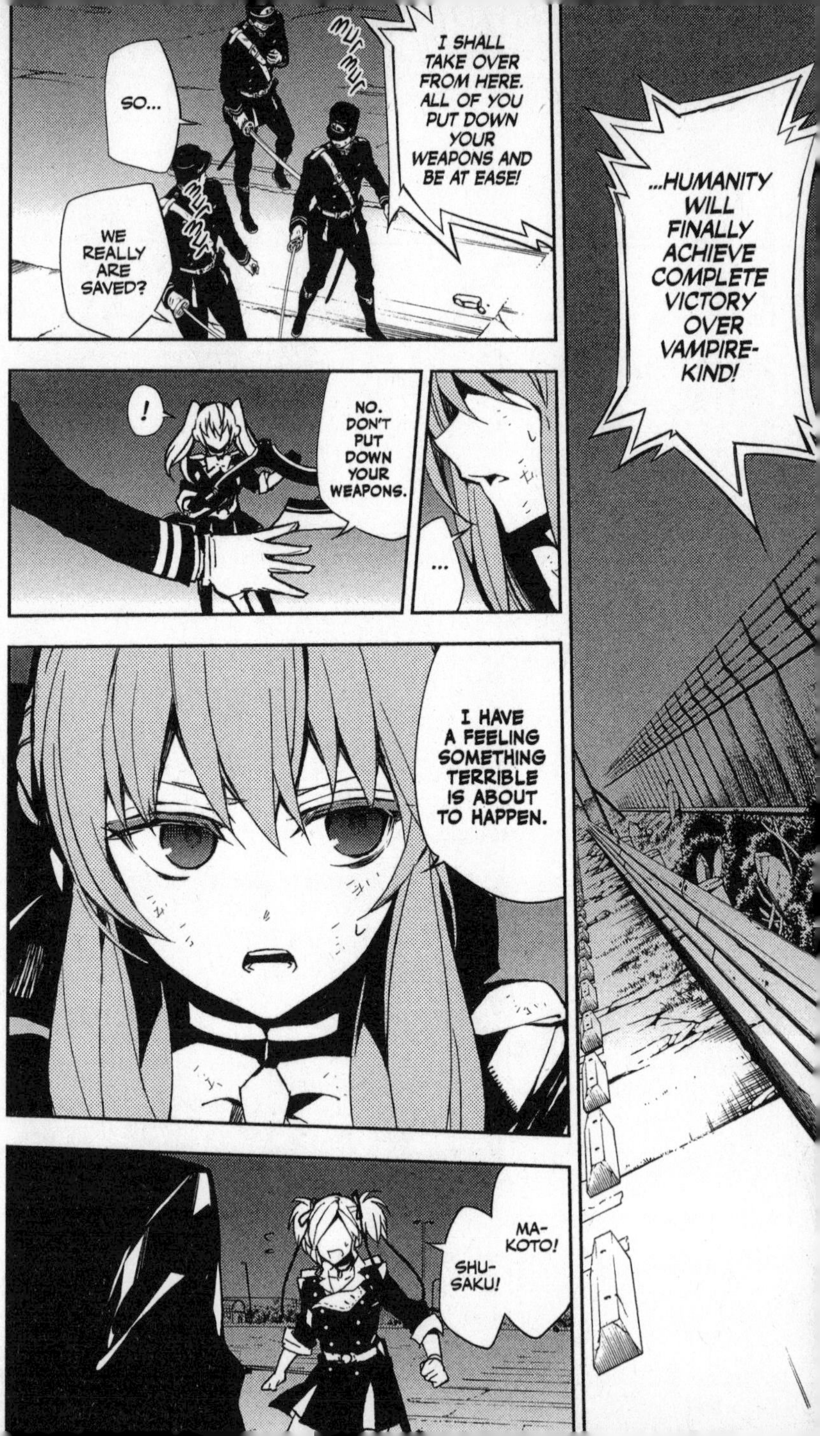

...HUMANITY WILL FINALLY ACHIEVE COMPLETE VICTORY OVER VAMPIRE-KIND!
I SHALL TAKE OVER FROM HERE. ALL OF YOU PUT DOWN YOUR WEAPONS AND BE AT EASE!
mur mur
SO...
mur mur
WE REALLY ARE SAVED?
...
NO. DON'T PUT DOWN YOUR WEAPONS.
!
I HAVE A FEELING SOMETHING TERRIBLE IS ABOUT TO HAPPEN.
MAKOTO!
SHUSAKU!

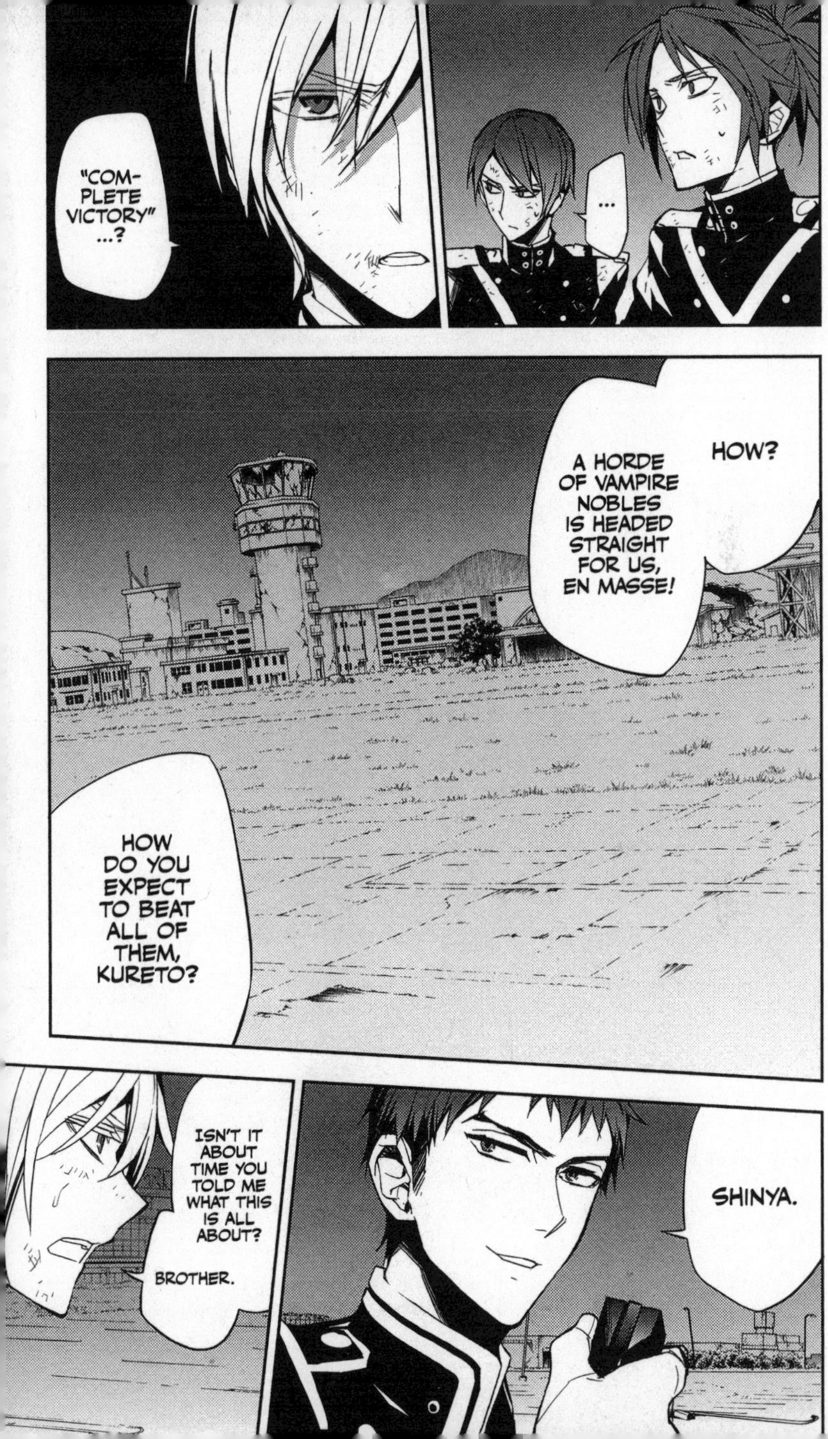
...
"COM-PLETE VICTORY" ...?
HOW?
A HORDE OF VAMPIRE NOBLES IS HEADED STRAIGHT FOR US, EN MASSE!
HOW DO YOU EXPECT TO BEAT ALL OF THEM, KURETO?
SHINYA.
ISN'T IT ABOUT TIME YOU TOLD ME WHAT THIS IS ALL ABOUT?
BROTHER.

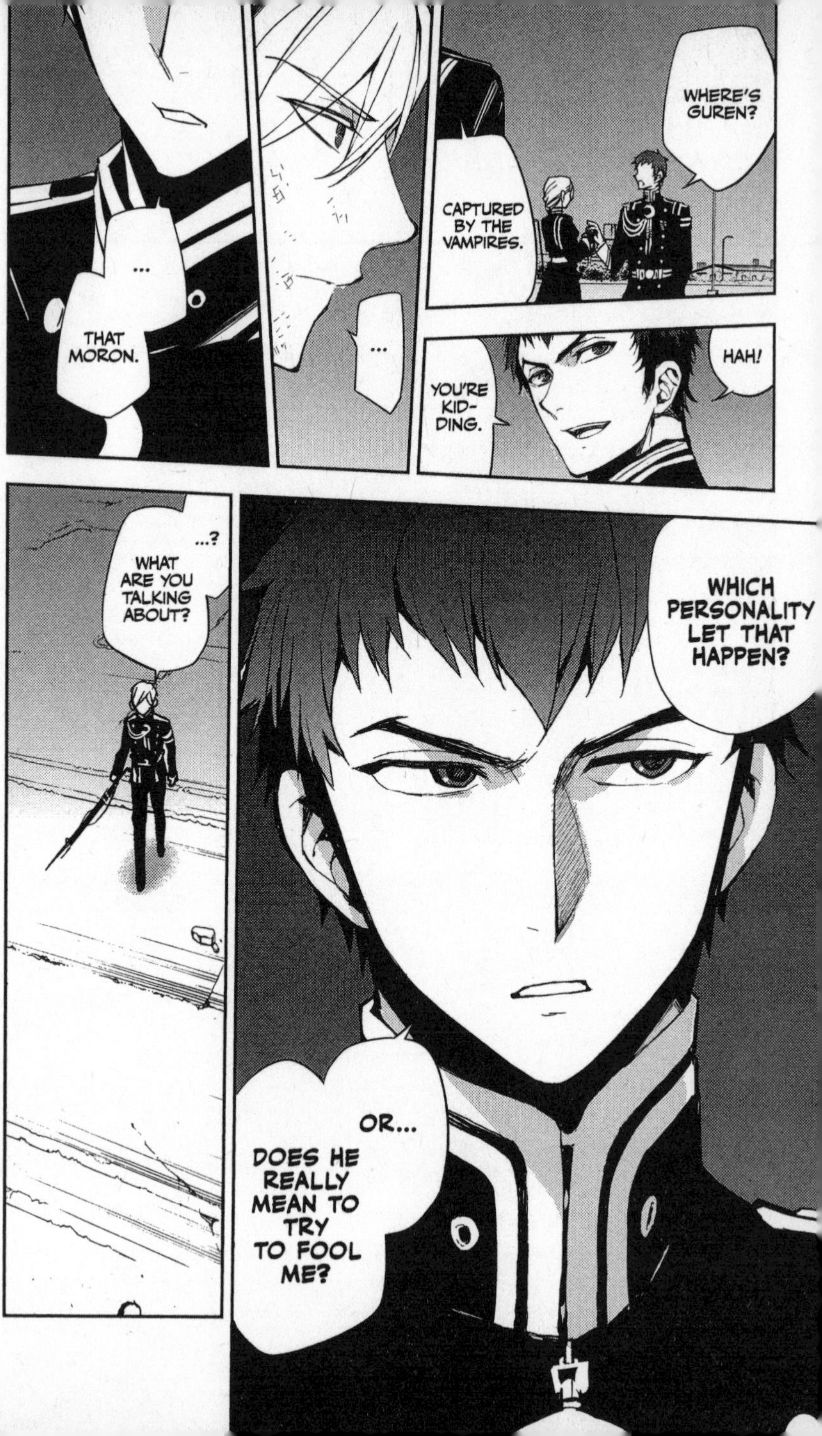
WHERE'S GUREN?
CAPTURED BY THE VAMPIRES.
HAH!
YOU'RE KID-DING.
...
...
THAT MORON.
WHICH PERSONALITY LET THAT HAPPEN?
OR...
DOES HE REALLY MEAN TO TRY TO FOOL ME?
...?
WHAT ARE YOU TALKING ABOUT?

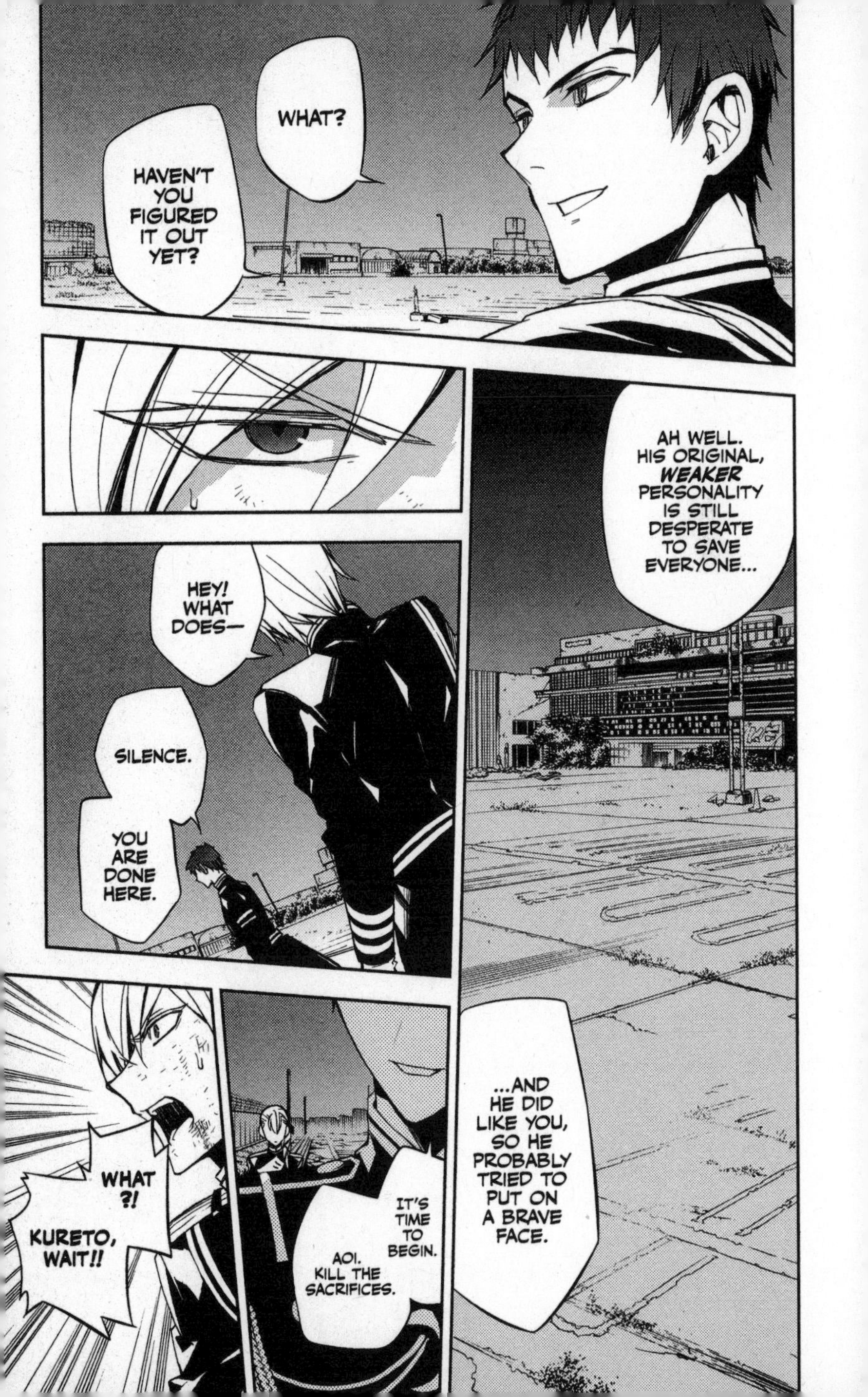
WHAT?
HAVEN'T YOU FIGURED IT OUT YET?
AH WELL. HIS ORIGINAL, ***WEAKER*** PERSONALITY IS STILL DESPERATE TO SAVE EVERYONE...
...AND HE DID LIKE YOU, SO HE PROBABLY TRIED TO PUT ON A BRAVE FACE.
HEY! WHAT DOES—
SILENCE.
YOU ARE DONE HERE.
IT'S TIME TO BEGIN.
AOI. KILL THE SACRIFICES.
WHAT ?!
KURETO, WAIT!!

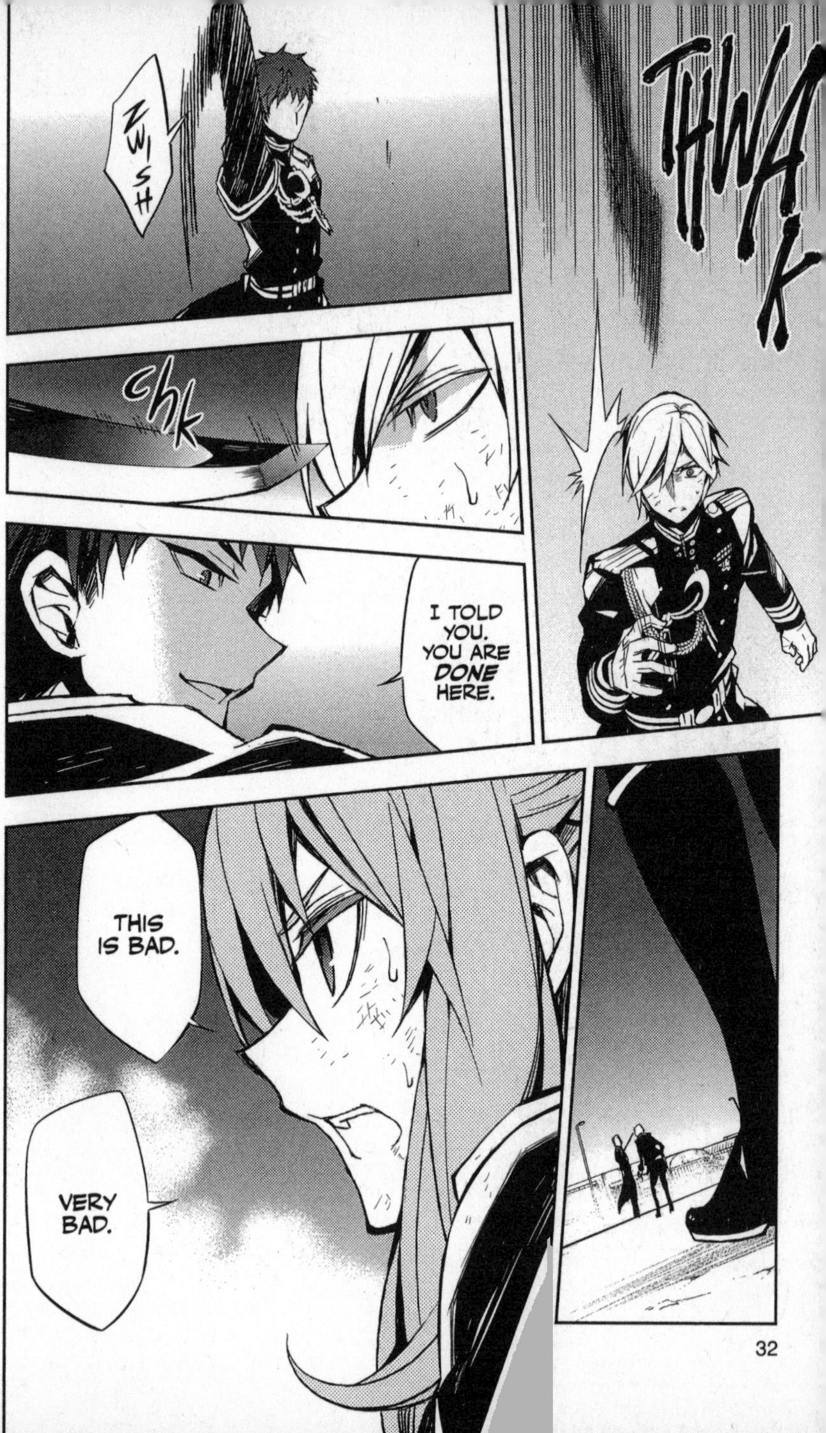

THWAK
ZWISH
chk
I TOLD YOU. YOU ARE DONE HERE.
THIS IS BAD.
VERY BAD.

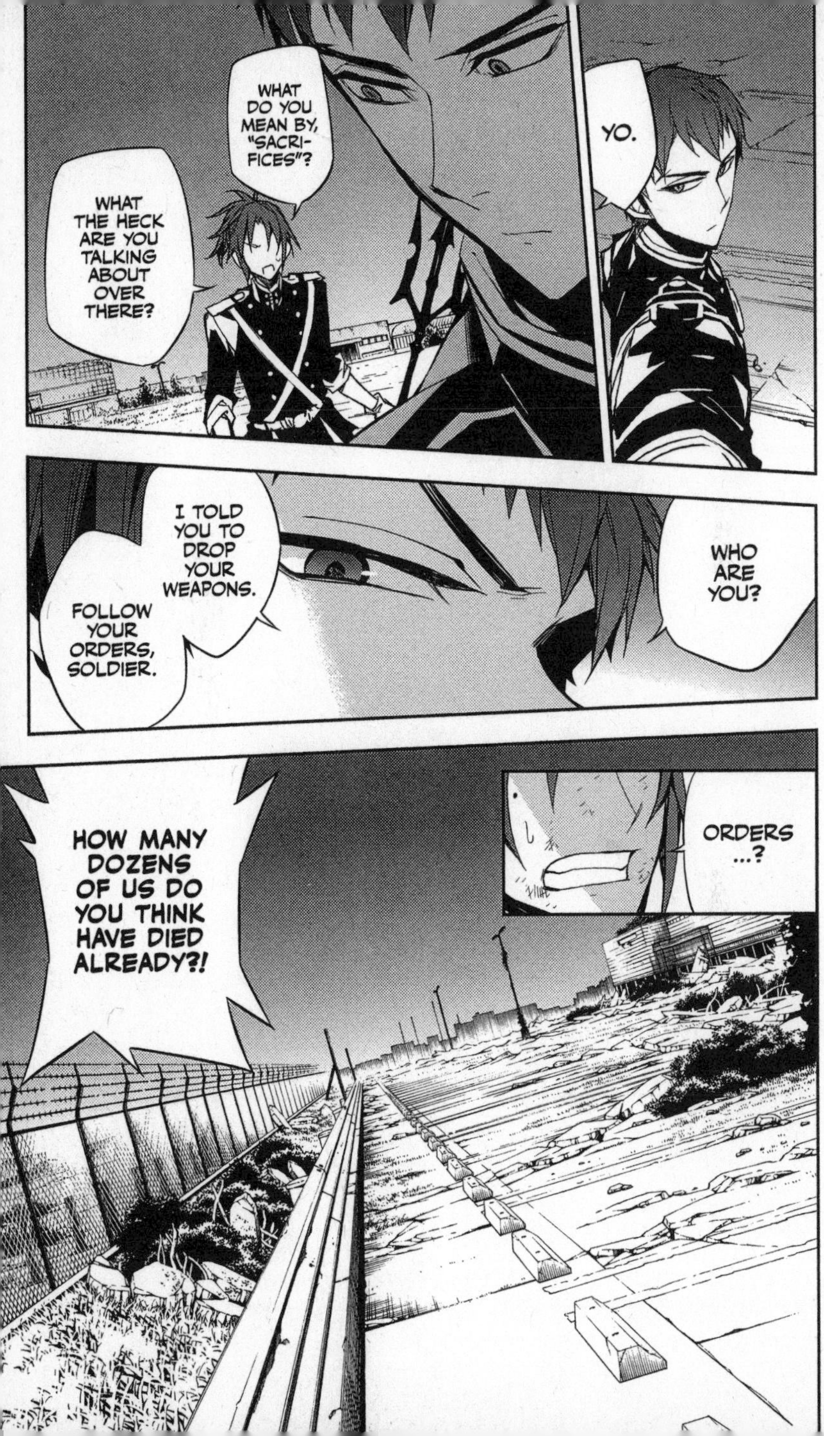
YO.
WHAT DO YOU MEAN BY, "SACRIFICES"?
WHAT THE HECK ARE YOU TALKING ABOUT OVER THERE?
WHO ARE YOU?
I TOLD YOU TO DROP YOUR WEAPONS.
FOLLOW YOUR ORDERS, SOLDIER.
ORDERS ...?
HOW MANY DOZENS OF US DO YOU THINK HAVE DIED ALREADY?!

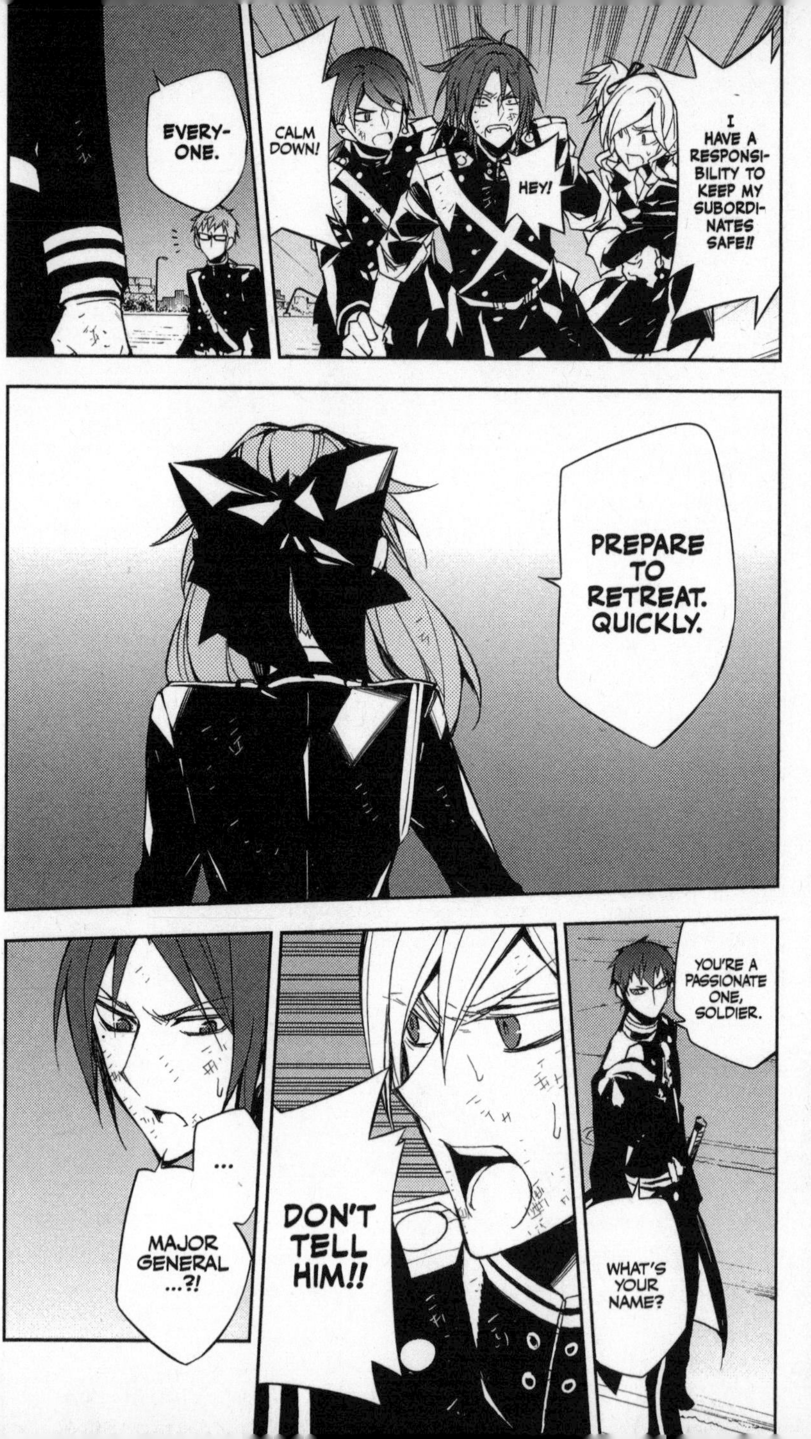
I HAVE A RESPONSIBILITY TO KEEP MY SUBORDINATES SAFE!!
CALM DOWN!
HEY!
EVERYONE.
PREPARE TO RETREAT. QUICKLY.
YOU'RE A PASSIONATE ONE, SOLDIER.
WHAT'S YOUR NAME?
DON'T TELL HIM!!
...
MAJOR GENERAL ...?!

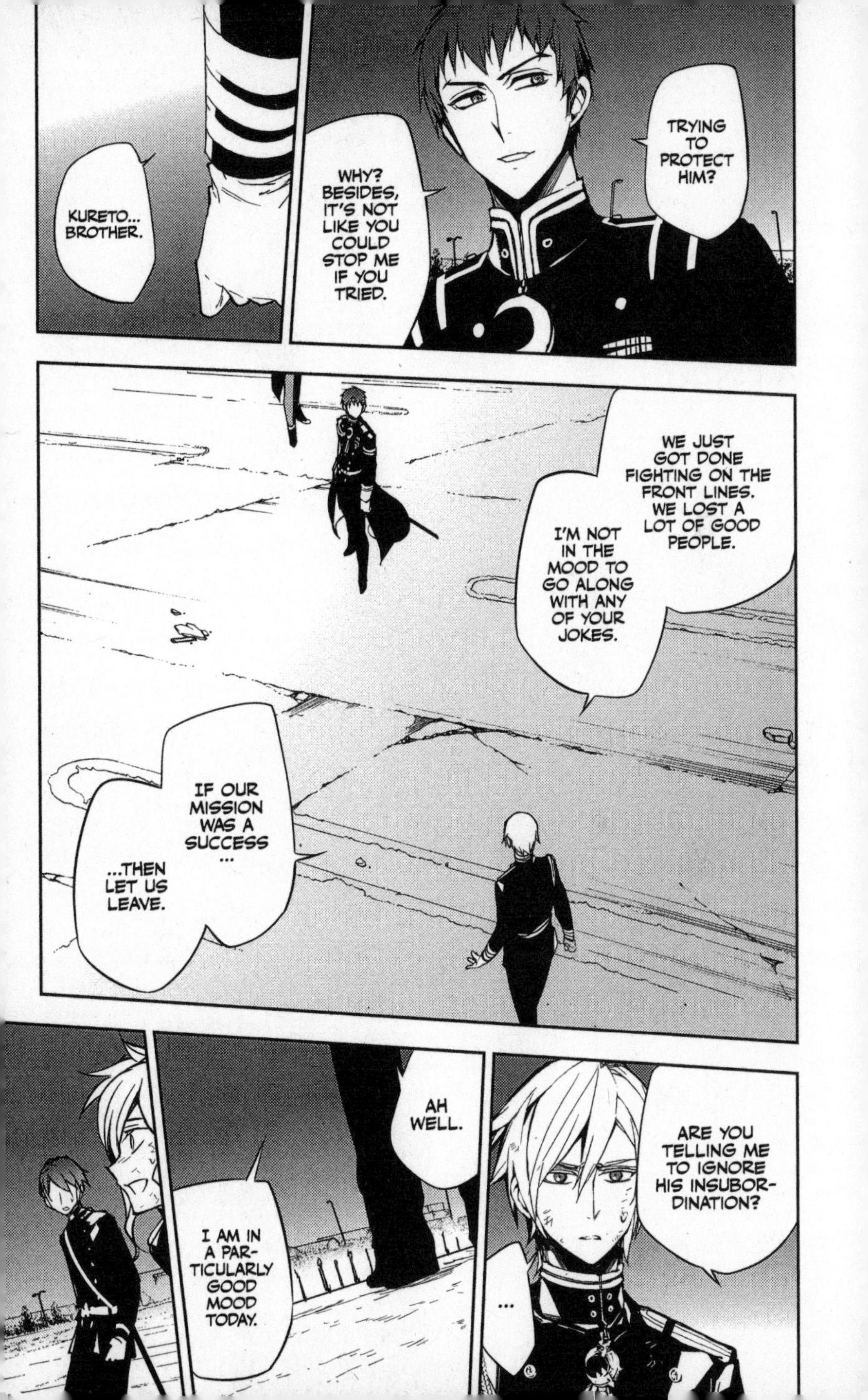
TRYING TO PROTECT HIM?
WHY? BESIDES, IT'S NOT LIKE YOU COULD STOP ME IF YOU TRIED.
KURETO... BROTHER.
WE JUST GOT DONE FIGHTING ON THE FRONT LINES. WE LOST A LOT OF GOOD PEOPLE.
I'M NOT IN THE MOOD TO GO ALONG WITH ANY OF YOUR JOKES.
IF OUR MISSION WAS A SUCCESS...
...THEN LET US LEAVE.
ARE YOU TELLING ME TO IGNORE HIS INSUBOR-DINATION?
...
AH WELL.
I AM IN A PAR-TICULARLY GOOD MOOD TODAY.

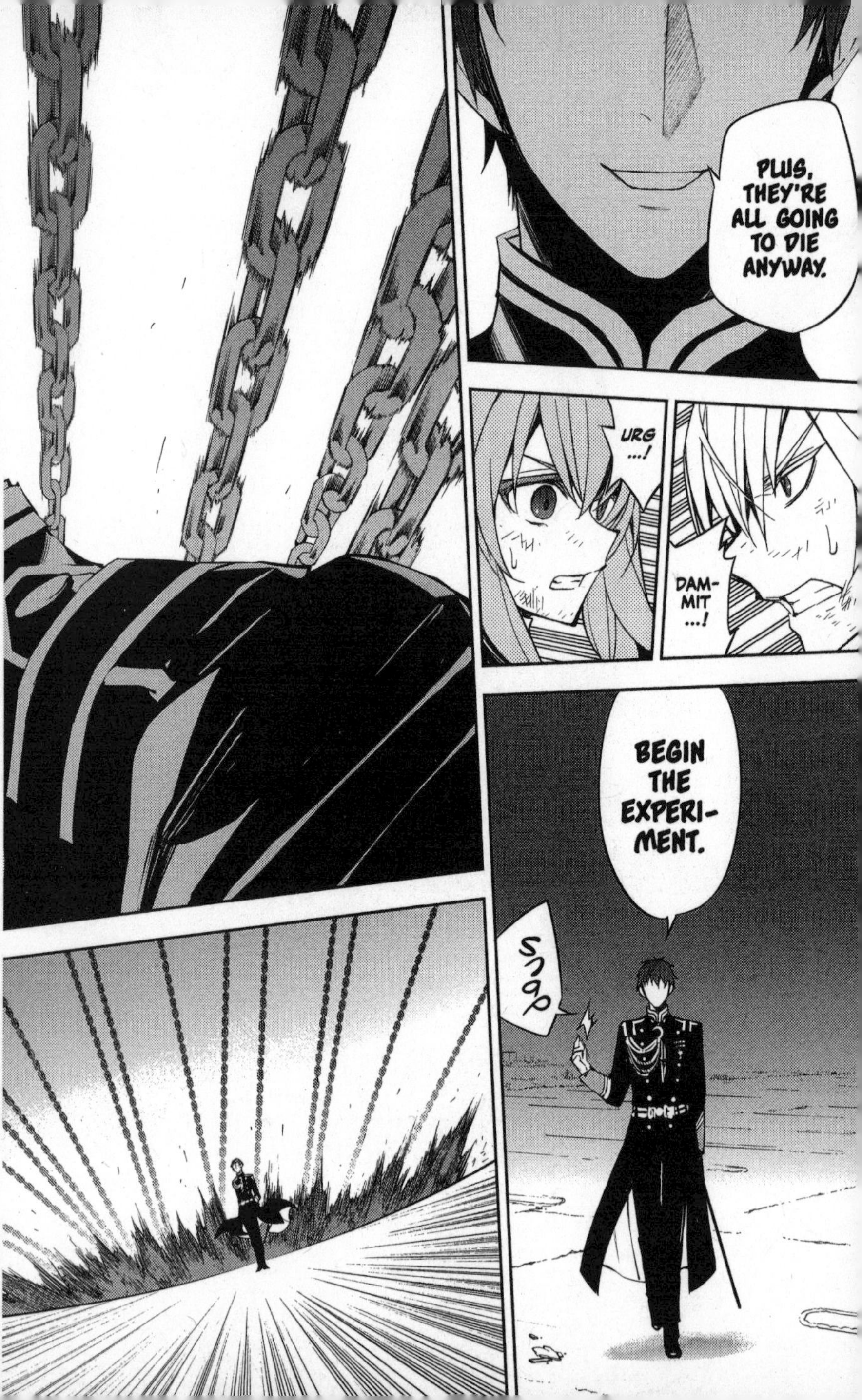
PLUS, THEY'RE ALL GOING TO DIE ANYWAY.
DAM-MIT ...!
URG ...!
BEGIN THE EXPERI-MENT.
SNAP

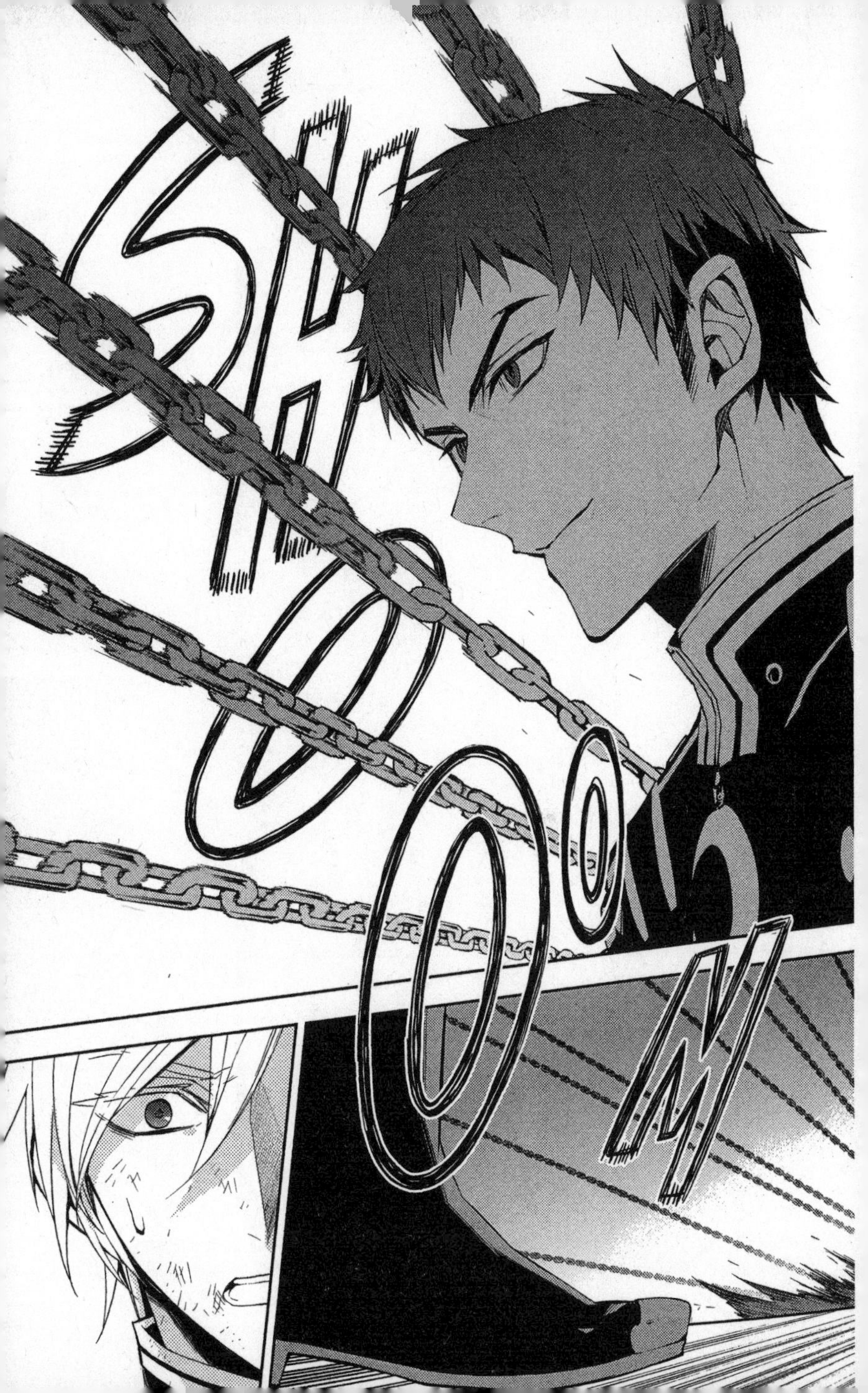
SHOOOM

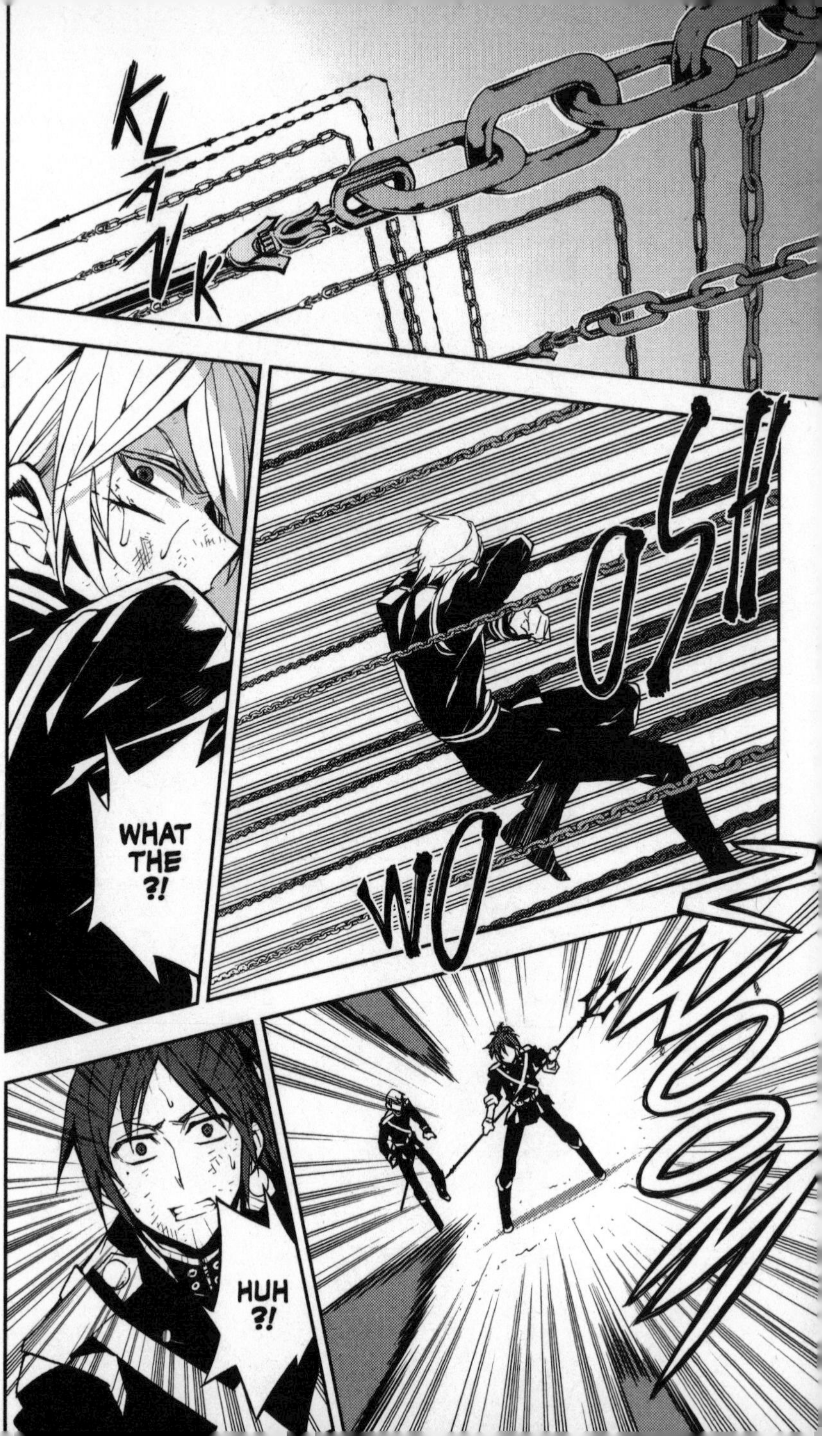
KLANK
WHOOSH
WHAT THE ?!
HUH ?!

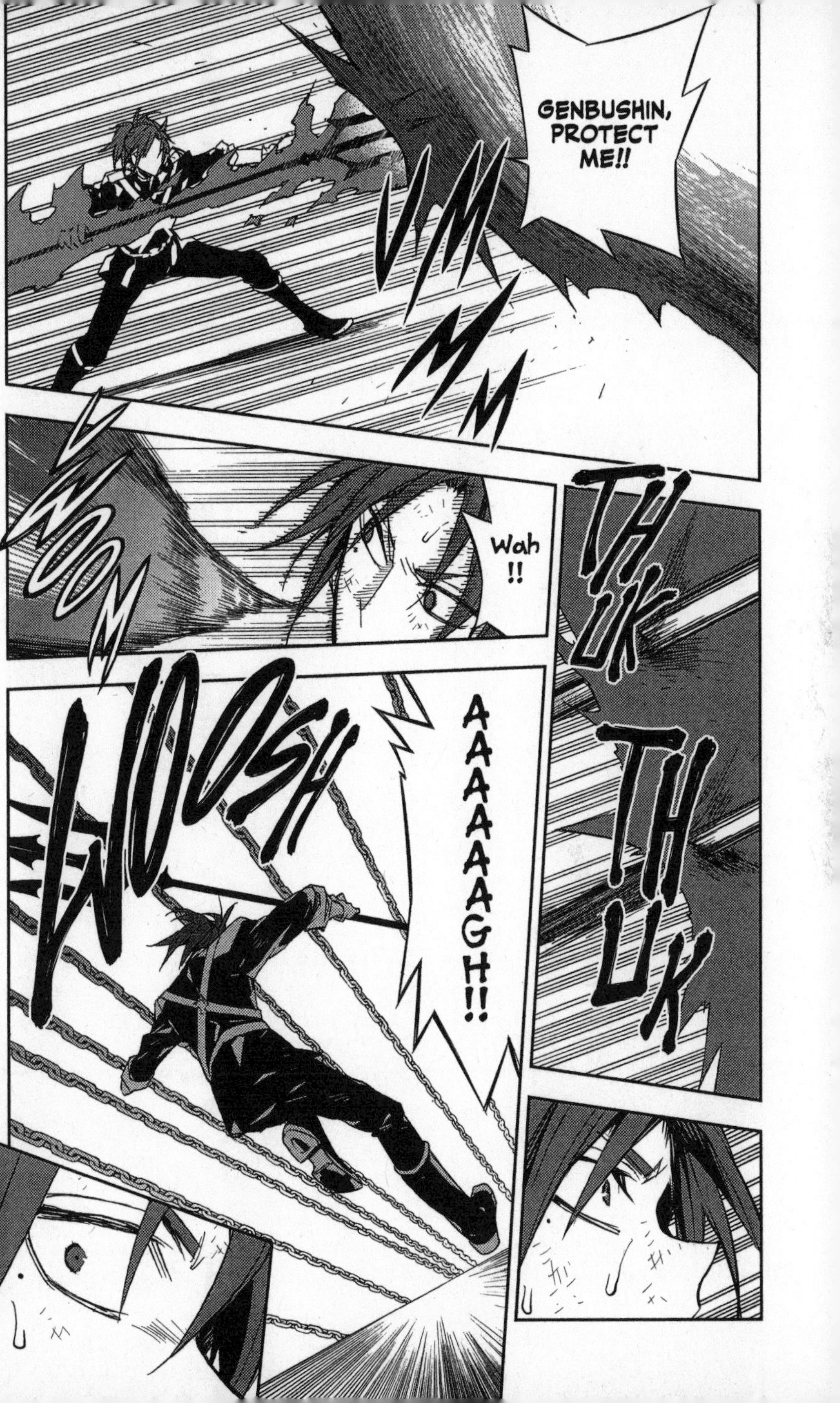
GENBUSHIN, PROTECT ME!!
VMMMMM
VWOOOM
THUK
Wah !!
THUK
WOOSH
AAAAAAAGH!!

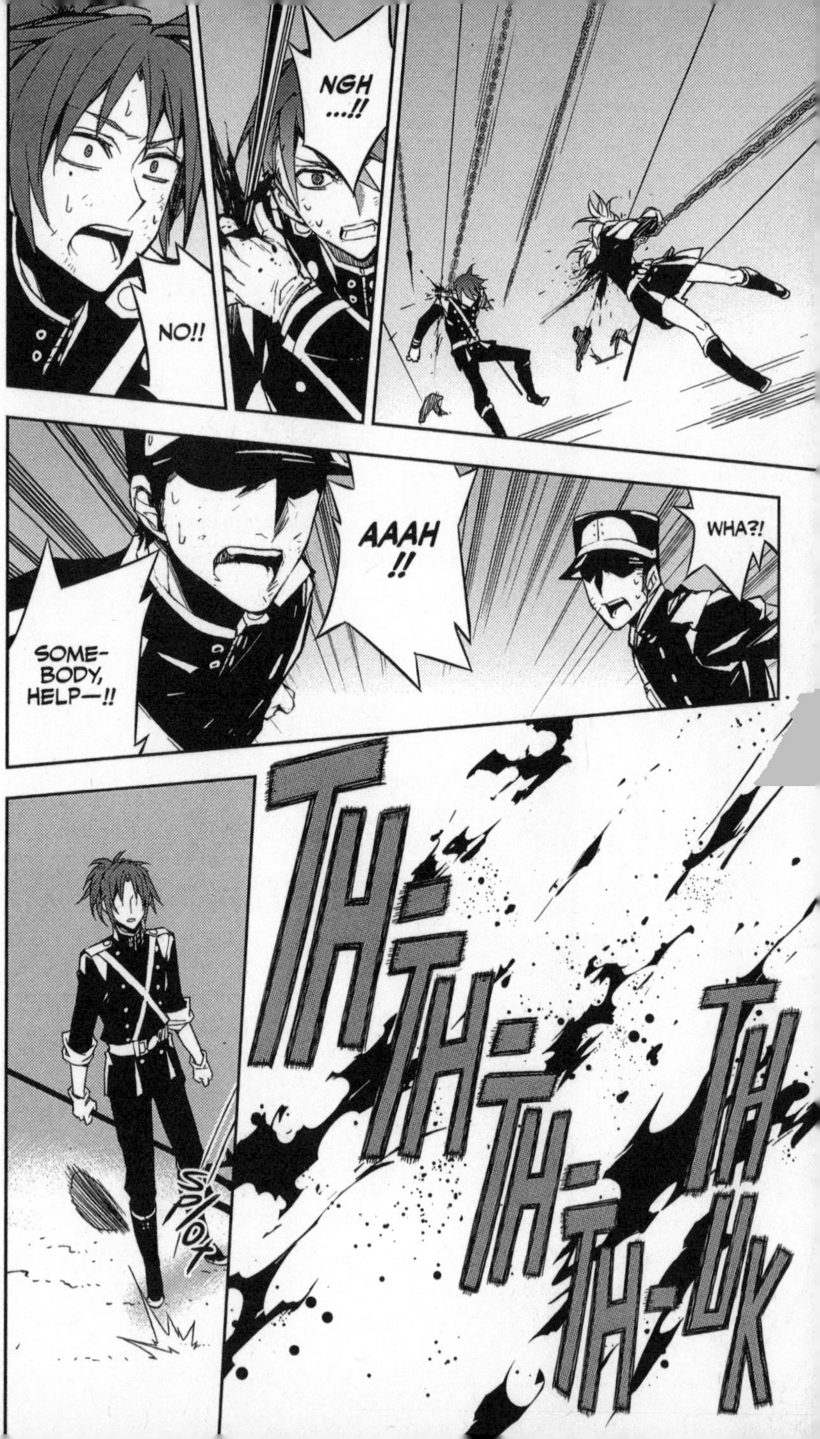
NGH ...!!
NO!!
WHA?!
AAAH !!
SOME-BODY, HELP—!!
TH-TH-TH-TH-TH-TH-UK

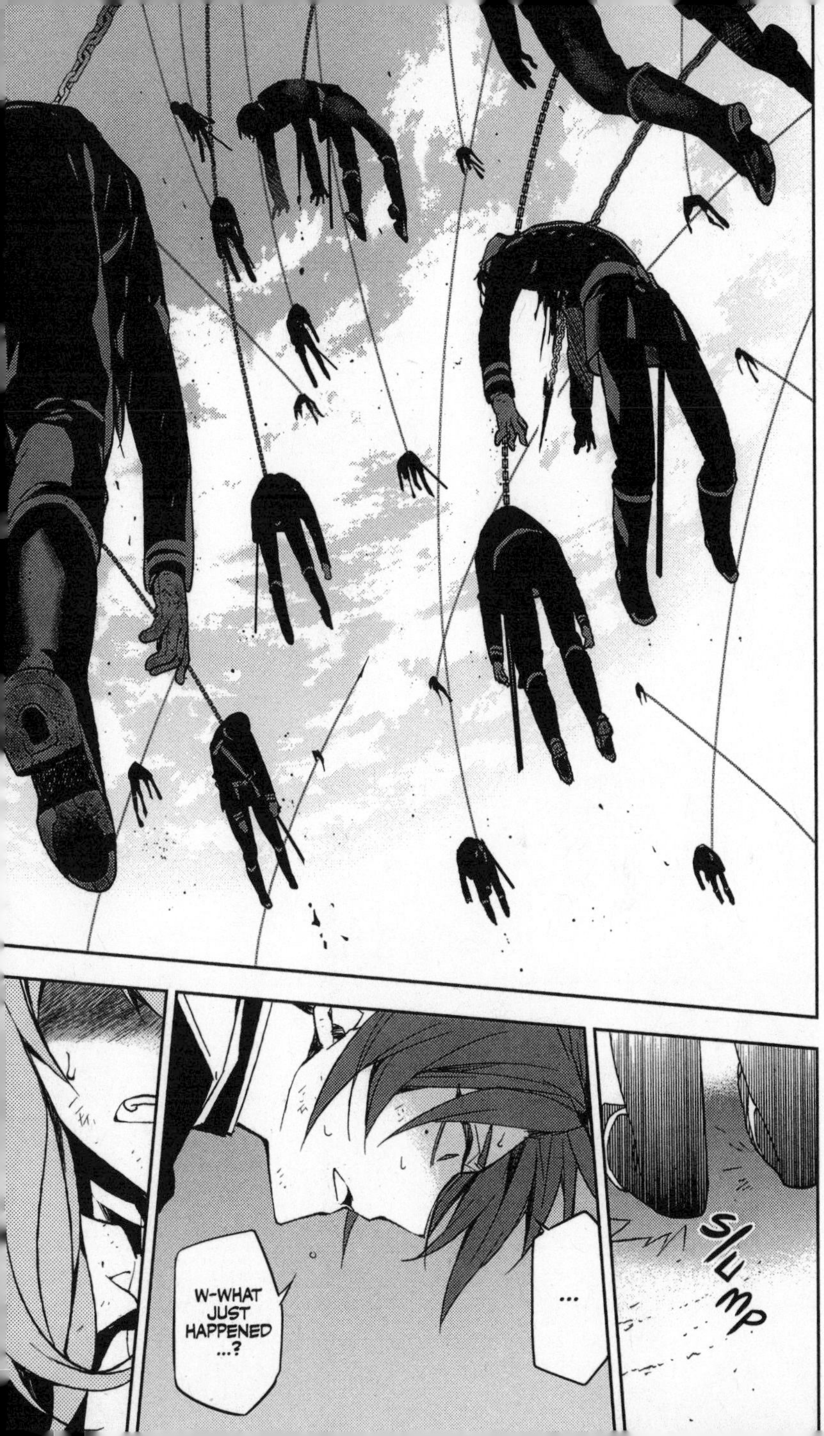
SLUMP
...
W-WHAT JUST HAPPENED ...?

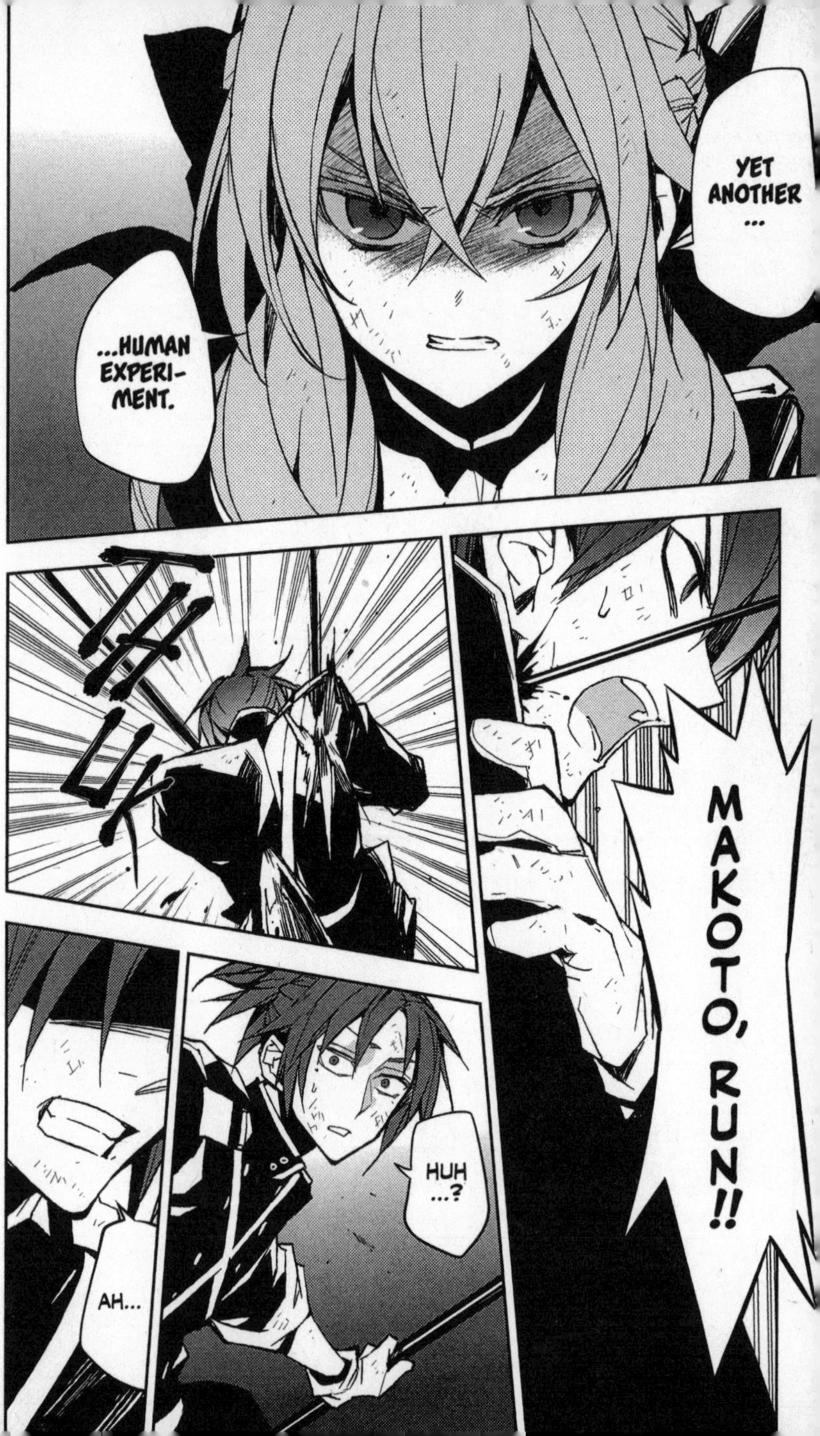
YET ANOTHER ...
...HUMAN EXPERI-MENT.
MAKOTO, RUN!!
THUK
HUH ...?
AH...

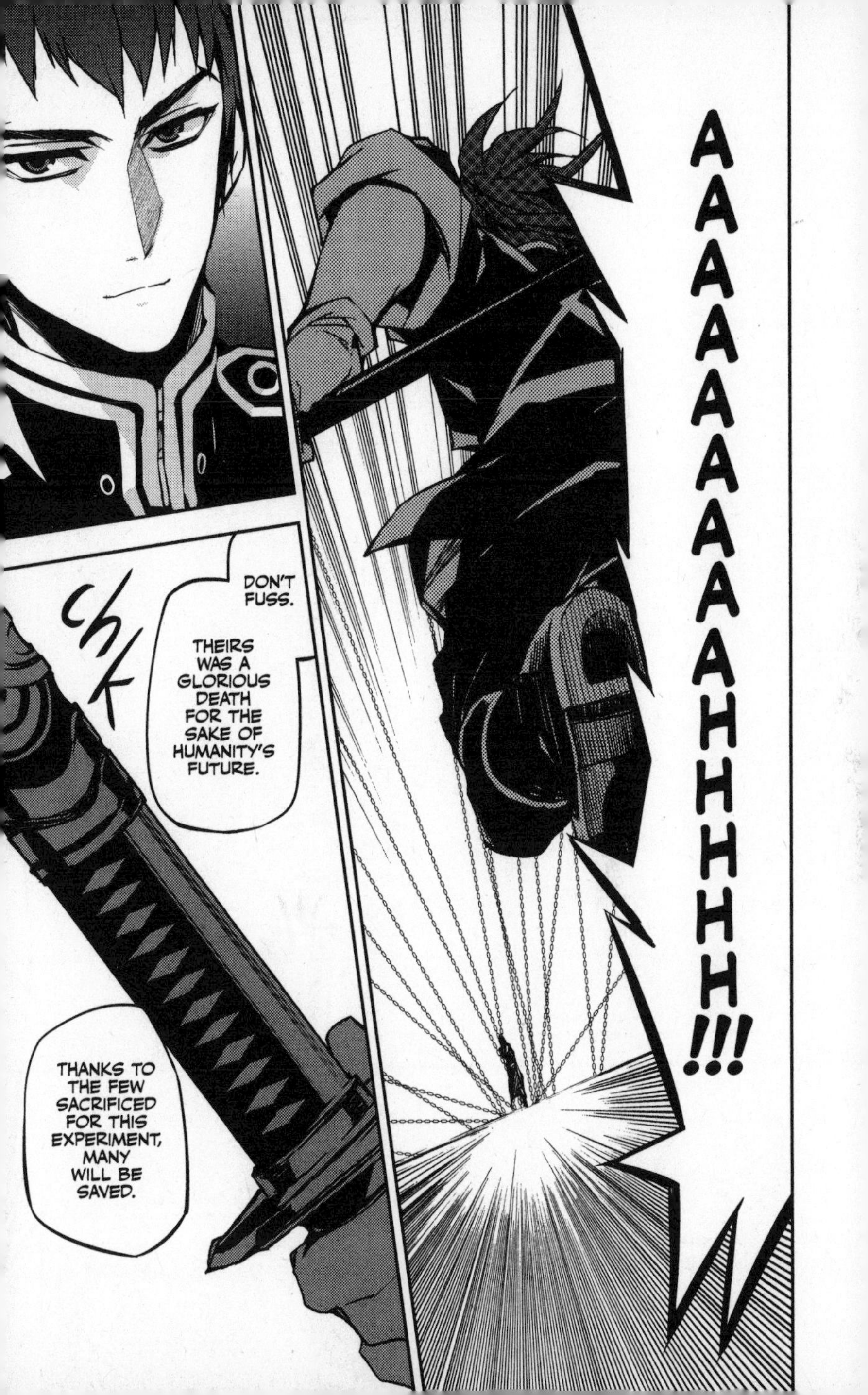
AAAAAAAAAHHHHH!!!
chk
DON'T FUSS.
THEIRS WAS A GLORIOUS DEATH FOR THE SAKE OF HUMANITY'S FUTURE.
THANKS TO THE FEW SACRIFICED FOR THIS EXPERIMENT, MANY WILL BE SAVED.

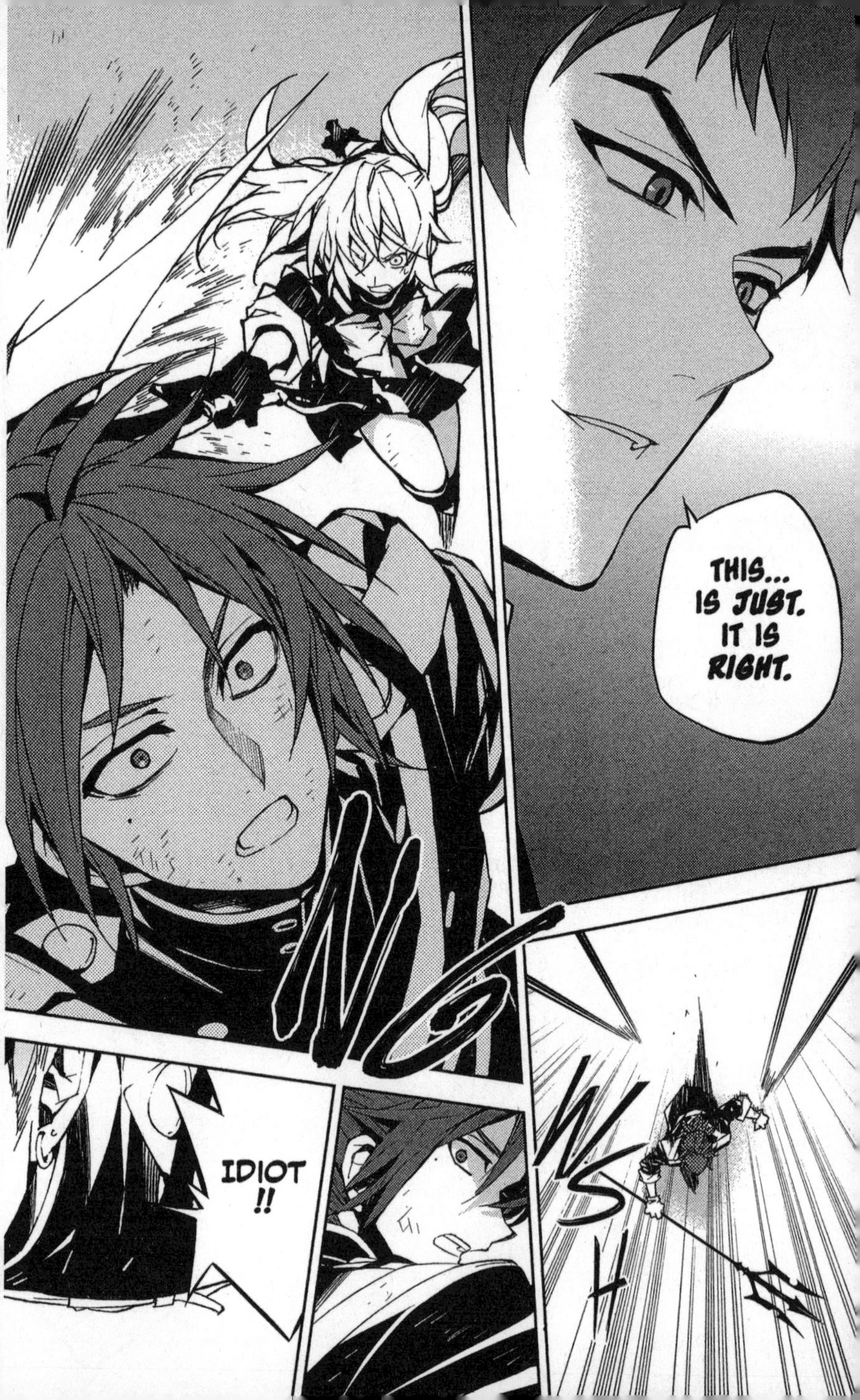
THIS... IS JUST. IT IS RIGHT.
NO
WSH
IDIOT!!

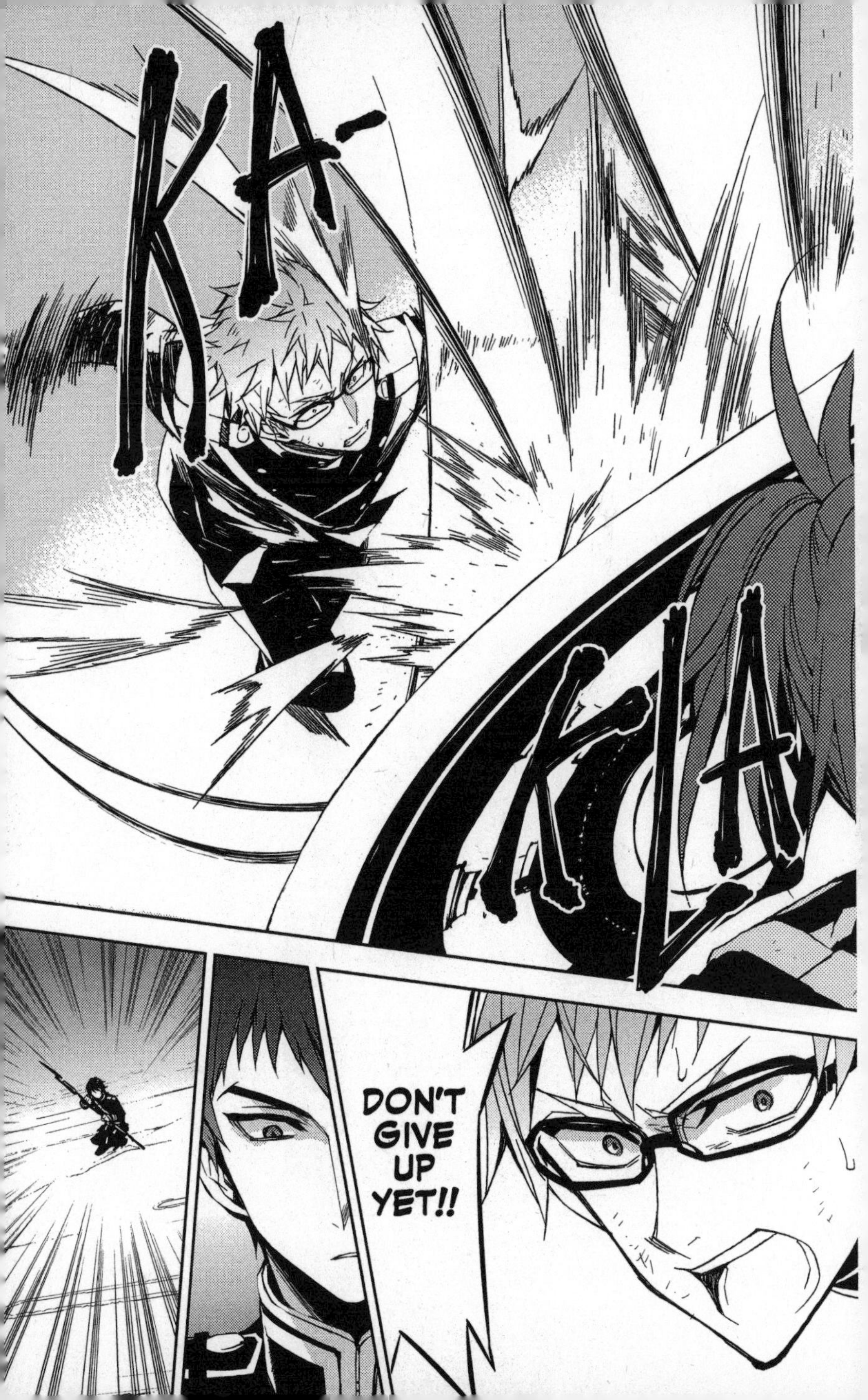
KA-
KA
DON'T GIVE UP YET!!

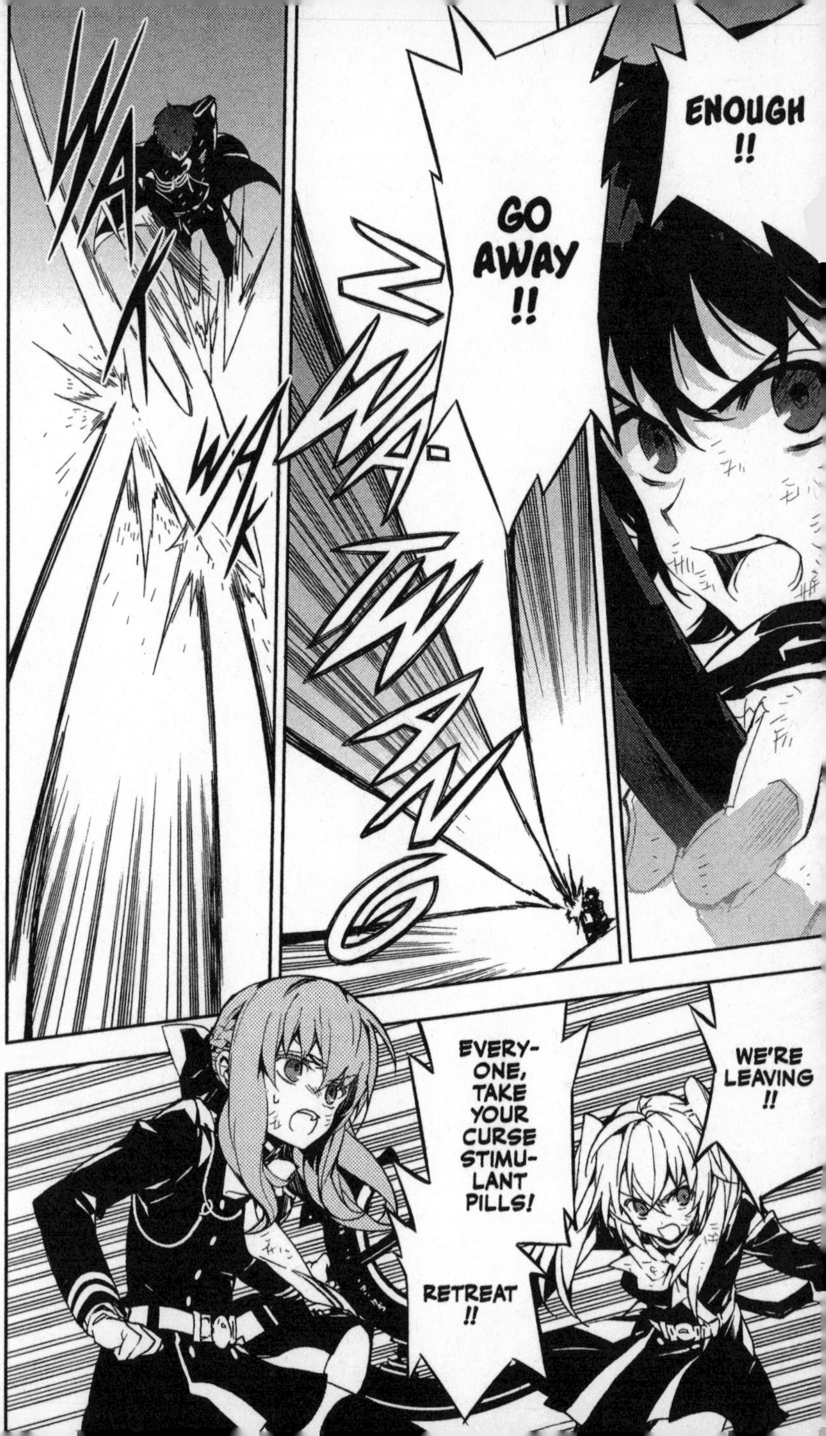

ENOUGH !!
GO AWAY !!
WE'RE LEAVING !!
EVERY-ONE, TAKE YOUR CURSE STIMU-LANT PILLS!
RETREAT !!

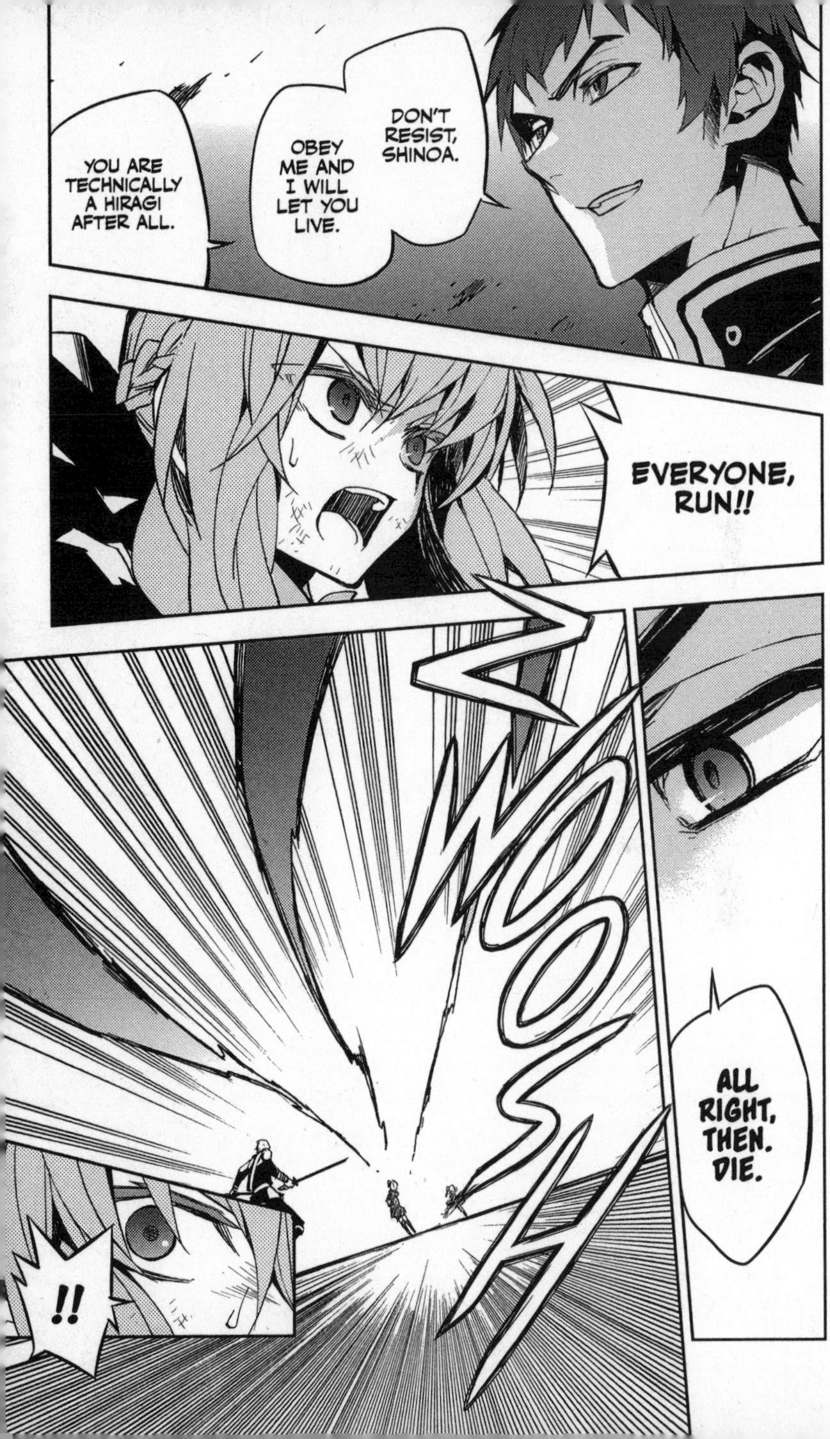

DON'T RESIST, SHINOA.
OBEY ME AND I WILL LET YOU LIVE.
YOU ARE TECHNICALLY A HIRAGI AFTER ALL.
EVERYONE, RUN!!
ALL RIGHT, THEN. DIE.
WHOOSH
!!

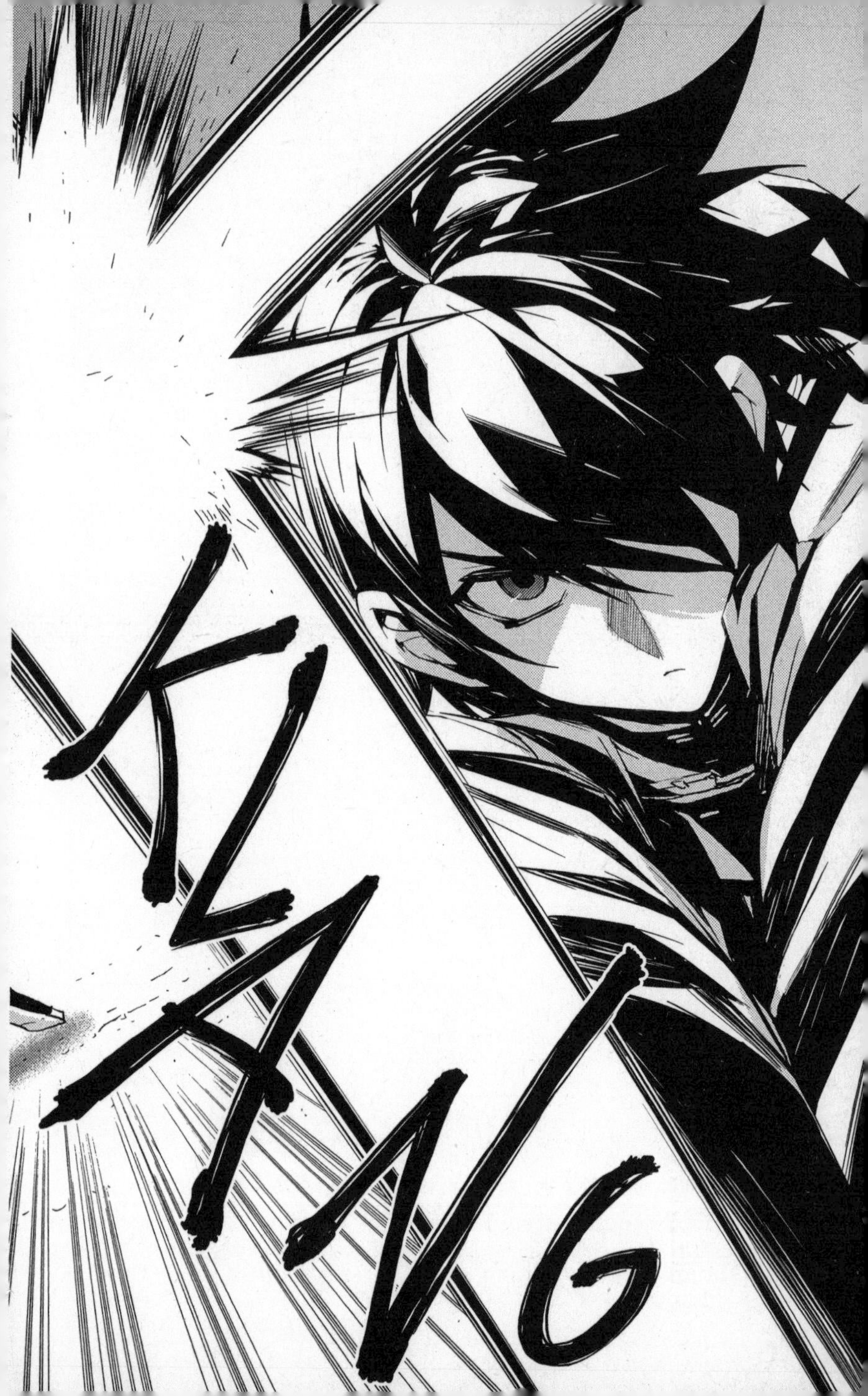
KLANG

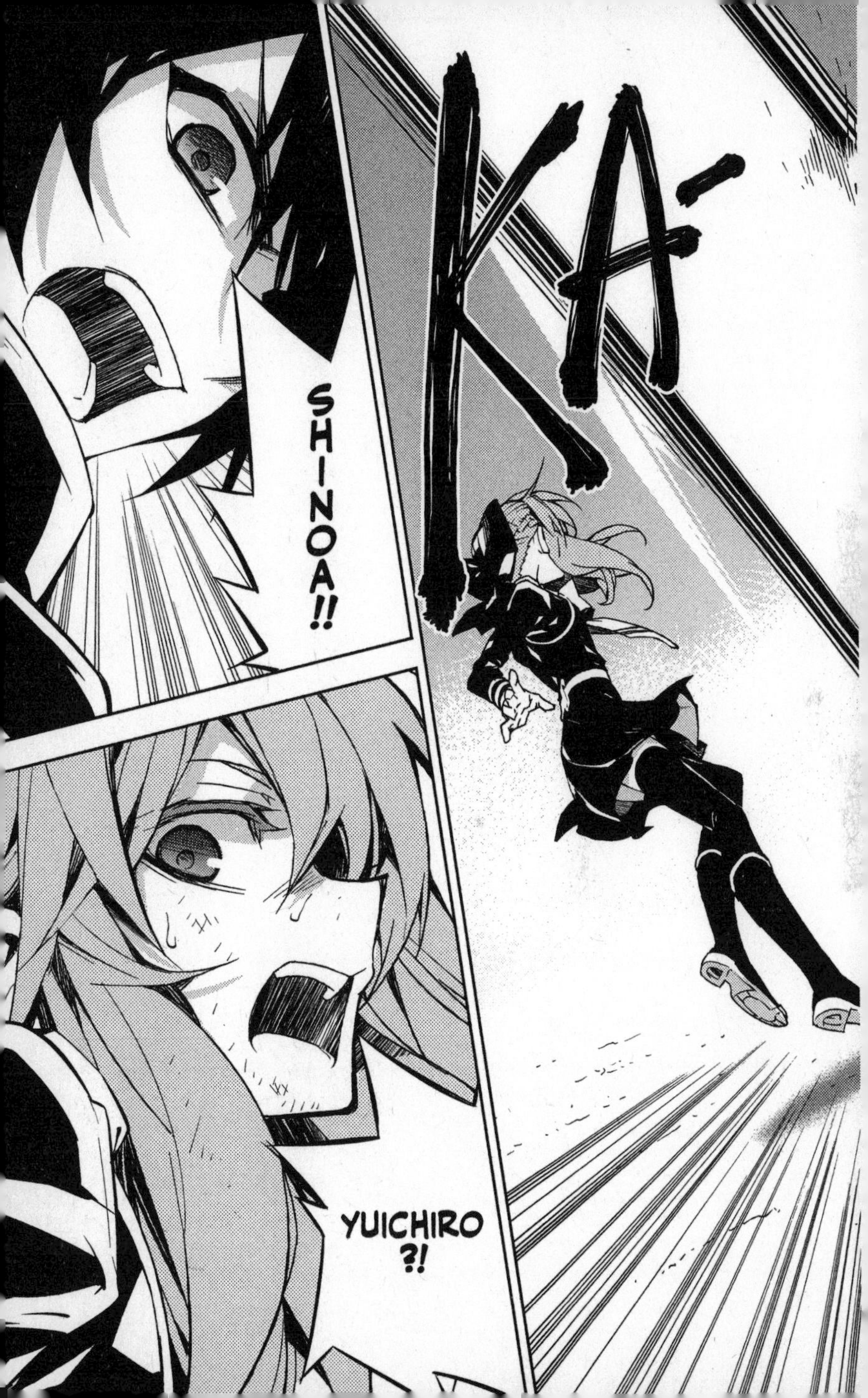
KA-
SHINOA!!
YUICHIRO ?!

Seraph of the End

VAMPIRE REIGN

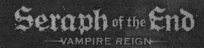

CHAPTER 40
Trumpet of the Apocalypse

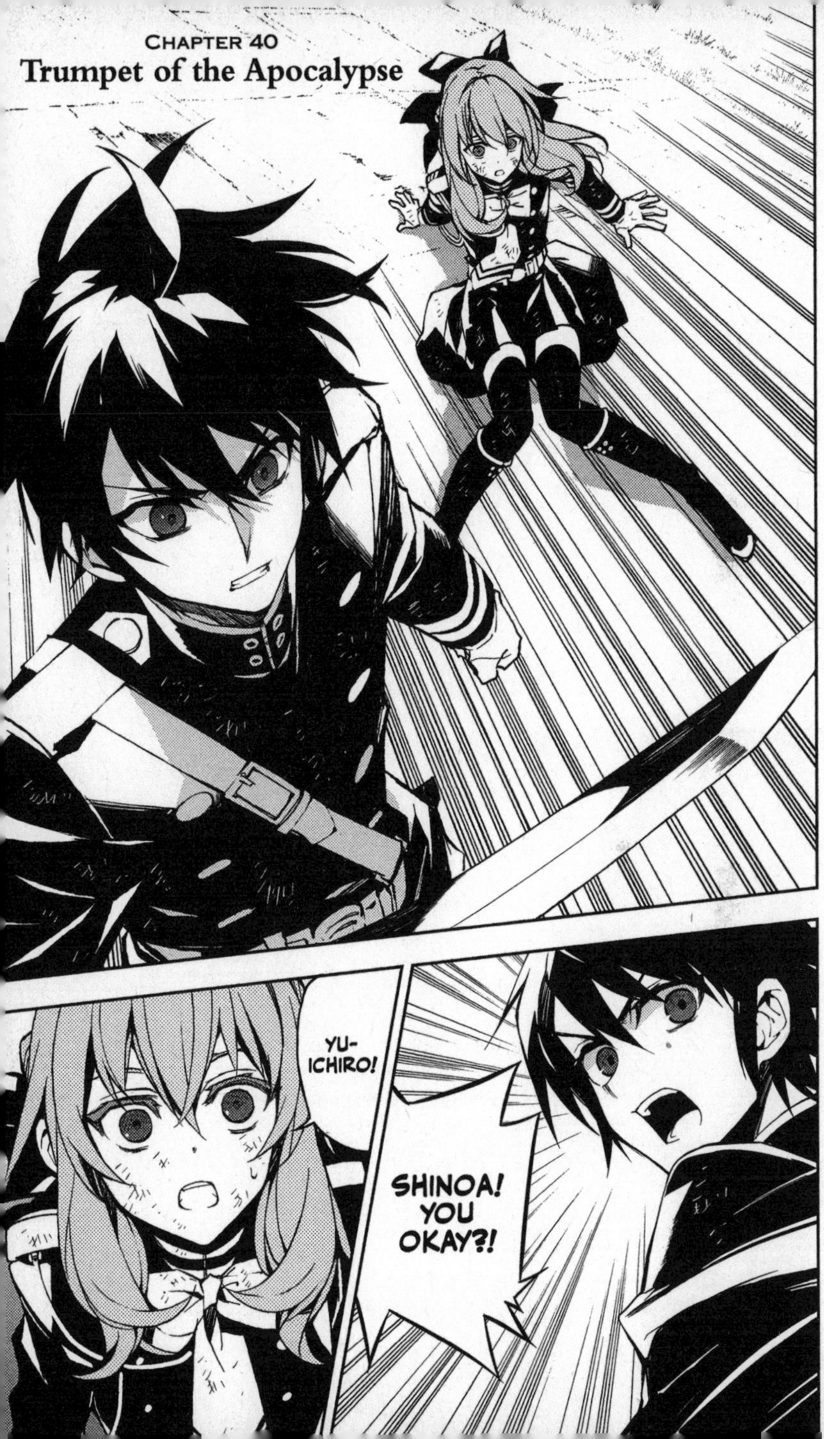
SHINOA! YOU OKAY?!
YU-ICHIRO!

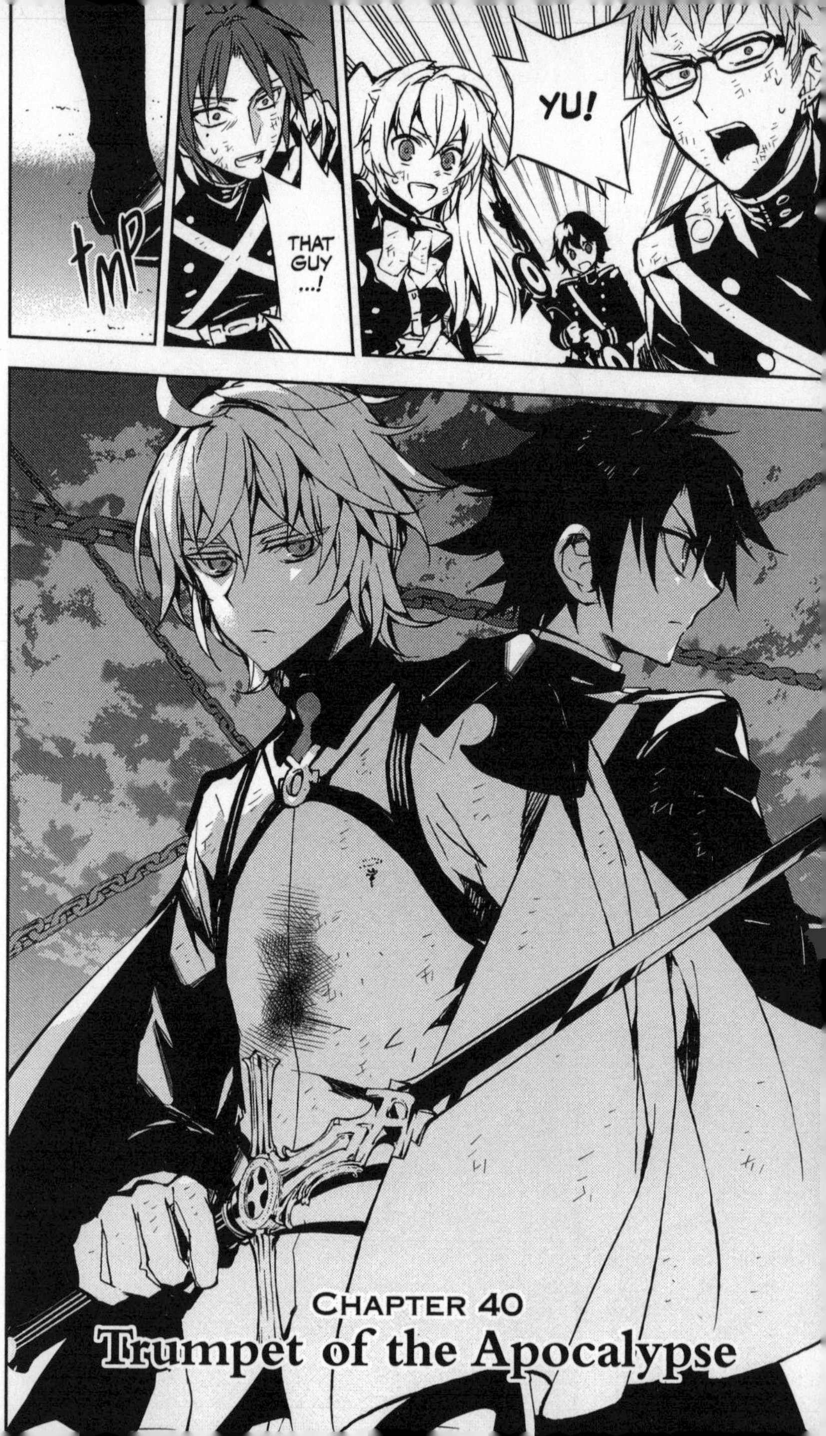
YU!
THAT GUY ...!
TMP
CHAPTER 40
Trumpet of the Apocalypse

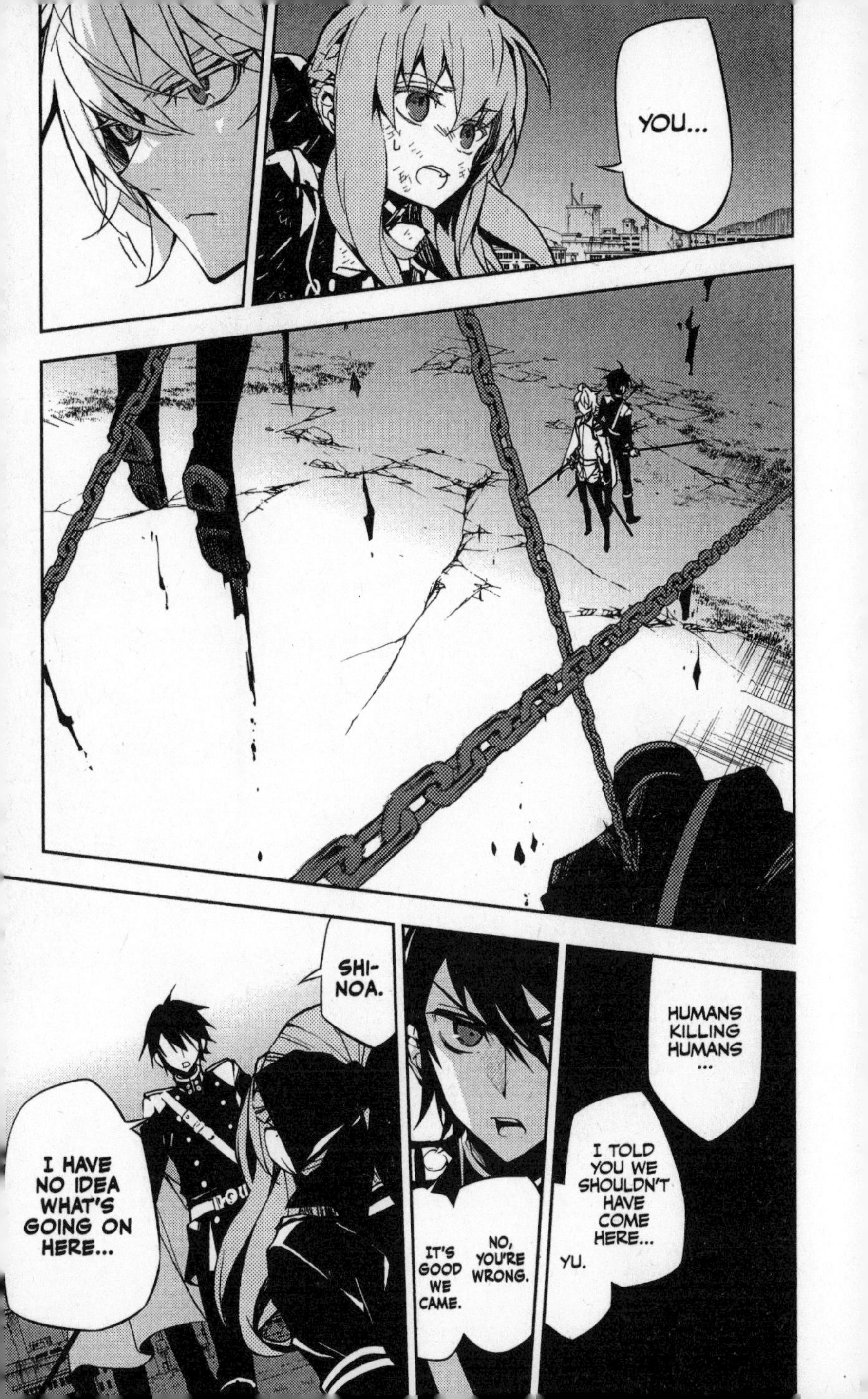
YOU...
HUMANS KILLING HUMANS...
I TOLD YOU WE SHOULDN'T HAVE COME HERE...
YU.
NO, YOU'RE WRONG.
IT'S GOOD WE CAME.
SHI-NOA.
I HAVE NO IDEA WHAT'S GOING ON HERE...

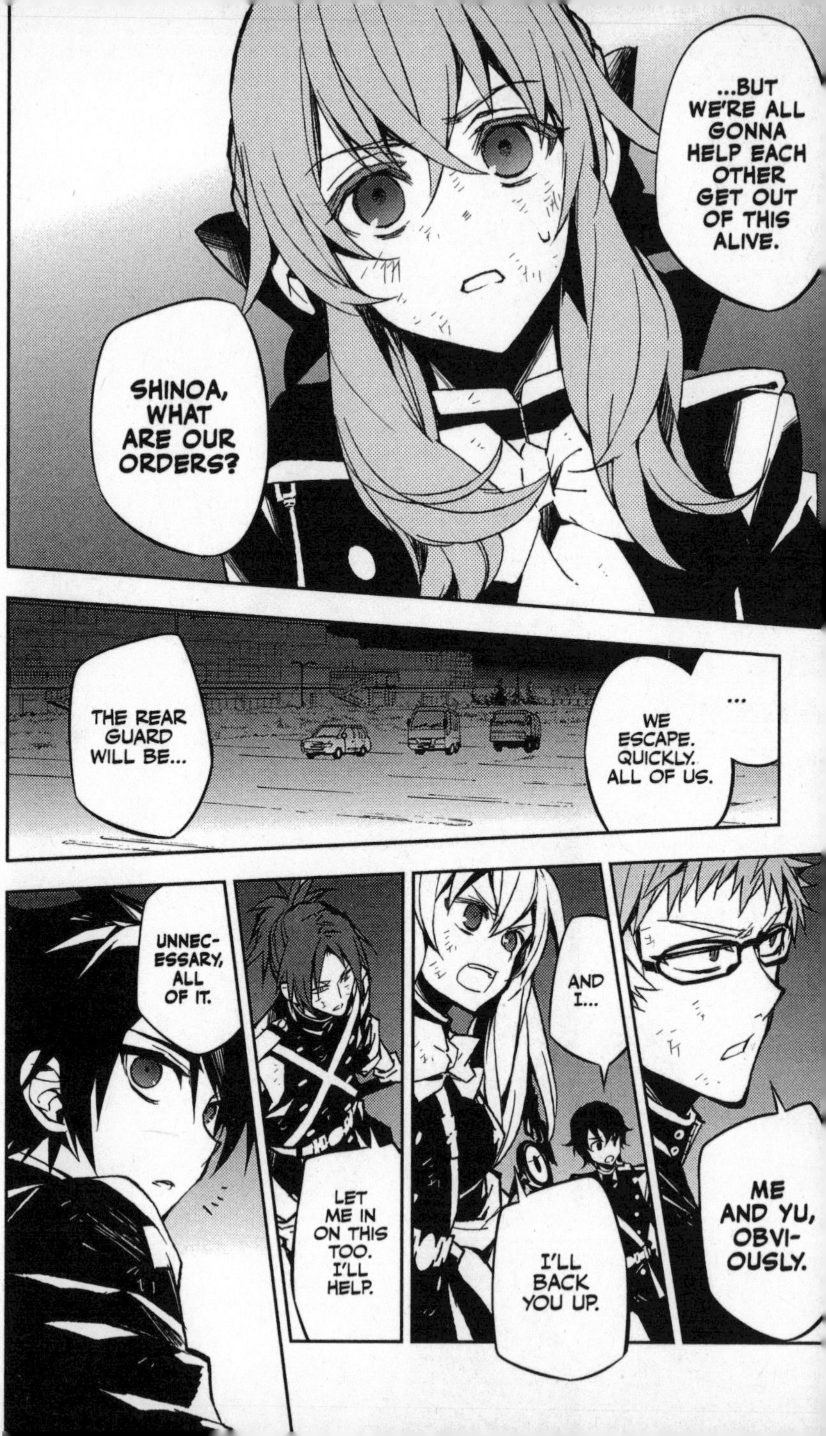
...BUT WE'RE ALL GONNA HELP EACH OTHER GET OUT OF THIS ALIVE.
SHINOA, WHAT ARE OUR ORDERS?
... WE ESCAPE. QUICKLY. ALL OF US.
THE REAR GUARD WILL BE...
ME AND YU, OBVIOUSLY.
AND I...
I'LL BACK YOU UP.
LET ME IN ON THIS TOO. I'LL HELP.
UNNECESSARY, ALL OF IT.

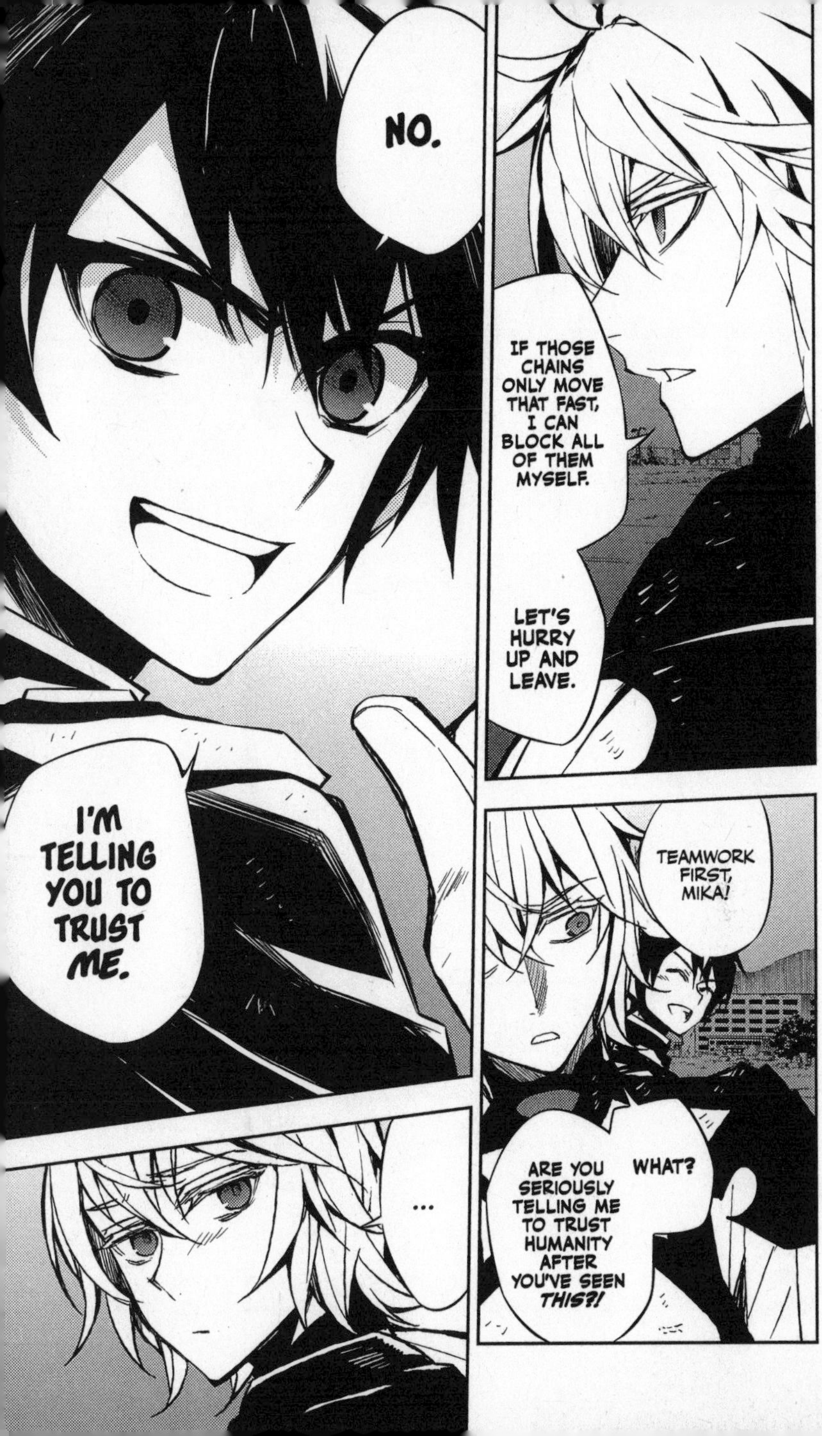
IF THOSE CHAINS ONLY MOVE THAT FAST, I CAN BLOCK ALL OF THEM MYSELF.
LET'S HURRY UP AND LEAVE.
NO.
I'M TELLING YOU TO TRUST ME.
TEAMWORK FIRST, MIKA!
WHAT?
ARE YOU SERIOUSLY TELLING ME TO TRUST HUMANITY AFTER YOU'VE SEEN THIS?!
...

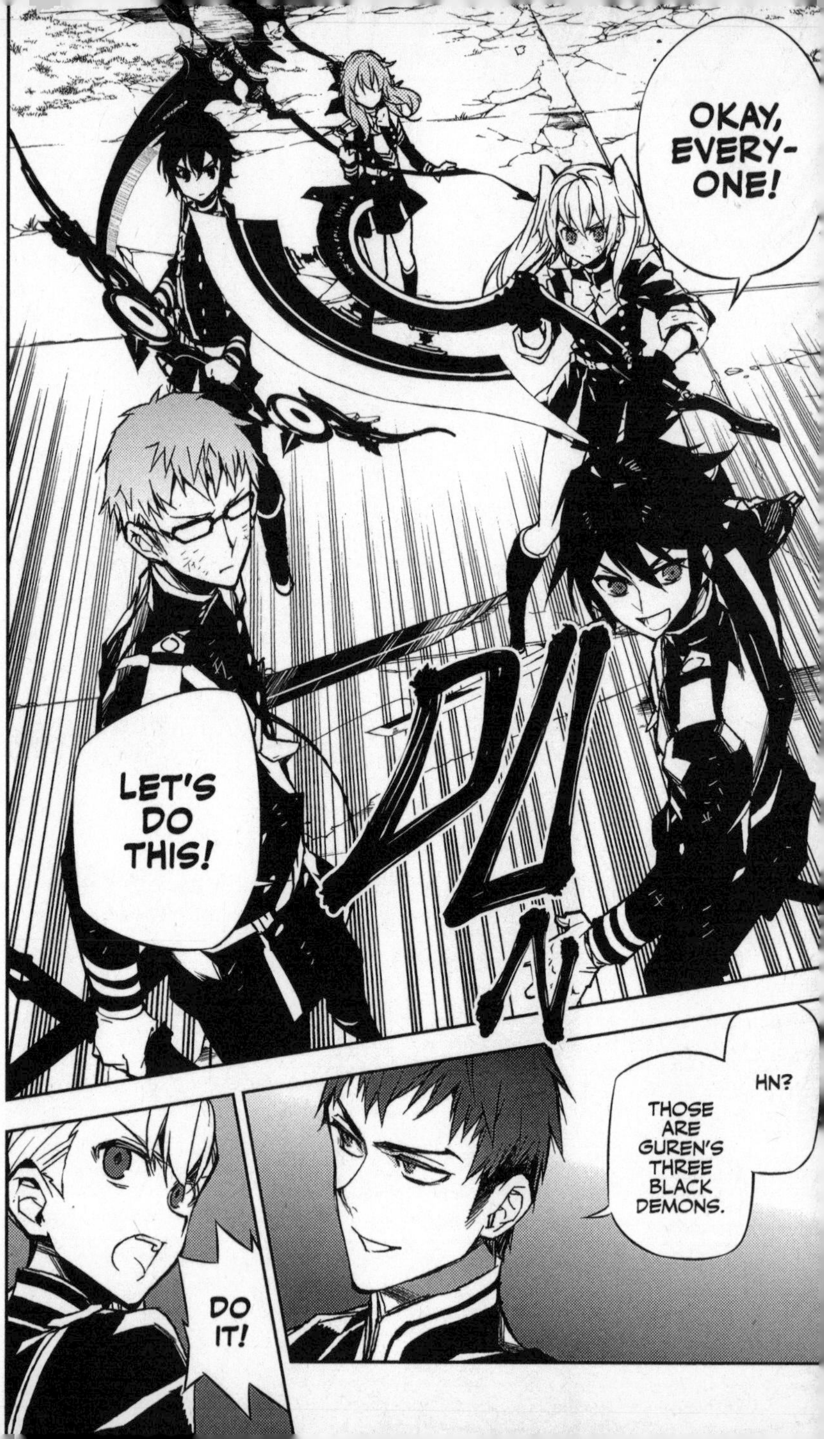
OKAY, EVERY-ONE!
LET'S DO THIS!
HN?
THOSE ARE GUREN'S THREE BLACK DEMONS.
DO IT!

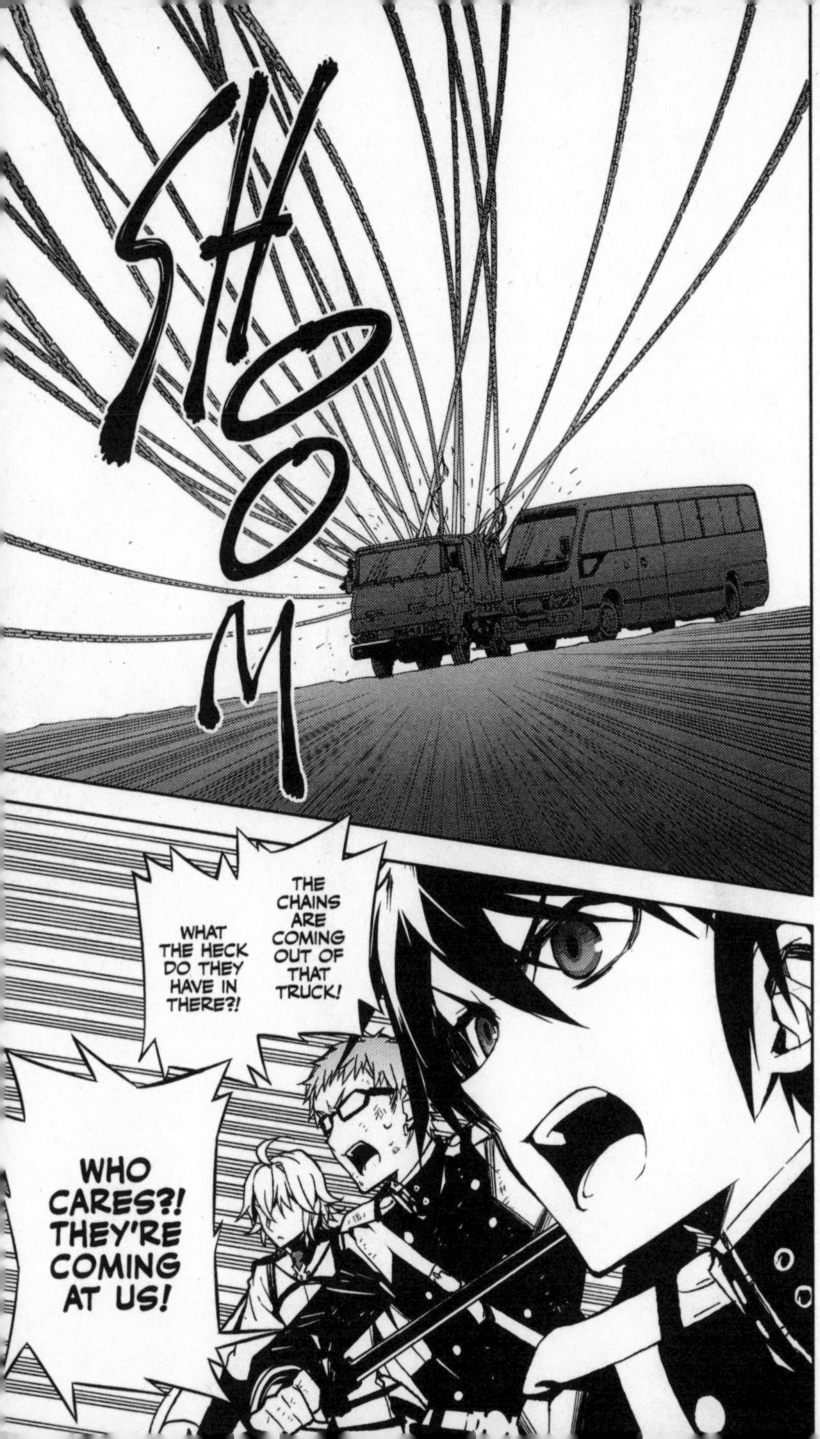
SHOOM
THE CHAINS ARE COMING OUT OF THAT TRUCK!
WHAT THE HECK DO THEY HAVE IN THERE?!
WHO CARES?! THEY'RE COMING AT US!

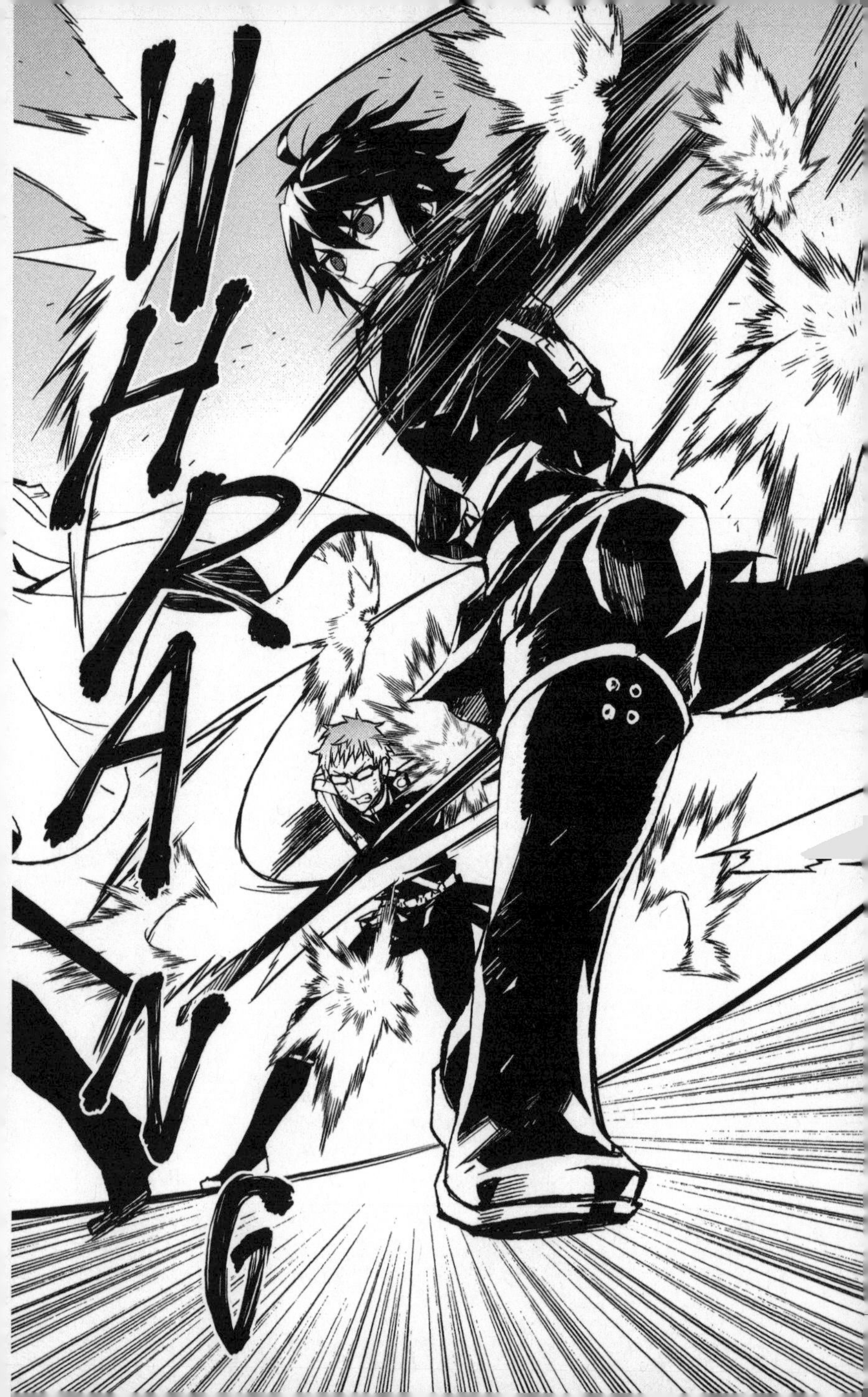
WHRANG

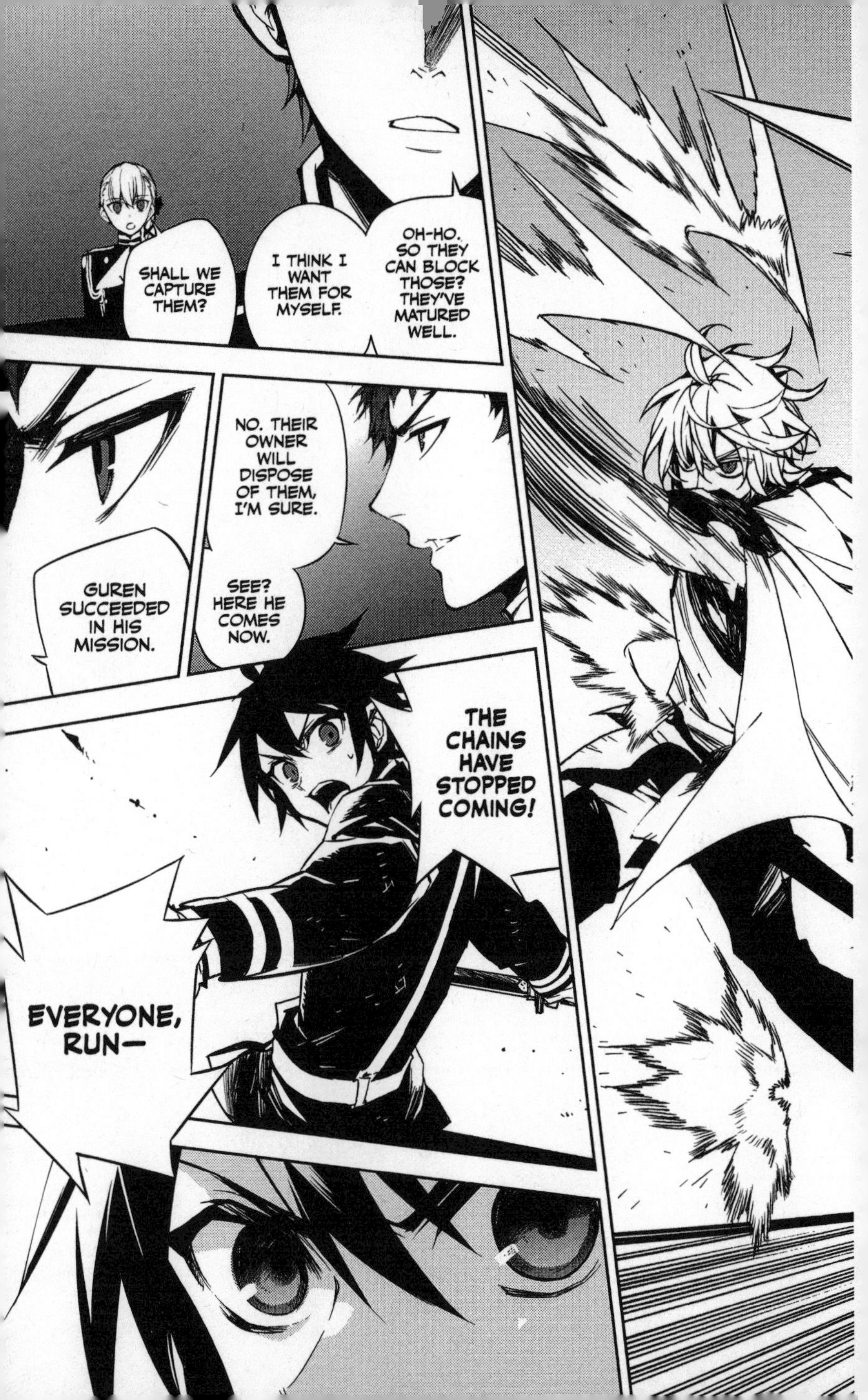
OH-HO. SO THEY CAN BLOCK THOSE? THEY'VE MATURED WELL.
I THINK I WANT THEM FOR MYSELF.
SHALL WE CAPTURE THEM?
NO. THEIR OWNER WILL DISPOSE OF THEM, I'M SURE.
SEE? HERE HE COMES NOW.
GUREN SUCCEEDED IN HIS MISSION.
THE CHAINS HAVE STOPPED COMING!
EVERYONE, RUN—

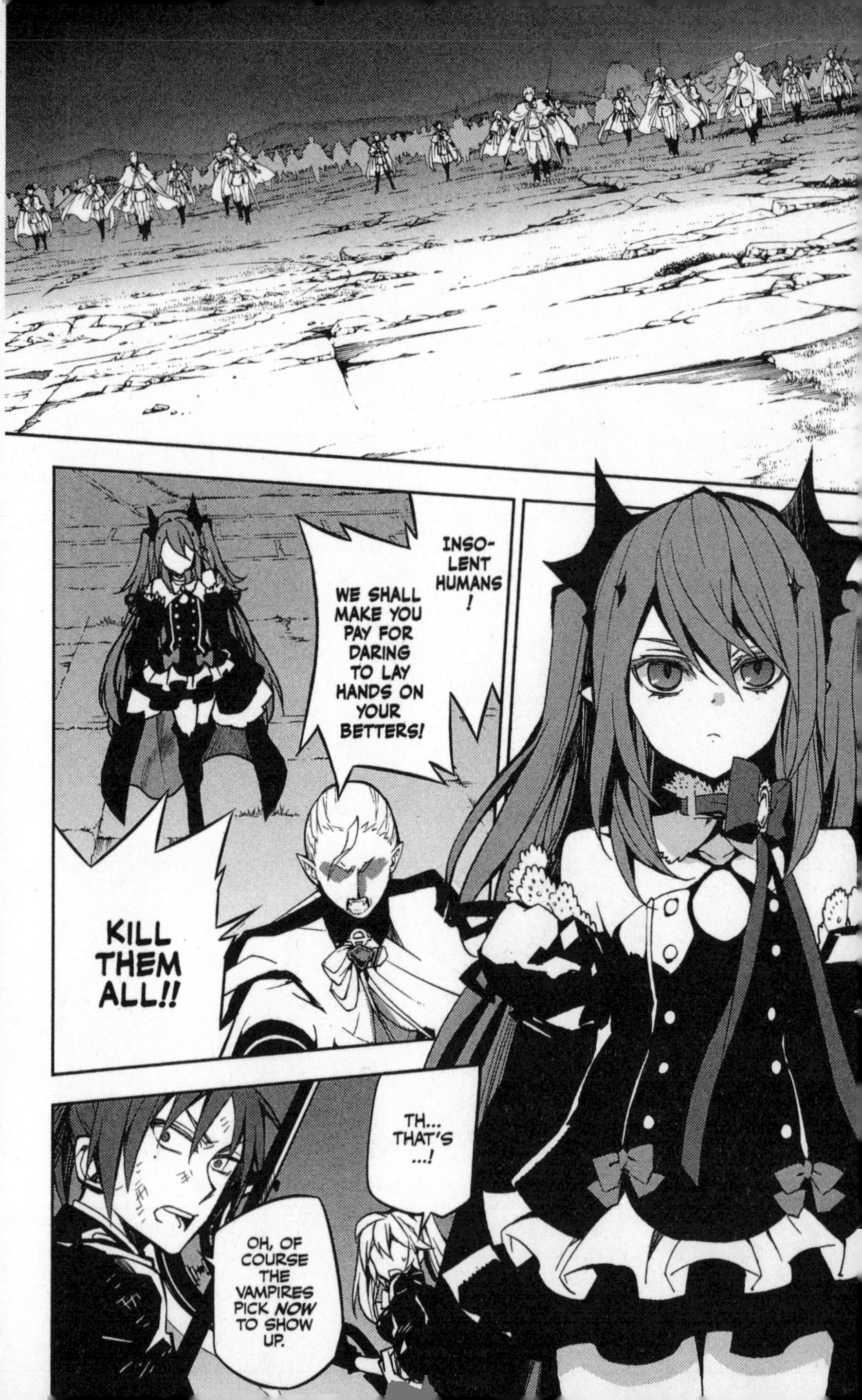
INSO-LENT HUMANS!
WE SHALL MAKE YOU PAY FOR DARING TO LAY HANDS ON YOUR BETTERS!
KILL THEM ALL!!
TH... THAT'S ...!
OH, OF COURSE THE VAMPIRES PICK *NOW* TO SHOW UP.

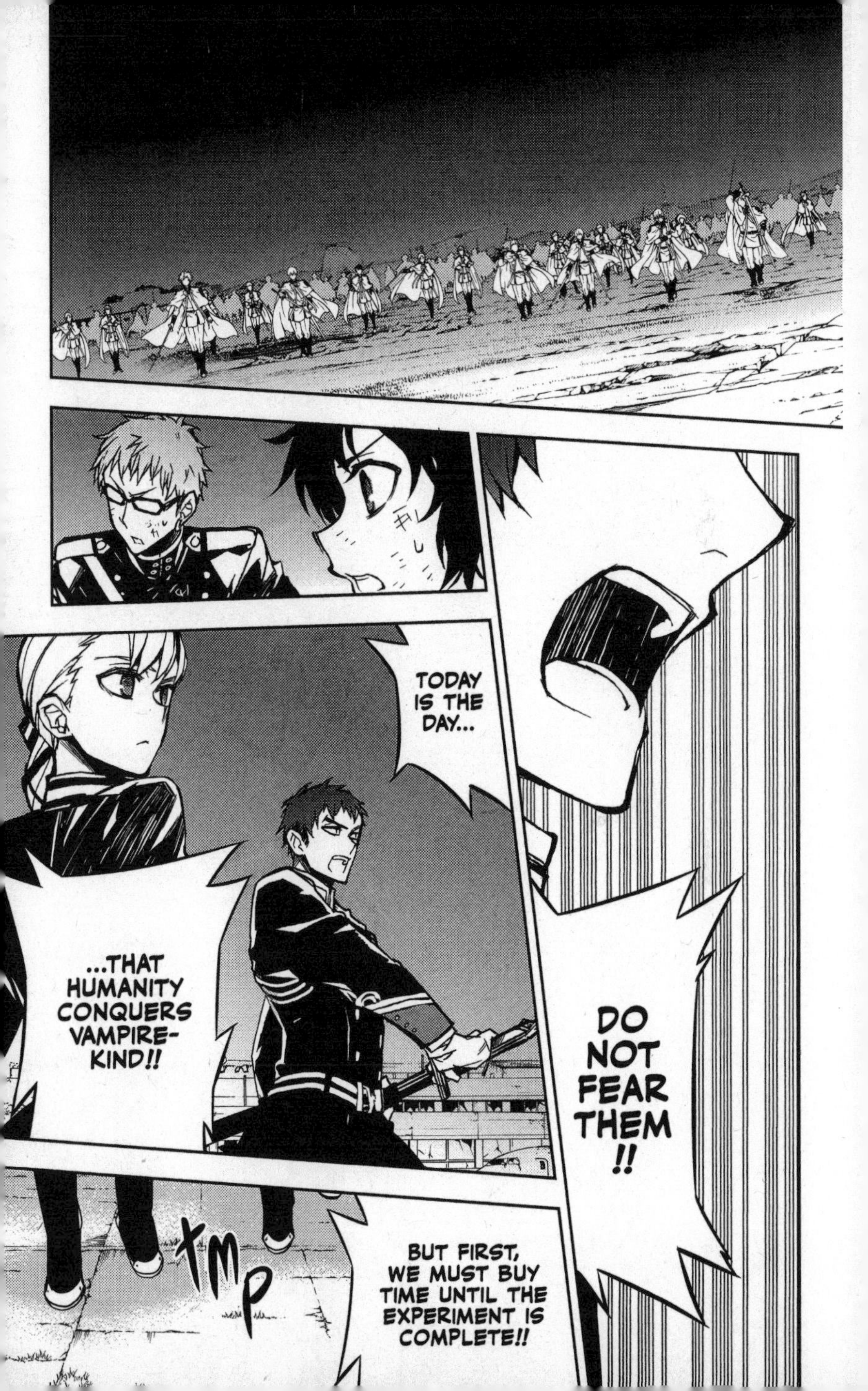
DO NOT FEAR THEM!!
TODAY IS THE DAY...
...THAT HUMANITY CONQUERS VAMPIRE-KIND!!
BUT FIRST, WE MUST BUY TIME UNTIL THE EXPERIMENT IS COMPLETE!!
TMP

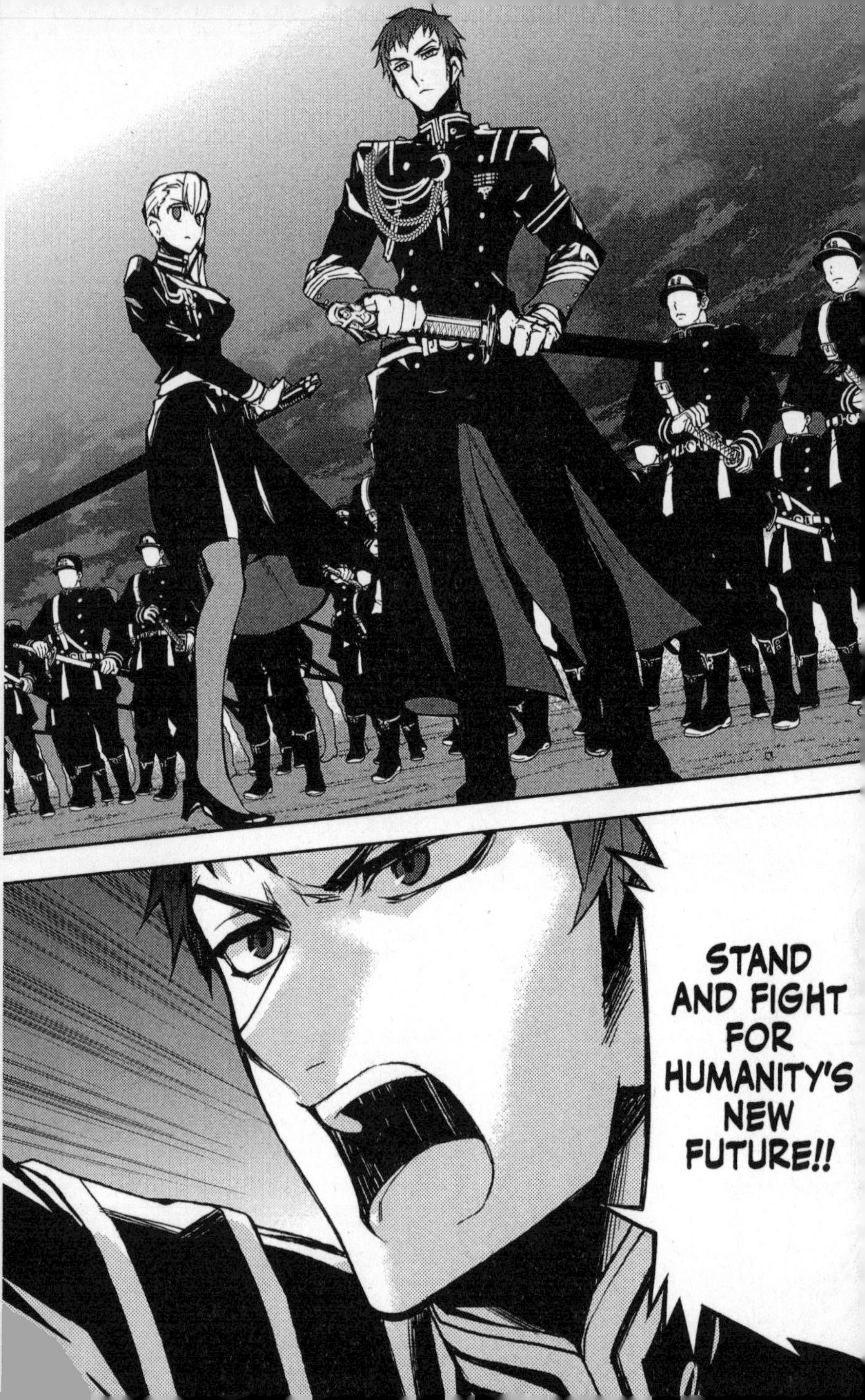
STAND AND FIGHT FOR HUMANITY'S NEW FUTURE!!

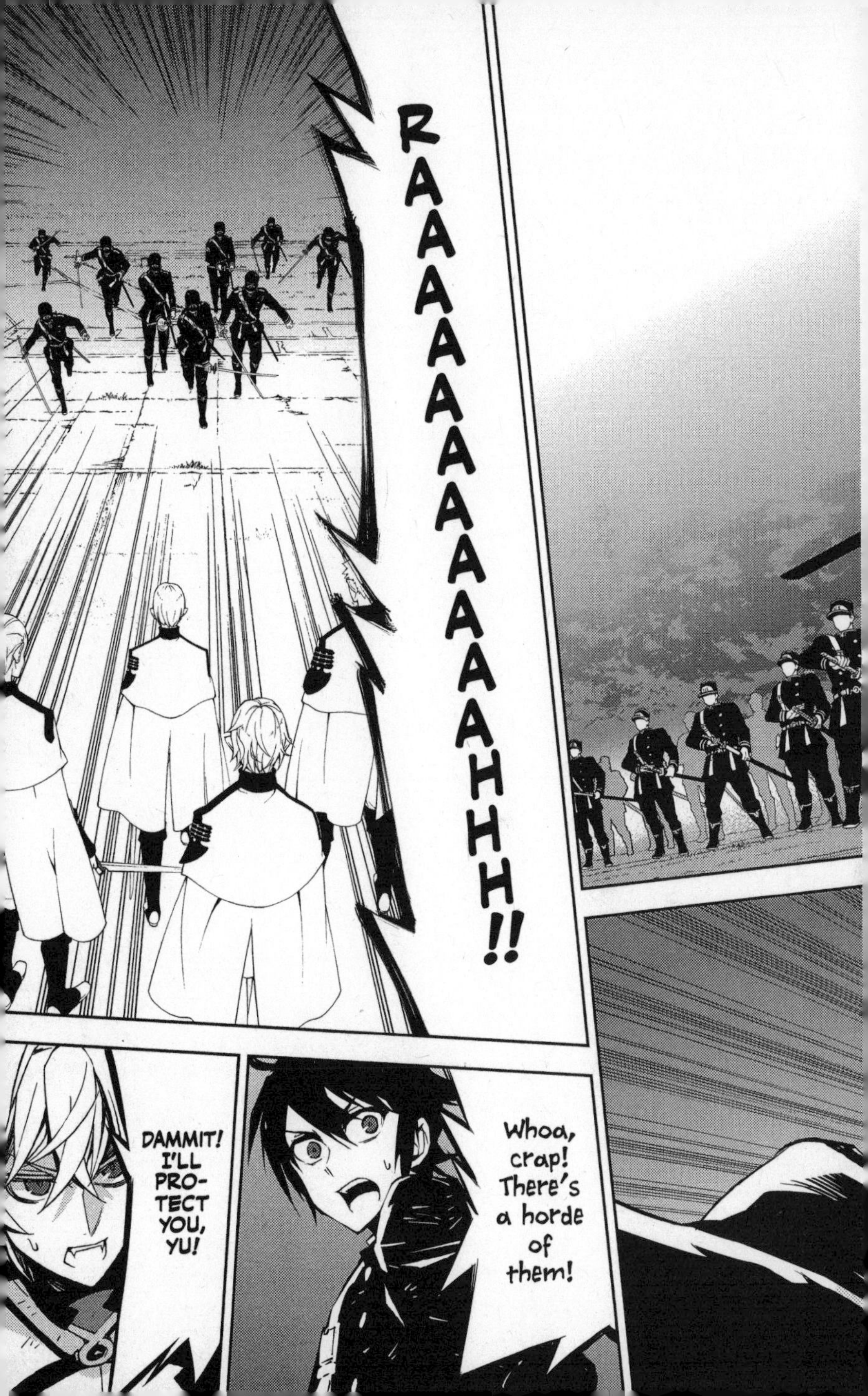
RAAAAAAAAAAAAHHH!!
Whoa, crap! There's a horde of them!
DAMMIT! I'LL PROTECT YOU, YU!

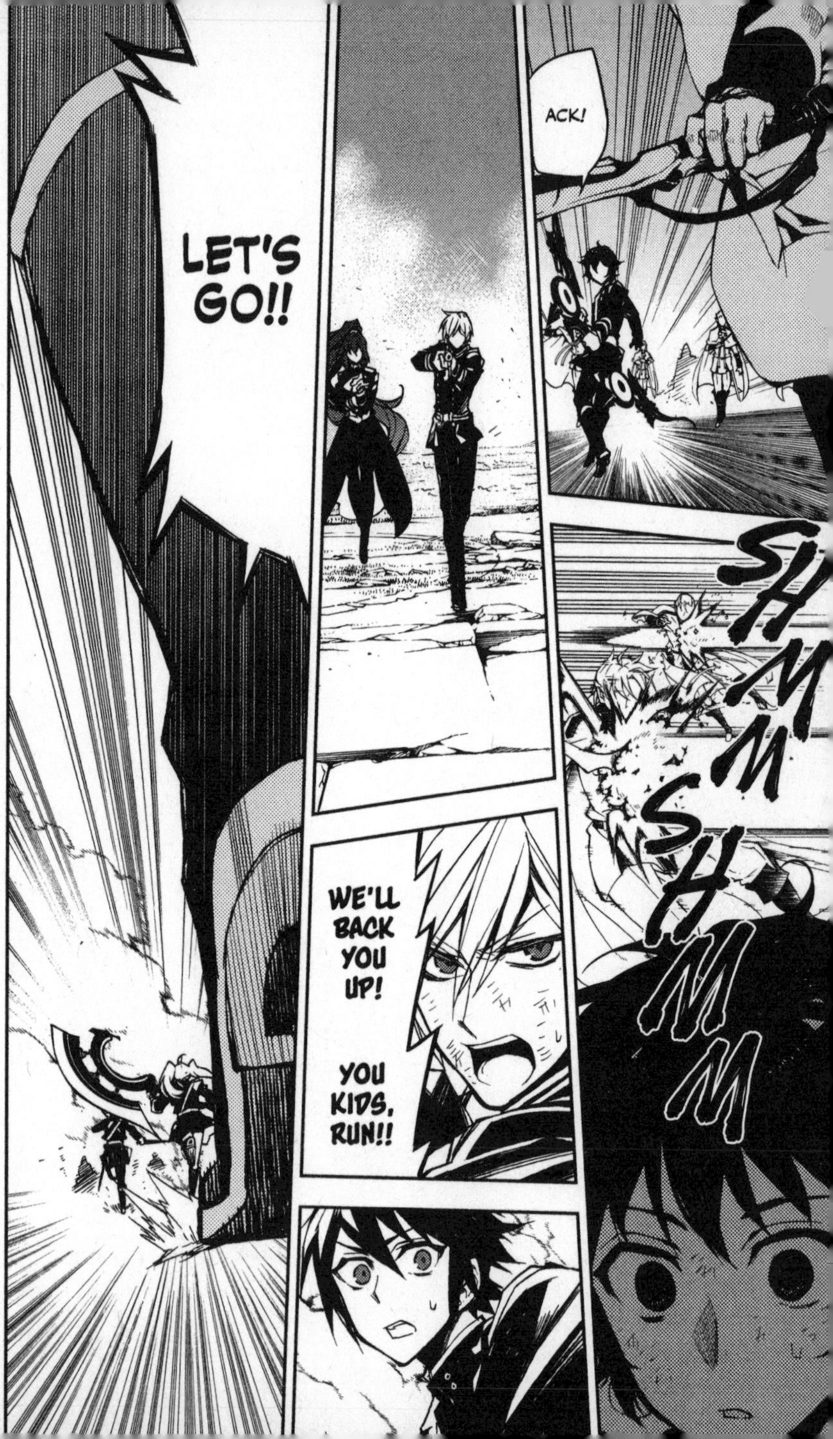
ACK!
SHMMM
SHMMM
WE'LL BACK YOU UP!
YOU KIDS, RUN!!
LET'S GO!!

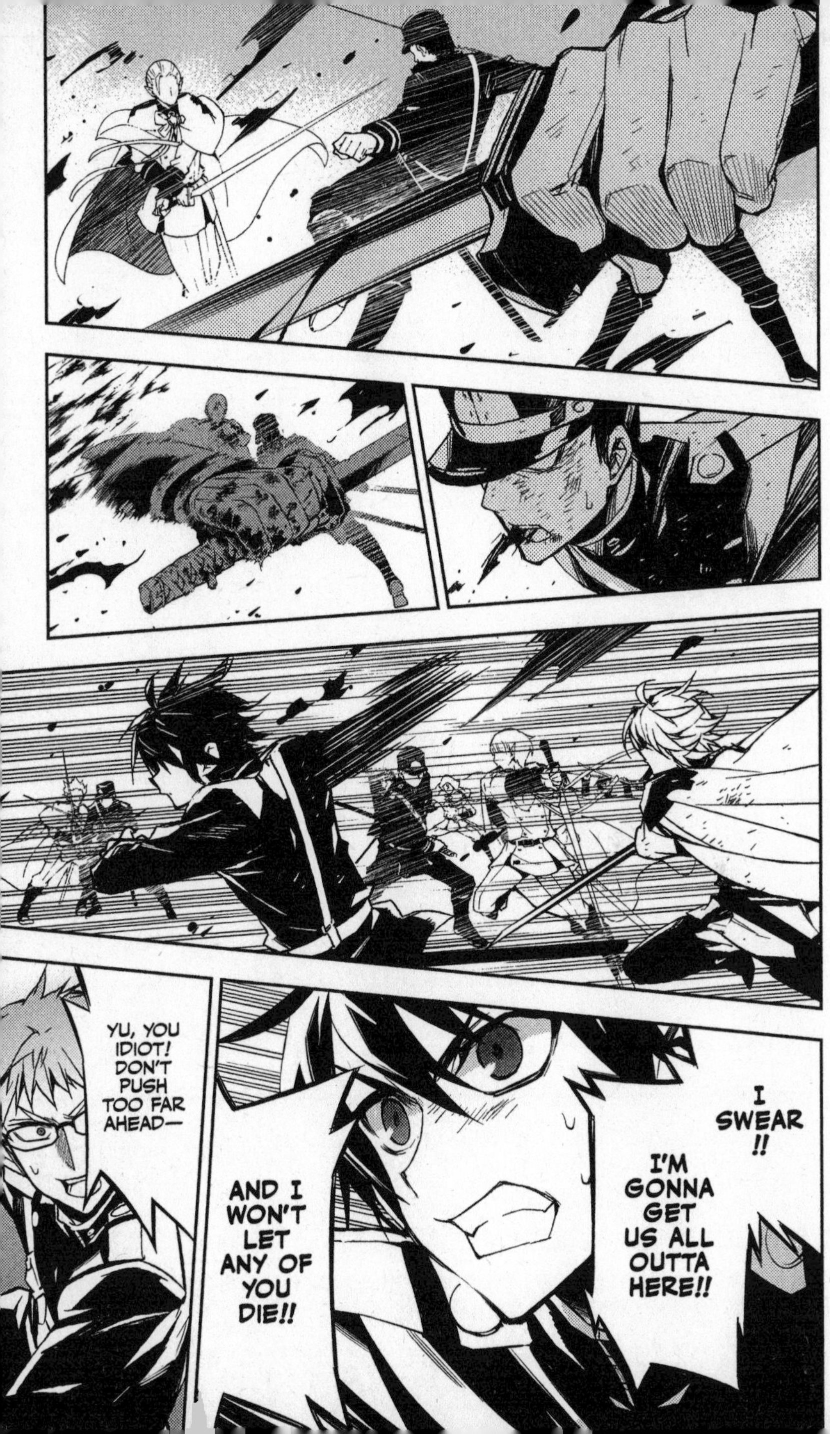
I SWEAR!!
I'M GONNA GET US ALL OUTTA HERE!!
AND I WON'T LET ANY OF YOU DIE!!
YU, YOU IDIOT! DON'T PUSH TOO FAR AHEAD—

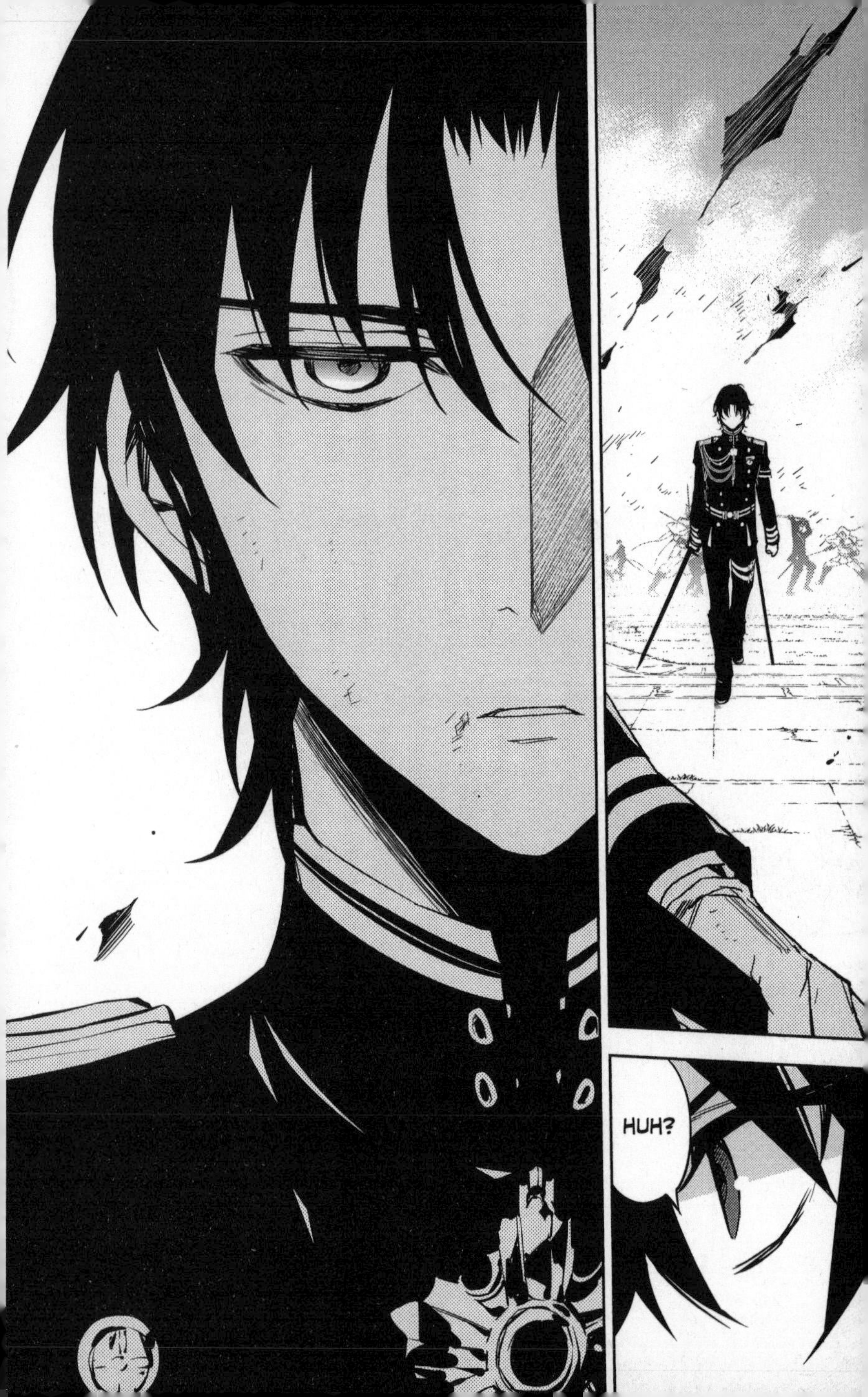
HUH?

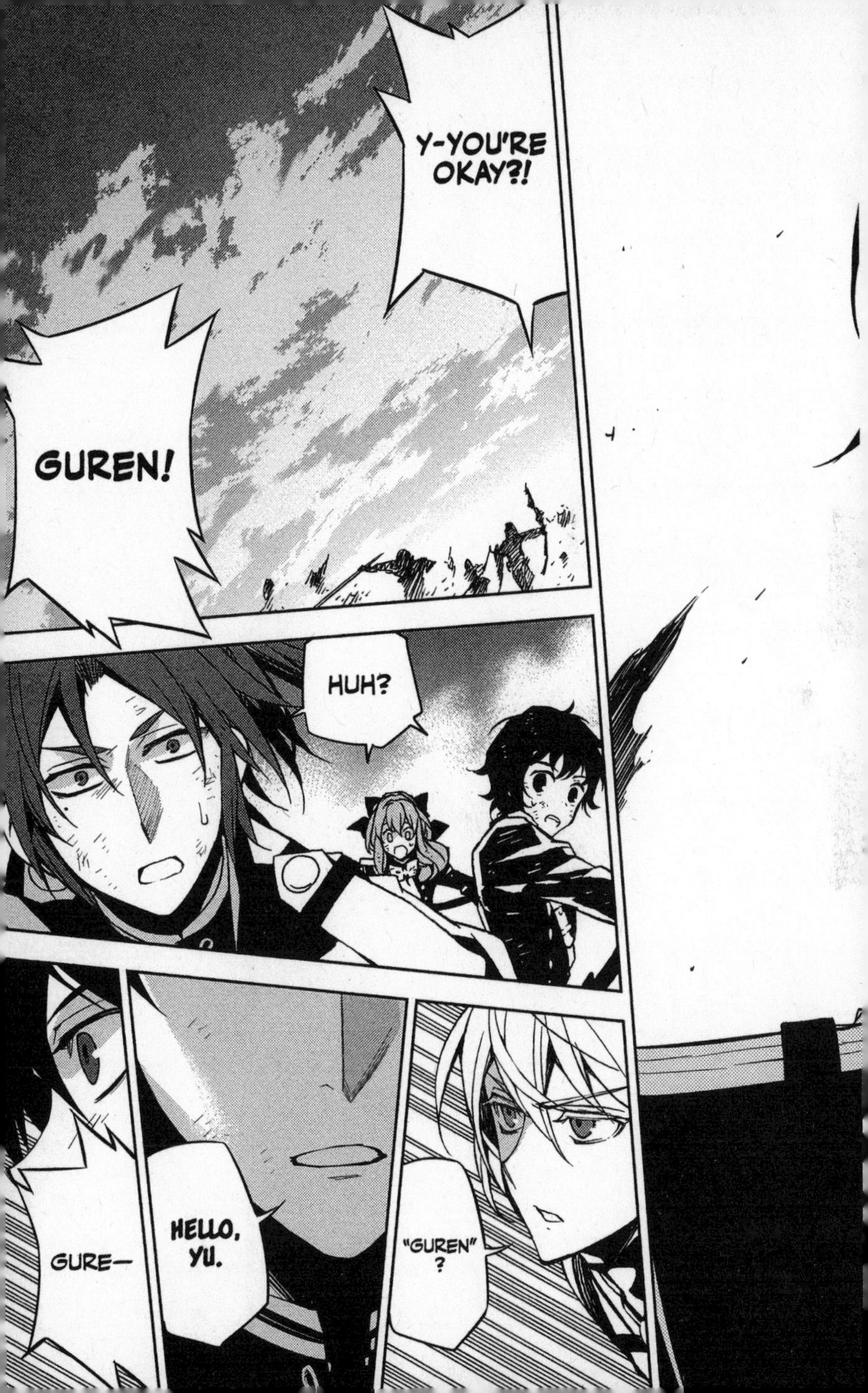
Y-YOU'RE OKAY?!
GUREN!
HUH?
"GUREN"?
HELLO, YU.
GURE—

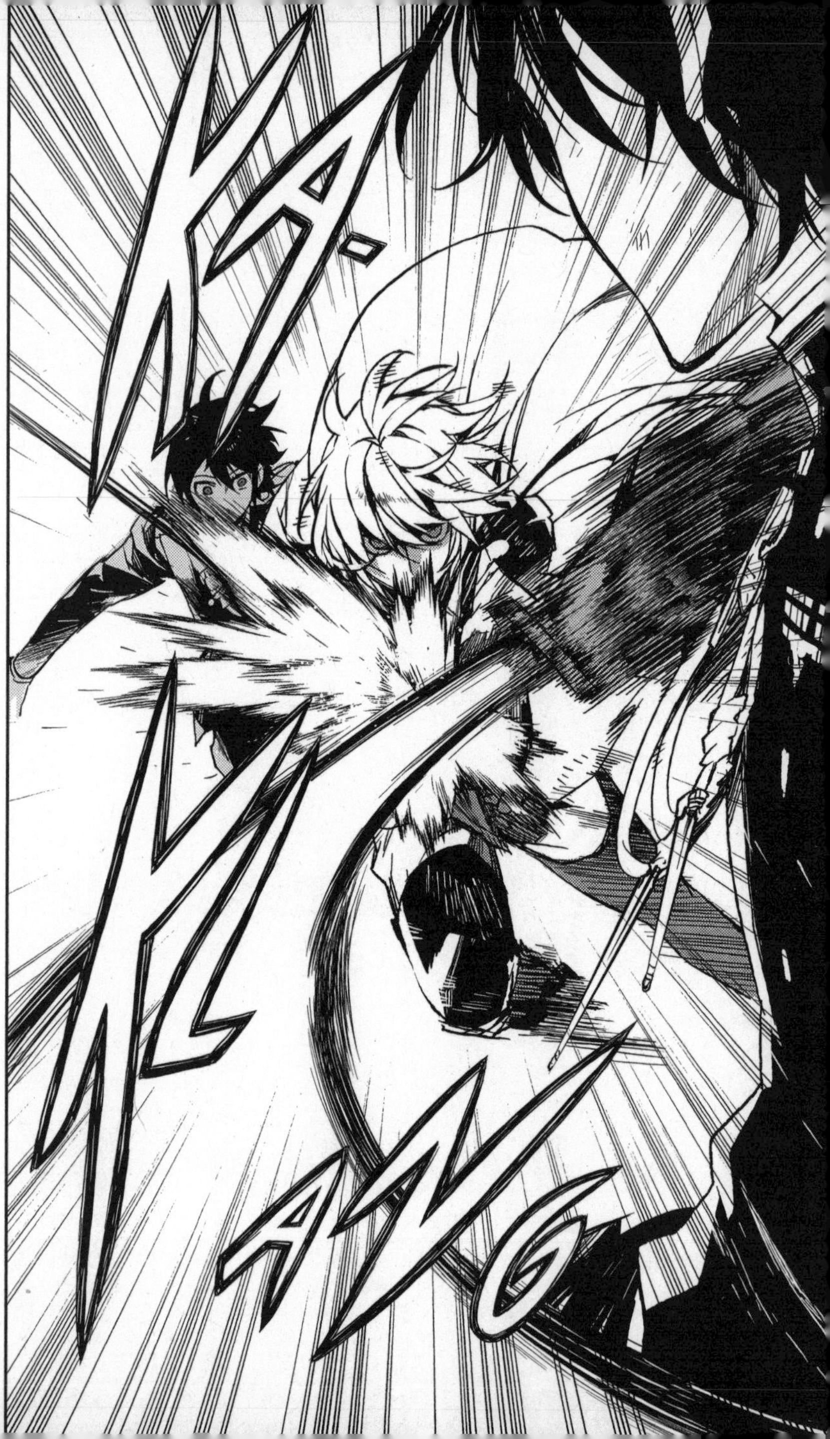
KA-KLANG

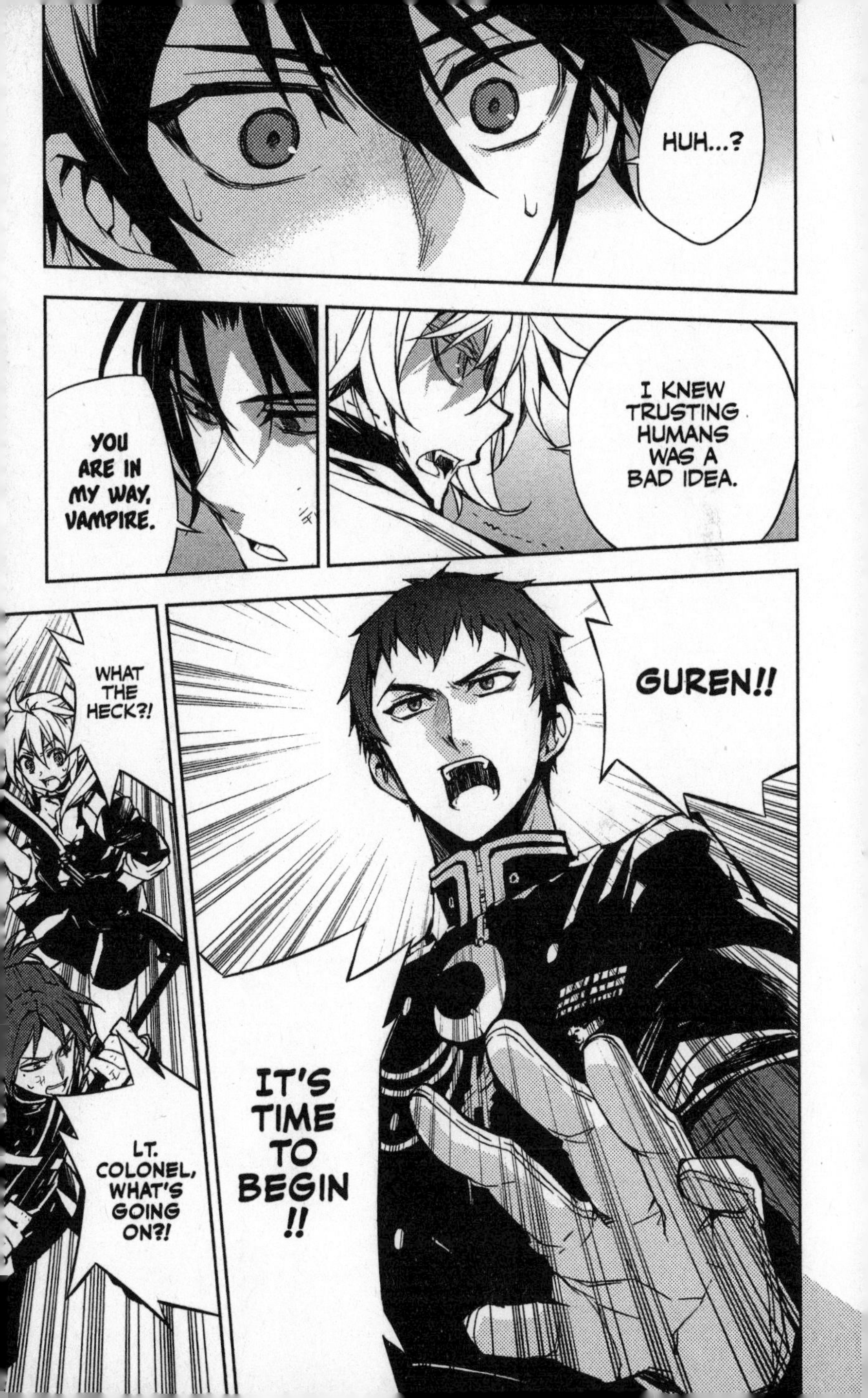
HUH...?
I KNEW TRUSTING HUMANS WAS A BAD IDEA.
YOU ARE IN MY WAY, VAMPIRE.
GUREN!!
IT'S TIME TO BEGIN!!
WHAT THE HECK?!
LT. COLONEL, WHAT'S GOING ON?!

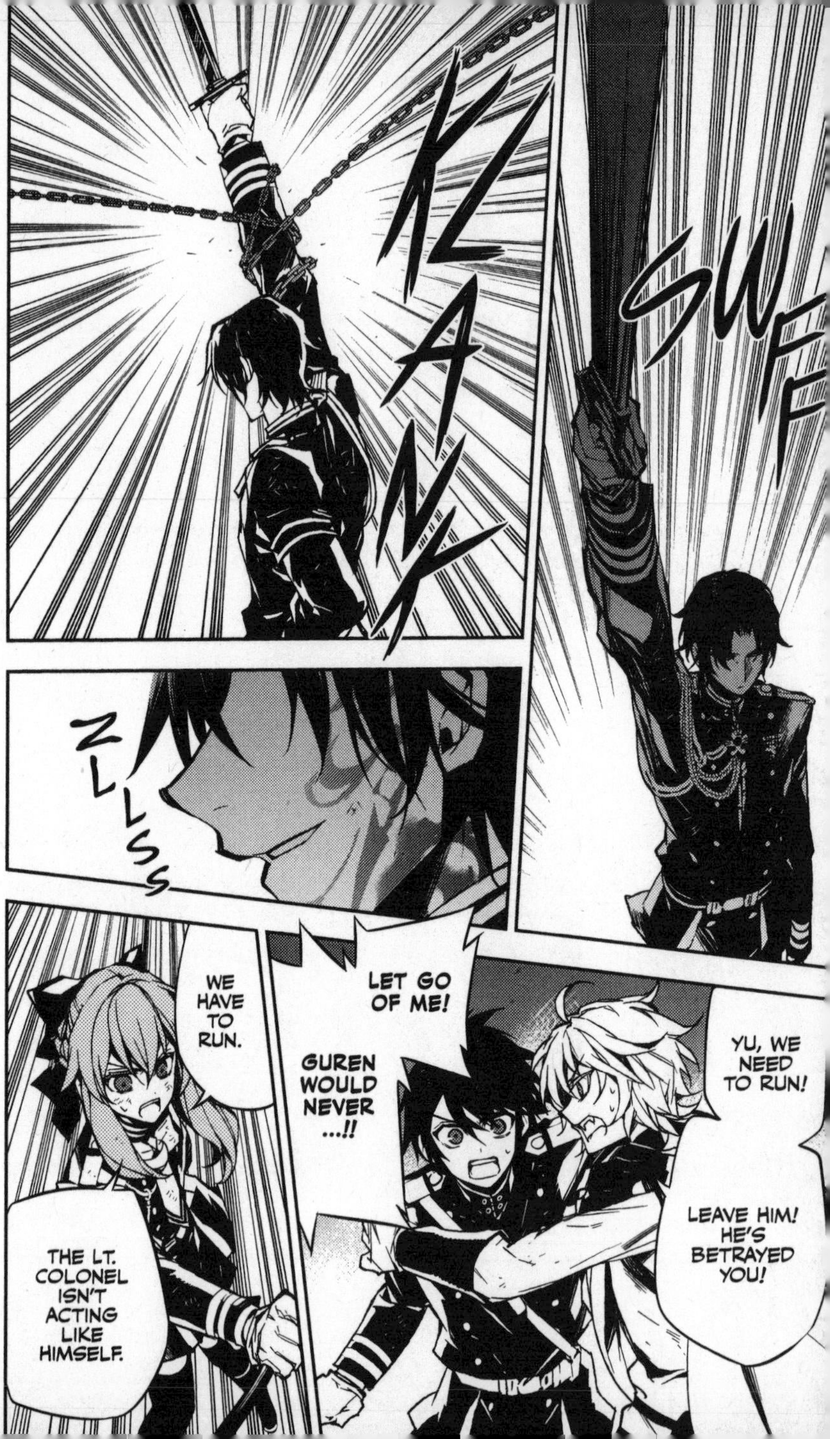
SWFF
KLANK
ZLLSSS
YU, WE NEED TO RUN!
LEAVE HIM! HE'S BETRAYED YOU!
LET GO OF ME!
GUREN WOULD NEVER ...!!
WE HAVE TO RUN.
THE LT. COLONEL ISN'T ACTING LIKE HIMSELF.

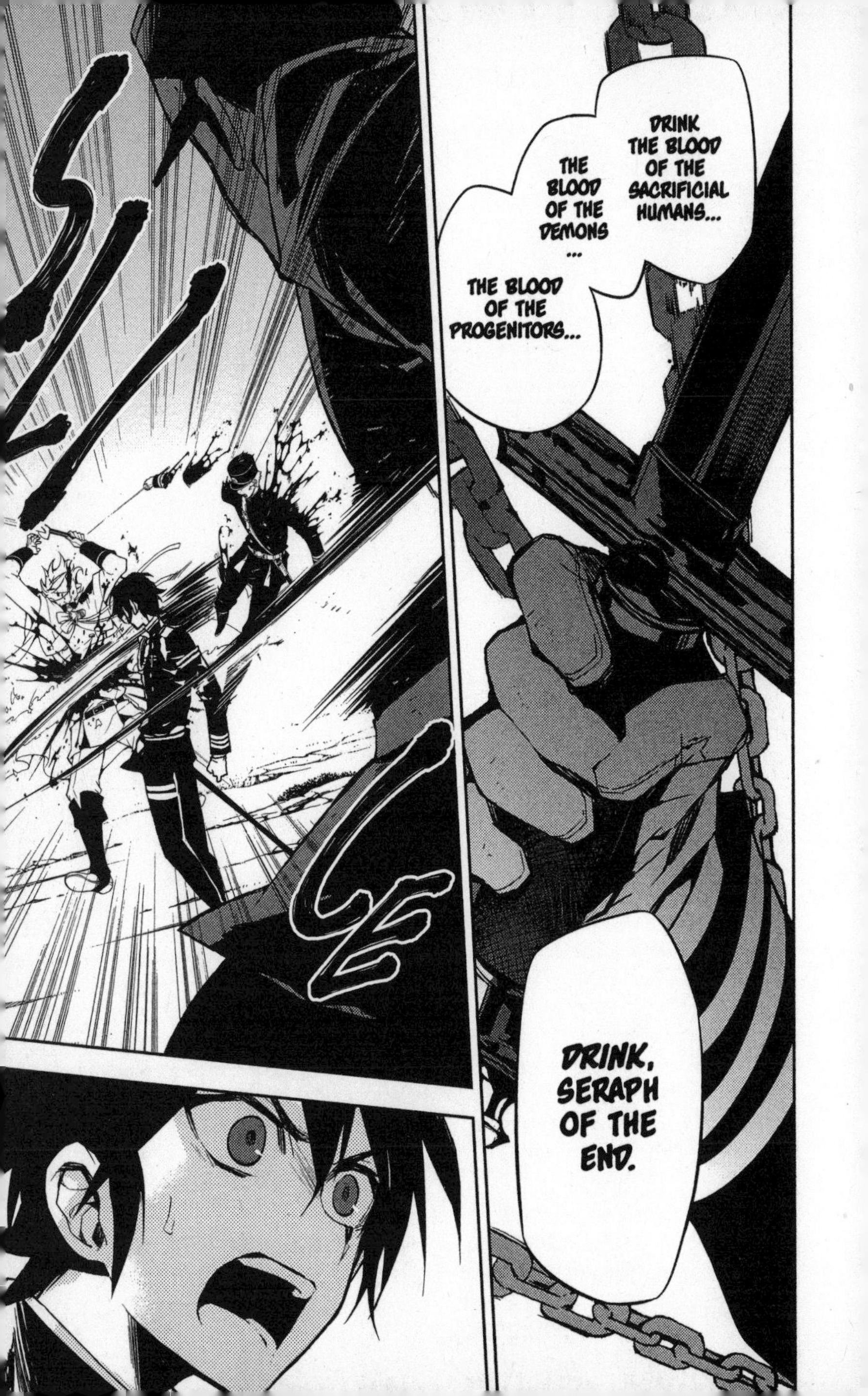
DRINK THE BLOOD OF THE SACRIFICIAL HUMANS...
THE BLOOD OF THE DEMONS ...
THE BLOOD OF THE PROGENITORS...
DRINK, SERAPH OF THE END.

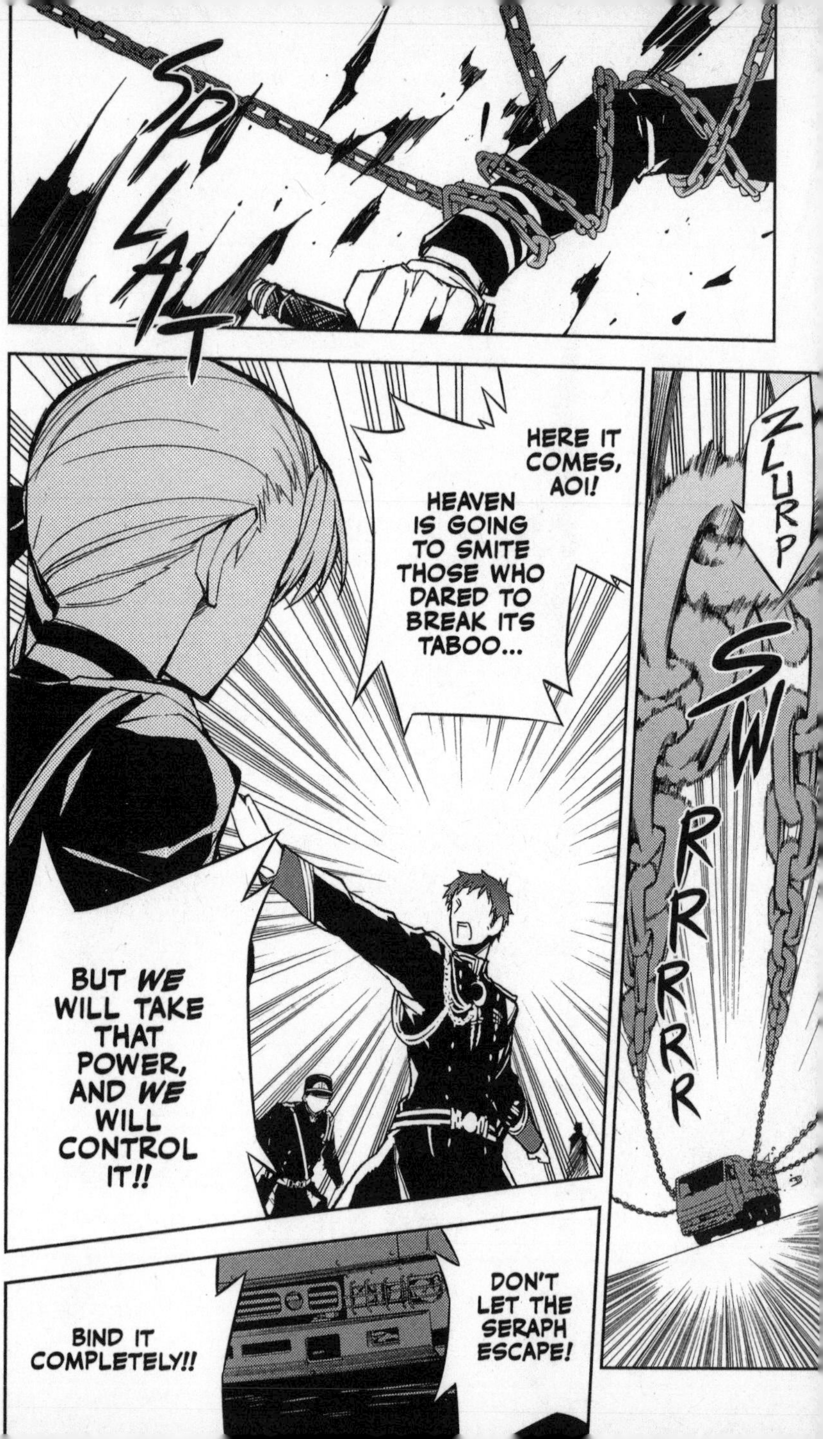
SPLAT
ZLURP
SWRRRRR
HERE IT COMES, AOI!
HEAVEN IS GOING TO SMITE THOSE WHO DARED TO BREAK ITS TABOO...
BUT *WE* WILL TAKE THAT POWER, AND *WE* WILL CONTROL IT!!
DON'T LET THE SERAPH ESCAPE!
BIND IT COMPLETELY!!

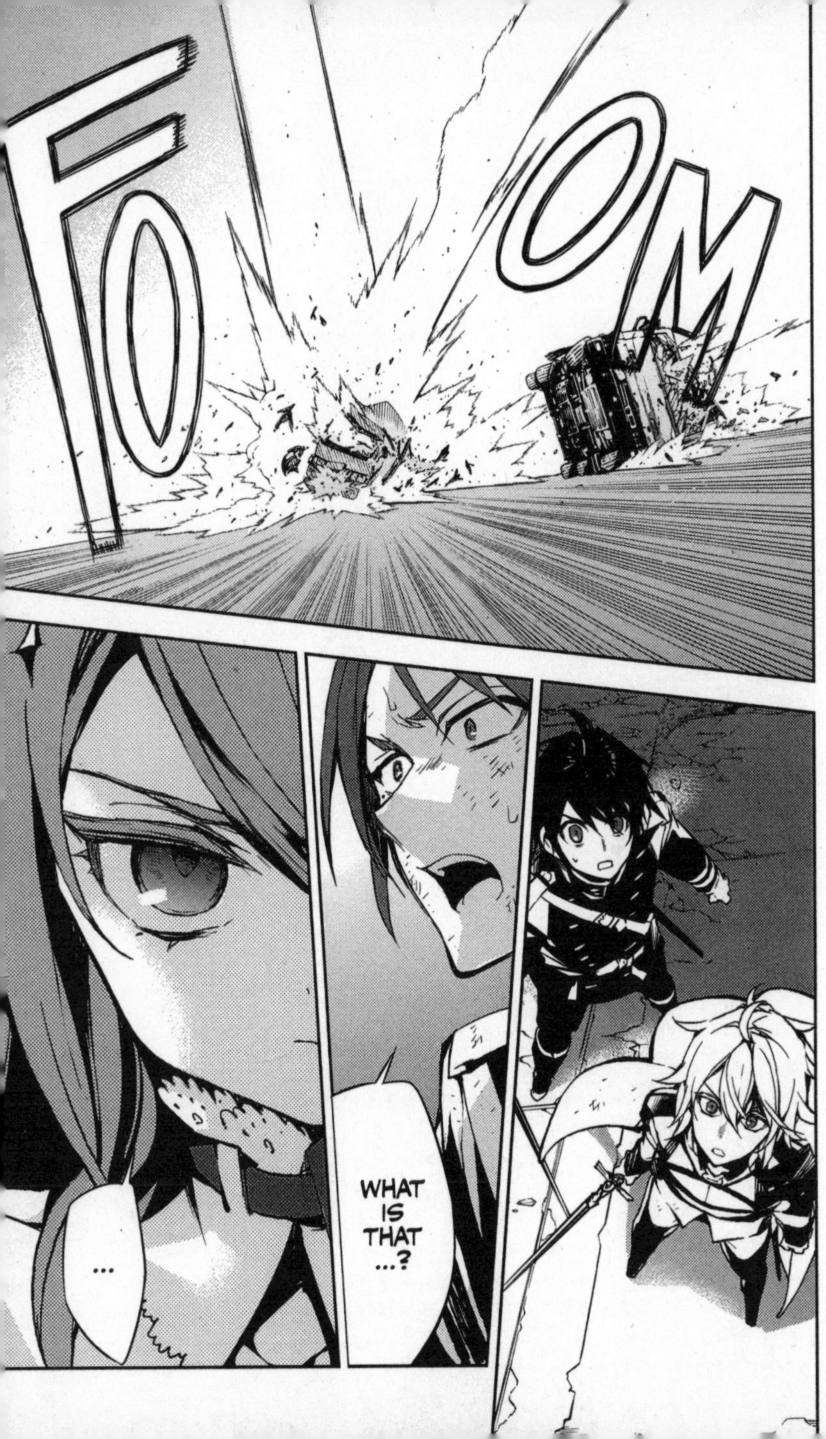
FOOM
WHAT IS THAT ...?
...

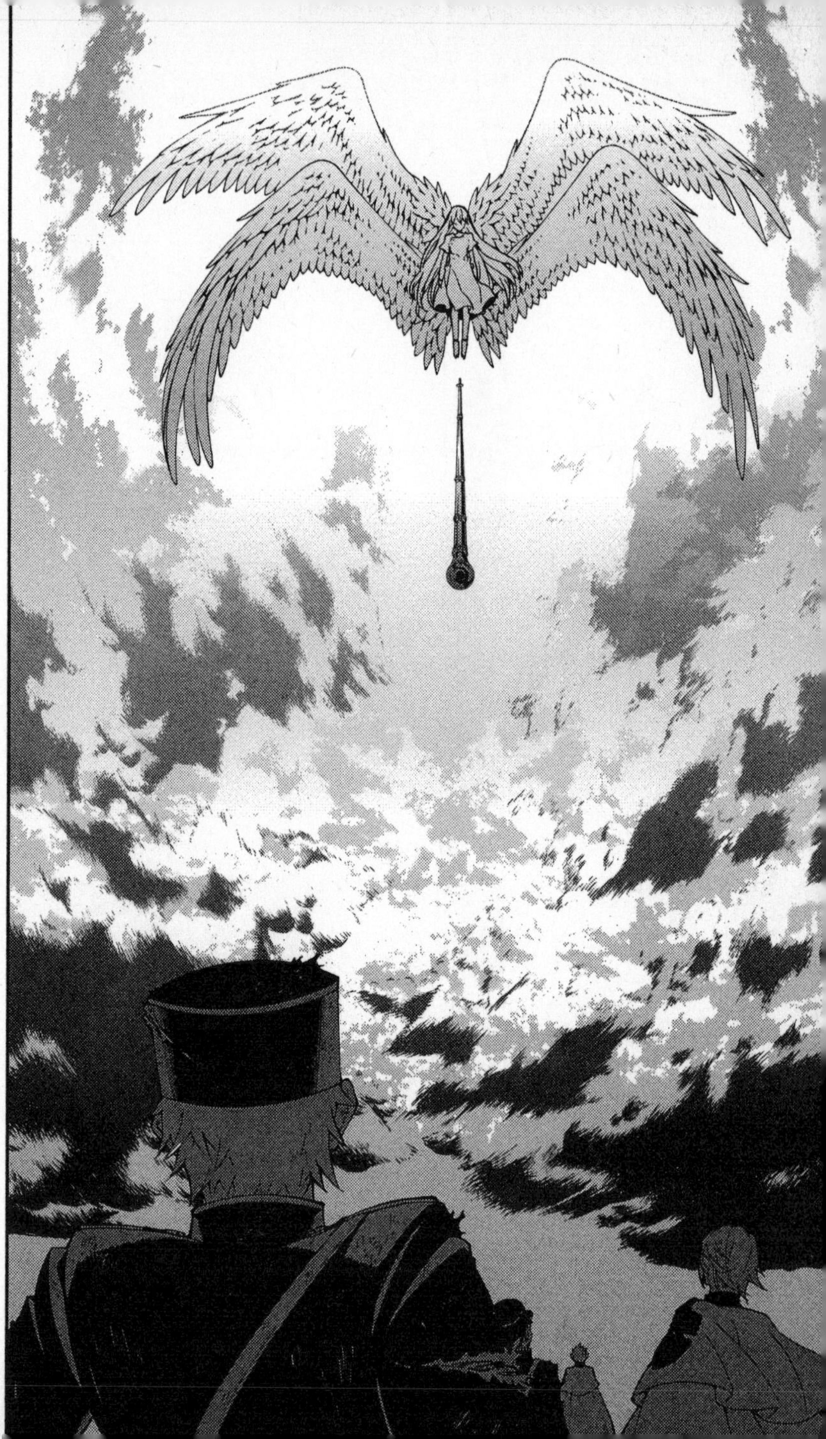

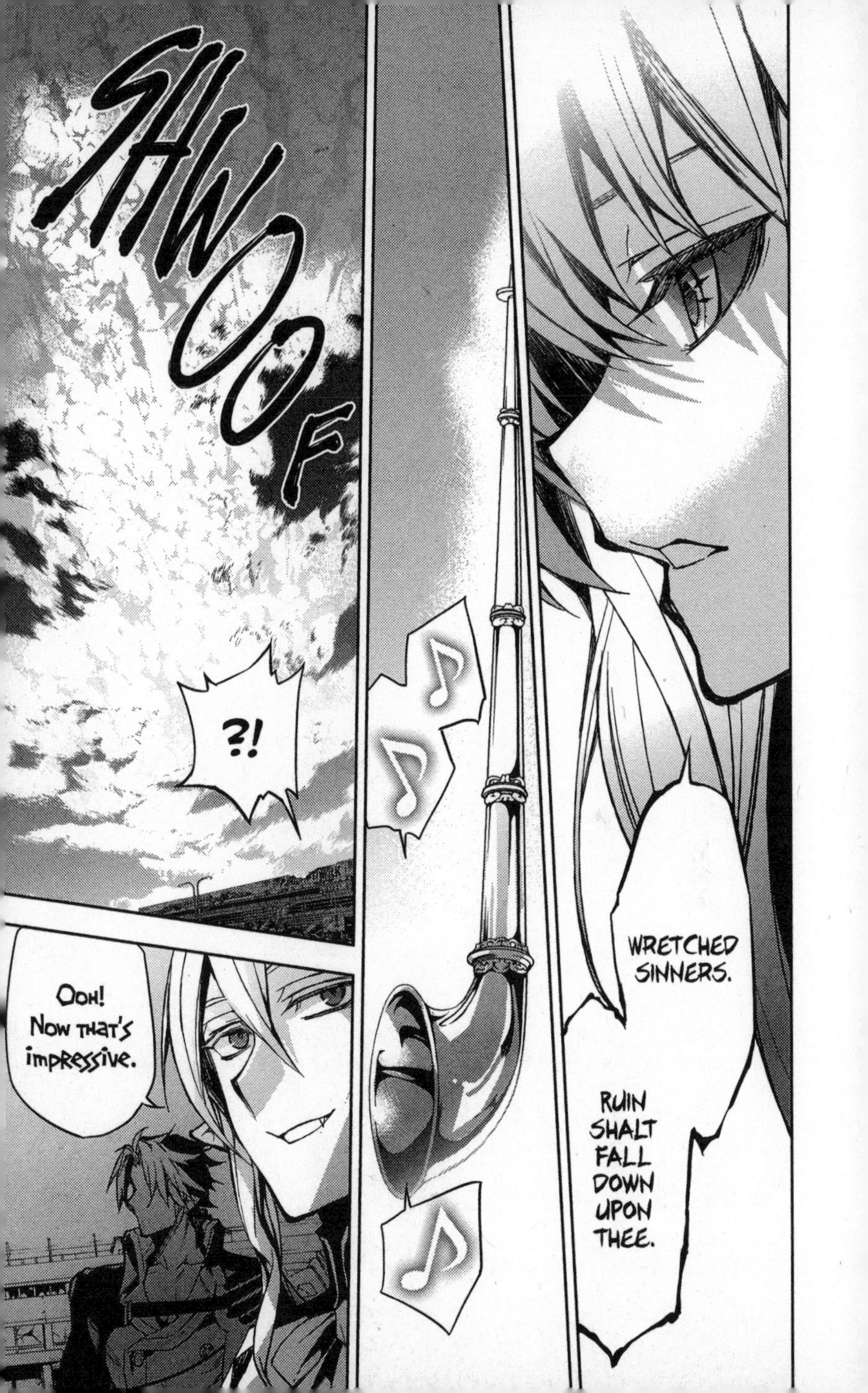
WRETCHED SINNERS.
RUIN SHALT FALL DOWN UPON THEE.
SHWOOF
?!
Ooh! Now that's impressive.

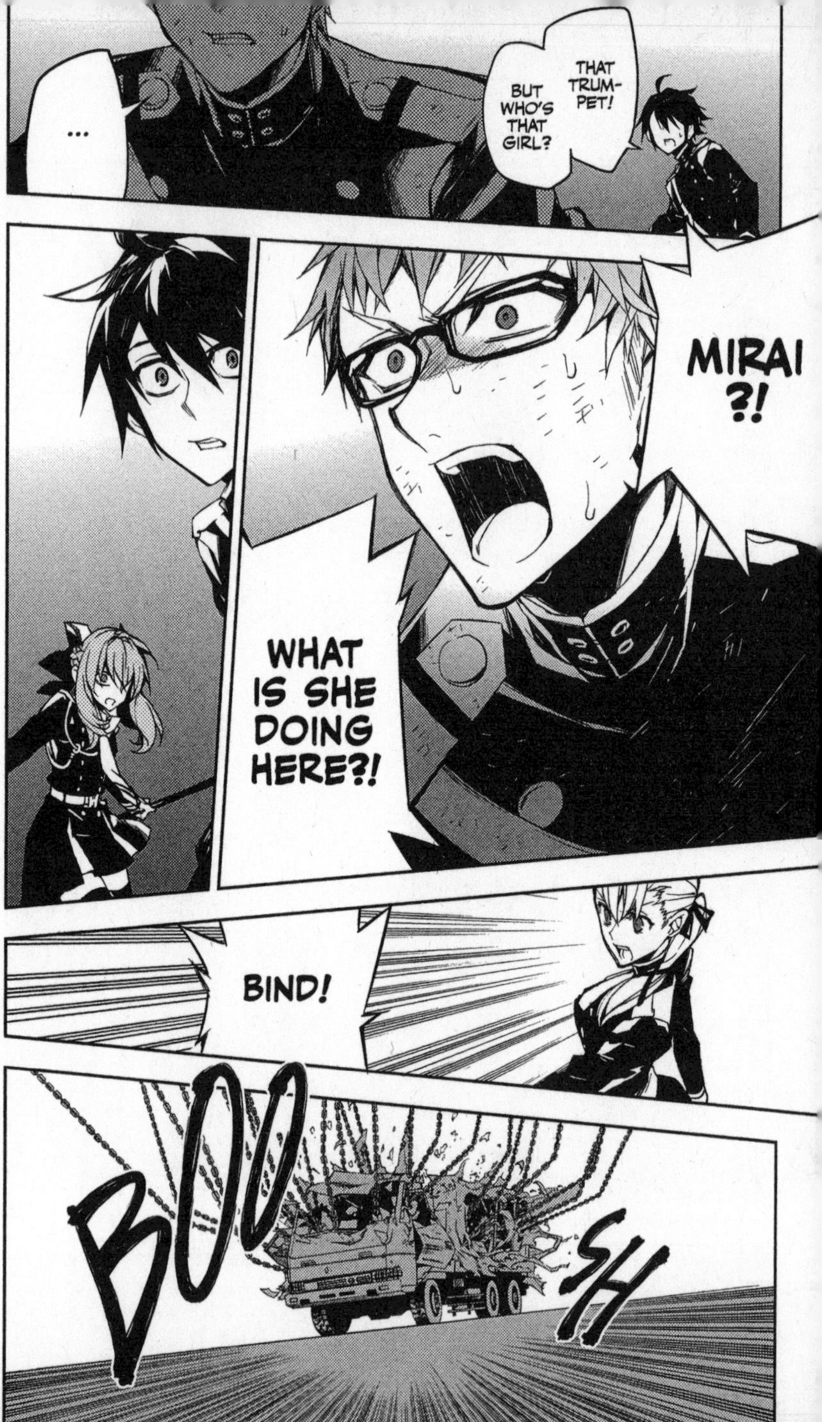
THAT TRUMPET! BUT WHO'S THAT GIRL?
...
MIRAI ?!
WHAT IS SHE DOING HERE?!
BIND!
BOOOSH

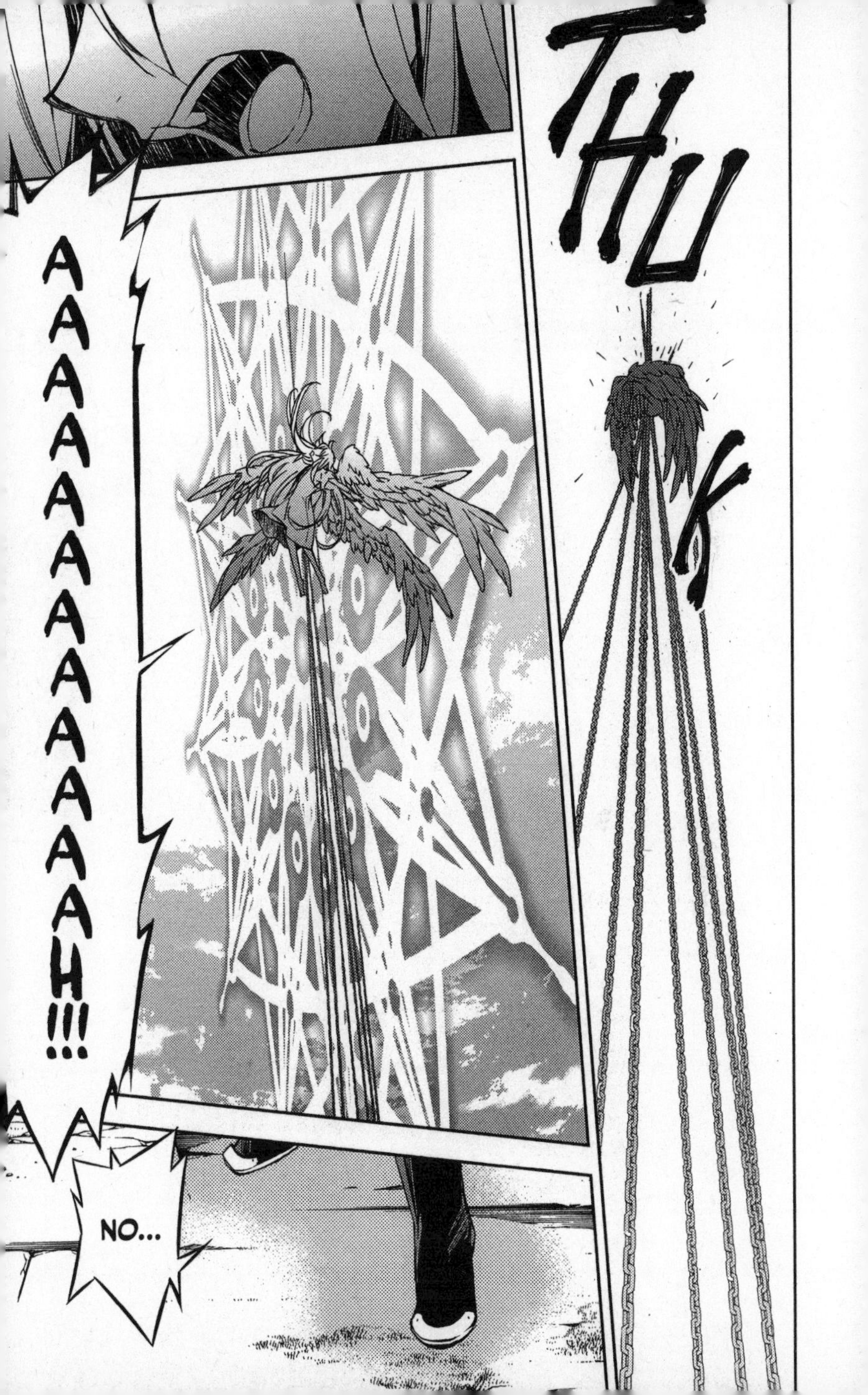
THUNK
AAAAAAAAAAAAAAAH!!!
NO...

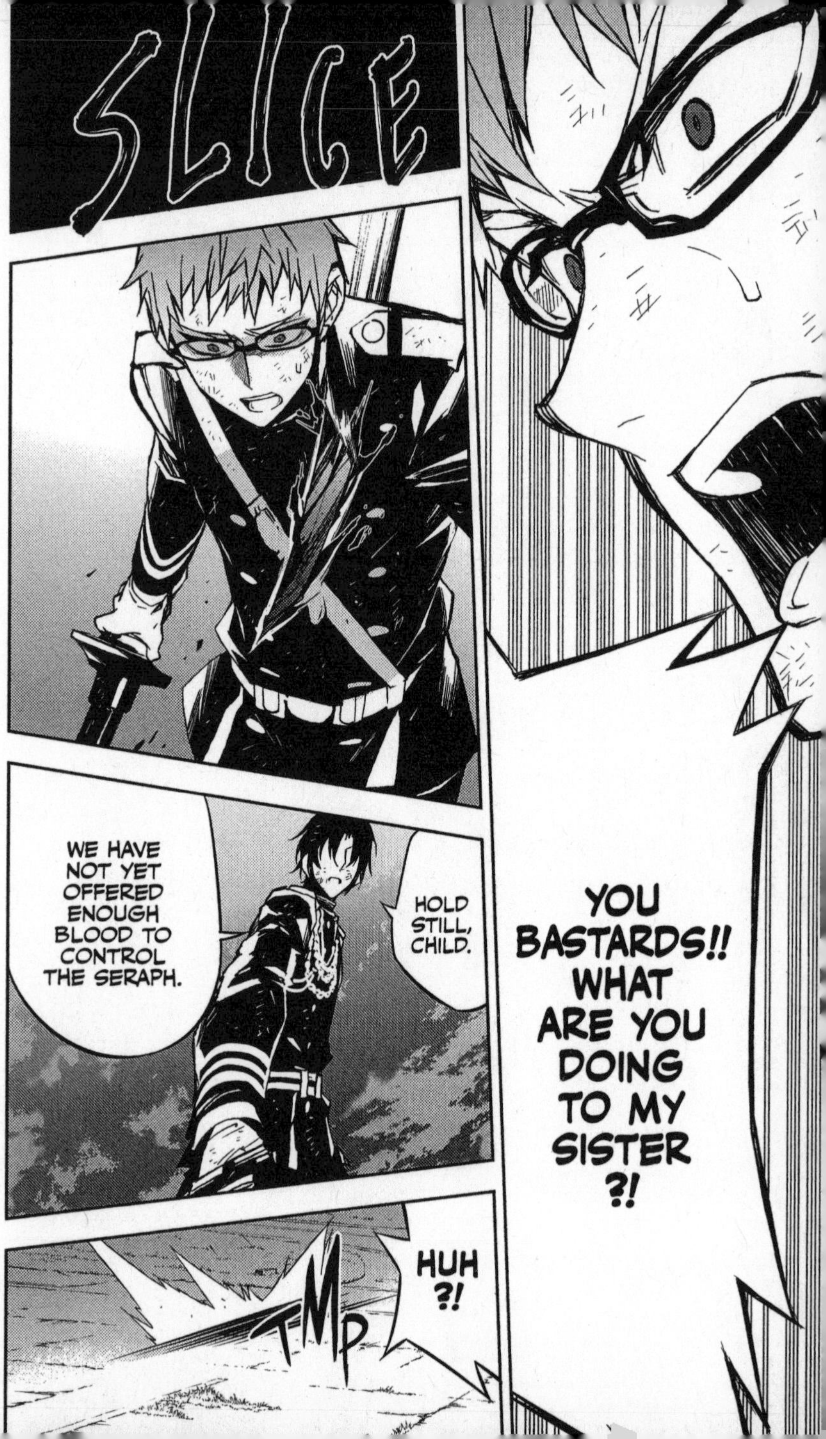
YOU BASTARDS!! WHAT ARE YOU DOING TO MY SISTER ?!
SLICE
HOLD STILL, CHILD.
WE HAVE NOT YET OFFERED ENOUGH BLOOD TO CONTROL THE SERAPH.
HUH ?!
TMP

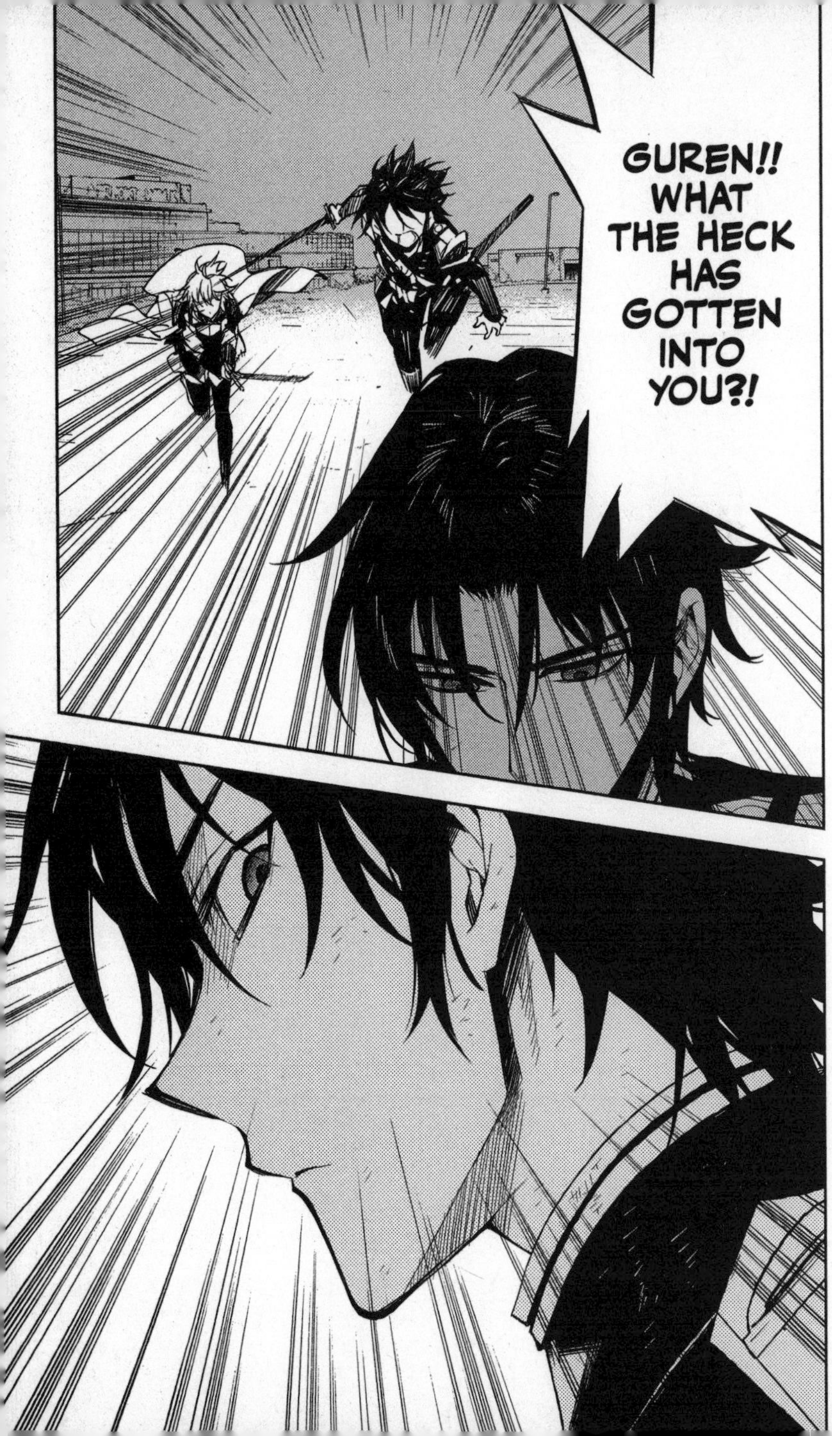
GUREN!! WHAT THE HECK HAS GOTTEN INTO YOU?!

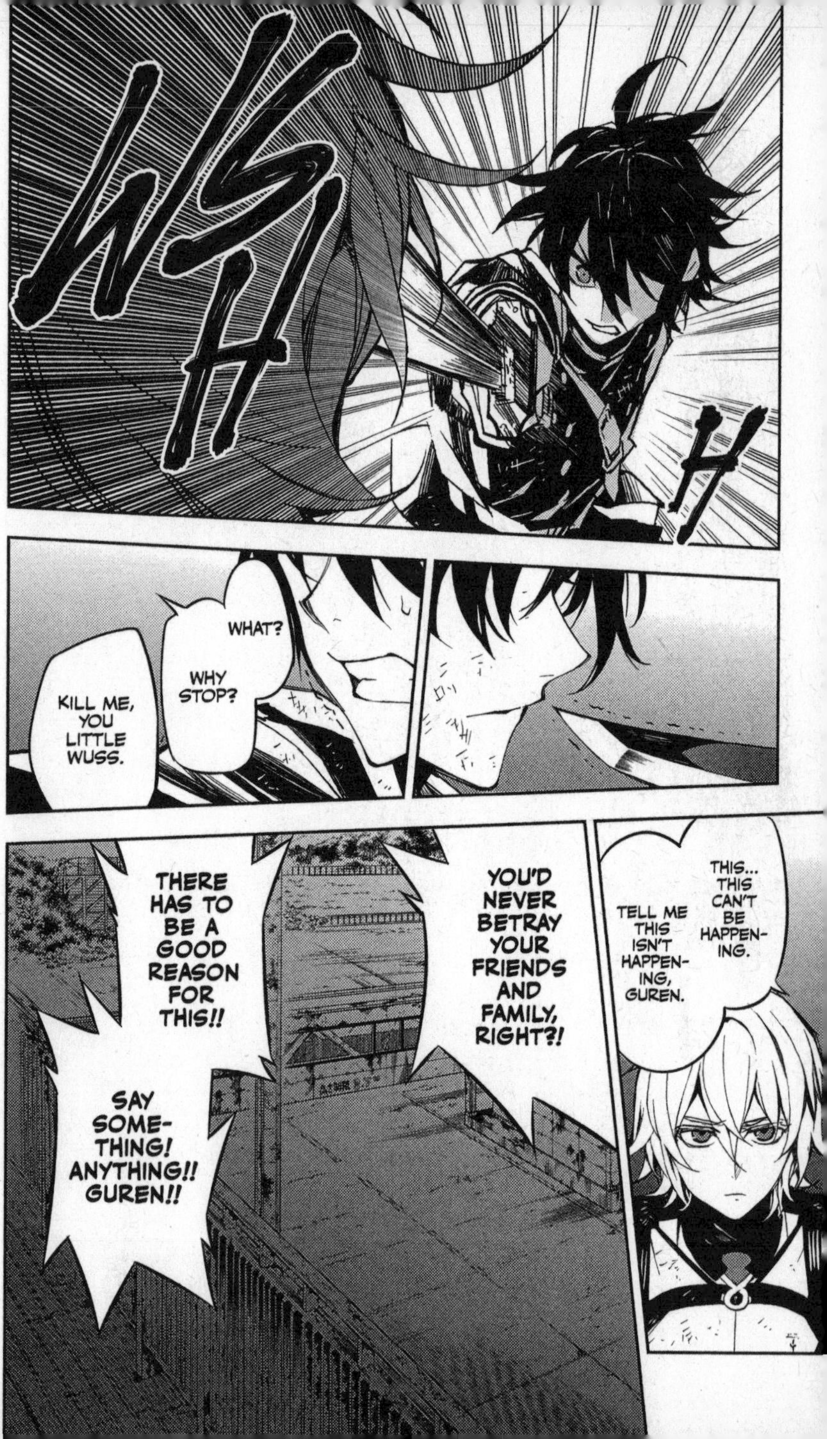
WSH
H
WHAT?
WHY STOP?
KILL ME, YOU LITTLE WUSS.
THIS... THIS CAN'T BE HAPPENING.
TELL ME THIS ISN'T HAPPENING, GUREN.
YOU'D NEVER BETRAY YOUR FRIENDS AND FAMILY, RIGHT?!
THERE HAS TO BE A GOOD REASON FOR THIS!!
SAY SOMETHING! ANYTHING!! GUREN!!

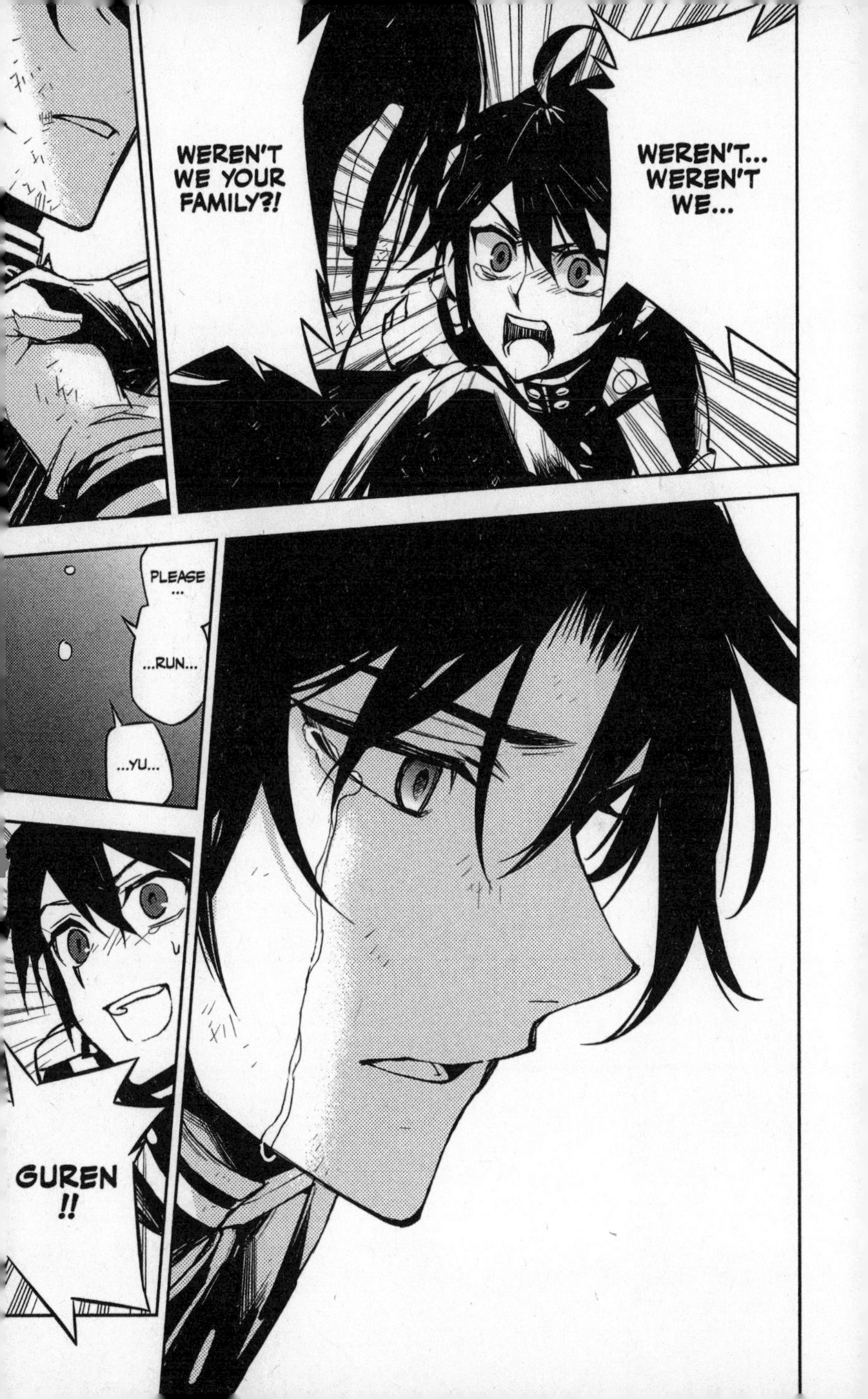
WEREN'T... WEREN'T WE...
WEREN'T WE YOUR FAMILY?!
PLEASE ...
...RUN...
...YU...
GUREN !!

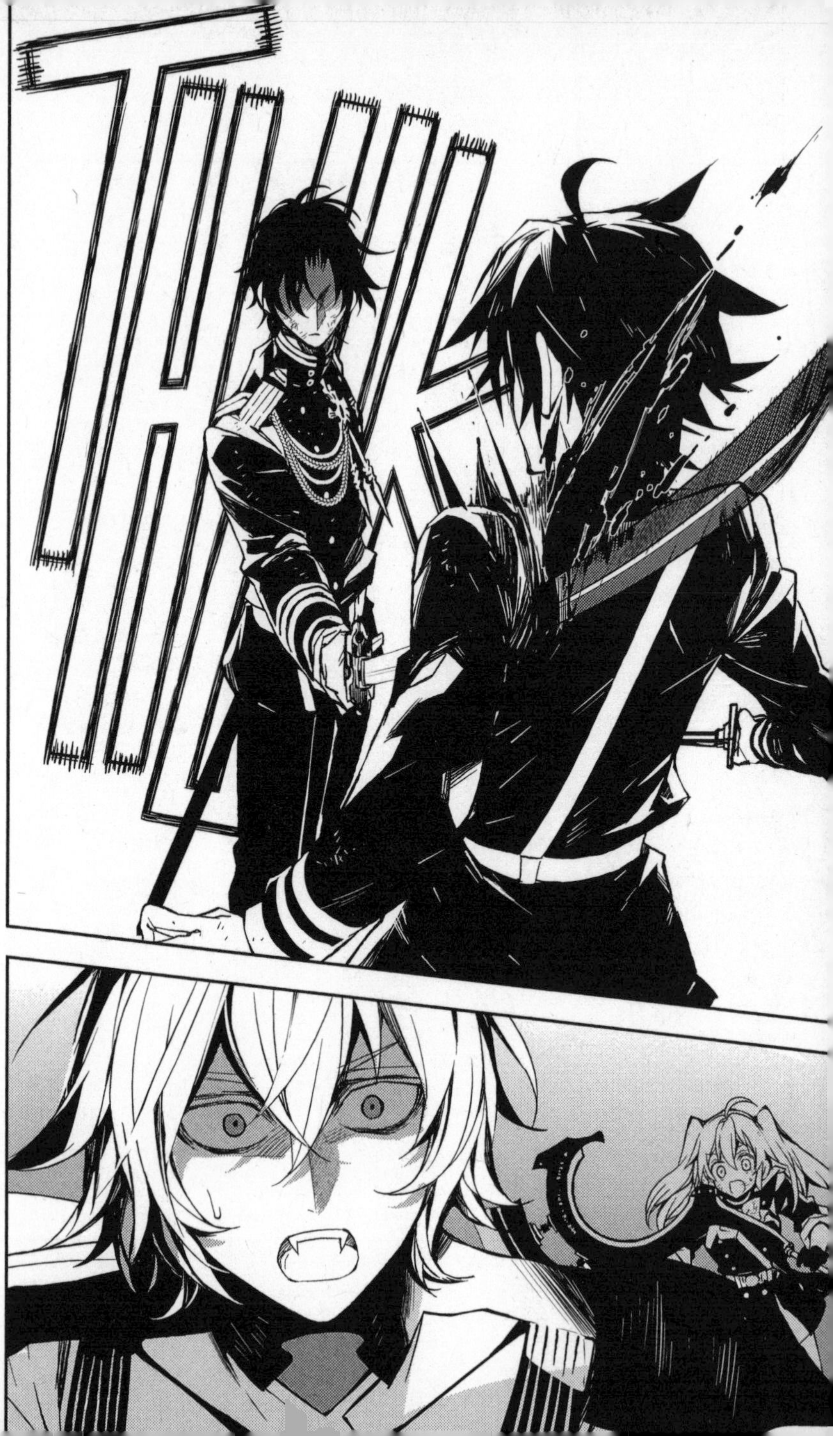

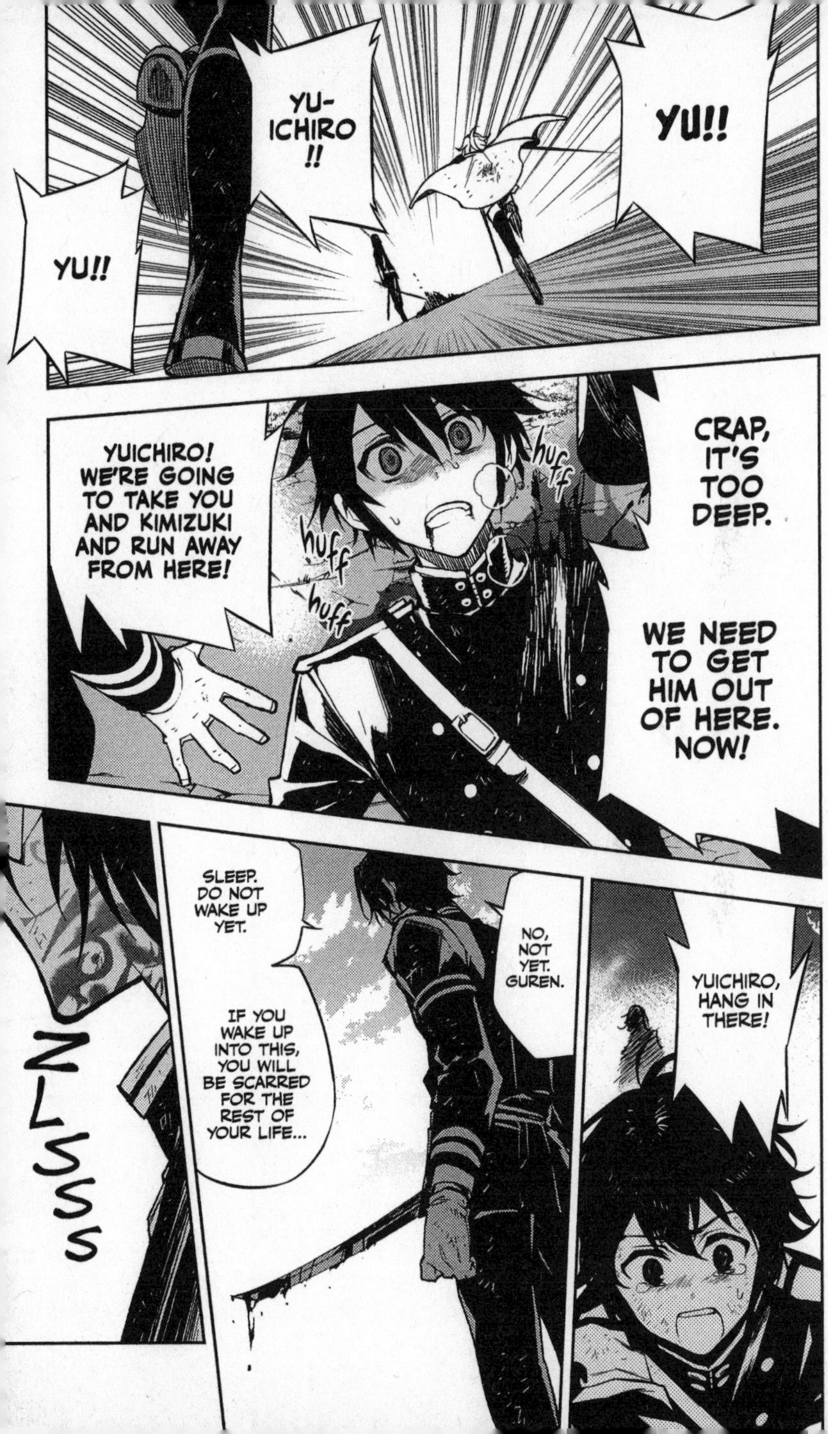
YU!!
YU-ICHIRO!!
YU!!
CRAP, IT'S TOO DEEP.
WE NEED TO GET HIM OUT OF HERE. NOW!
huff
huff
huff
YUICHIRO! WE'RE GOING TO TAKE YOU AND KIMIZUKI AND RUN AWAY FROM HERE!
YUICHIRO, HANG IN THERE!
NO, NOT YET. GUREN.
SLEEP. DO NOT WAKE UP YET.
IF YOU WAKE UP INTO THIS, YOU WILL BE SCARRED FOR THE REST OF YOUR LIFE...
ZLSSS

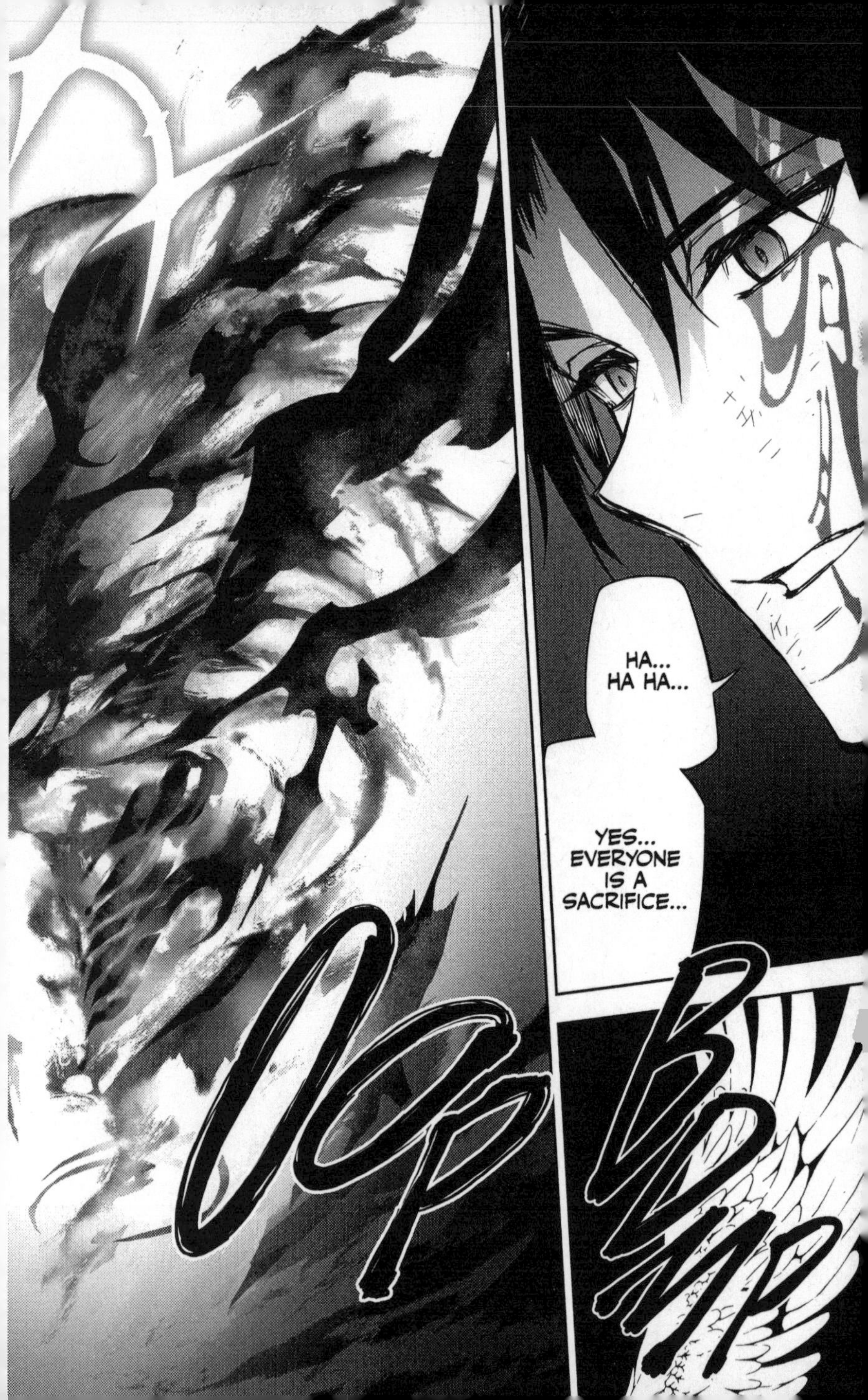
HA... HA HA...
YES... EVERYONE IS A SACRIFICE...

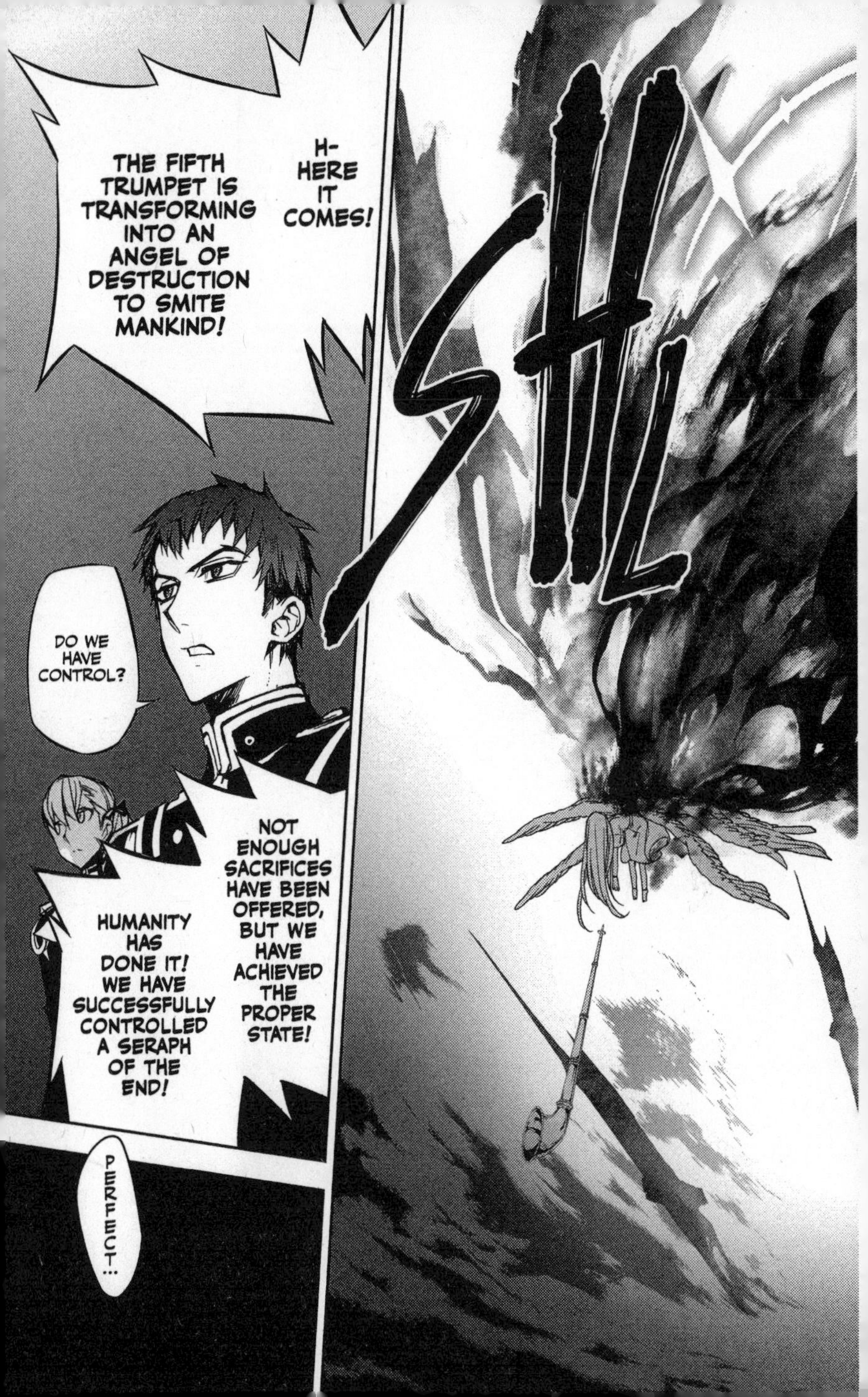
H- HERE IT COMES!
THE FIFTH TRUMPET IS TRANSFORMING INTO AN ANGEL OF DESTRUCTION TO SMITE MANKIND!
DO WE HAVE CONTROL?
NOT ENOUGH SACRIFICES HAVE BEEN OFFERED, BUT WE HAVE ACHIEVED THE PROPER STATE!
HUMANITY HAS DONE IT! WE HAVE SUCCESSFULLY CONTROLLED A SERAPH OF THE END!
PERFECT...

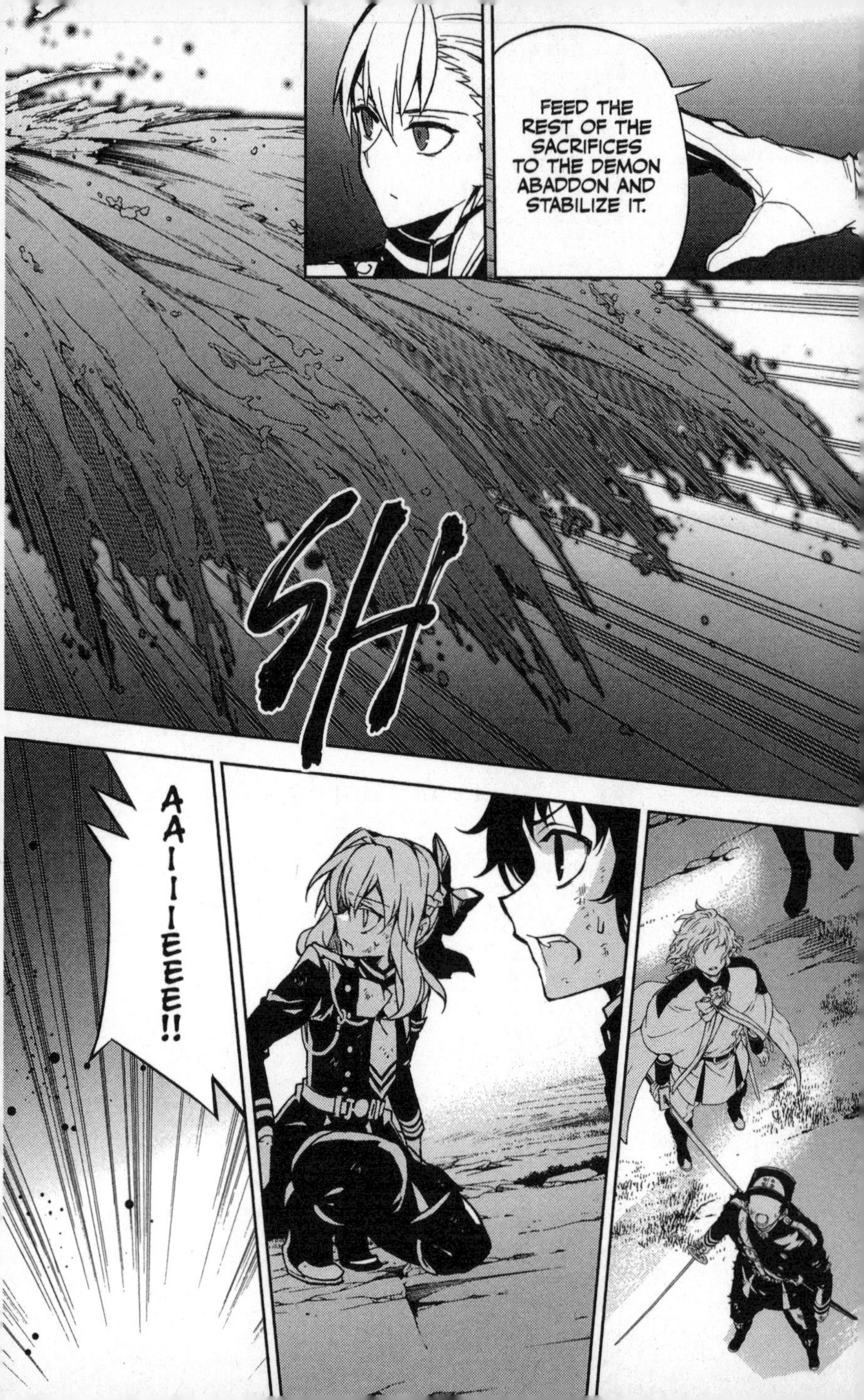
FEED THE REST OF THE SACRIFICES TO THE DEMON ABADDON AND STABILIZE IT.
SH
AAIIIIEEEE!!

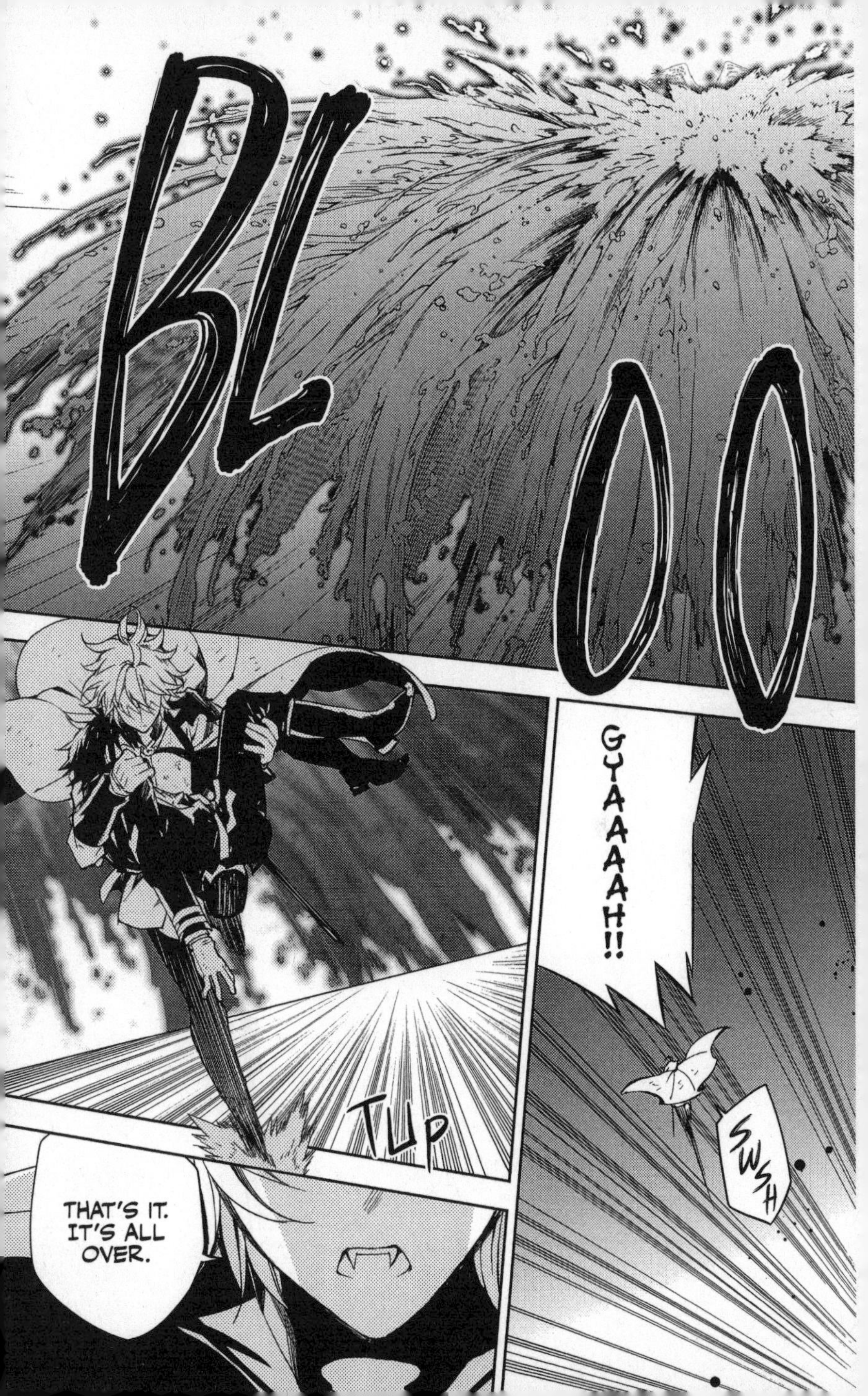
BLOOO
GYAAAAAH!!
SWSH
TUP
THAT'S IT. IT'S ALL OVER.

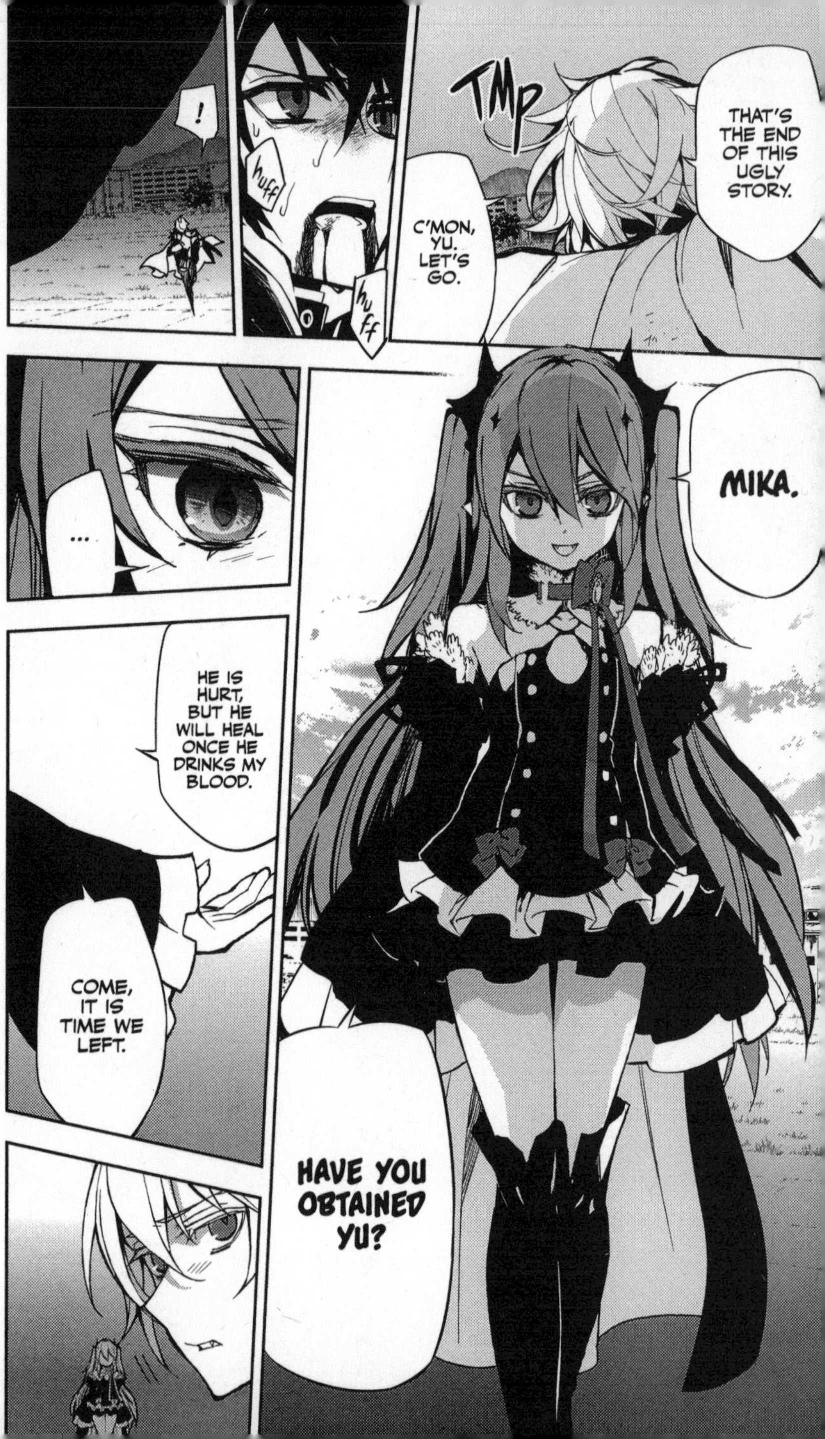

THAT'S THE END OF THIS UGLY STORY.
TMP
C'MON, YU. LET'S GO.
huff
huff
!
MIKA.
...
HE IS HURT, BUT HE WILL HEAL ONCE HE DRINKS MY BLOOD.
COME, IT IS TIME WE LEFT.
HAVE YOU OBTAINED YU?

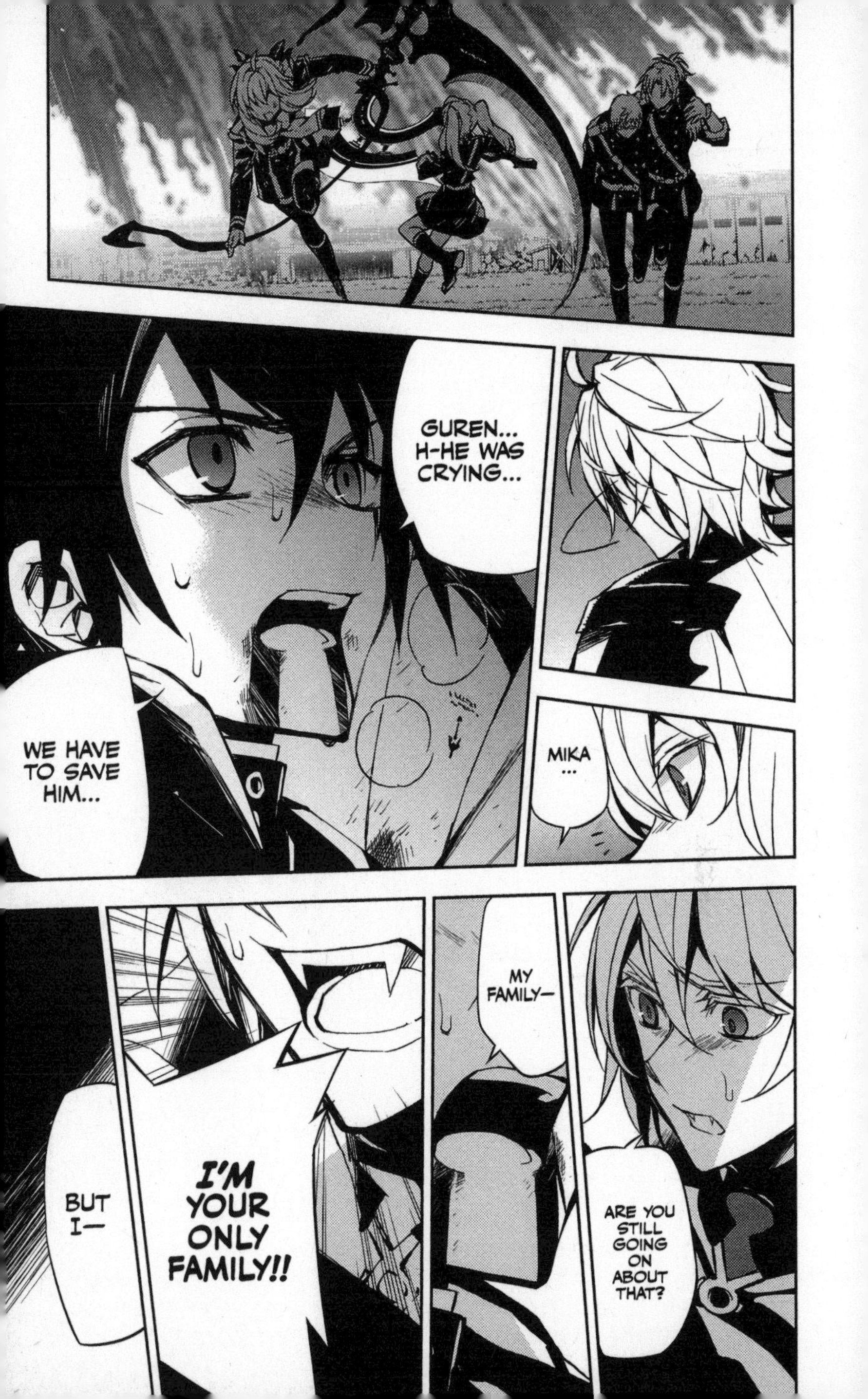
MIKA ...
GUREN... H-HE WAS CRYING...
WE HAVE TO SAVE HIM...
ARE YOU STILL GOING ON ABOUT THAT?
MY FAMILY—
I'M YOUR ONLY FAMILY!!
BUT I—

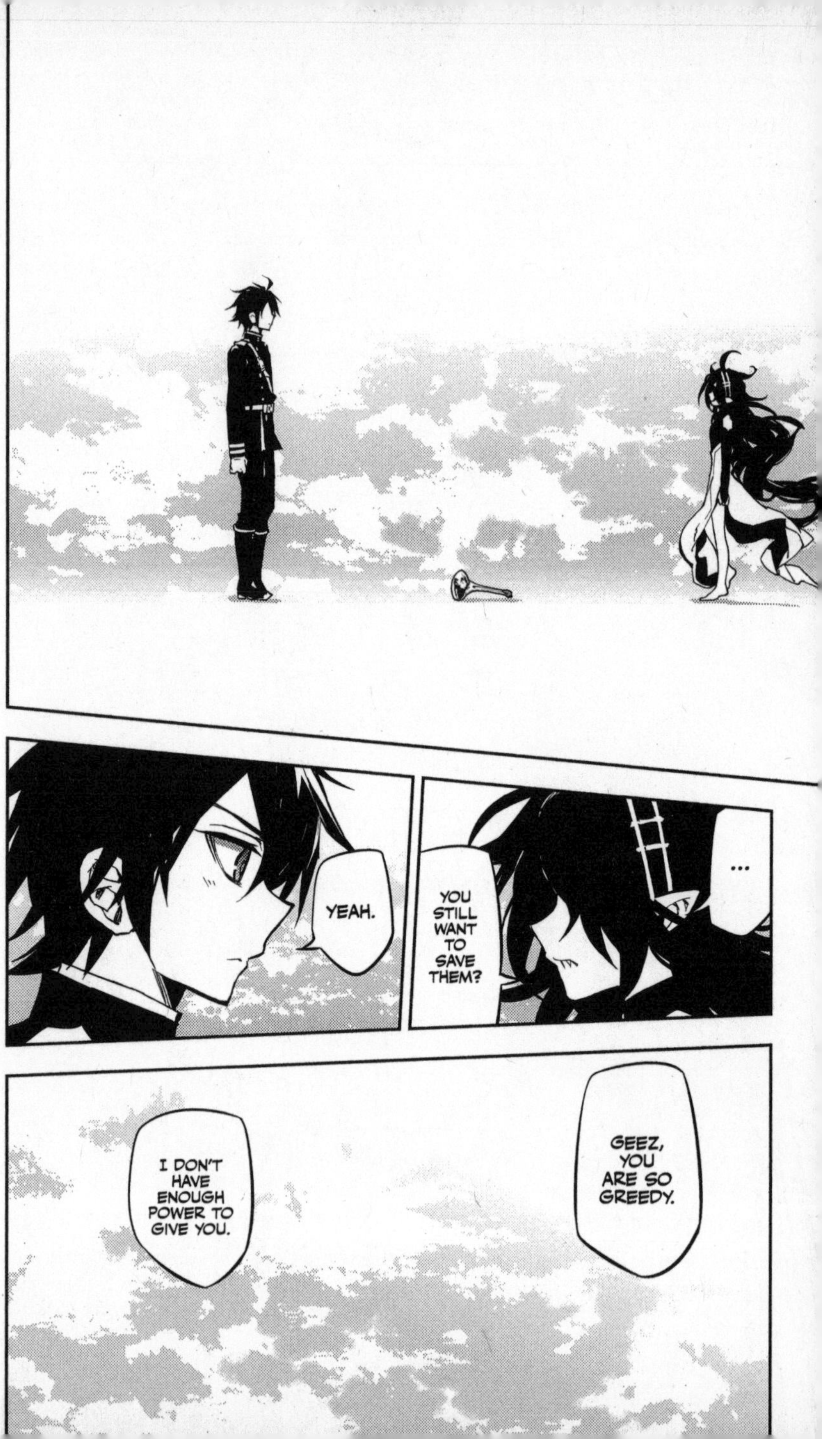
...
YOU STILL WANT TO SAVE THEM?
YEAH.
GEEZ, YOU ARE SO GREEDY.
I DON'T HAVE ENOUGH POWER TO GIVE YOU.

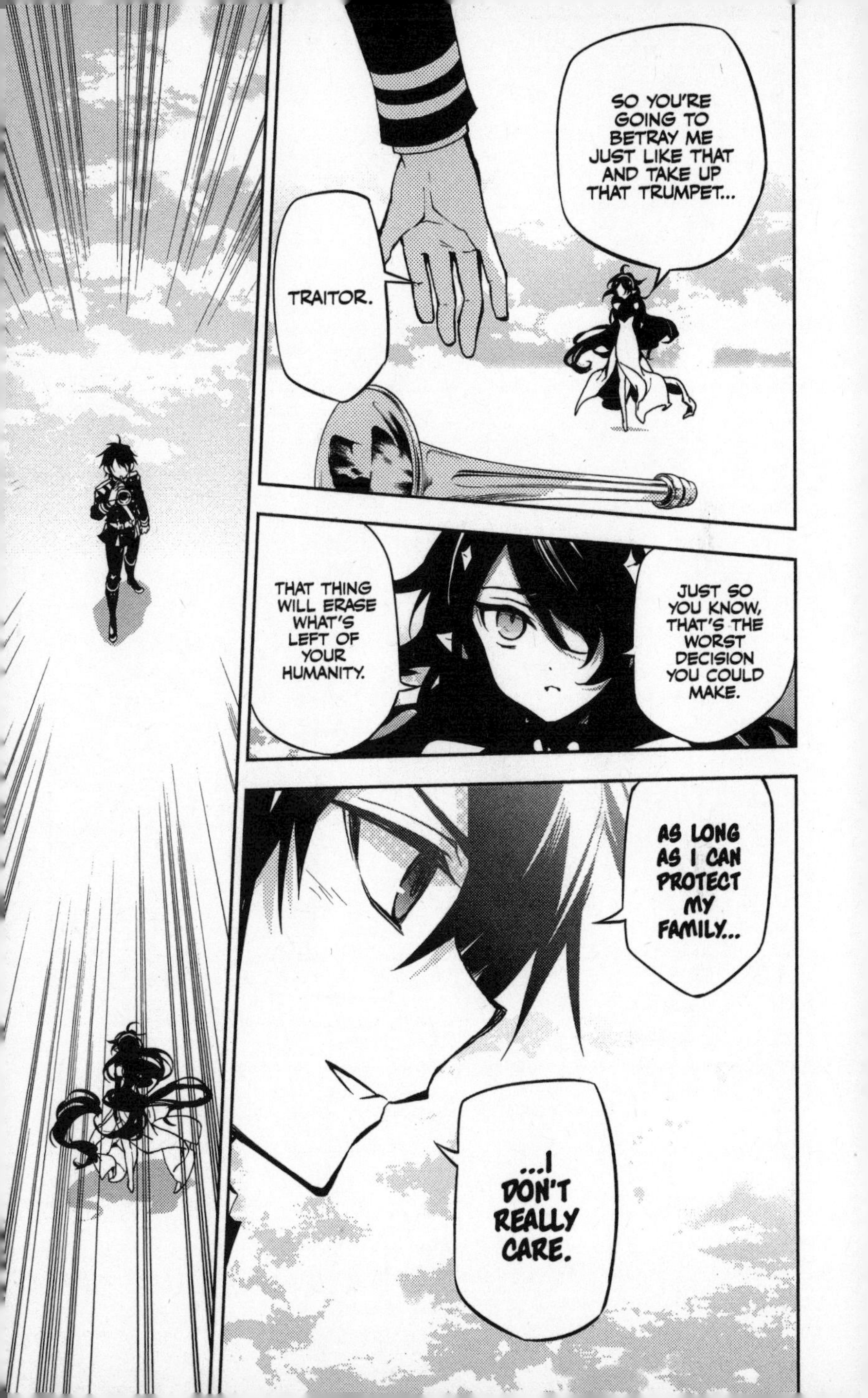
SO YOU'RE GOING TO BETRAY ME JUST LIKE THAT AND TAKE UP THAT TRUMPET...
TRAITOR.
JUST SO YOU KNOW, THAT'S THE WORST DECISION YOU COULD MAKE.
THAT THING WILL ERASE WHAT'S LEFT OF YOUR HUMANITY.
AS LONG AS I CAN PROTECT MY FAMILY...
...I DON'T REALLY CARE.

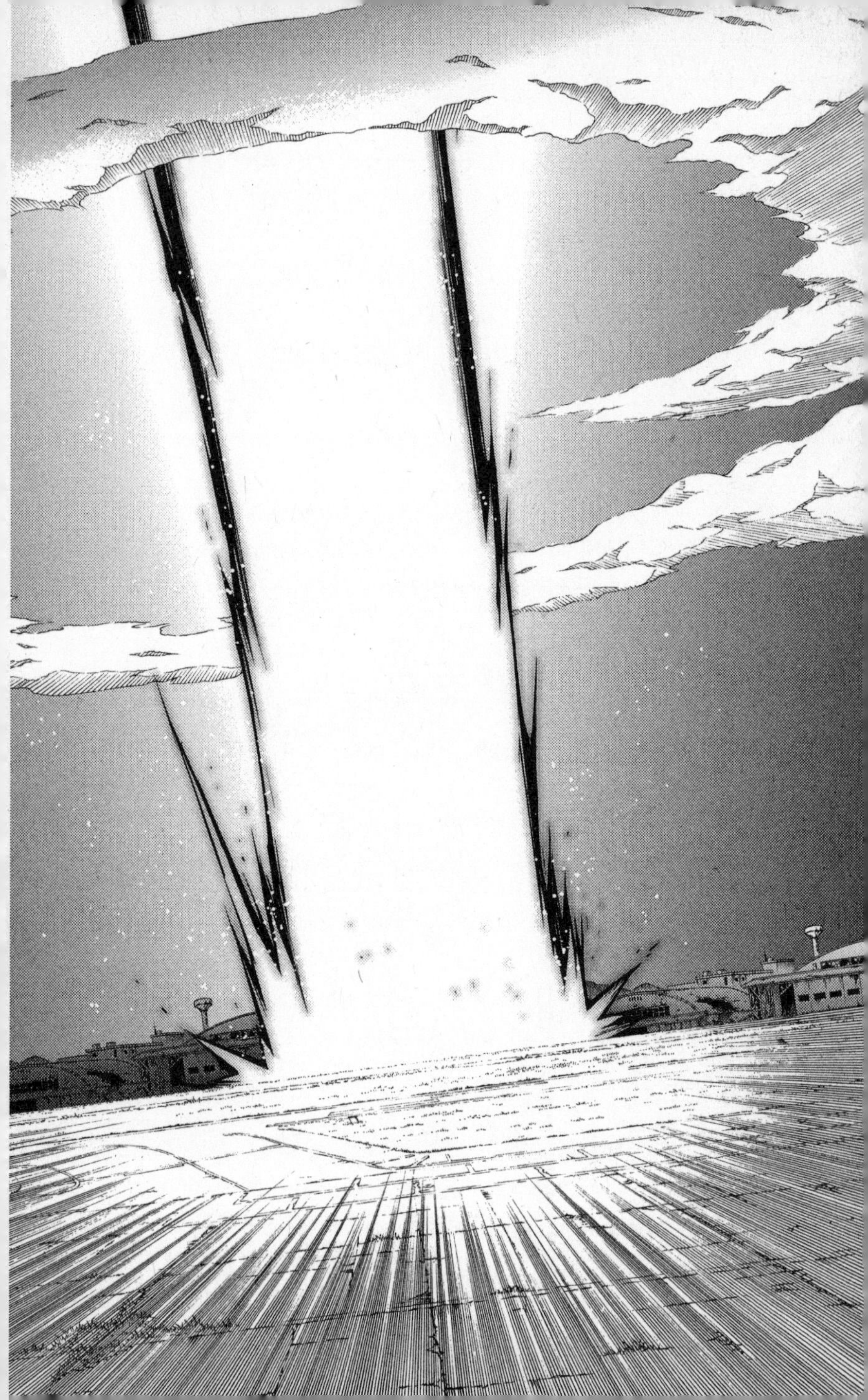

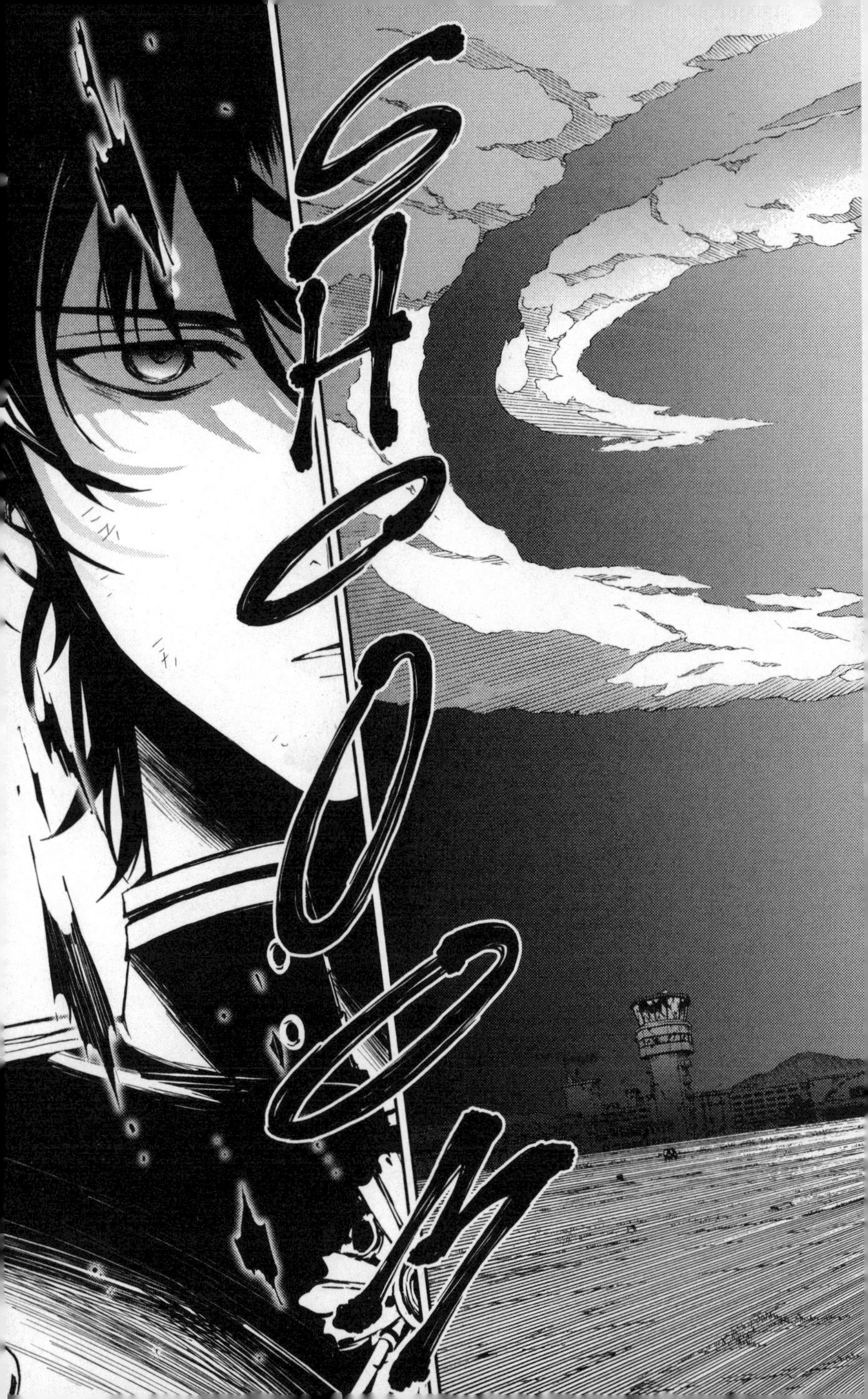
SHOOOM

Seraph of the End

VAMPIRE REIGN

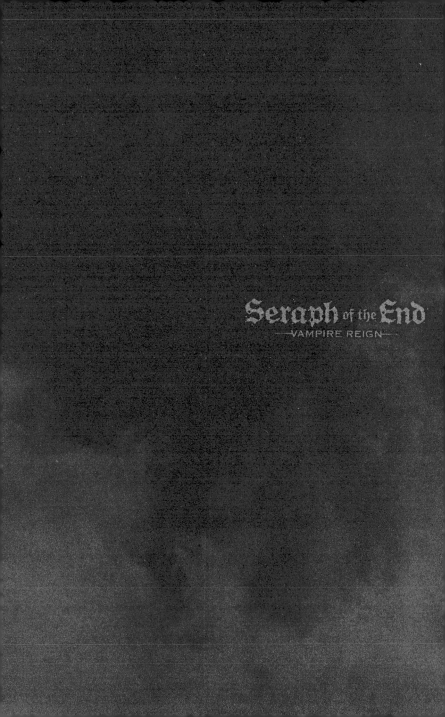

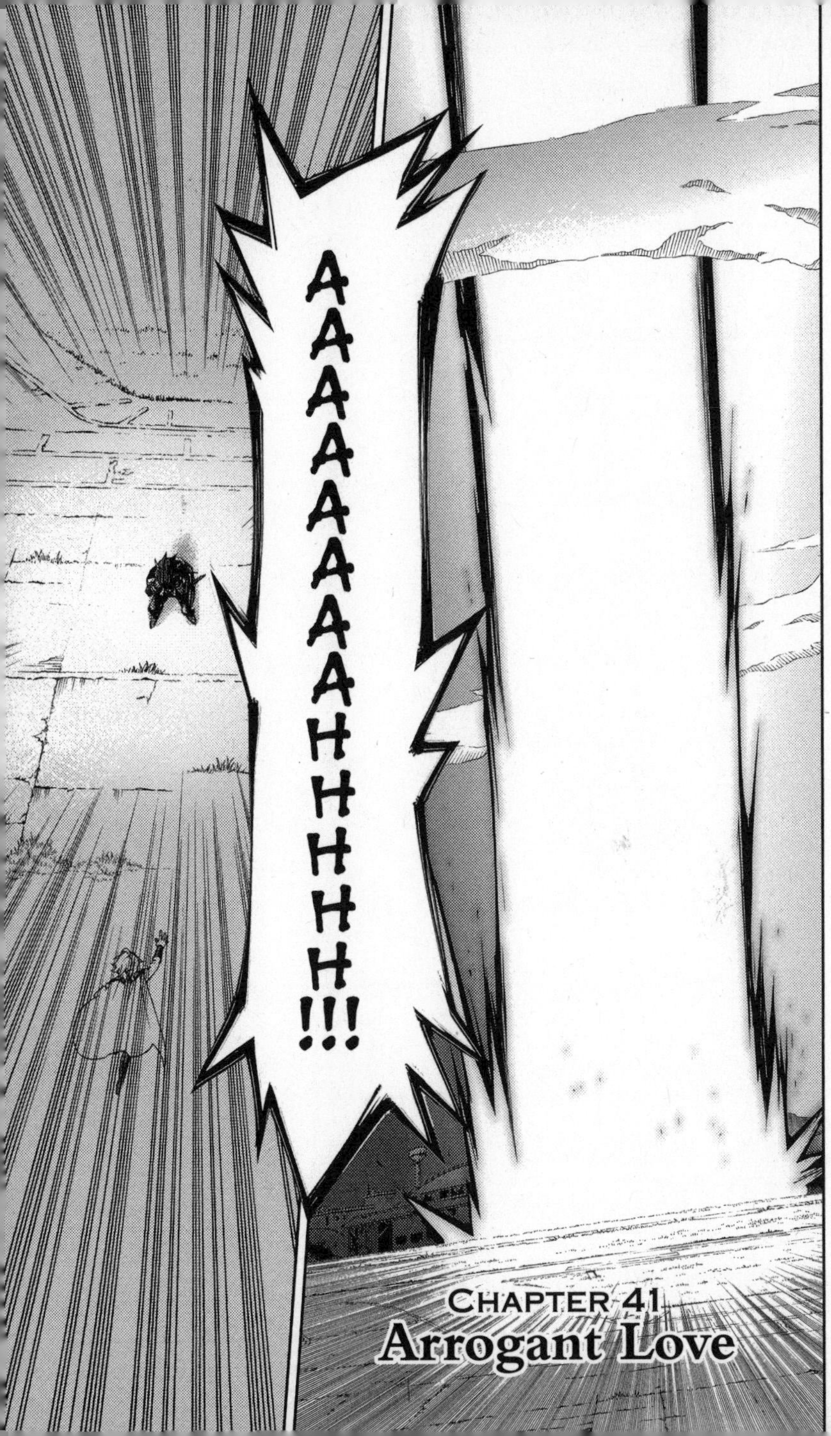
AAAAAAAAAHHHHHH!!!

CHAPTER 41
Arrogant Love

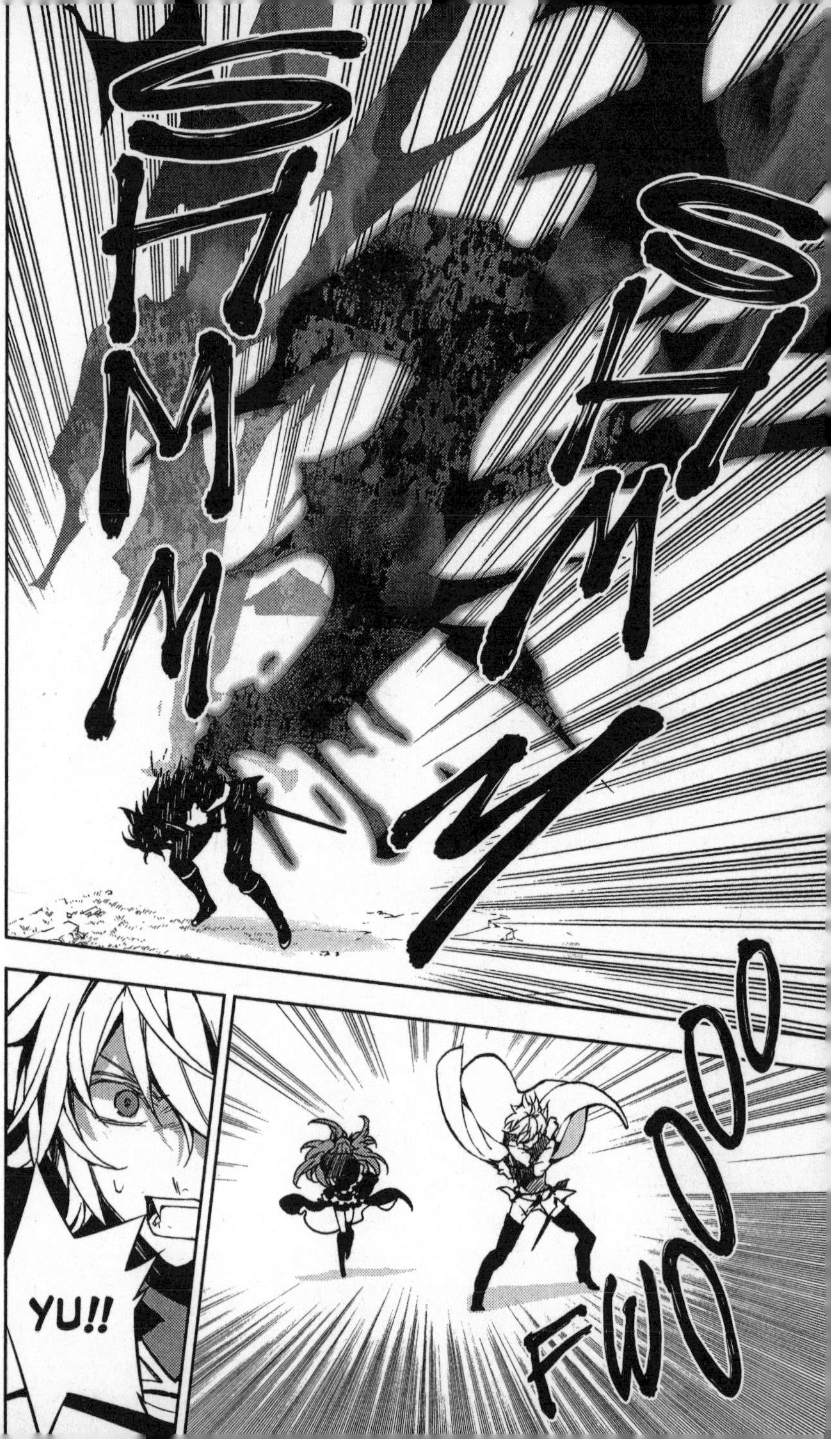
SHMM
SHMM
FWOOOO
YU!!

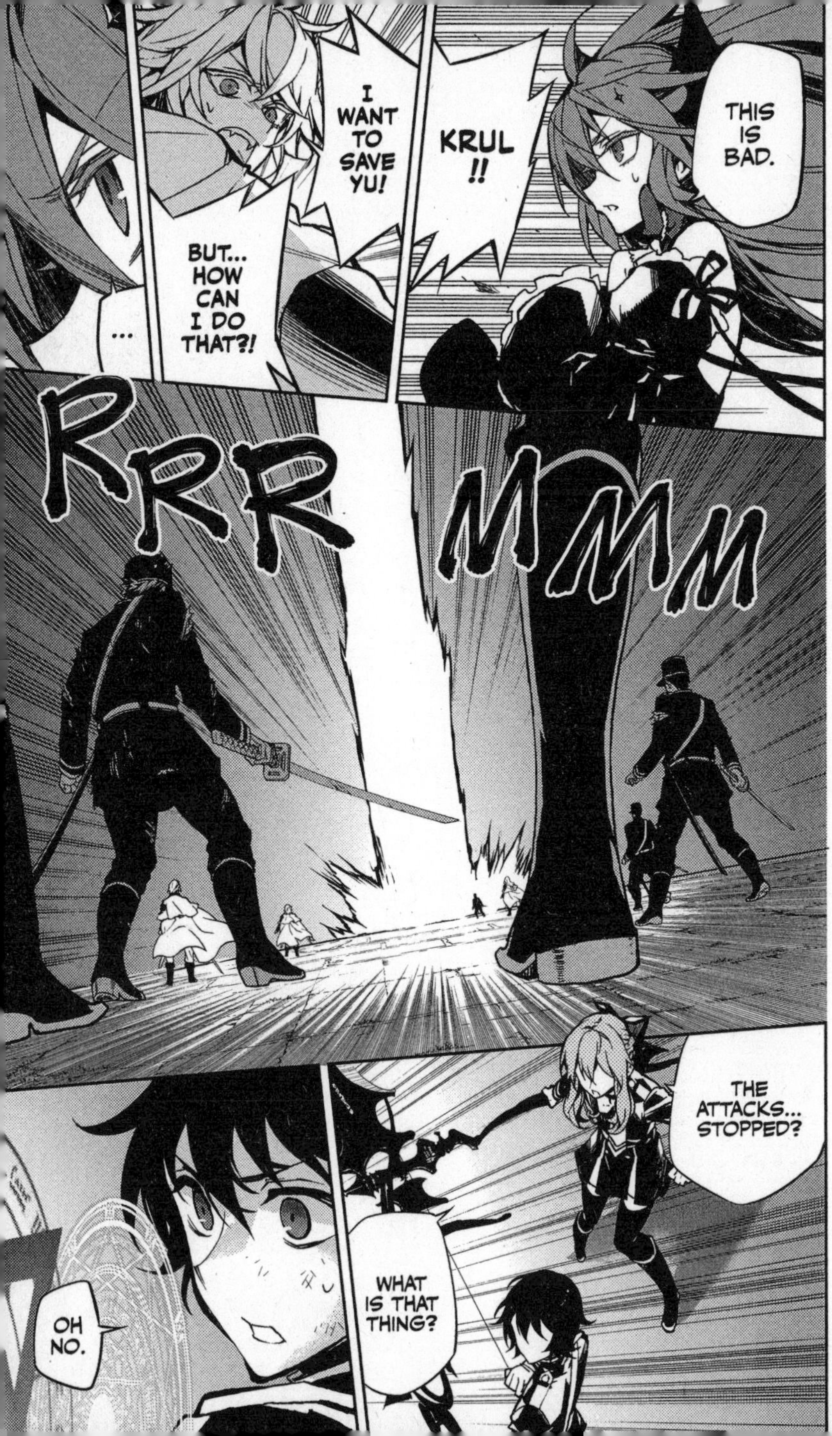
THIS IS BAD.
KRUL!!
I WANT TO SAVE YU!
BUT... HOW CAN I DO THAT?!
...
RRRMMM
THE ATTACKS... STOPPED?
WHAT IS THAT THING?
OH NO.

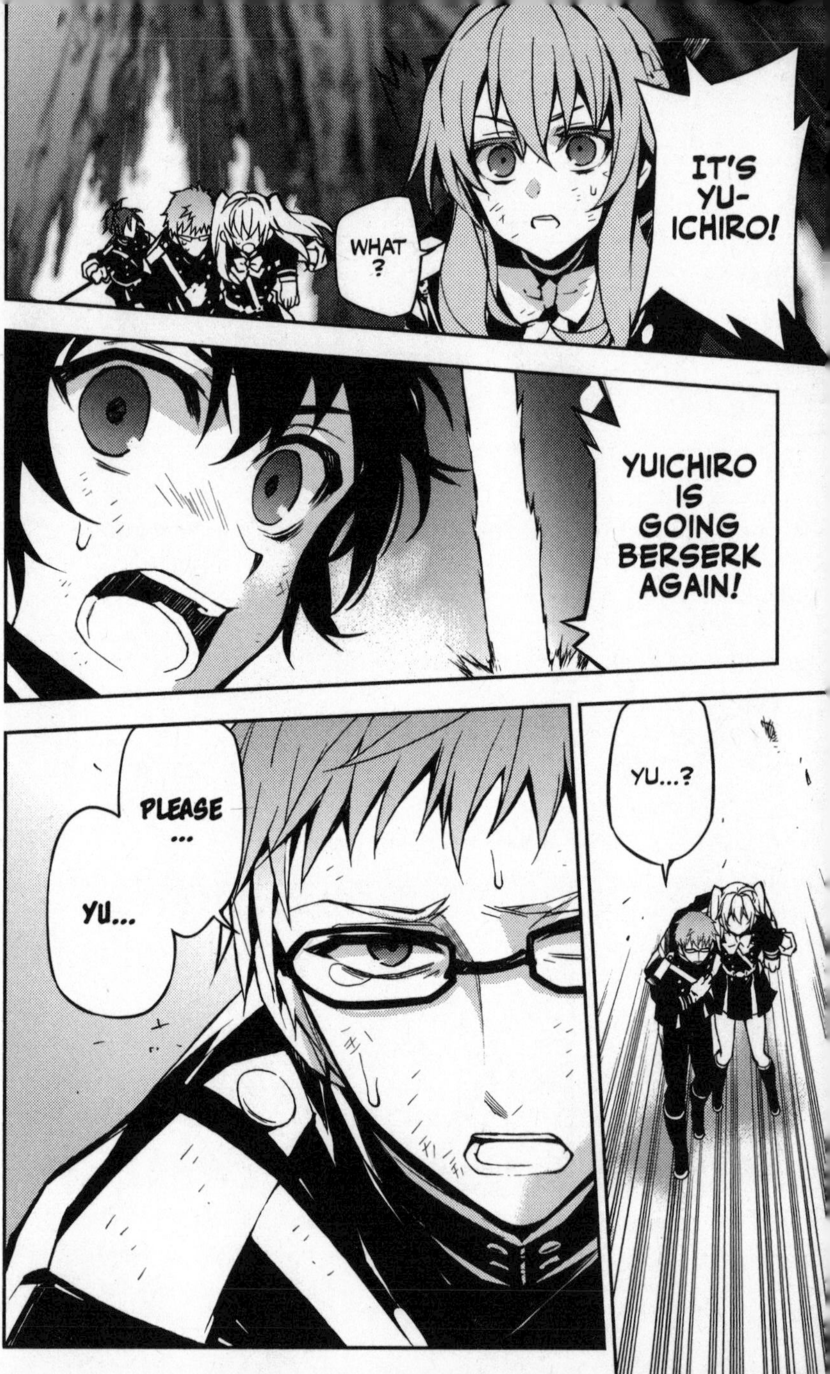
IT'S YU-ICHIRO!
WHAT?
YUICHIRO IS GOING BERSERK AGAIN!
YU...?
PLEASE...
YU...

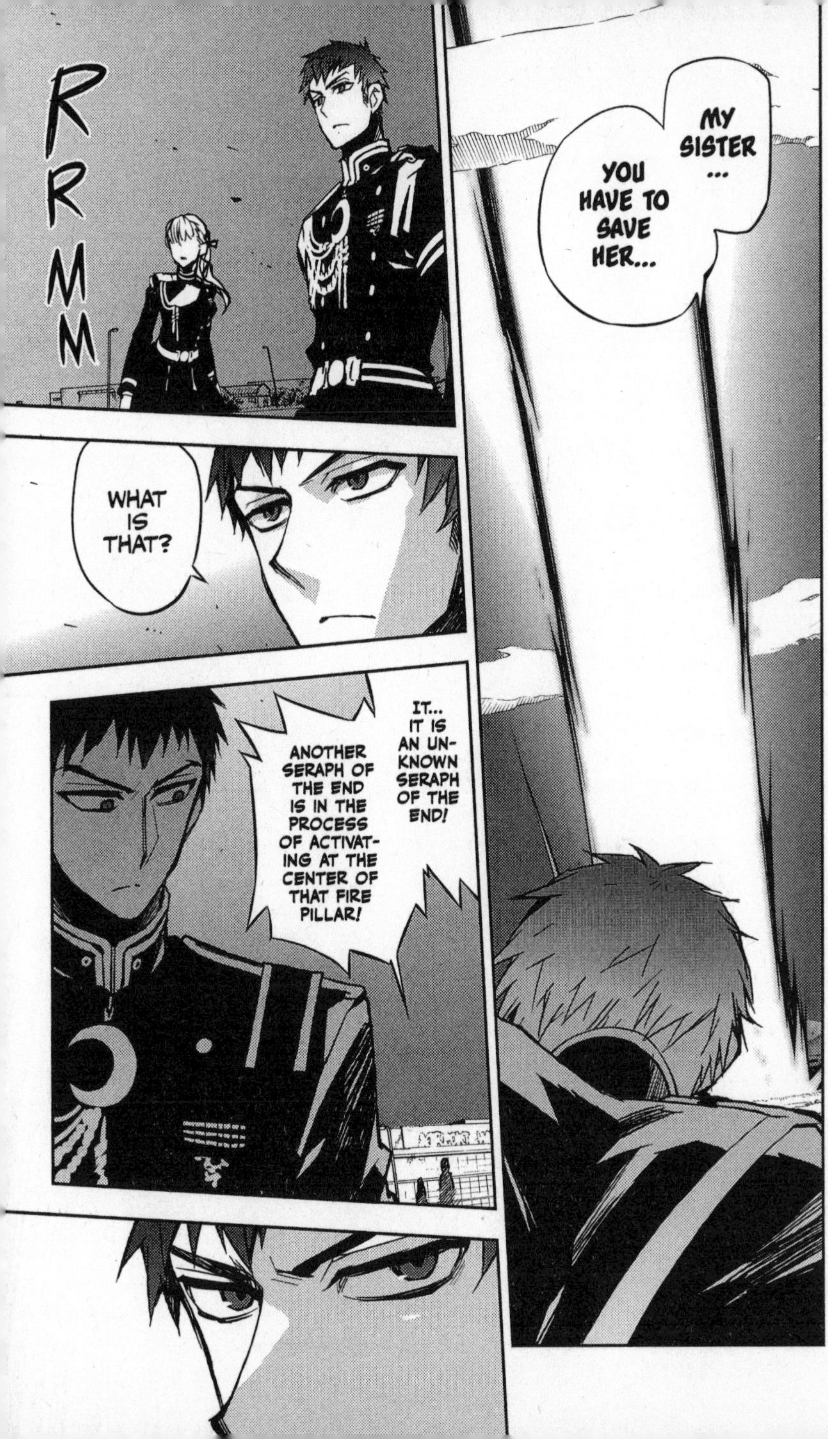
MY SISTER...
YOU HAVE TO SAVE HER...
RRMM
WHAT IS THAT?
IT... IT IS AN UNKNOWN SERAPH OF THE END!
ANOTHER SERAPH OF THE END IS IN THE PROCESS OF ACTIVATING AT THE CENTER OF THAT FIRE PILLAR!

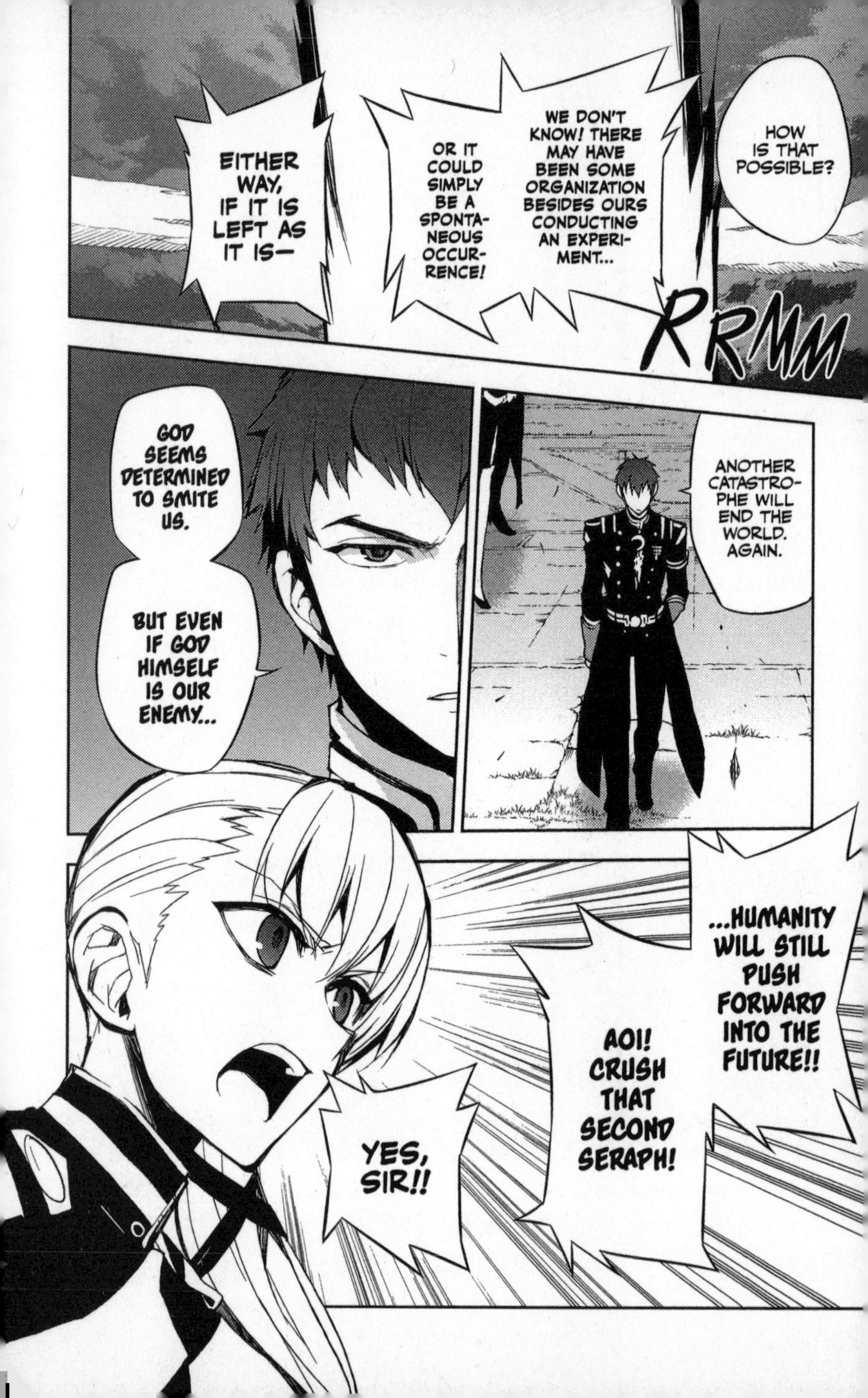
HOW IS THAT POSSIBLE?
WE DON'T KNOW! THERE MAY HAVE BEEN SOME ORGANIZATION BESIDES OURS CONDUCTING AN EXPERIMENT...
OR IT COULD SIMPLY BE A SPONTANEOUS OCCURRENCE!
EITHER WAY, IF IT IS LEFT AS IT IS—
RRMM
ANOTHER CATASTROPHE WILL END THE WORLD. AGAIN.
GOD SEEMS DETERMINED TO SMITE US.
BUT EVEN IF GOD HIMSELF IS OUR ENEMY...
...HUMANITY WILL STILL PUSH FORWARD INTO THE FUTURE!!
AOI! CRUSH THAT SECOND SERAPH!
YES, SIR!!

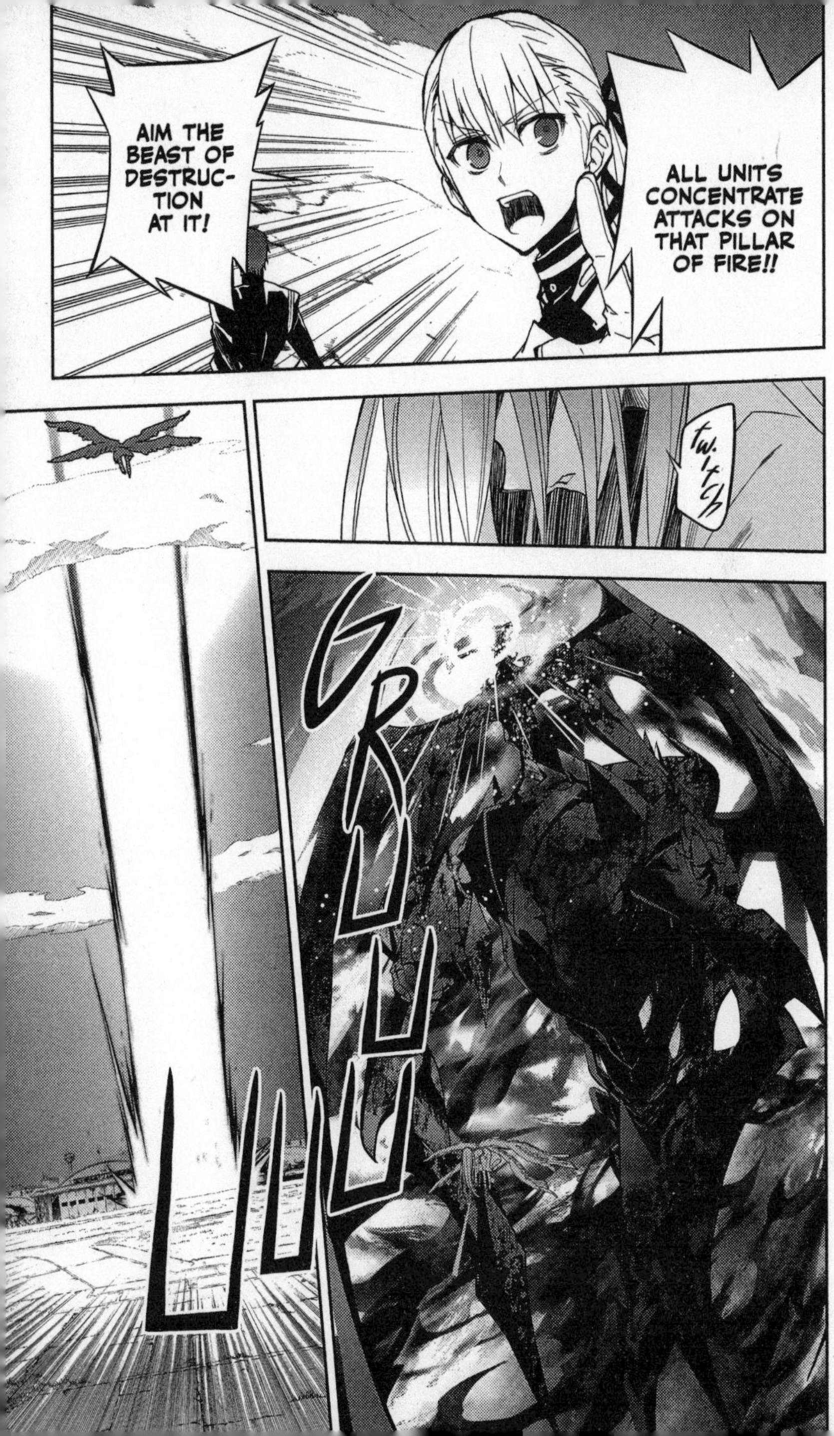
ALL UNITS CONCENTRATE ATTACKS ON THAT PILLAR OF FIRE!!
AIM THE BEAST OF DESTRUC-TION AT IT!
twitch
GRUUUU

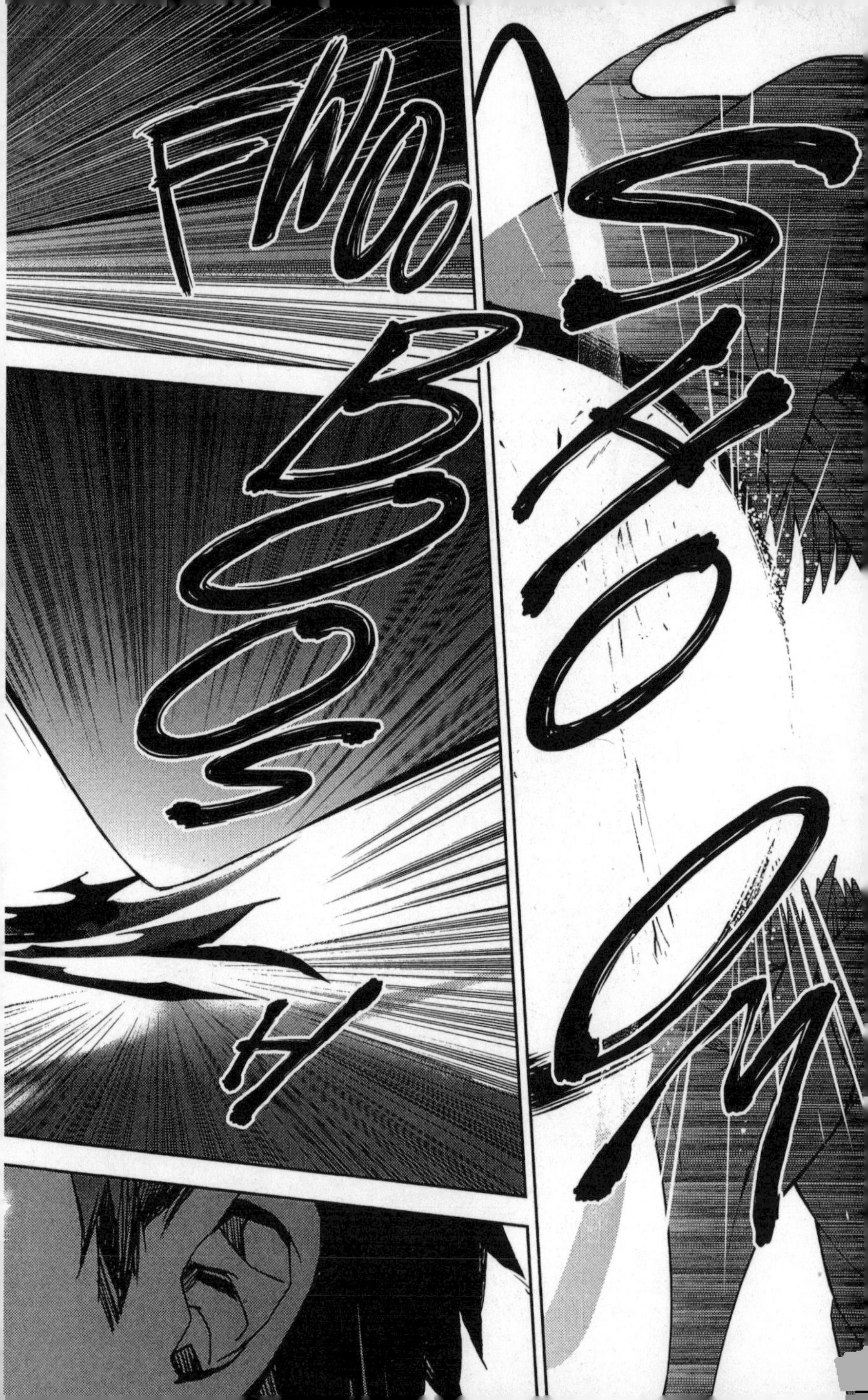
SHOOM
FWOOO
SWOOSH

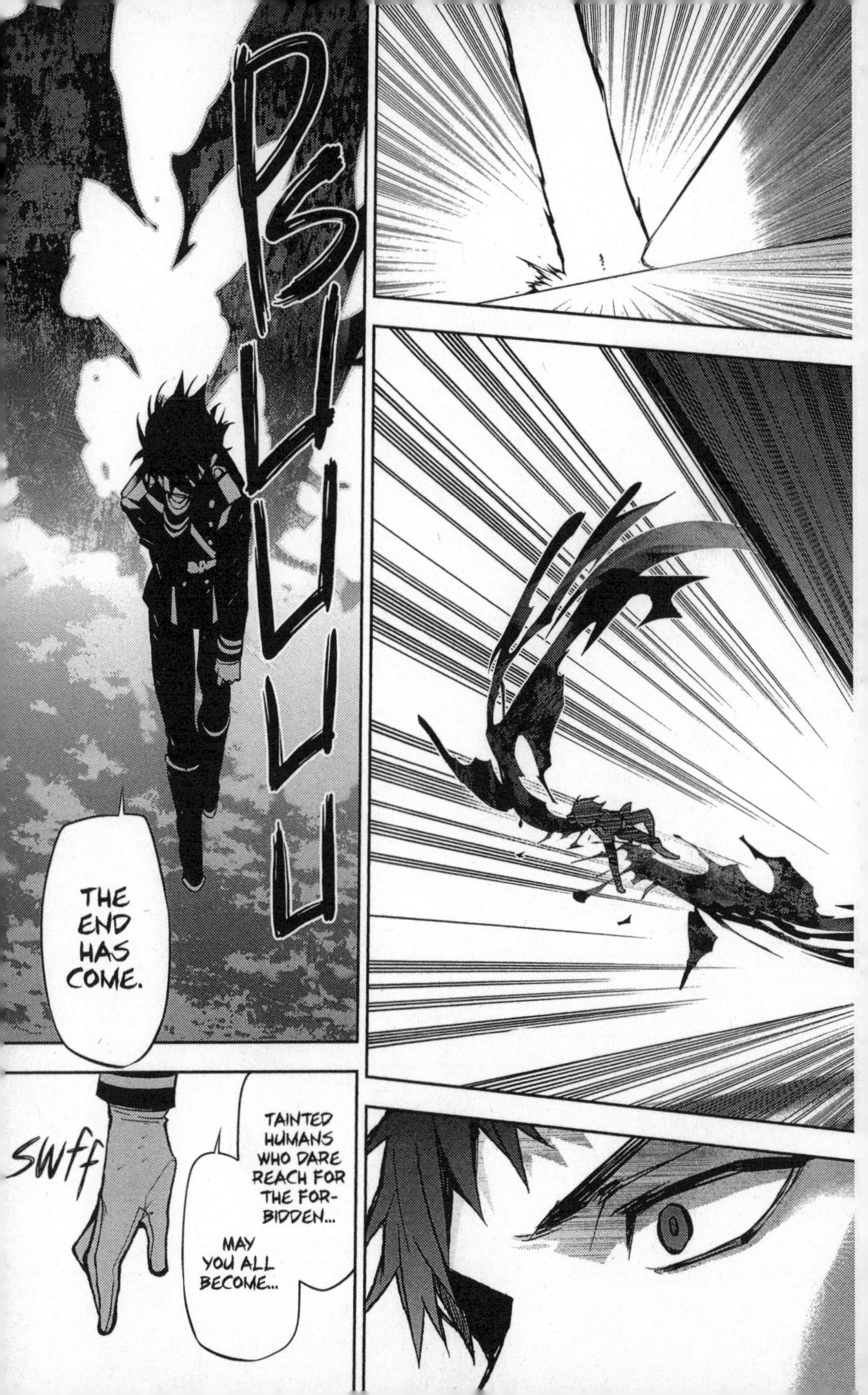
PSUUUU
THE END HAS COME.
SWFF
TAINTED HUMANS WHO DARE REACH FOR THE FOR-BIDDEN...
MAY YOU ALL BECOME...

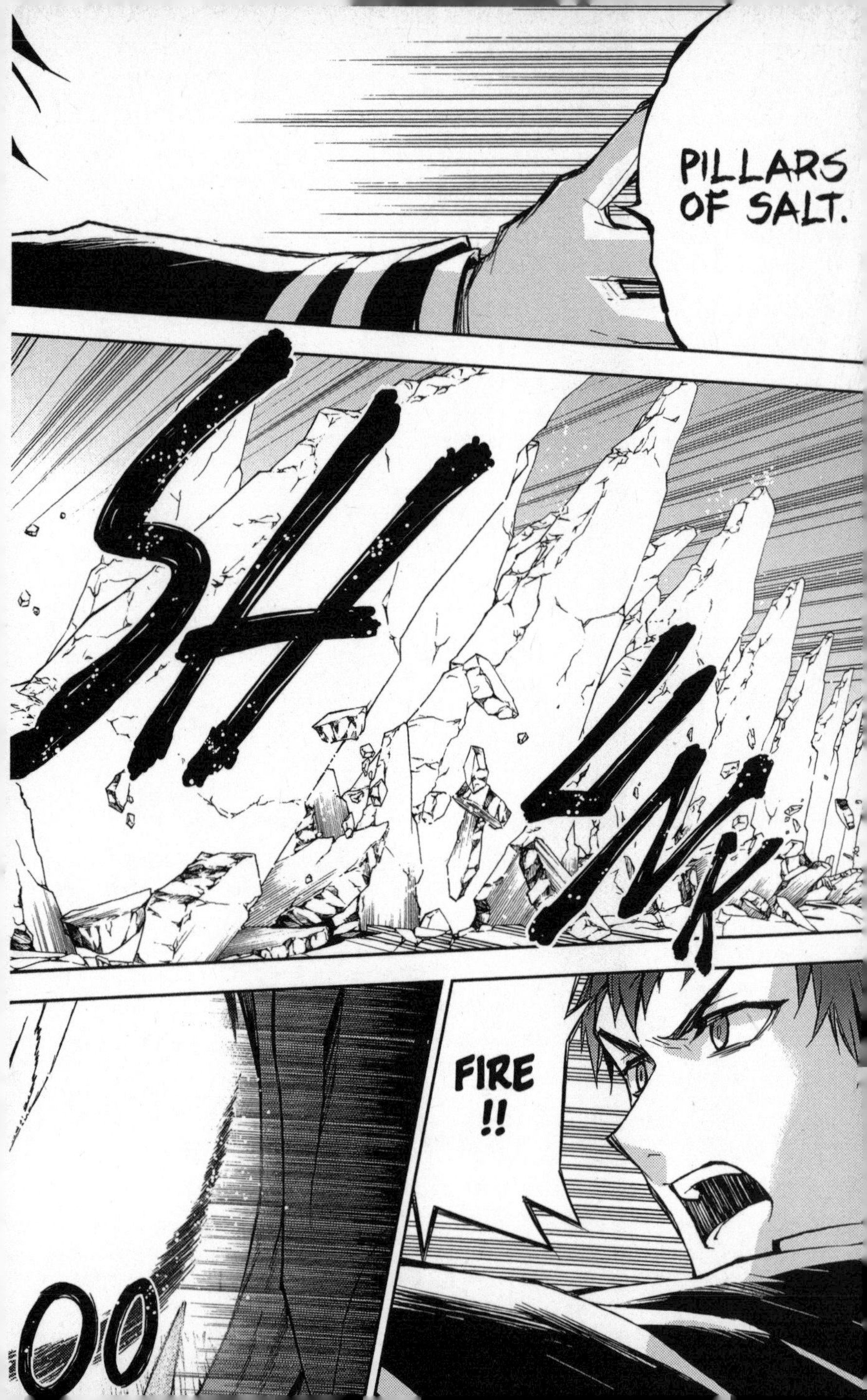
PILLARS OF SALT.
SHUNK
FIRE!!
OO

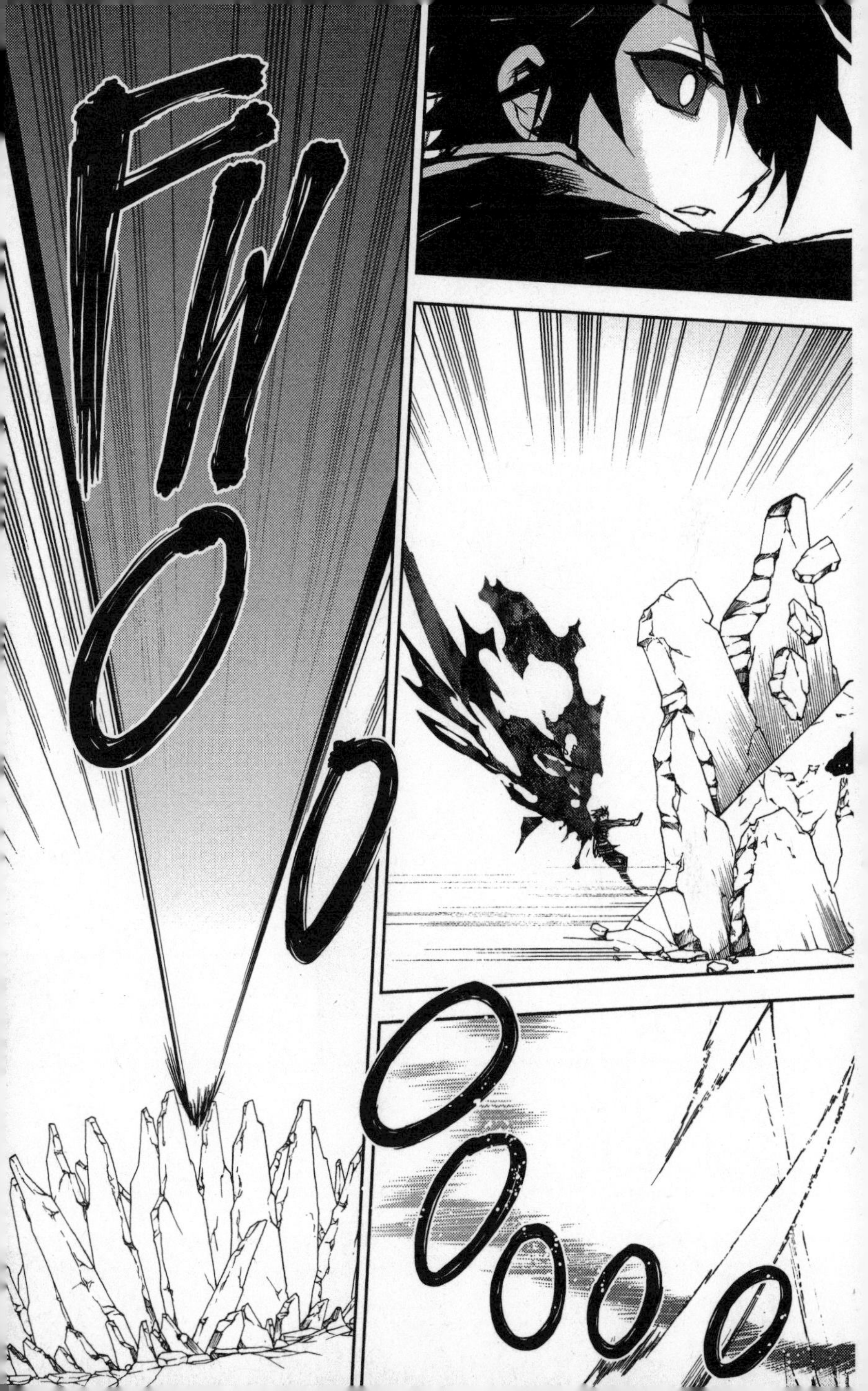
FWOOOOOOOOO

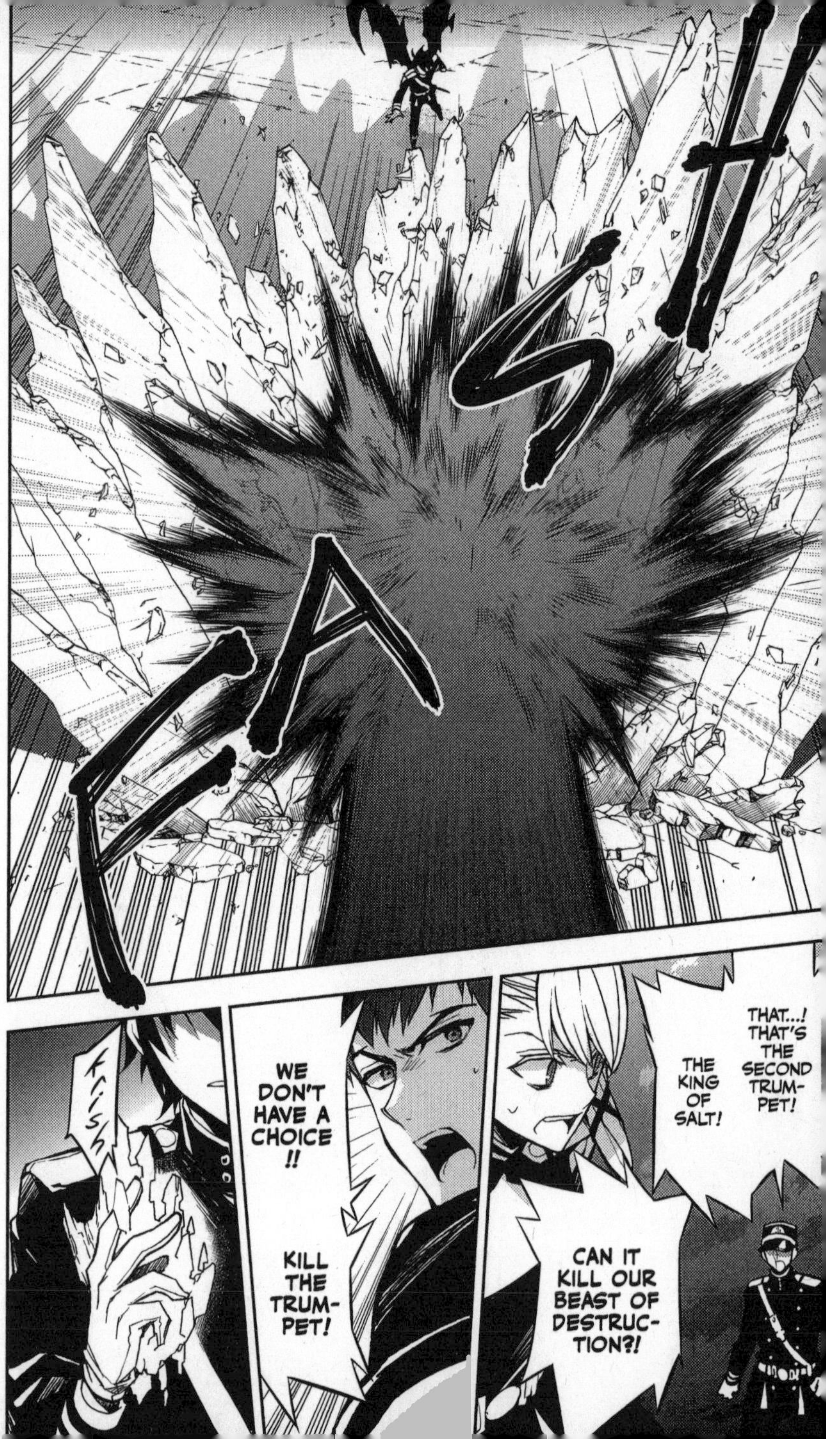
KASH!!
THAT...! THAT'S THE SECOND TRUM-PET!
THE KING OF SALT!
CAN IT KILL OUR BEAST OF DESTRUC-TION?!
WE DON'T HAVE A CHOICE!!
KILL THE TRUM-PET!
krish

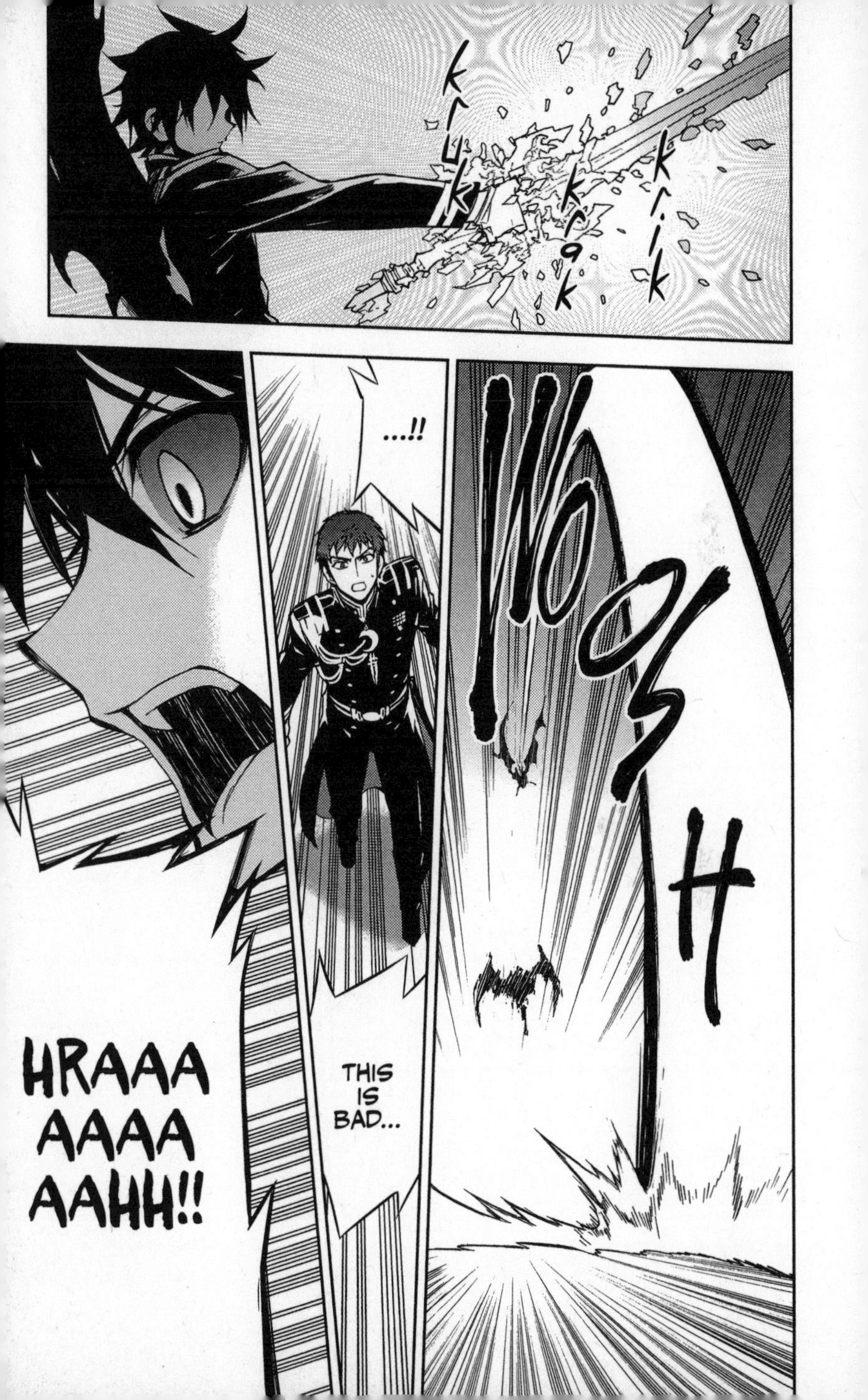
kriik
krak
kruk
WOOSH
...!!
THIS IS BAD...
HRAAAAAAAAAHH!!

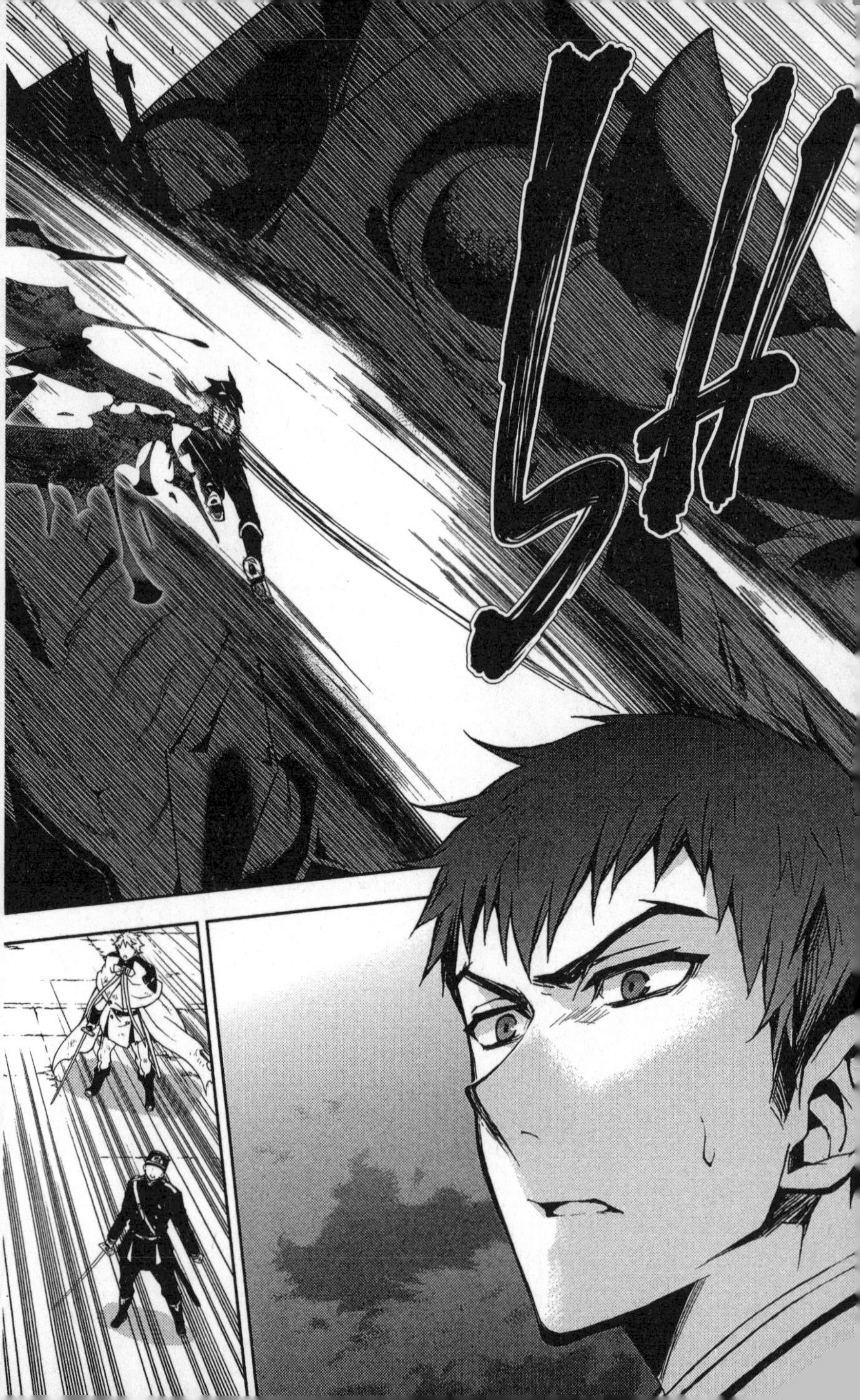
SHH

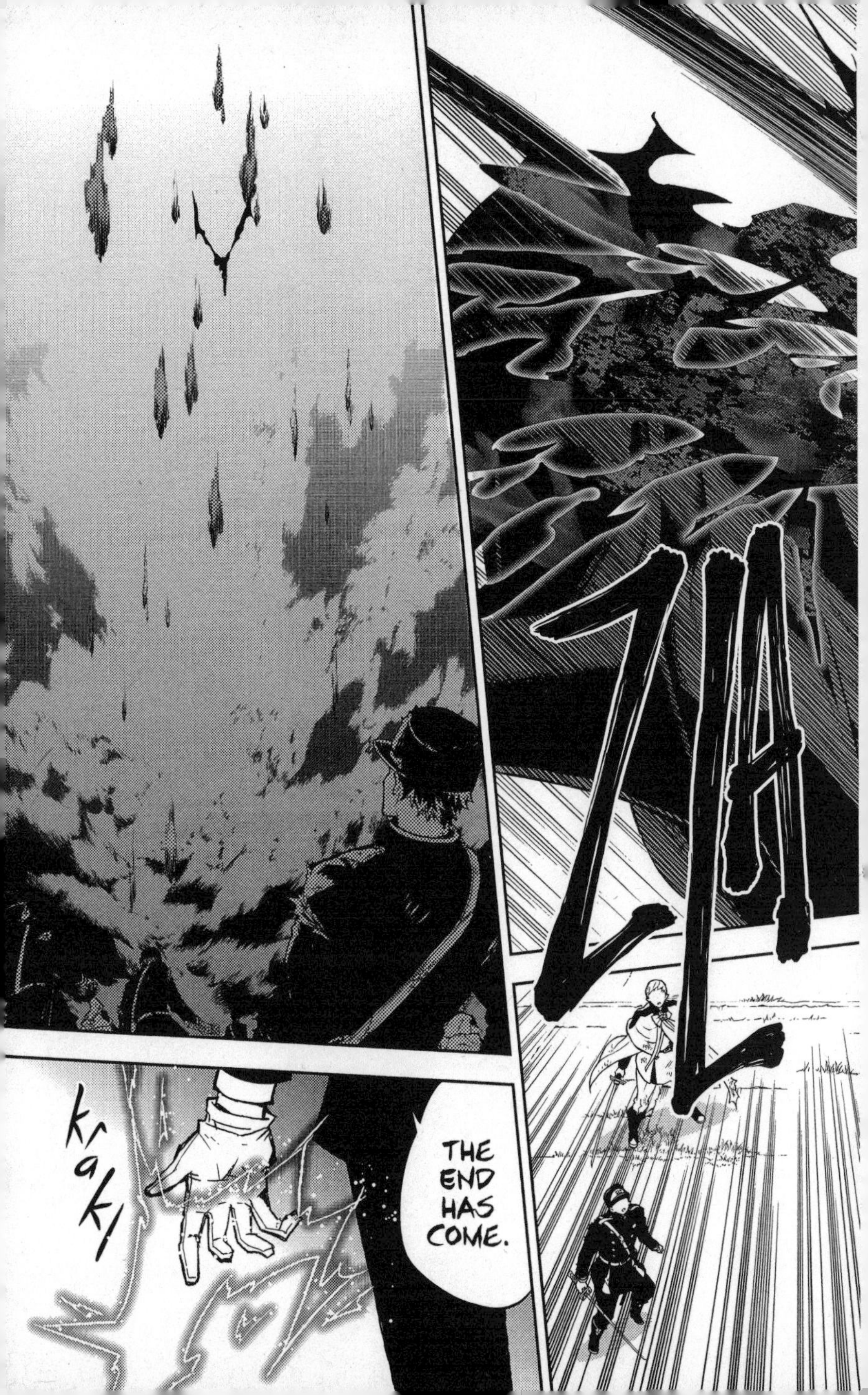

THE END HAS COME.
KRAKI

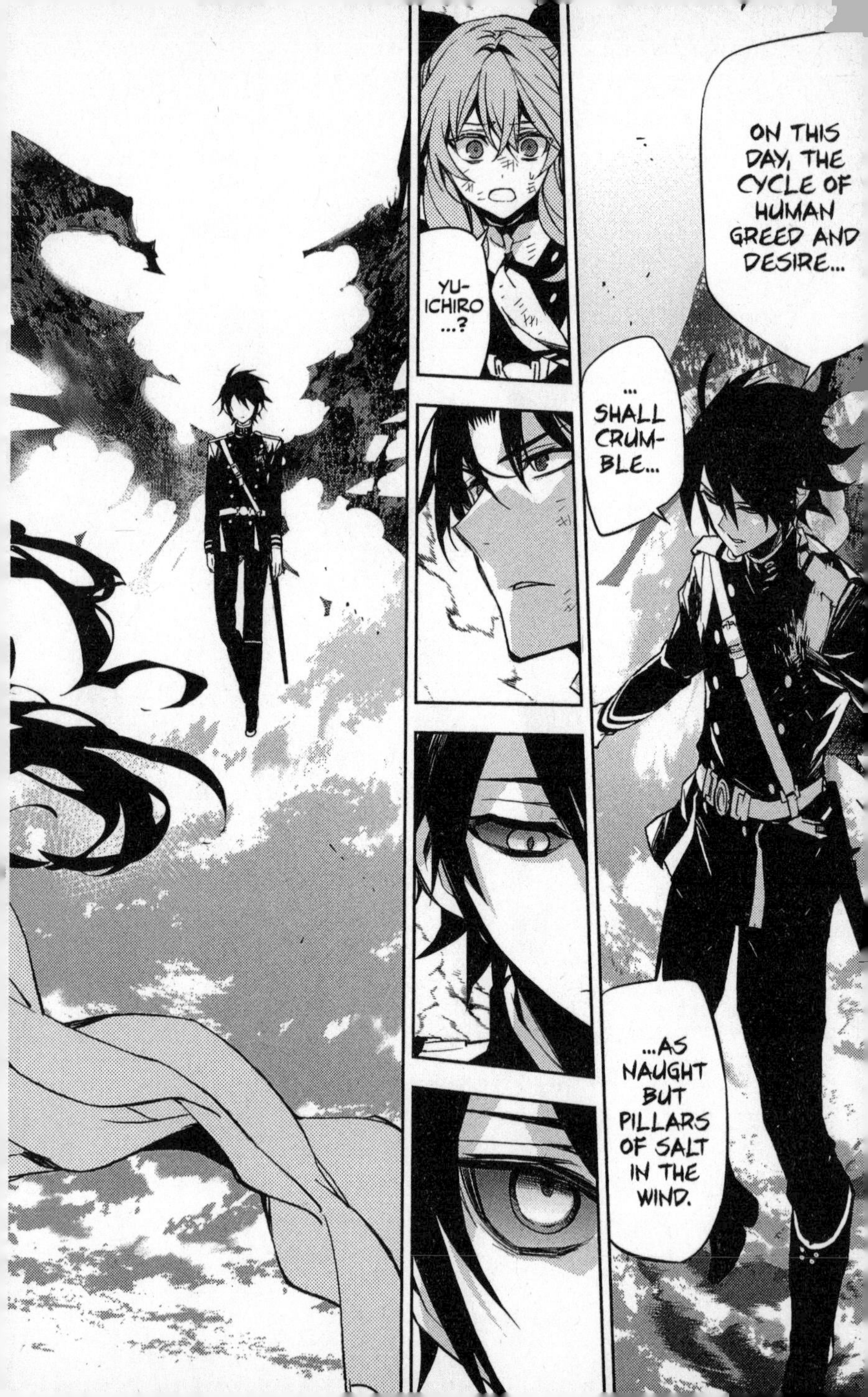
ON THIS DAY, THE CYCLE OF HUMAN GREED AND DESIRE...
...SHALL CRUMBLE...
...AS NAUGHT BUT PILLARS OF SALT IN THE WIND.
YU-ICHIRO...?

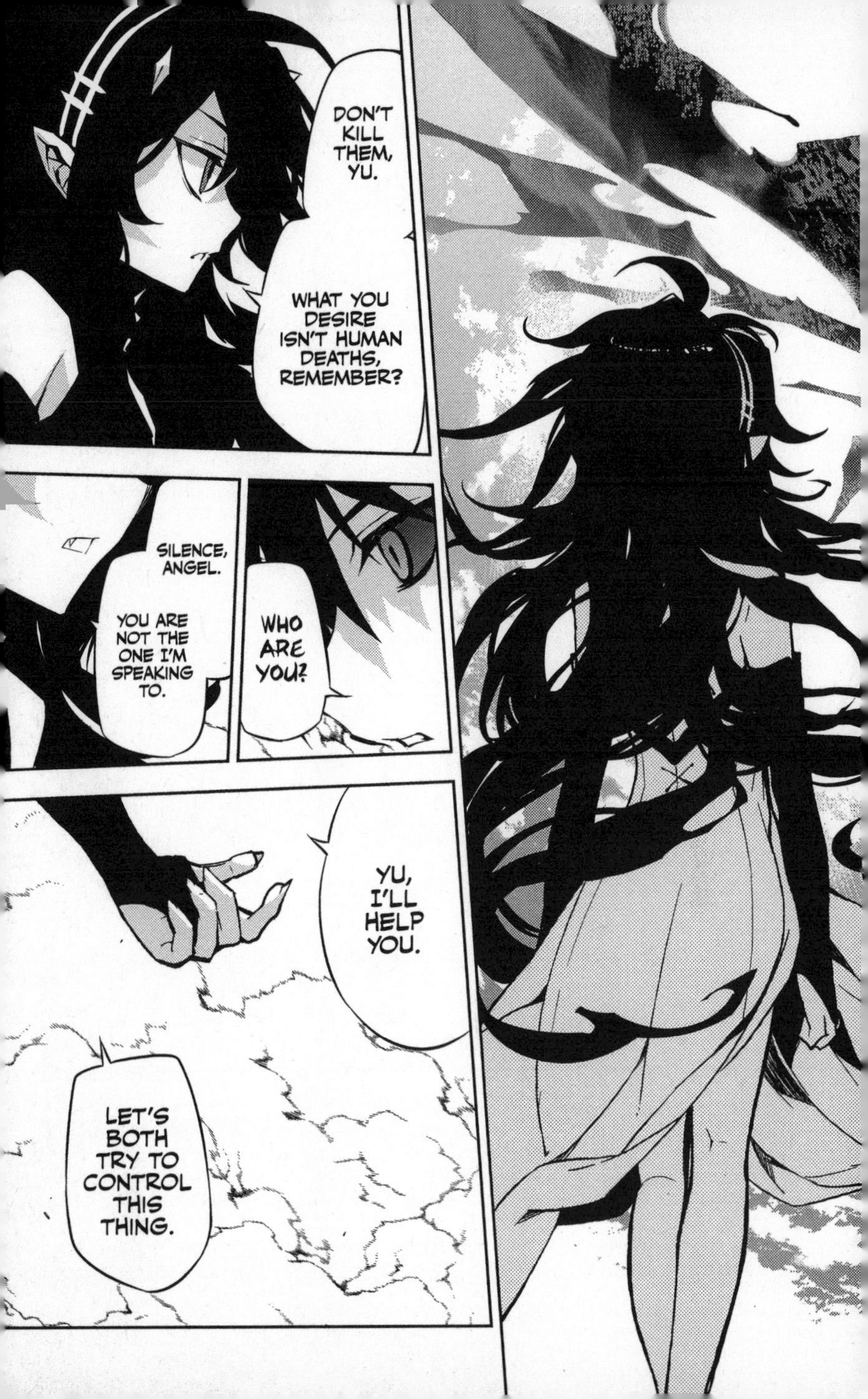
DON'T KILL THEM, YU.
WHAT YOU DESIRE ISN'T HUMAN DEATHS, REMEMBER?
WHO ARE YOU?
SILENCE, ANGEL.
YOU ARE NOT THE ONE I'M SPEAKING TO.
YU, I'LL HELP YOU.
LET'S BOTH TRY TO CONTROL THIS THING.

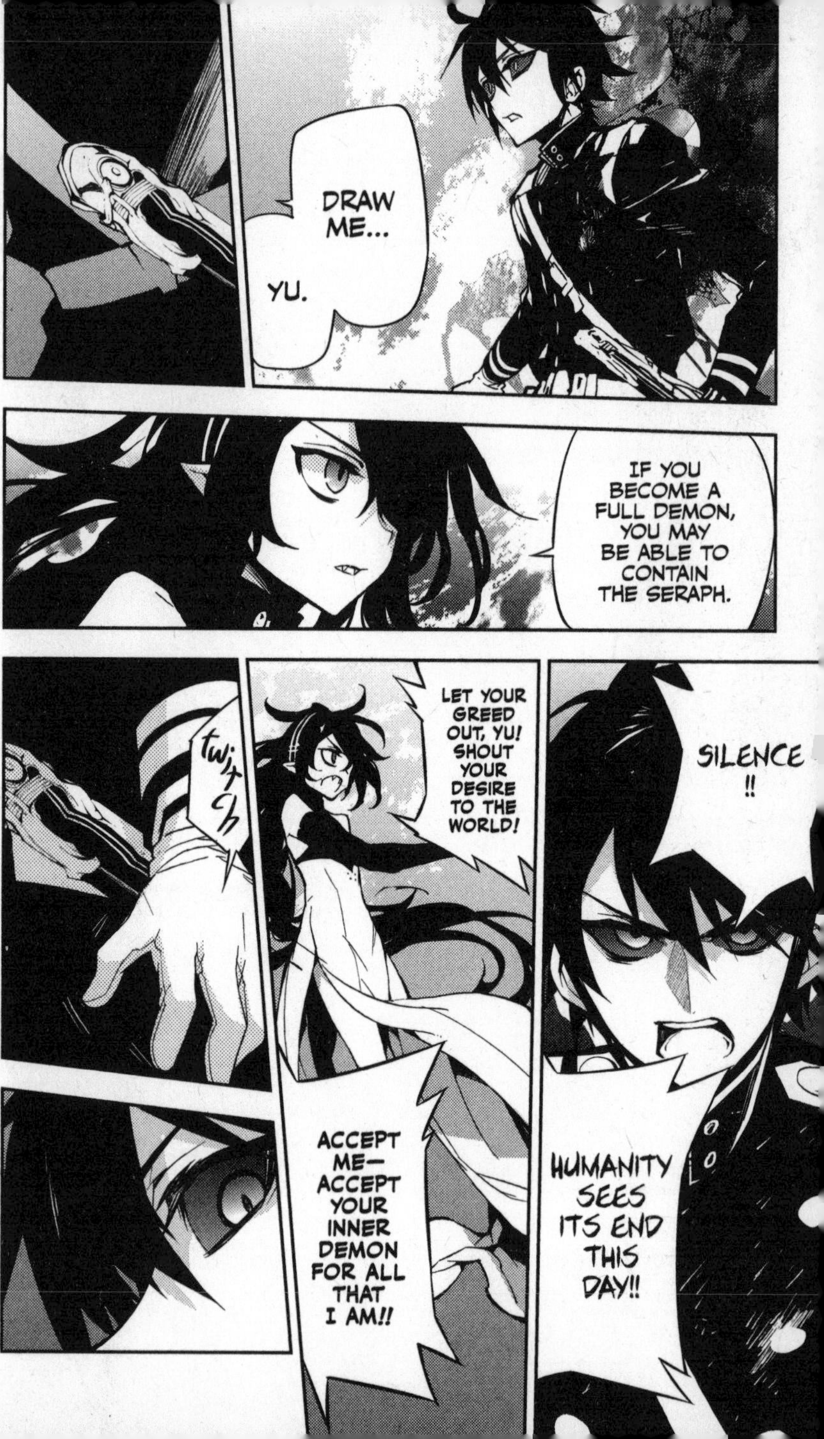
DRAW ME... YU.
IF YOU BECOME A FULL DEMON, YOU MAY BE ABLE TO CONTAIN THE SERAPH.
SILENCE!!
LET YOUR GREED OUT, YU! SHOUT YOUR DESIRE TO THE WORLD!
twitch
HUMANITY SEES ITS END THIS DAY!!
ACCEPT ME—ACCEPT YOUR INNER DEMON FOR ALL THAT I AM!!

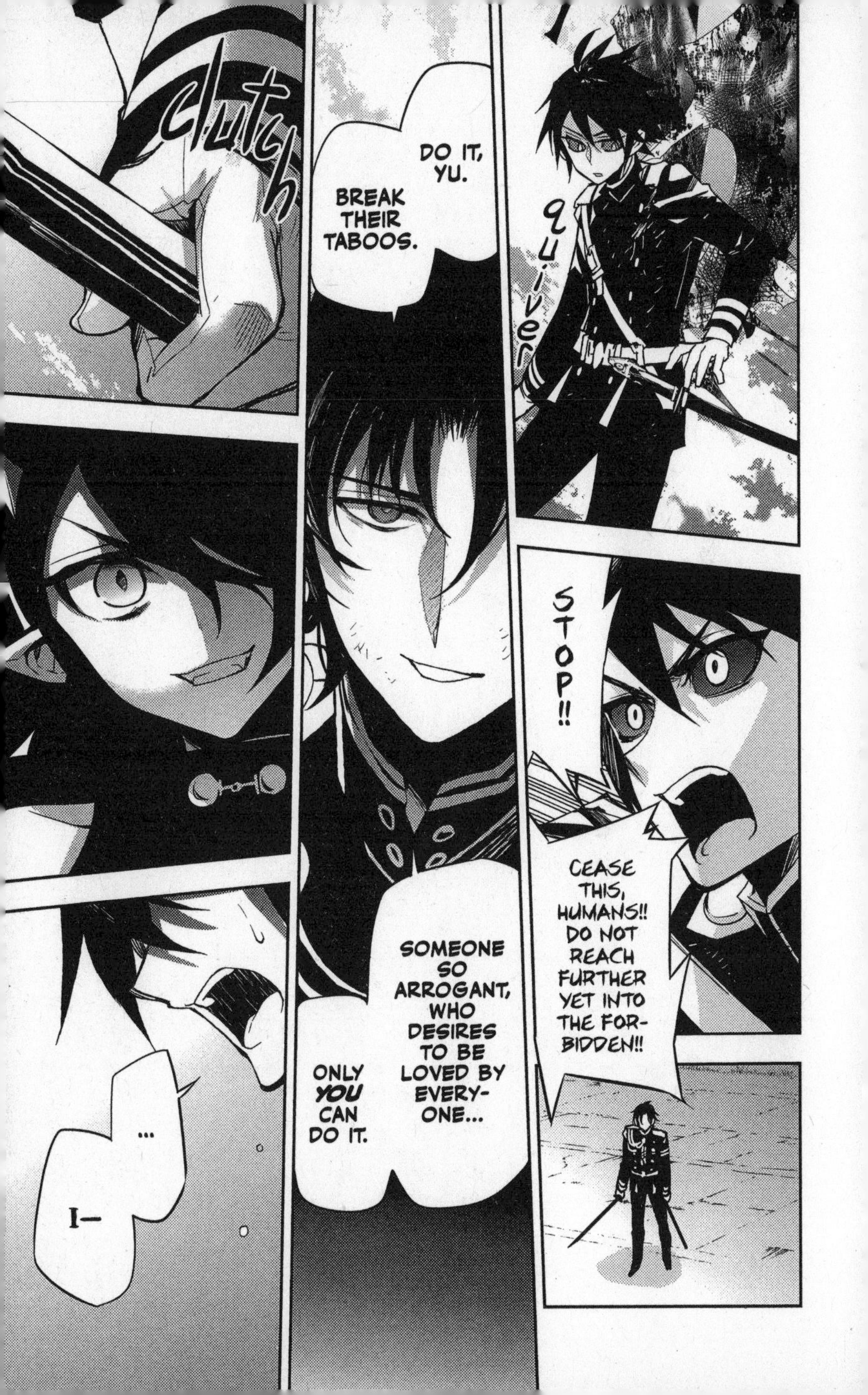
quiver
STOP!!
CEASE THIS, HUMANS!! DO NOT REACH FURTHER YET INTO THE FOR-BIDDEN!!
DO IT, YU.
BREAK THEIR TABOOS.
SOMEONE SO ARROGANT, WHO DESIRES TO BE LOVED BY EVERY-ONE...
ONLY *YOU* CAN DO IT.
clutch
...
I—

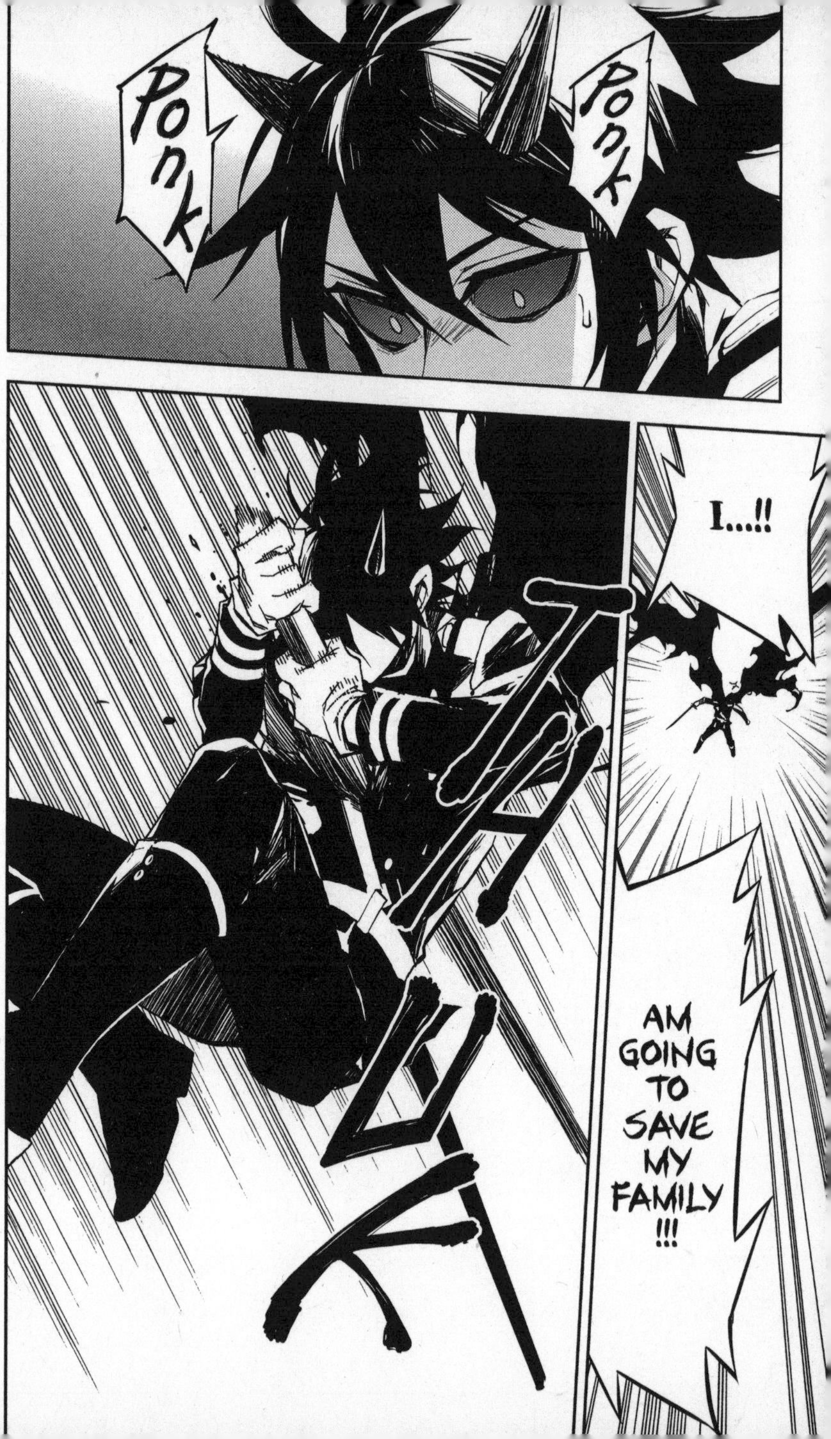
PONK
PONK
I...!!
AM GOING TO SAVE MY FAMILY!!!

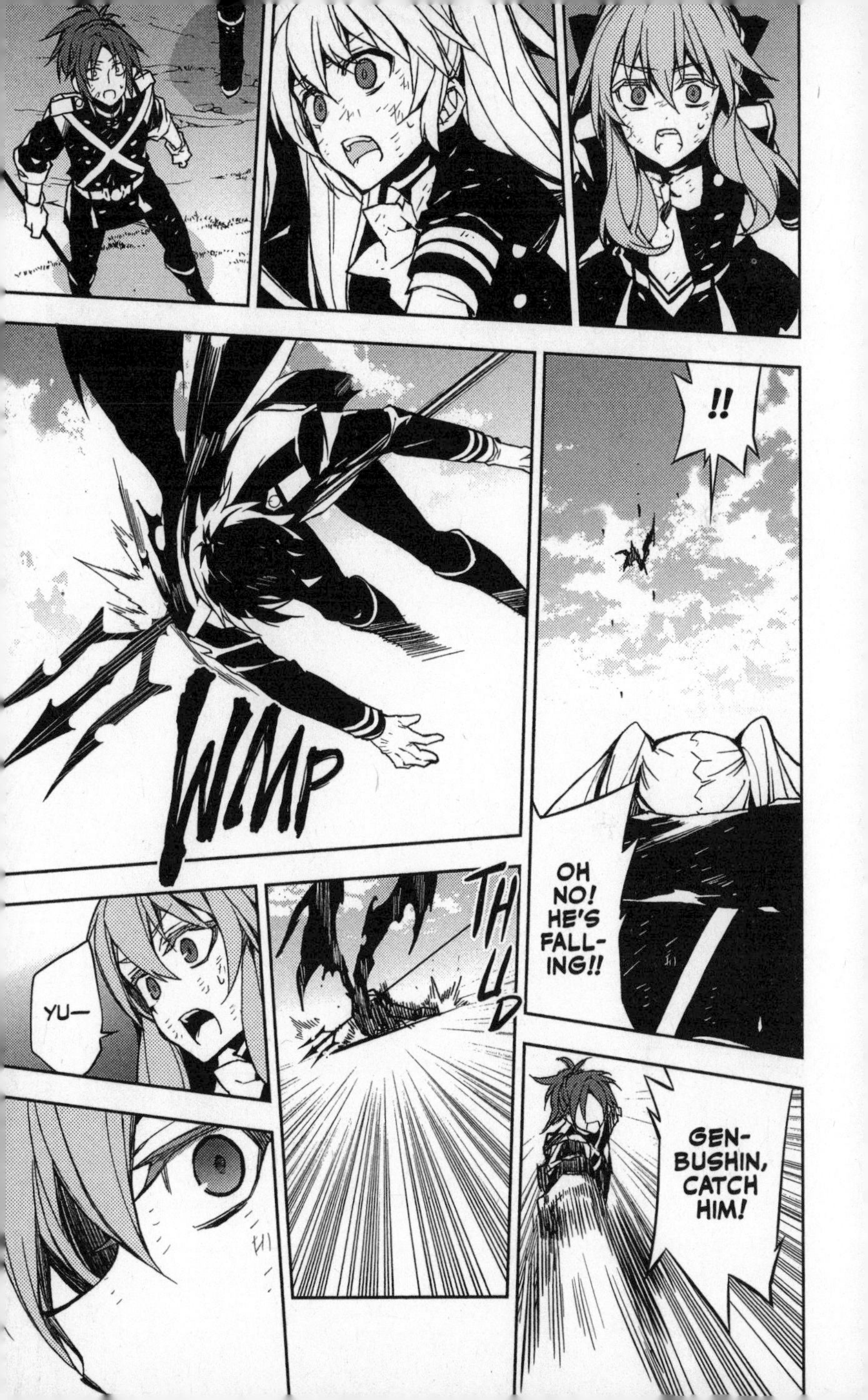
!!
WMP
OH NO! HE'S FALLING!!
THUD
YU—
GEN-BUSHIN, CATCH HIM!

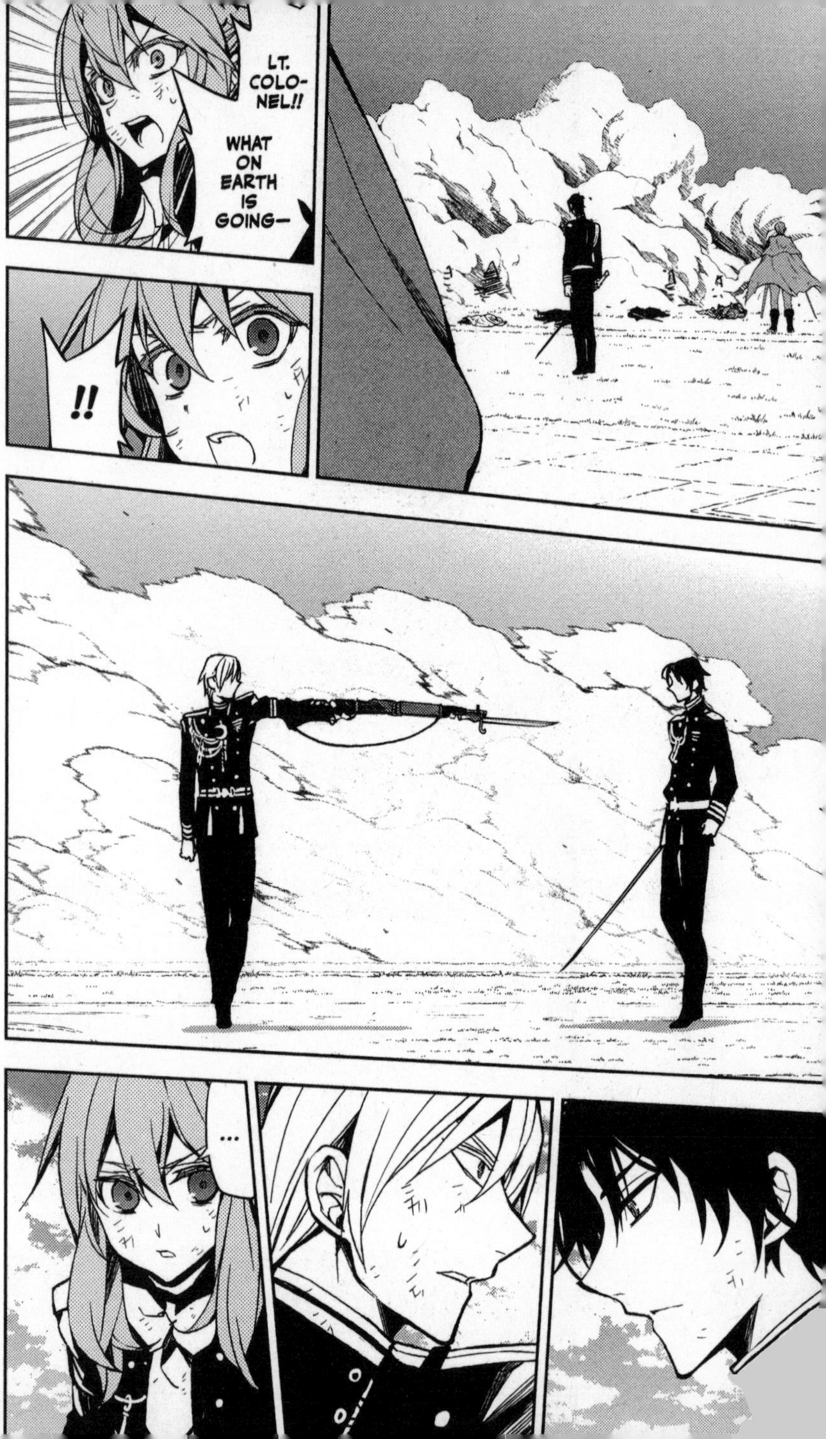
LT. COLONEL!!
WHAT ON EARTH IS GOING—
!!
...

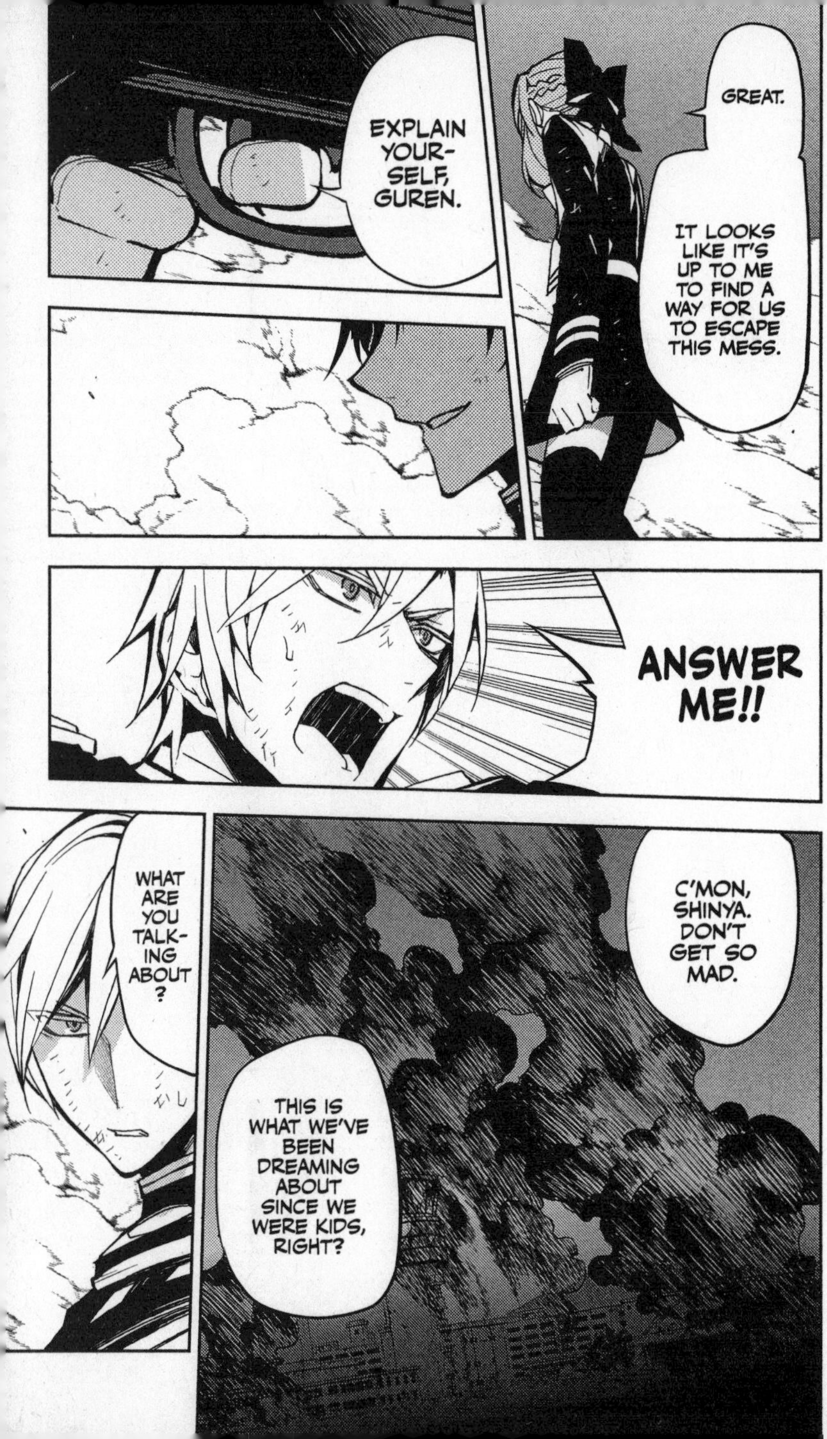
GREAT.
IT LOOKS LIKE IT'S UP TO ME TO FIND A WAY FOR US TO ESCAPE THIS MESS.
EXPLAIN YOUR-SELF, GUREN.
ANSWER ME!!
C'MON, SHINYA. DON'T GET SO MAD.
THIS IS WHAT WE'VE BEEN DREAMING ABOUT SINCE WE WERE KIDS, RIGHT?
WHAT ARE YOU TALKING ABOUT?

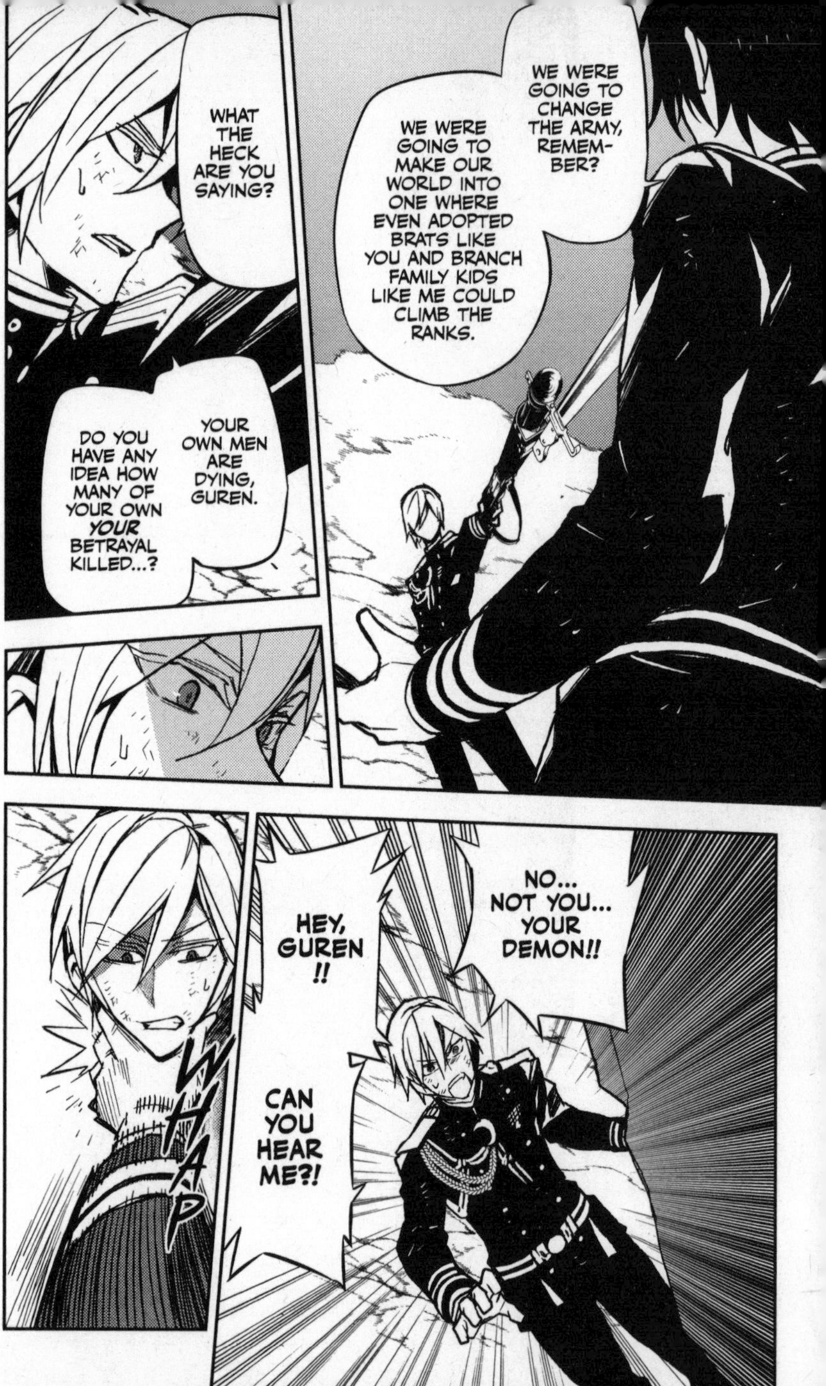
WE WERE GOING TO CHANGE THE ARMY, REMEMBER?
WE WERE GOING TO MAKE OUR WORLD INTO ONE WHERE EVEN ADOPTED BRATS LIKE YOU AND BRANCH FAMILY KIDS LIKE ME COULD CLIMB THE RANKS.
WHAT THE HECK ARE YOU SAYING?
YOUR OWN MEN ARE DYING, GUREN.
DO YOU HAVE ANY IDEA HOW MANY OF YOUR OWN *YOUR* BETRAYAL KILLED...?
NO... NOT YOU... YOUR DEMON!!
HEY, GUREN!!
CAN YOU HEAR ME?!
WHAP

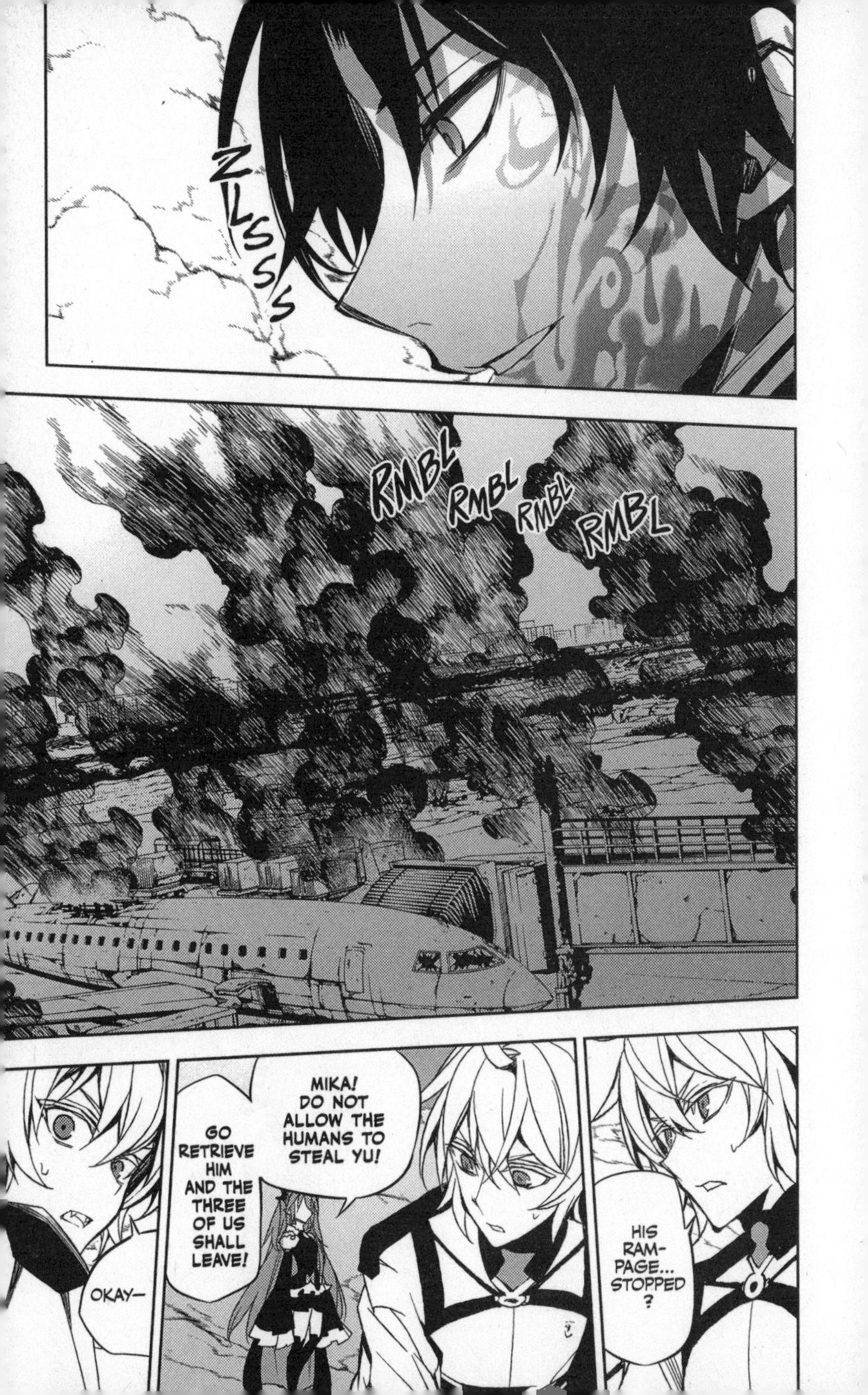
ZLSSSS
RMBL RMBL RMBL RMBL
HIS RAM-PAGE... STOPPED?
MIKA! DO NOT ALLOW THE HUMANS TO STEAL YU!
GO RETRIEVE HIM AND THE THREE OF US SHALL LEAVE!
OKAY—

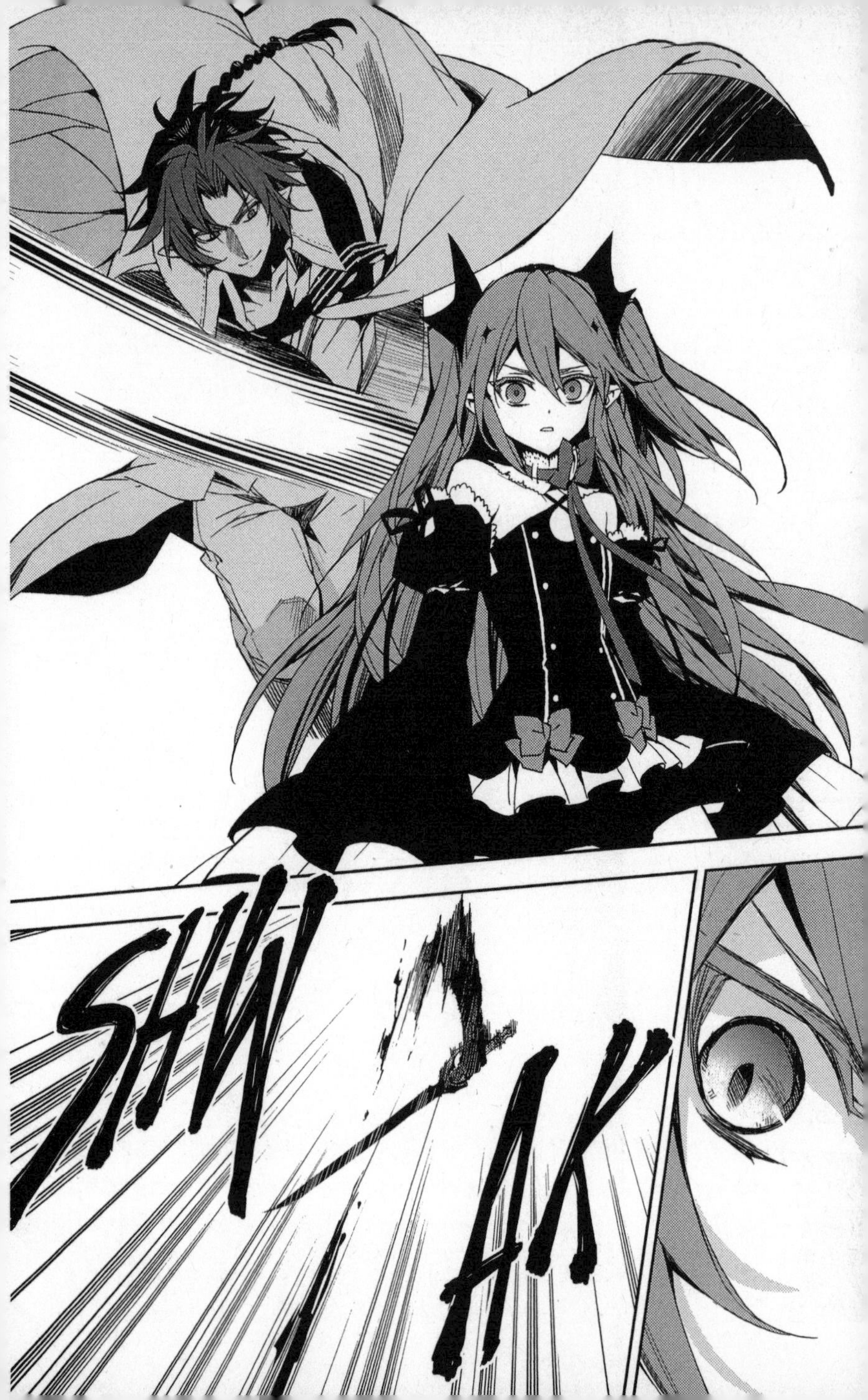
SHWAK

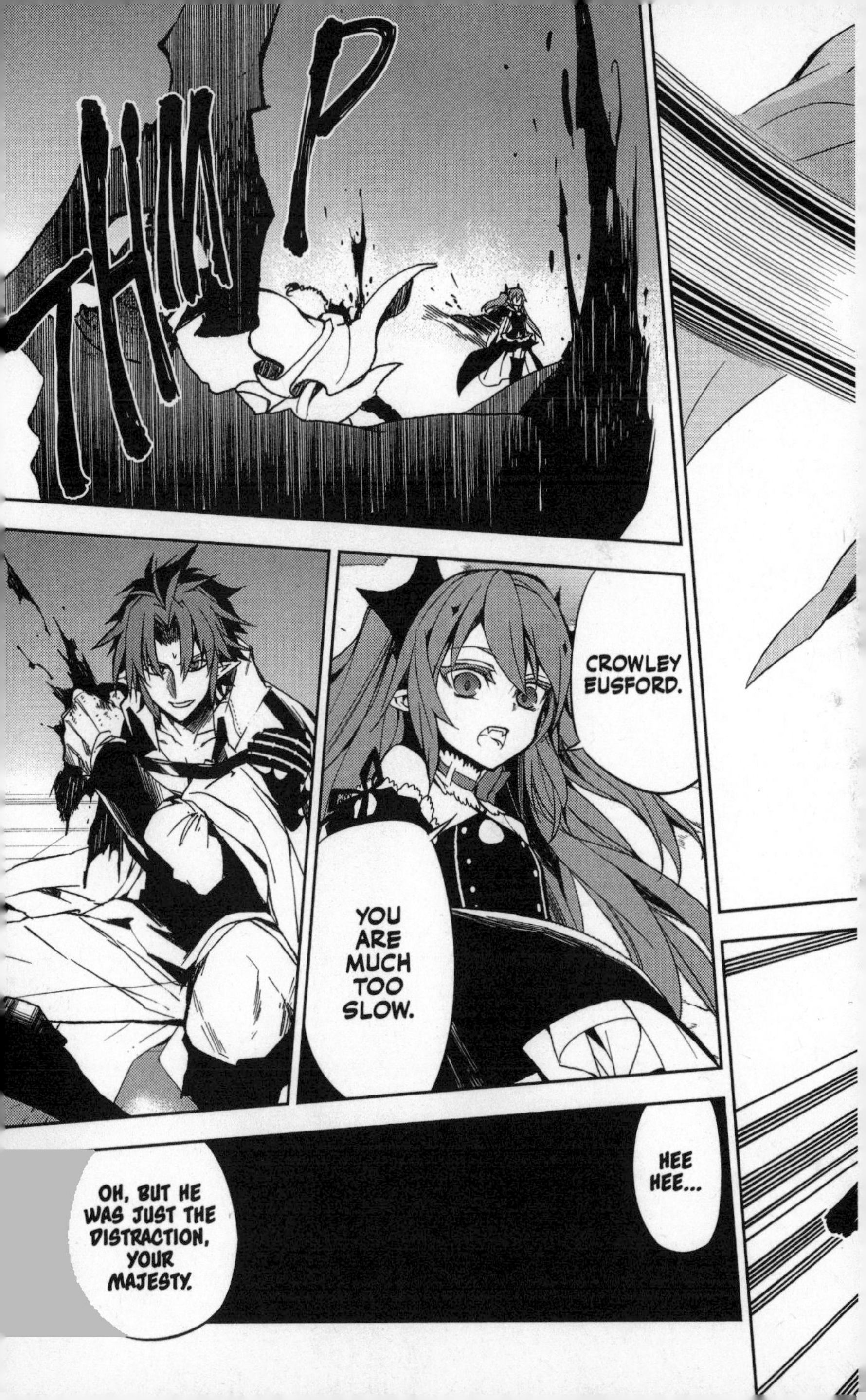
THUMP
CROWLEY EUSFORD.
YOU ARE MUCH TOO SLOW.
HEE HEE...
OH, BUT HE WAS JUST THE DISTRACTION, YOUR MAJESTY.

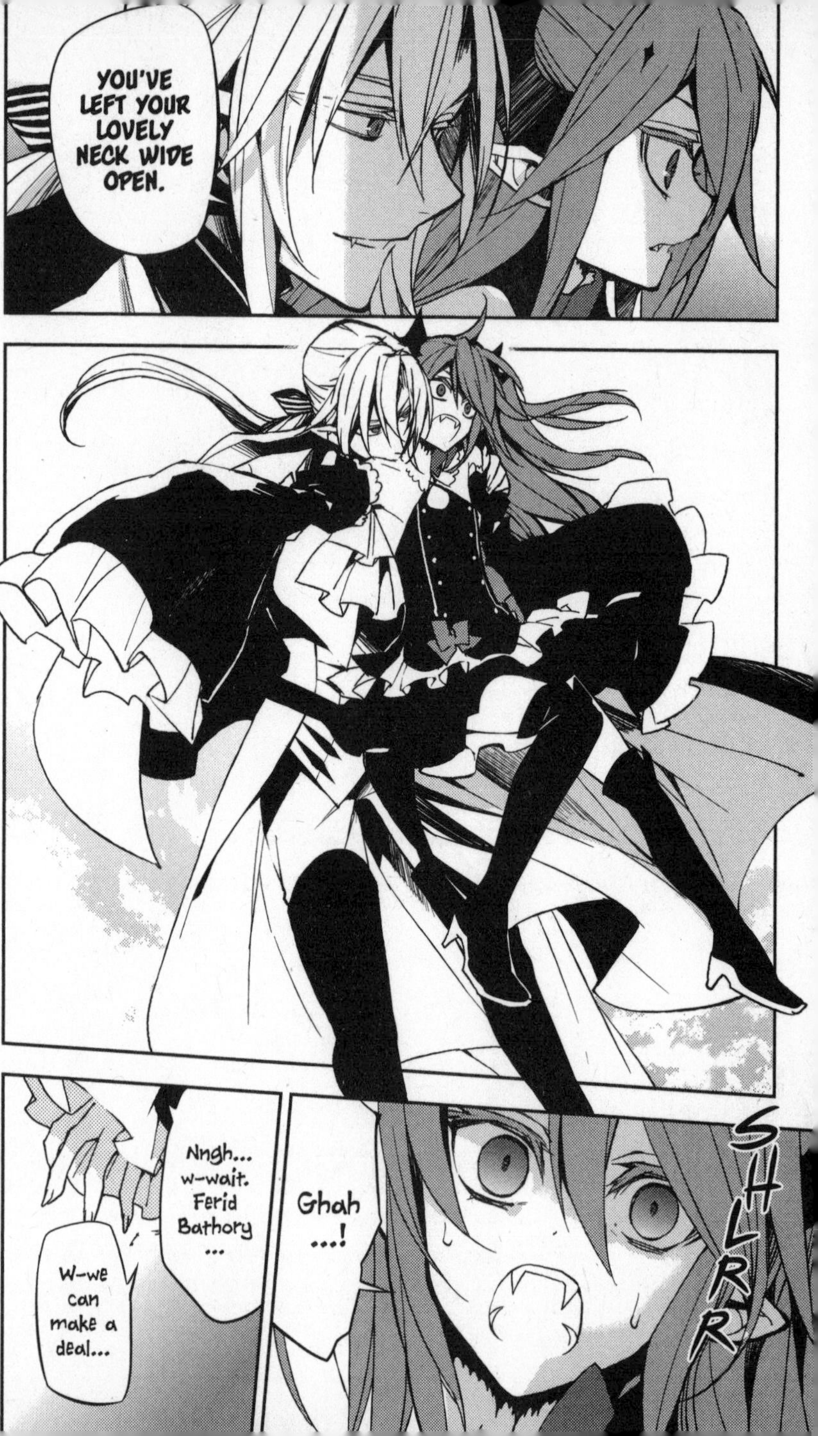
YOU'VE LEFT YOUR LOVELY NECK WIDE OPEN.
SHLRRR
Ghah ...!
Nngh... w-wait. Ferid Bathory ...
W-we can make a deal...

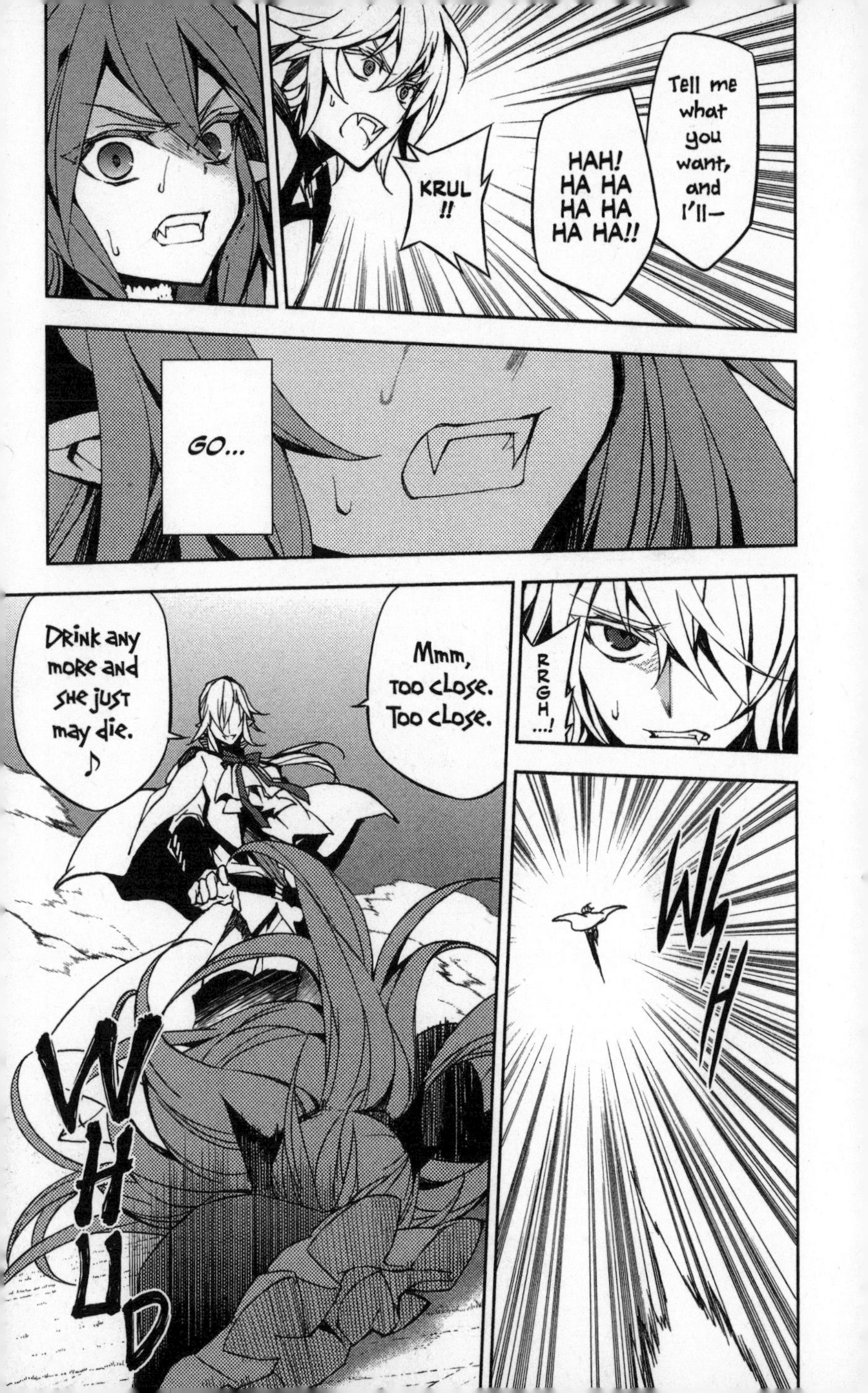
Tell me what you want, and I'll—
HAH! HA HA HA HA HA HA!!
KRUL!!
GO...
RRGH...!
Mmm, too close. Too close.
Drink any more and she just may die. ♪
WSH
WHUD

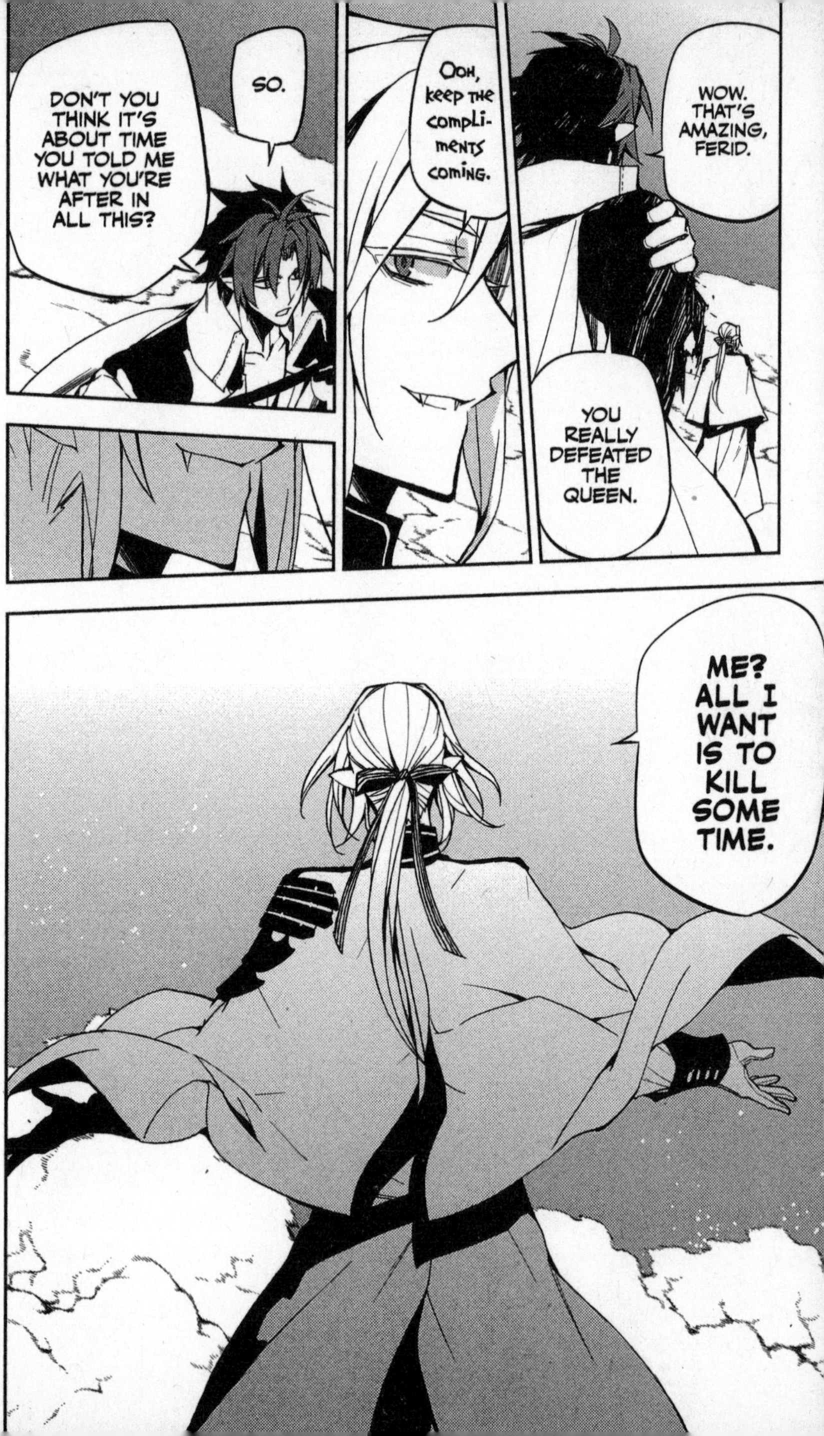
WOW. THAT'S AMAZING, FERID.
YOU REALLY DEFEATED THE QUEEN.
Ooh, keep the compliments coming.
SO.
DON'T YOU THINK IT'S ABOUT TIME YOU TOLD ME WHAT YOU'RE AFTER IN ALL THIS?
ME? ALL I WANT IS TO KILL SOME TIME.

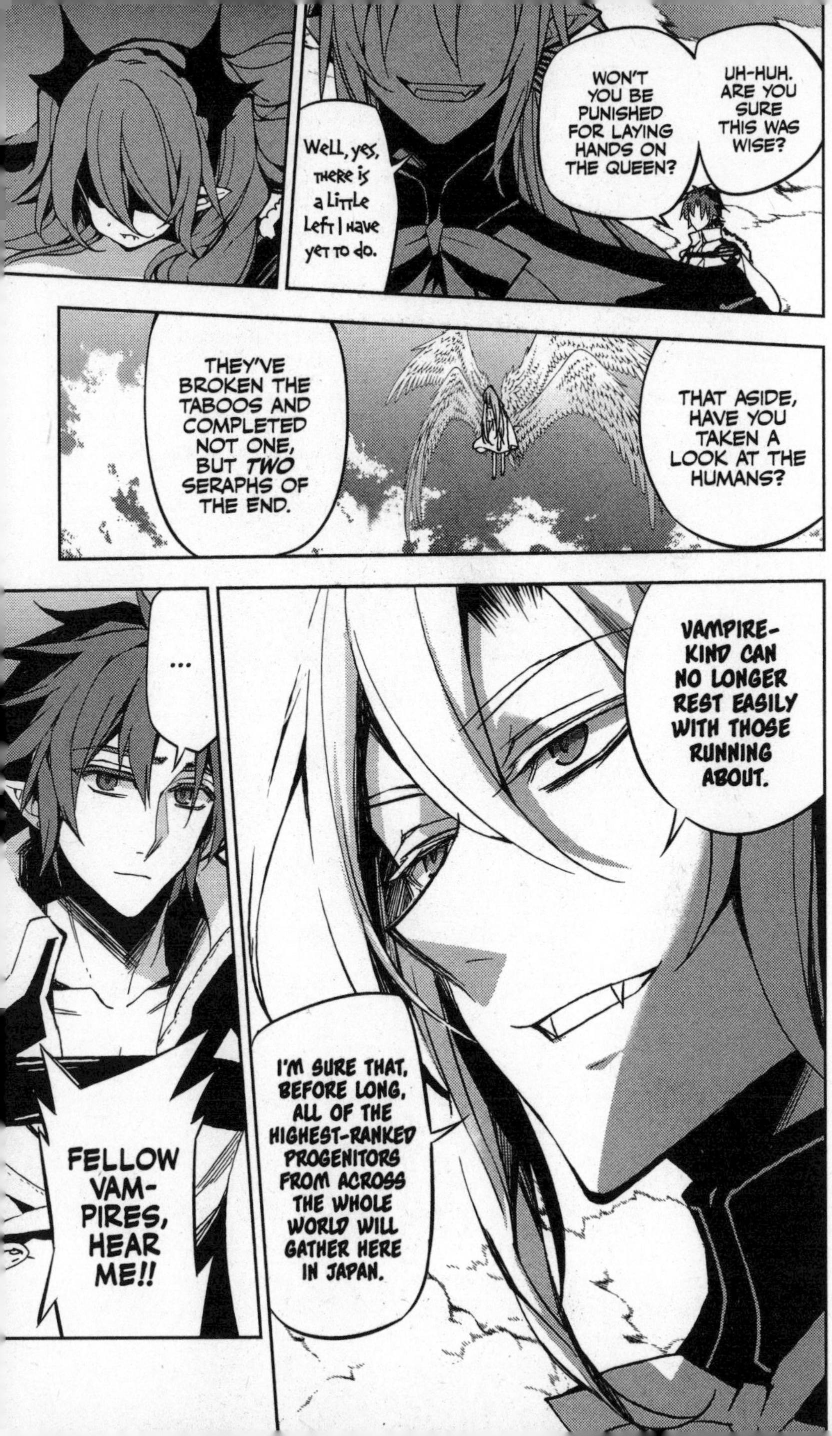
UH-HUH. ARE YOU SURE THIS WAS WISE?
WON'T YOU BE PUNISHED FOR LAYING HANDS ON THE QUEEN?
Well, yes, there is a little left I have yet to do.
THAT ASIDE, HAVE YOU TAKEN A LOOK AT THE HUMANS?
THEY'VE BROKEN THE TABOOS AND COMPLETED NOT ONE, BUT *TWO* SERAPHS OF THE END.
VAMPIRE-KIND CAN NO LONGER REST EASILY WITH THOSE RUNNING ABOUT.
I'M SURE THAT, BEFORE LONG, ALL OF THE HIGHEST-RANKED PROGENITORS FROM ACROSS THE WHOLE WORLD WILL GATHER HERE IN JAPAN.
...
FELLOW VAMPIRES, HEAR ME!!

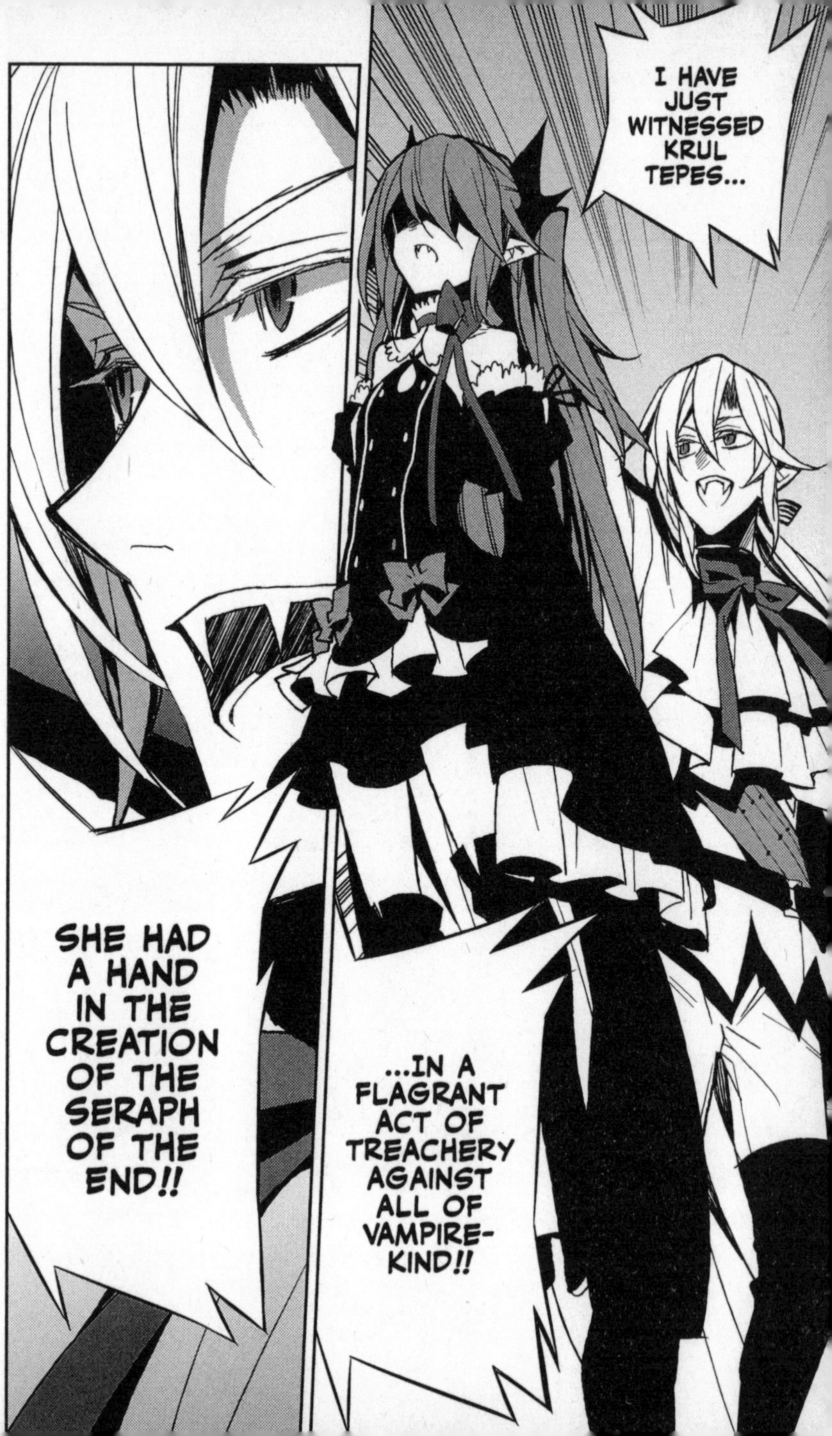
I HAVE JUST WITNESSED KRUL TEPES...
SHE HAD A HAND IN THE CREATION OF THE SERAPH OF THE END!!
...IN A FLAGRANT ACT OF TREACHERY AGAINST ALL OF VAMPIRE-KIND!!

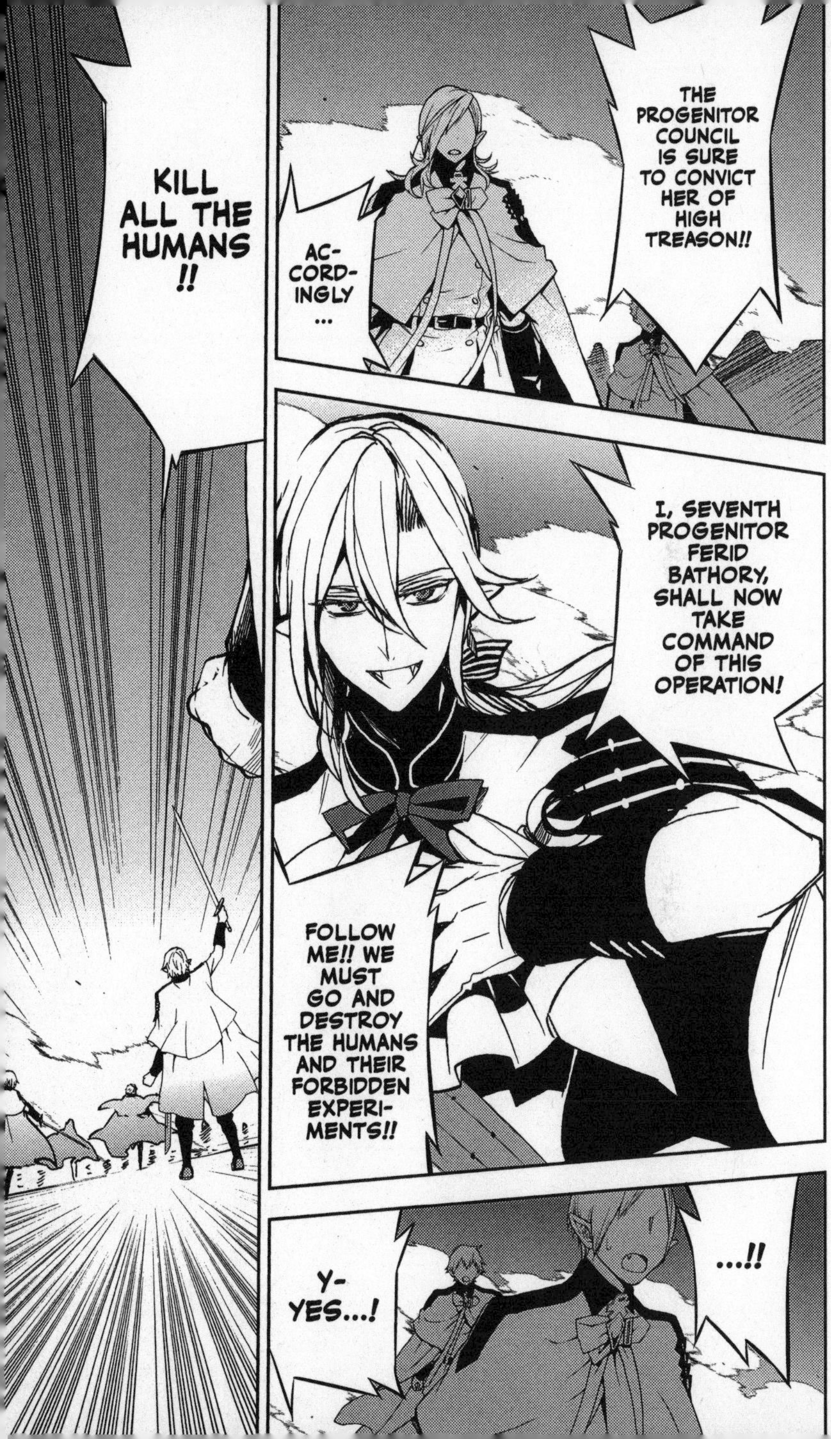
THE PROGENITOR COUNCIL IS SURE TO CONVICT HER OF HIGH TREASON!!
AC-CORD-INGLY...
I, SEVENTH PROGENITOR FERID BATHORY, SHALL NOW TAKE COMMAND OF THIS OPERATION!
FOLLOW ME!! WE MUST GO AND DESTROY THE HUMANS AND THEIR FORBIDDEN EXPERI-MENTS!!
...!!
Y-YES...!
KILL ALL THE HUMANS!!

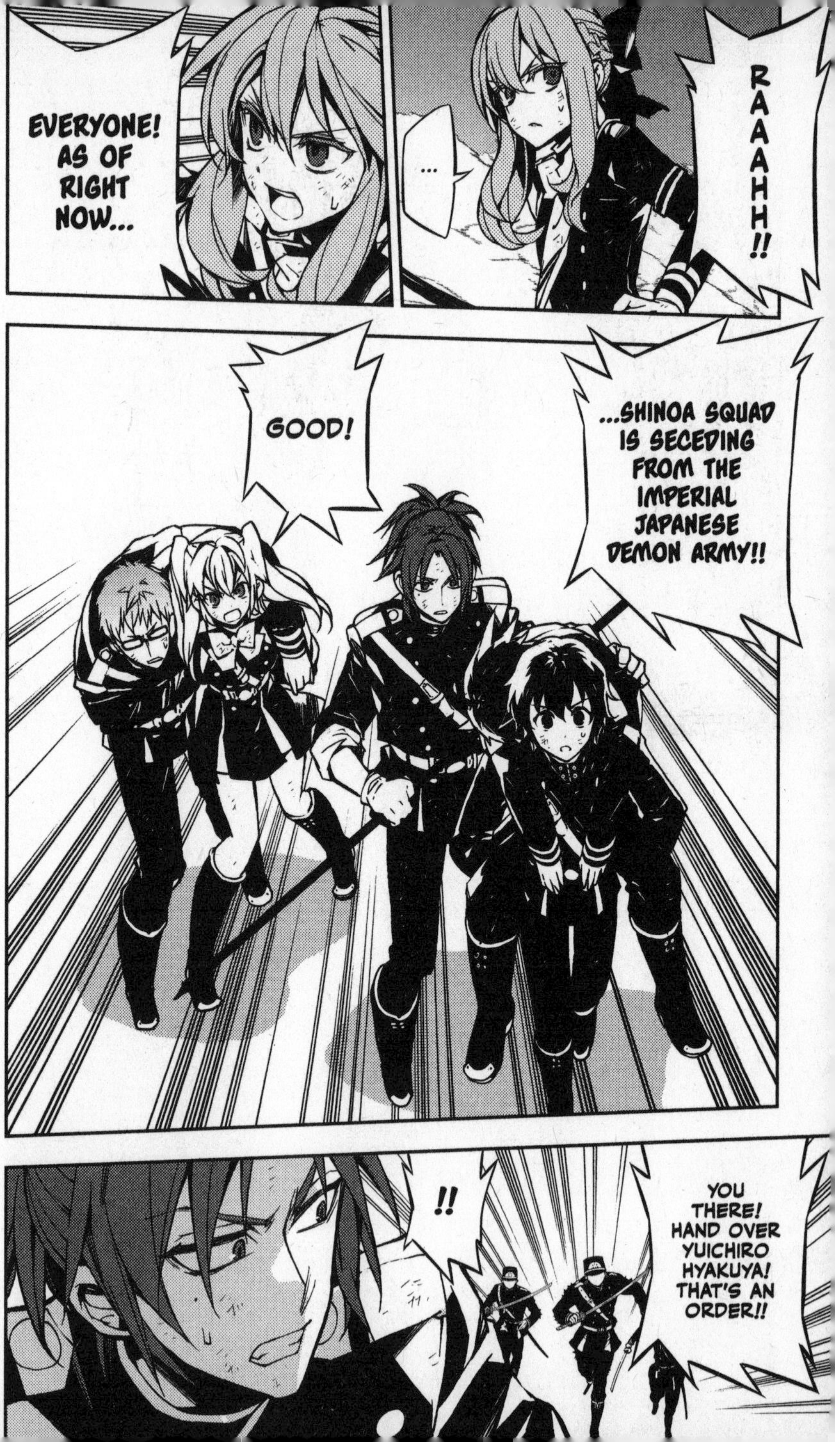
RAAAAHH!!
...
EVERYONE! AS OF RIGHT NOW...
...SHINOA SQUAD IS SECEDING FROM THE IMPERIAL JAPANESE DEMON ARMY!!
GOOD!
YOU THERE! HAND OVER YUICHIRO HYAKUYA! THAT'S AN ORDER!!
!!

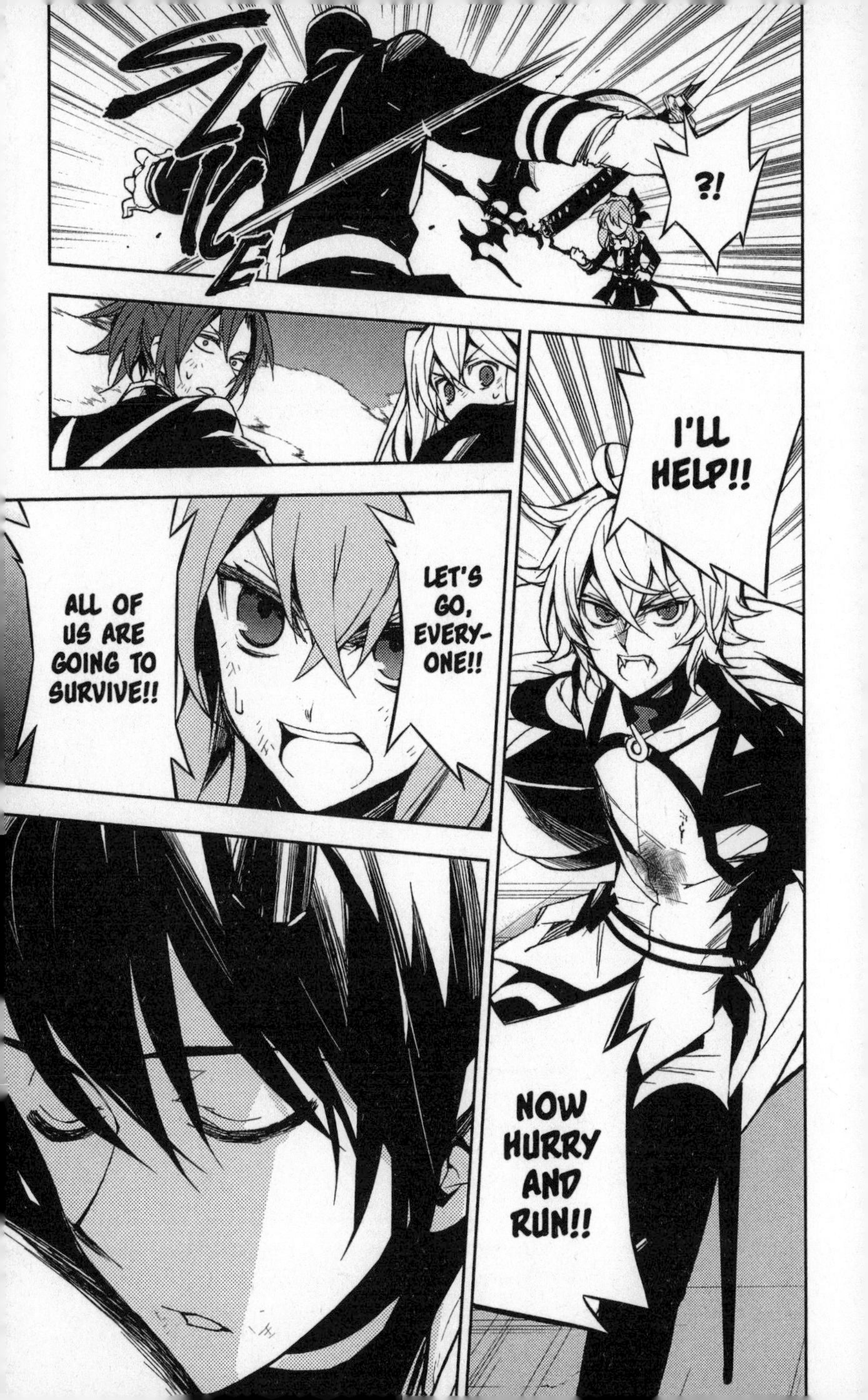
?!
SLICE
I'LL HELP!!
NOW HURRY AND RUN!!
LET'S GO, EVERY-ONE!!
ALL OF US ARE GOING TO SURVIVE!!

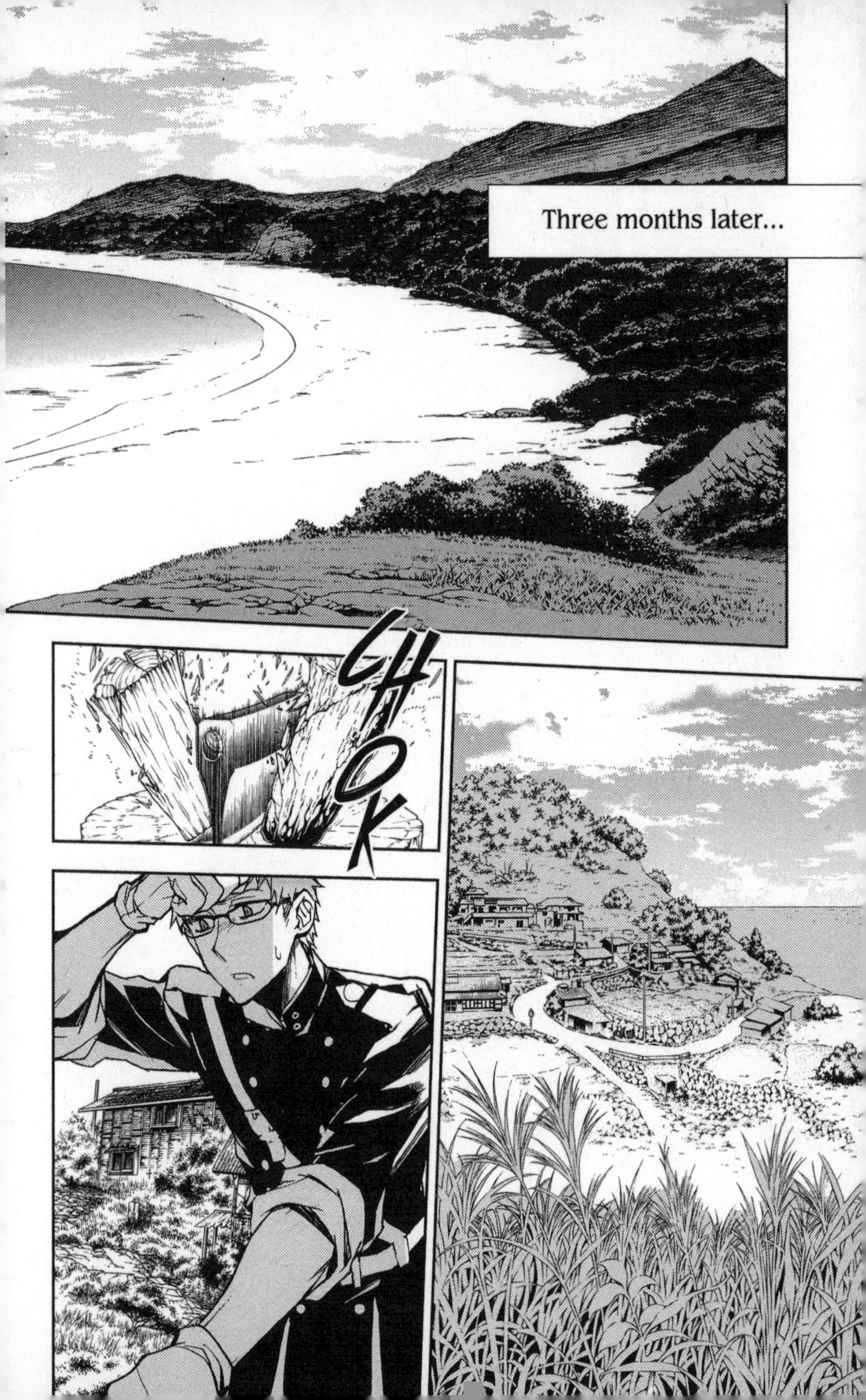
Three months later...
CHOK

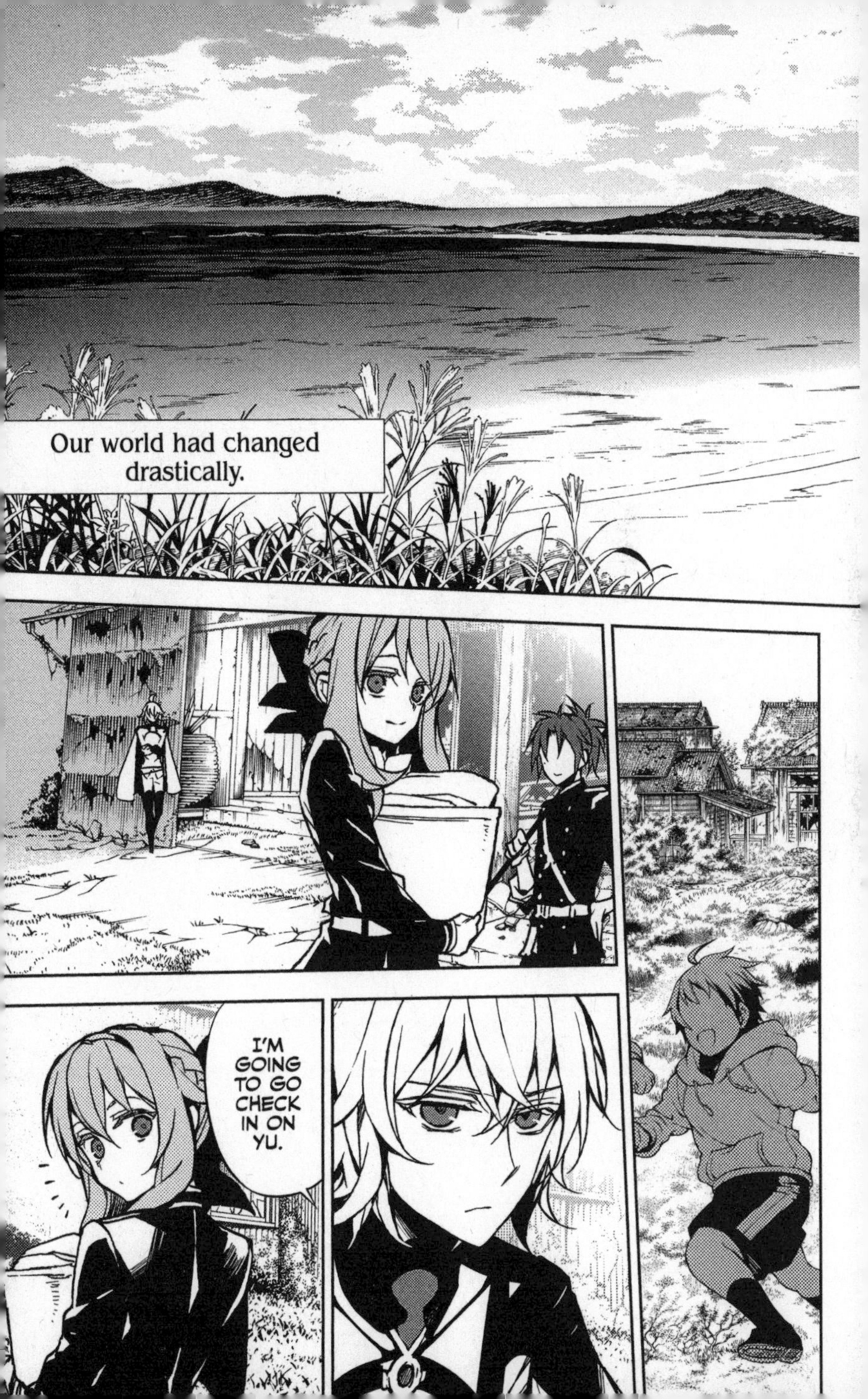
Our world had changed drastically.
I'M GOING TO GO CHECK IN ON YU.

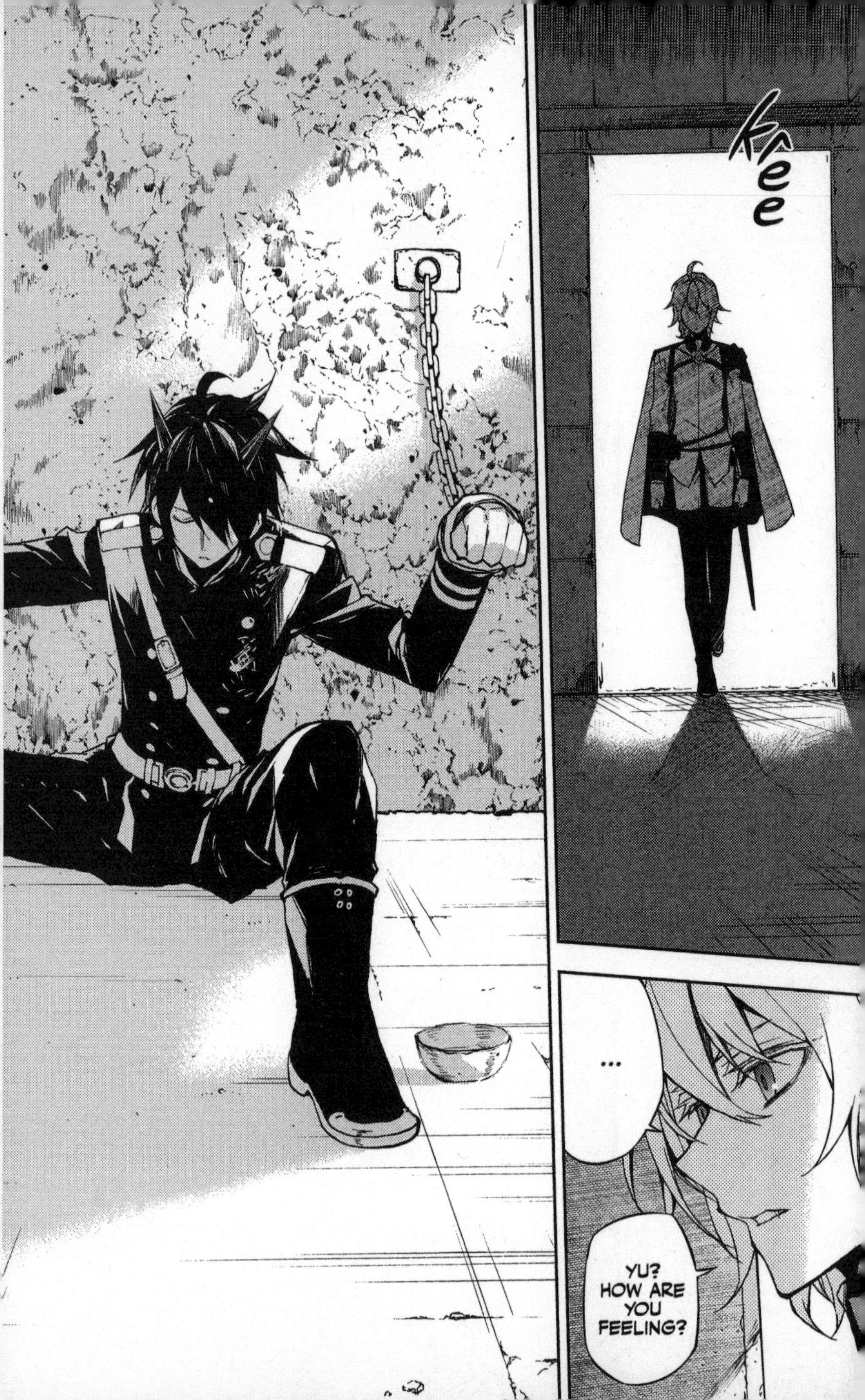
kree
...
YU? HOW ARE YOU FEELING?

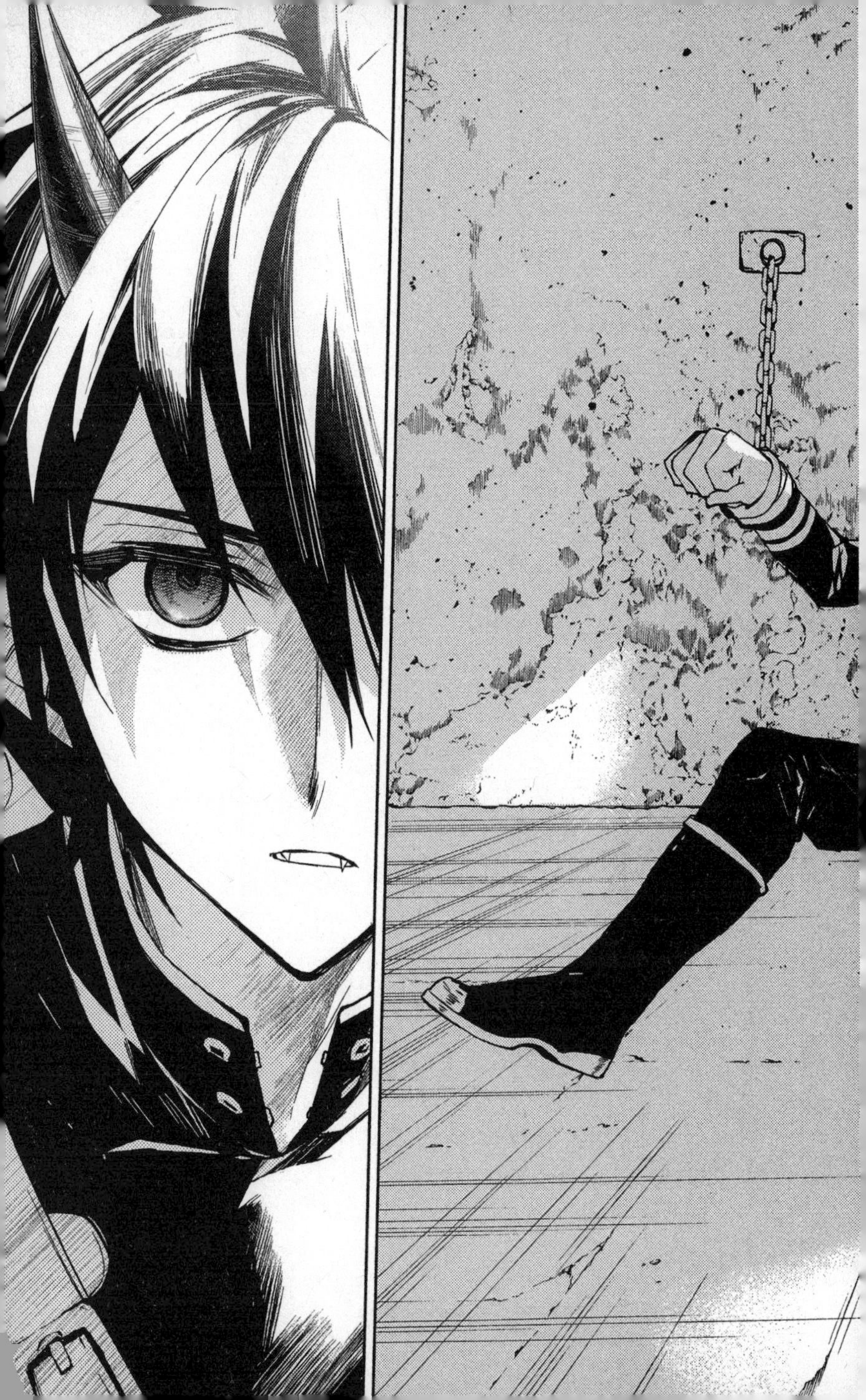

Seraph of the End

VAMPIRE REIGN

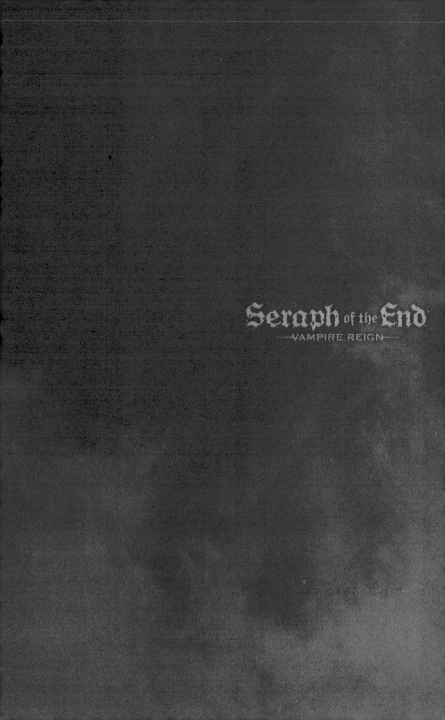

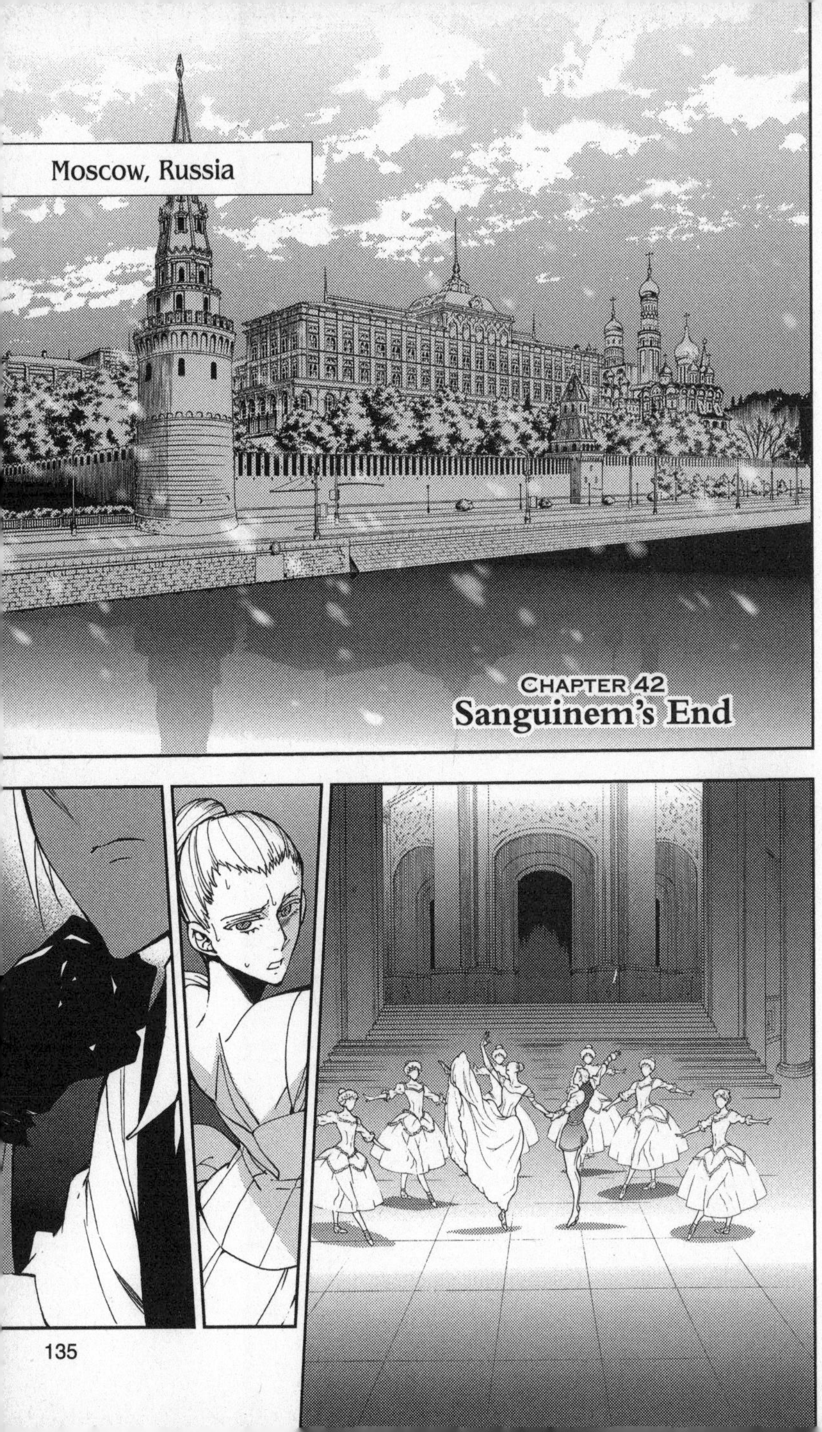
Moscow, Russia
Chapter 42
Sanguinem's End

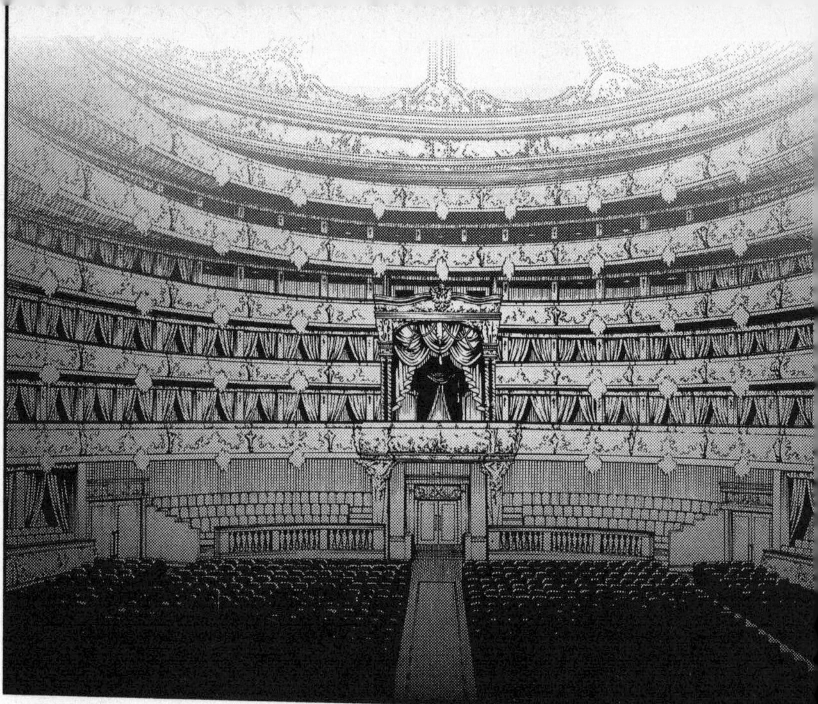

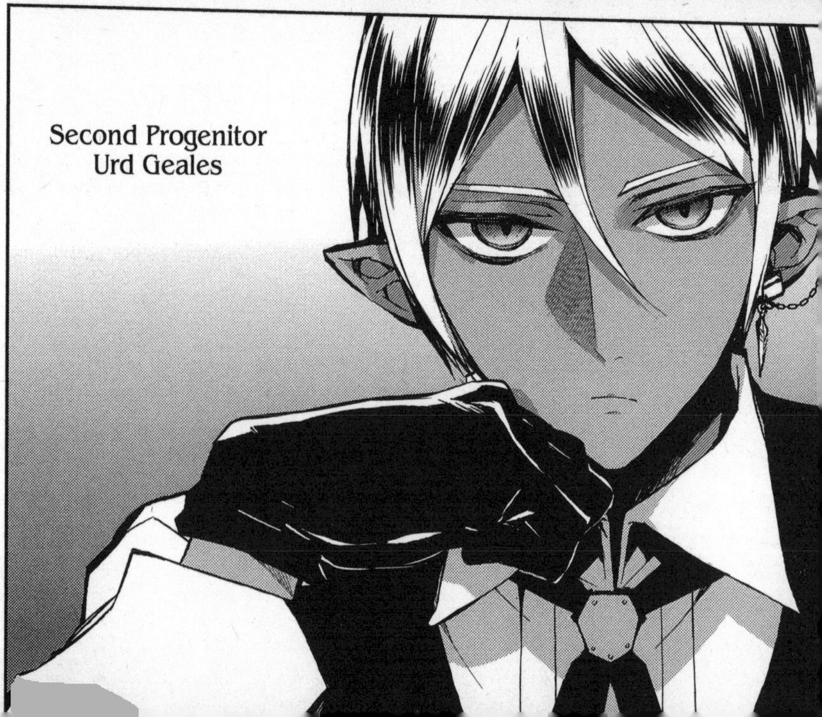
Second Progenitor
Urd Geales

CHAPTER 42 Sanguinem's End

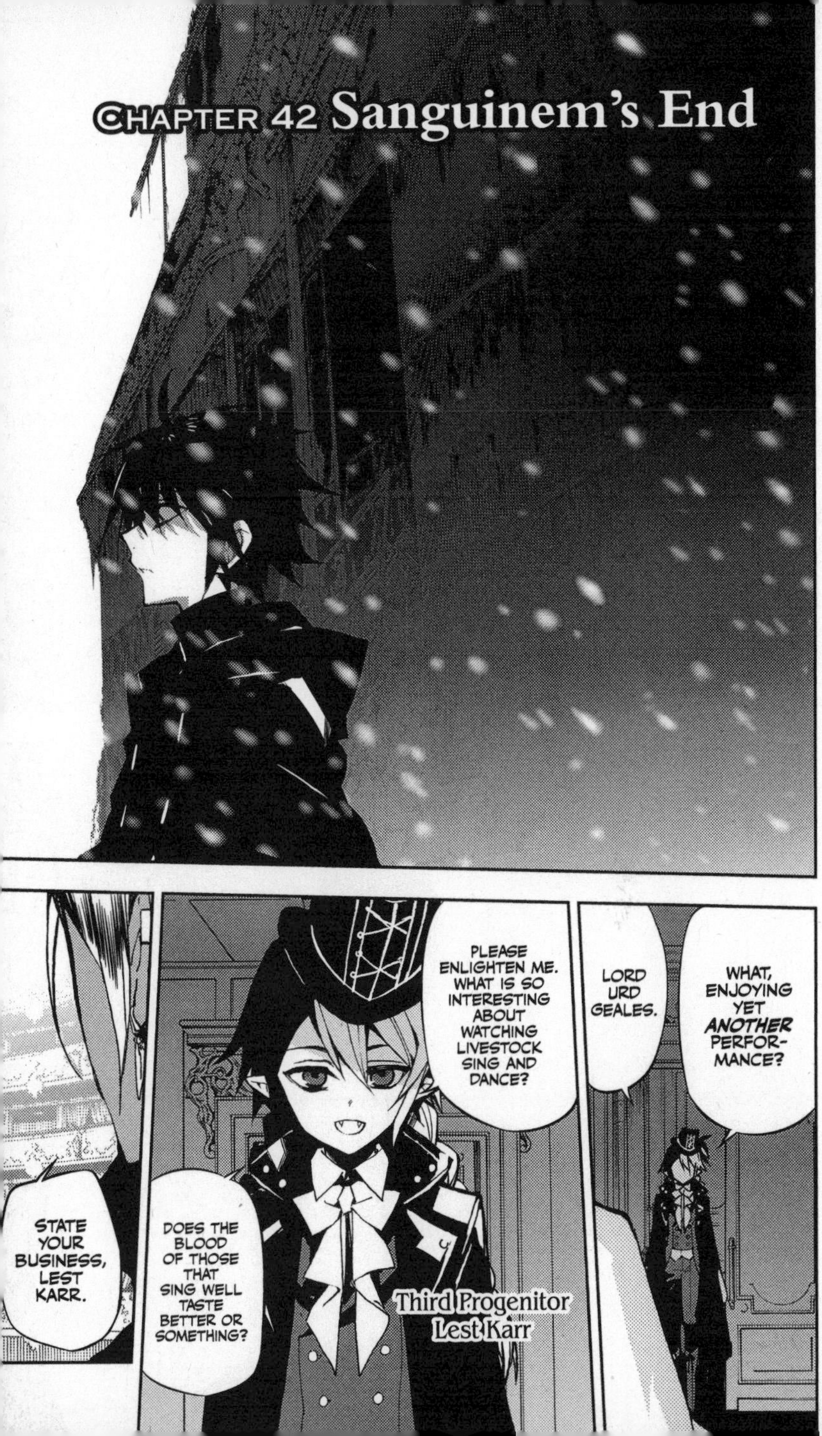
WHAT, ENJOYING YET *ANOTHER* PERFORMANCE?
LORD URD GEALES.
PLEASE ENLIGHTEN ME. WHAT IS SO INTERESTING ABOUT WATCHING LIVESTOCK SING AND DANCE?
Third Progenitor Lest Karr
DOES THE BLOOD OF THOSE THAT SING WELL TASTE BETTER OR SOMETHING?
STATE YOUR BUSINESS, LEST KARR.

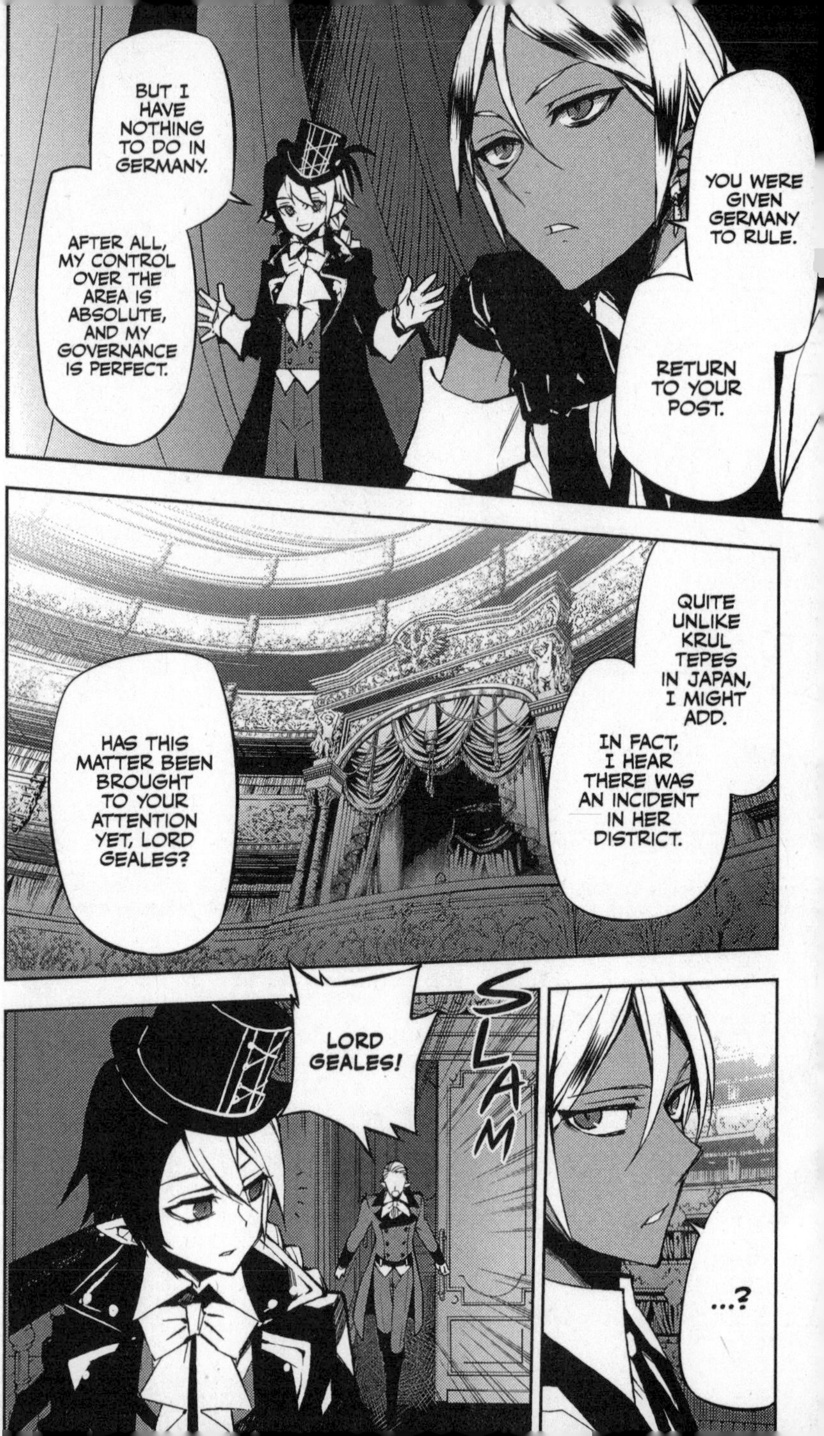
YOU WERE GIVEN GERMANY TO RULE.
RETURN TO YOUR POST.
BUT I HAVE NOTHING TO DO IN GERMANY.
AFTER ALL, MY CONTROL OVER THE AREA IS ABSOLUTE, AND MY GOVERNANCE IS PERFECT.
QUITE UNLIKE KRUL TEPES IN JAPAN, I MIGHT ADD.
IN FACT, I HEAR THERE WAS AN INCIDENT IN HER DISTRICT.
HAS THIS MATTER BEEN BROUGHT TO YOUR ATTENTION YET, LORD GEALES?
...?
SLAM
LORD GEALES!

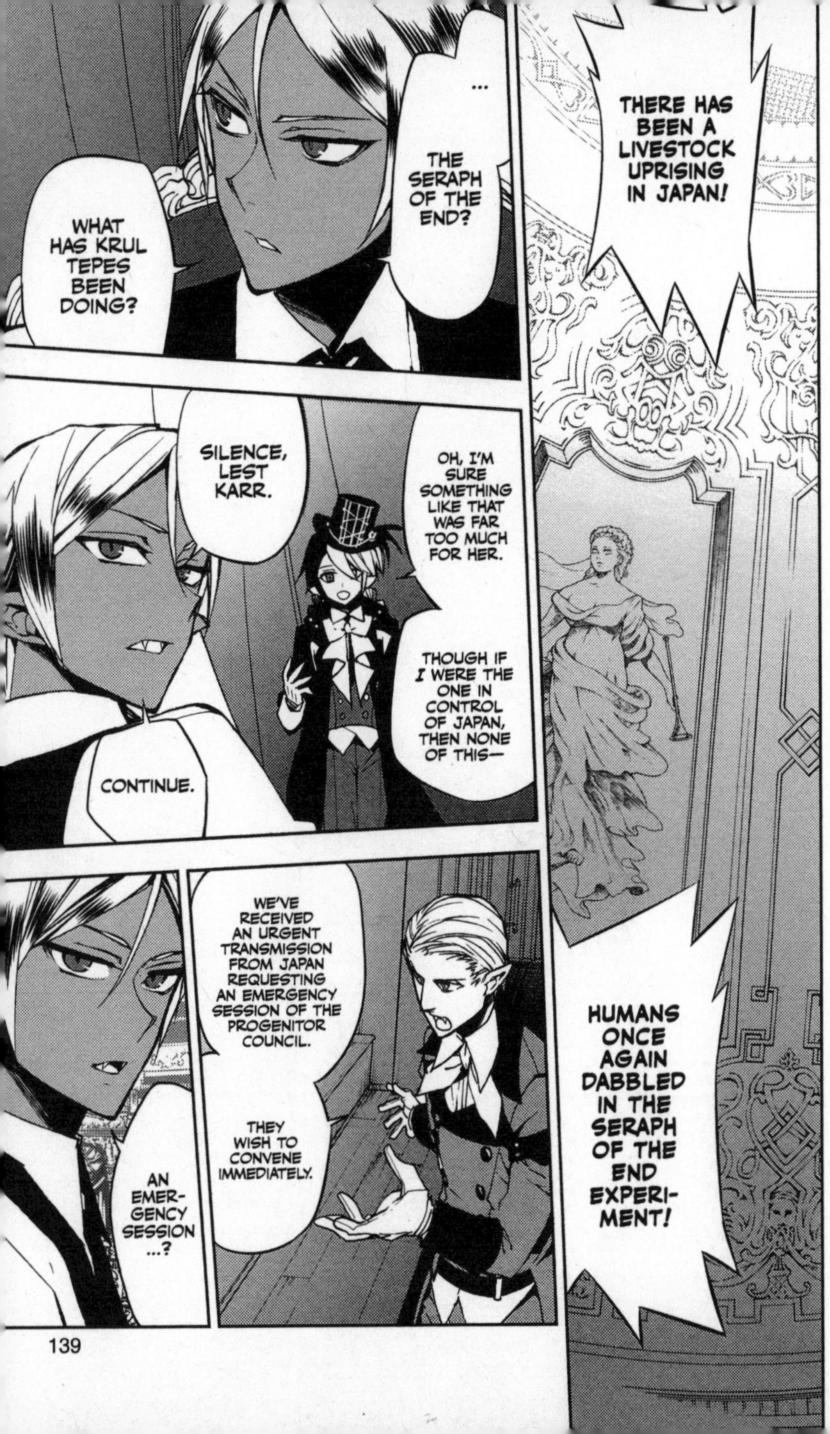
THERE HAS BEEN A LIVESTOCK UPRISING IN JAPAN!
HUMANS ONCE AGAIN DABBLED IN THE SERAPH OF THE END EXPERIMENT!
...
THE SERAPH OF THE END?
WHAT HAS KRUL TEPES BEEN DOING?
OH, I'M SURE SOMETHING LIKE THAT WAS FAR TOO MUCH FOR HER.
THOUGH IF *I* WERE THE ONE IN CONTROL OF JAPAN, THEN NONE OF THIS—
SILENCE, LEST KARR.
CONTINUE.
WE'VE RECEIVED AN URGENT TRANSMISSION FROM JAPAN REQUESTING AN EMERGENCY SESSION OF THE PROGENITOR COUNCIL.
THEY WISH TO CONVENE IMMEDIATELY.
AN EMER-GENCY SESSION ...?

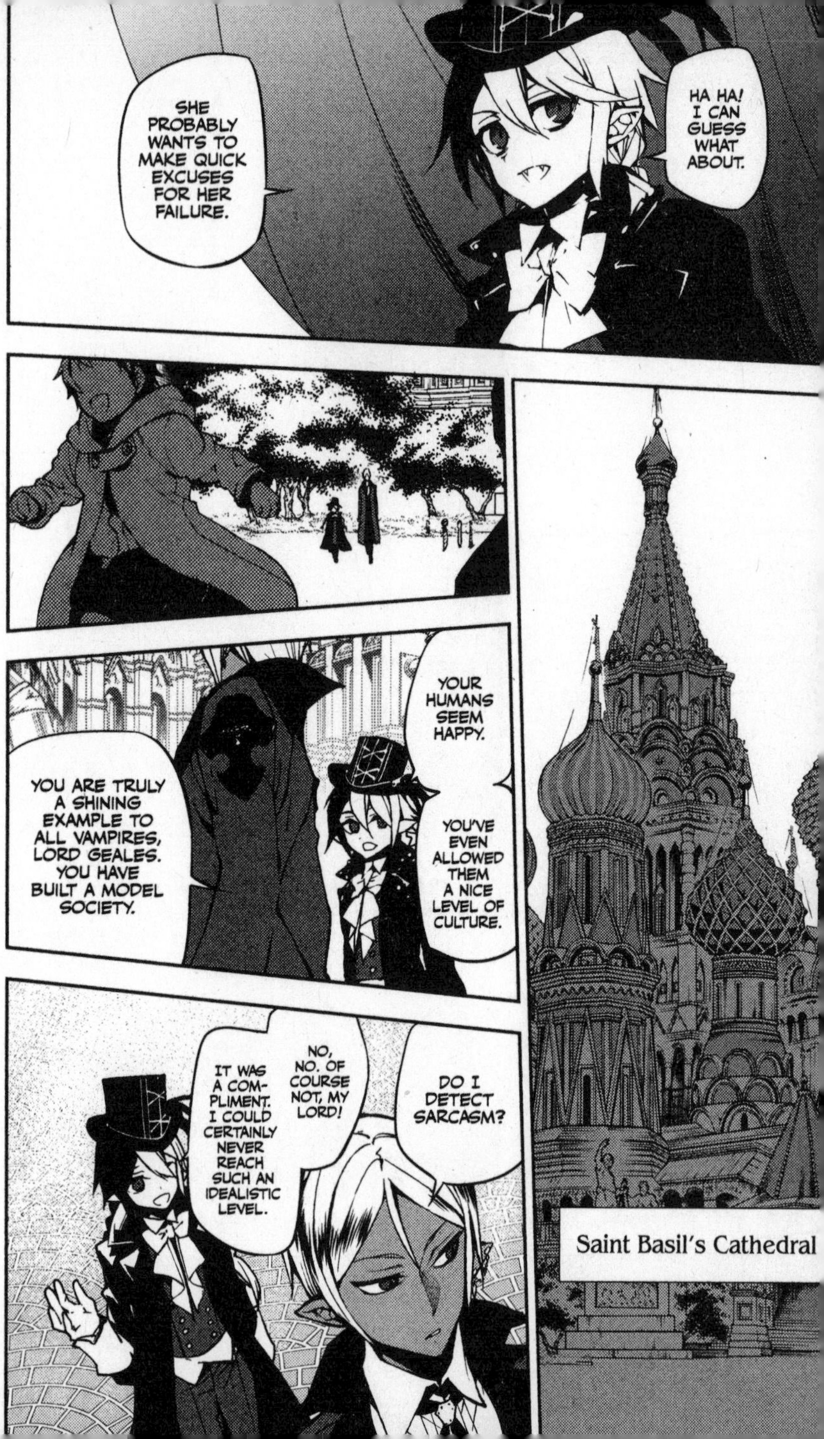
HA HA! I CAN GUESS WHAT ABOUT.
SHE PROBABLY WANTS TO MAKE QUICK EXCUSES FOR HER FAILURE.
Saint Basil's Cathedral
YOUR HUMANS SEEM HAPPY.
YOU'VE EVEN ALLOWED THEM A NICE LEVEL OF CULTURE.
YOU ARE TRULY A SHINING EXAMPLE TO ALL VAMPIRES, LORD GEALES. YOU HAVE BUILT A MODEL SOCIETY.
DO I DETECT SARCASM?
NO, NO. OF COURSE NOT, MY LORD!
IT WAS A COMPLIMENT. I COULD CERTAINLY NEVER REACH SUCH AN IDEALISTIC LEVEL.

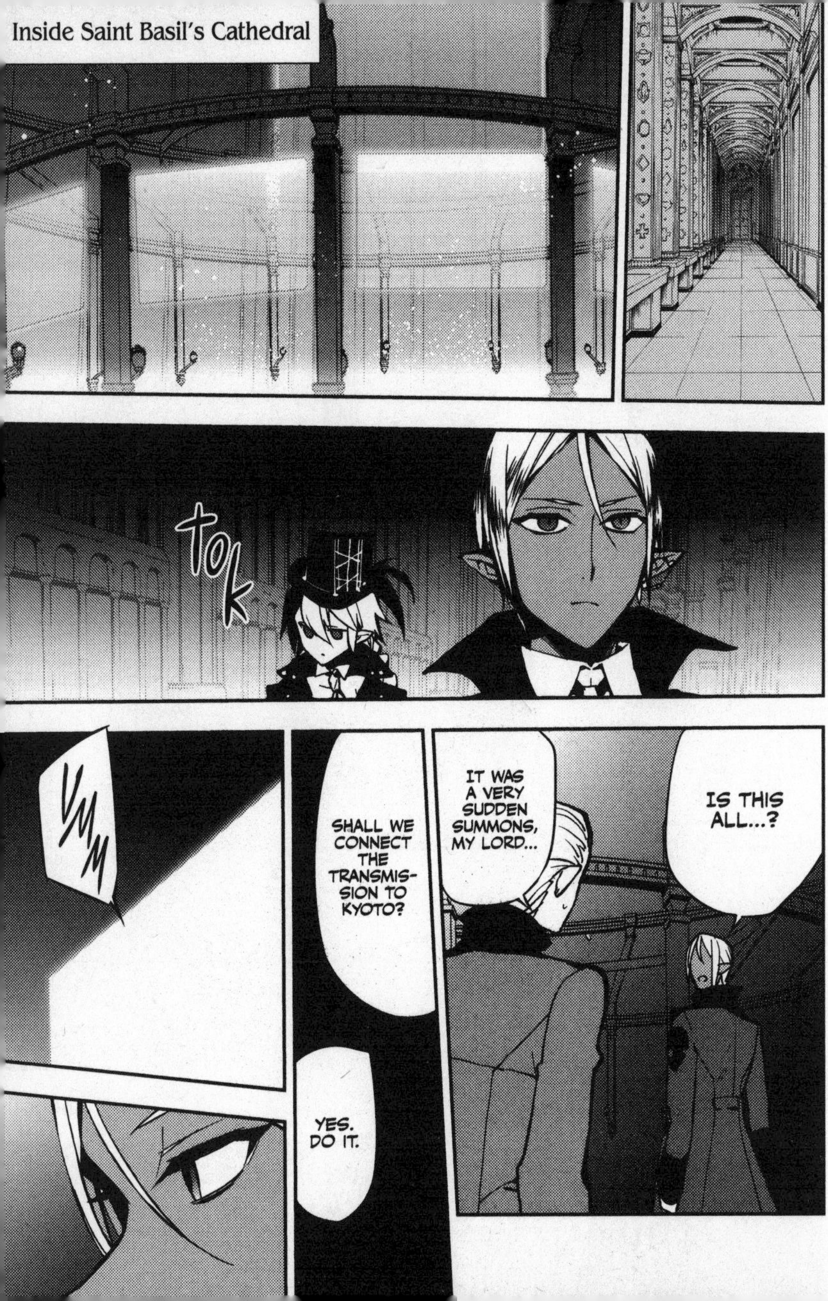
Inside Saint Basil's Cathedral
tok
IS THIS ALL...?
IT WAS A VERY SUDDEN SUMMONS, MY LORD...
SHALL WE CONNECT THE TRANSMIS-SION TO KYOTO?
YES. DO IT.
VMM

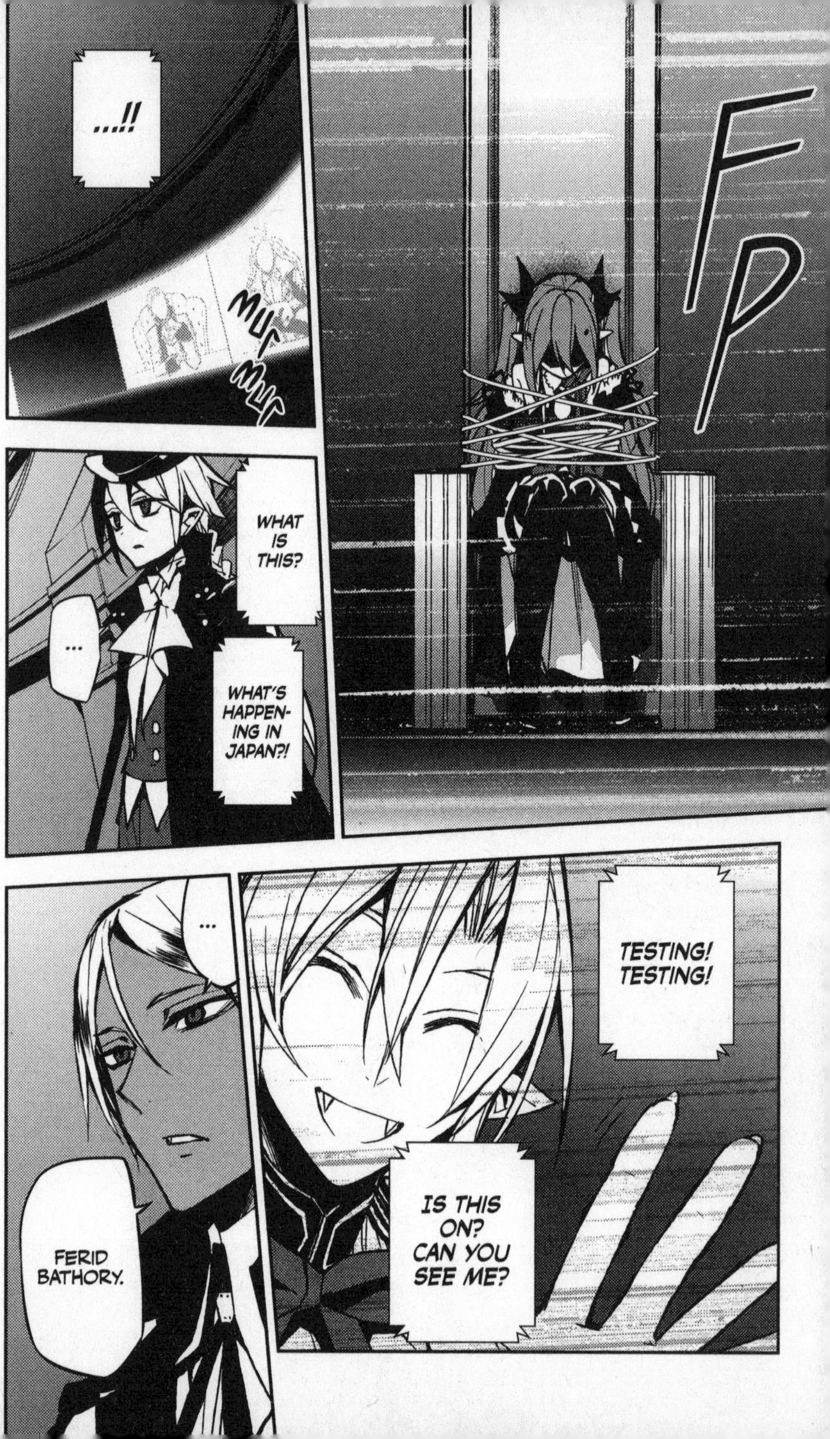
FP
...!!
MUT MUT
WHAT IS THIS?
WHAT'S HAPPEN-ING IN JAPAN?!
...
TESTING! TESTING!
IS THIS ON? CAN YOU SEE ME?
...
FERID BATHORY.

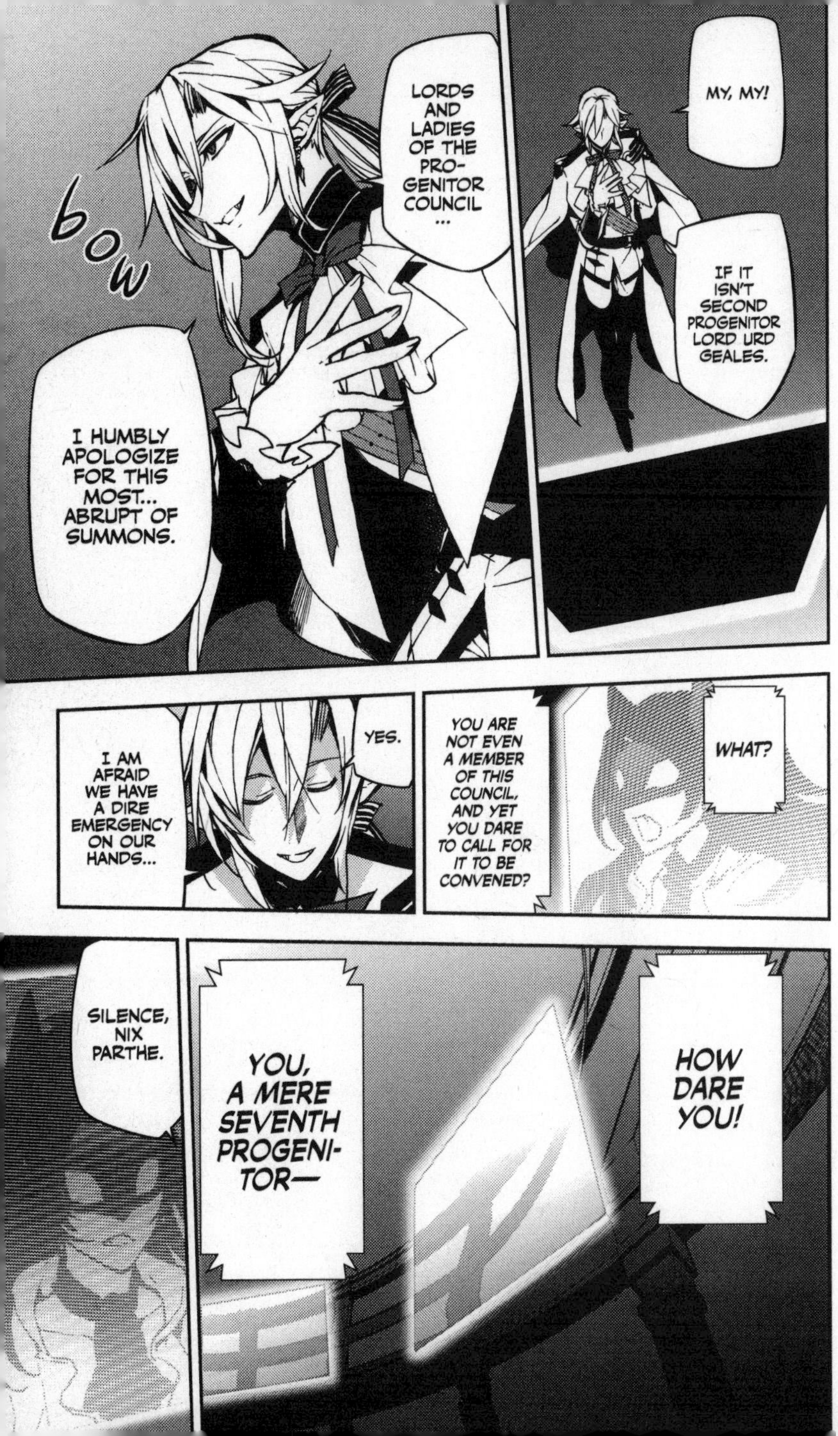
MY, MY!
IF IT ISN'T SECOND PROGENITOR LORD URD GEALES.
LORDS AND LADIES OF THE PRO-GENITOR COUNCIL...
bow
I HUMBLY APOLOGIZE FOR THIS MOST... ABRUPT OF SUMMONS.
WHAT?
YOU ARE NOT EVEN A MEMBER OF THIS COUNCIL, AND YET YOU DARE TO CALL FOR IT TO BE CONVENED?
YES.
I AM AFRAID WE HAVE A DIRE EMERGENCY ON OUR HANDS...
HOW DARE YOU!
YOU, A MERE SEVENTH PROGENI-TOR—
SILENCE, NIX PARTHE.

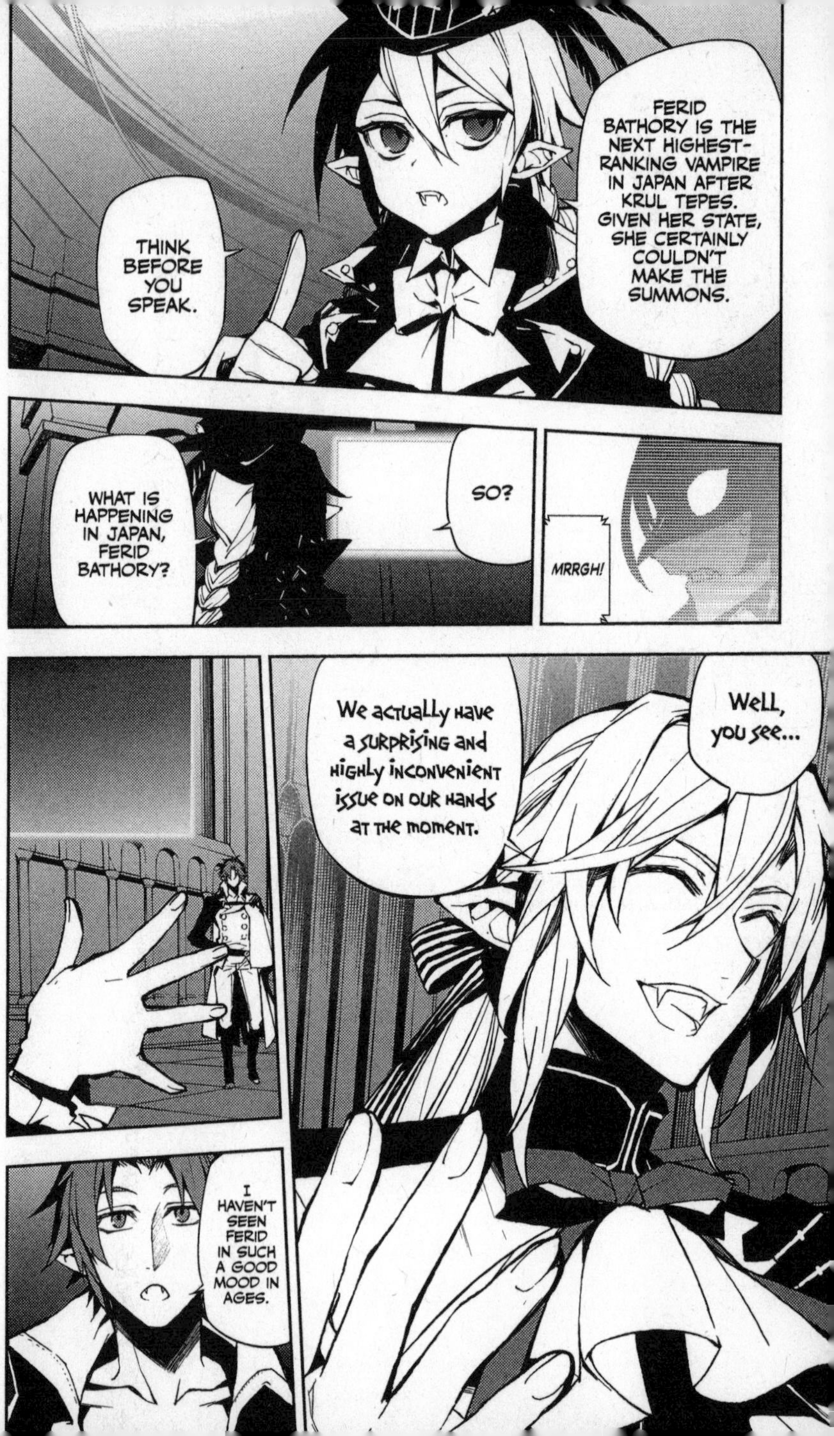
FERID BATHORY IS THE NEXT HIGHEST-RANKING VAMPIRE IN JAPAN AFTER KRUL TEPES. GIVEN HER STATE, SHE CERTAINLY COULDN'T MAKE THE SUMMONS.
THINK BEFORE YOU SPEAK.
MRRGH!
SO?
WHAT IS HAPPENING IN JAPAN, FERID BATHORY?
Well, you see...
We actually have a surprising and highly inconvenient issue on our hands at the moment.
I HAVEN'T SEEN FERID IN SUCH A GOOD MOOD IN AGES.

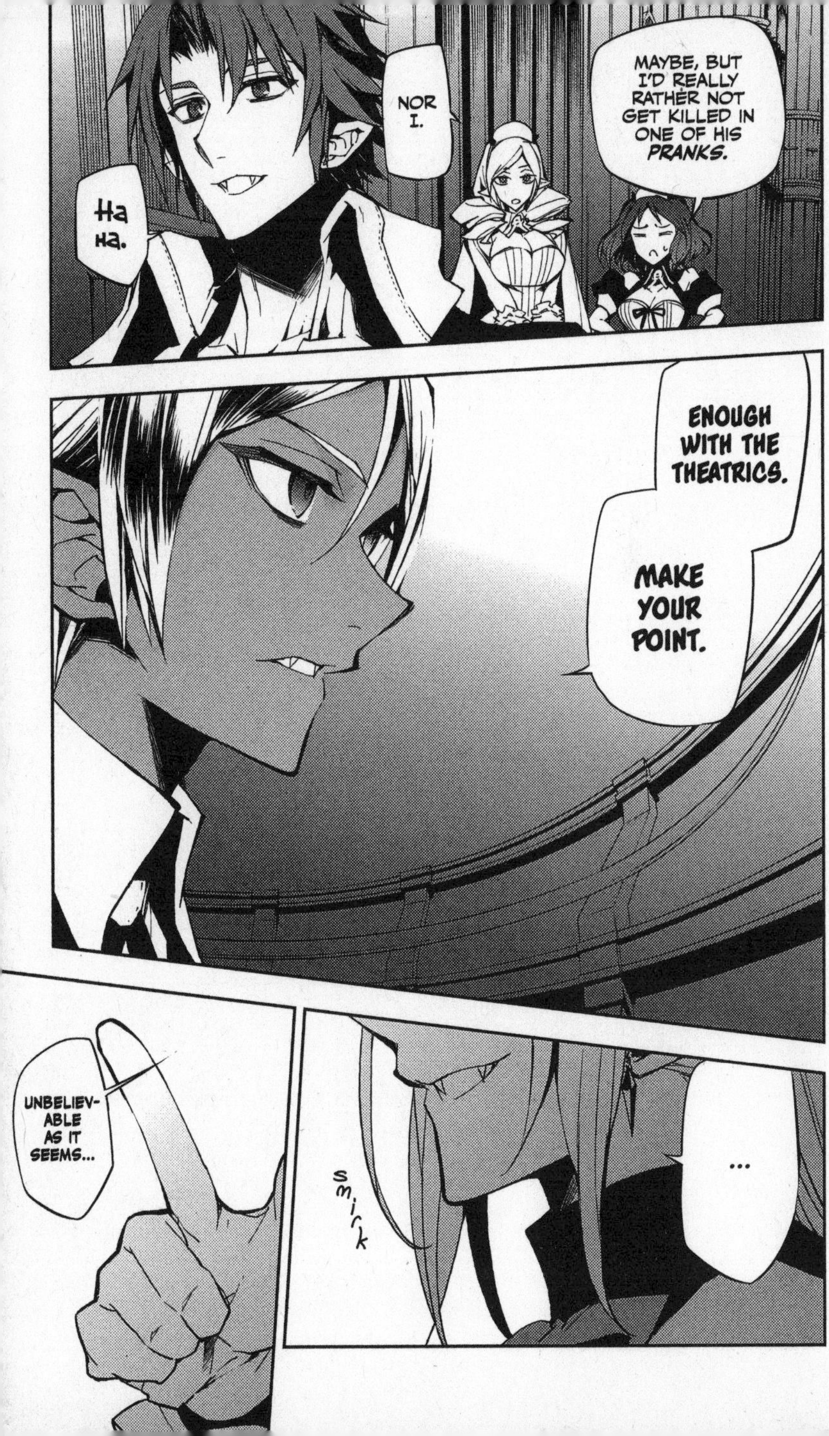
MAYBE, BUT I'D REALLY RATHER NOT GET KILLED IN ONE OF HIS *PRANKS.*
NOR I.
Ha ha.
ENOUGH WITH THE THEATRICS.
MAKE YOUR POINT.
...
smirk
UNBELIEV-ABLE AS IT SEEMS...

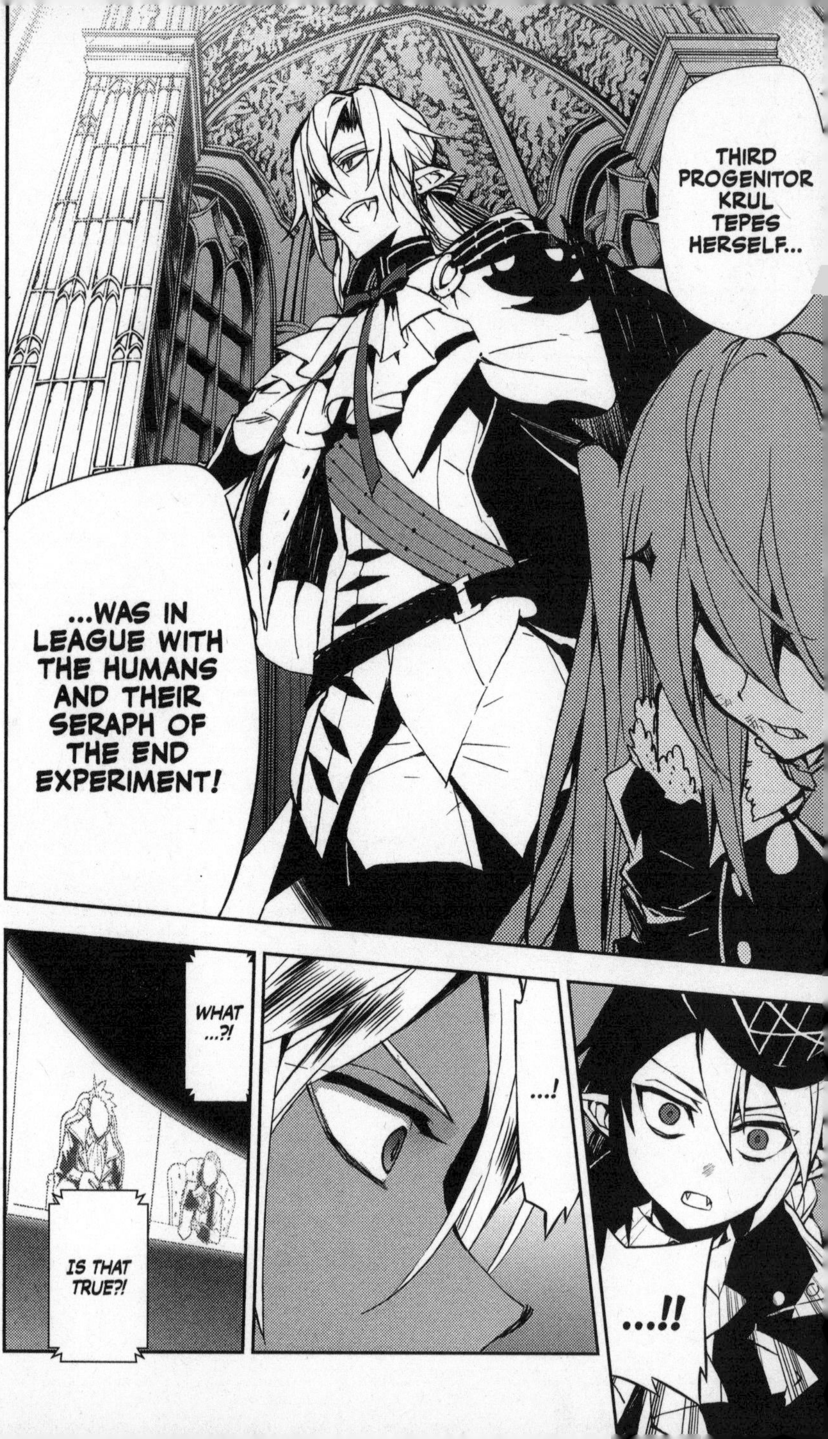

THIRD PROGENITOR KRUL TEPES HERSELF...
...WAS IN LEAGUE WITH THE HUMANS AND THEIR SERAPH OF THE END EXPERIMENT!
...!!
...!
WHAT ...?!
IS THAT TRUE?!

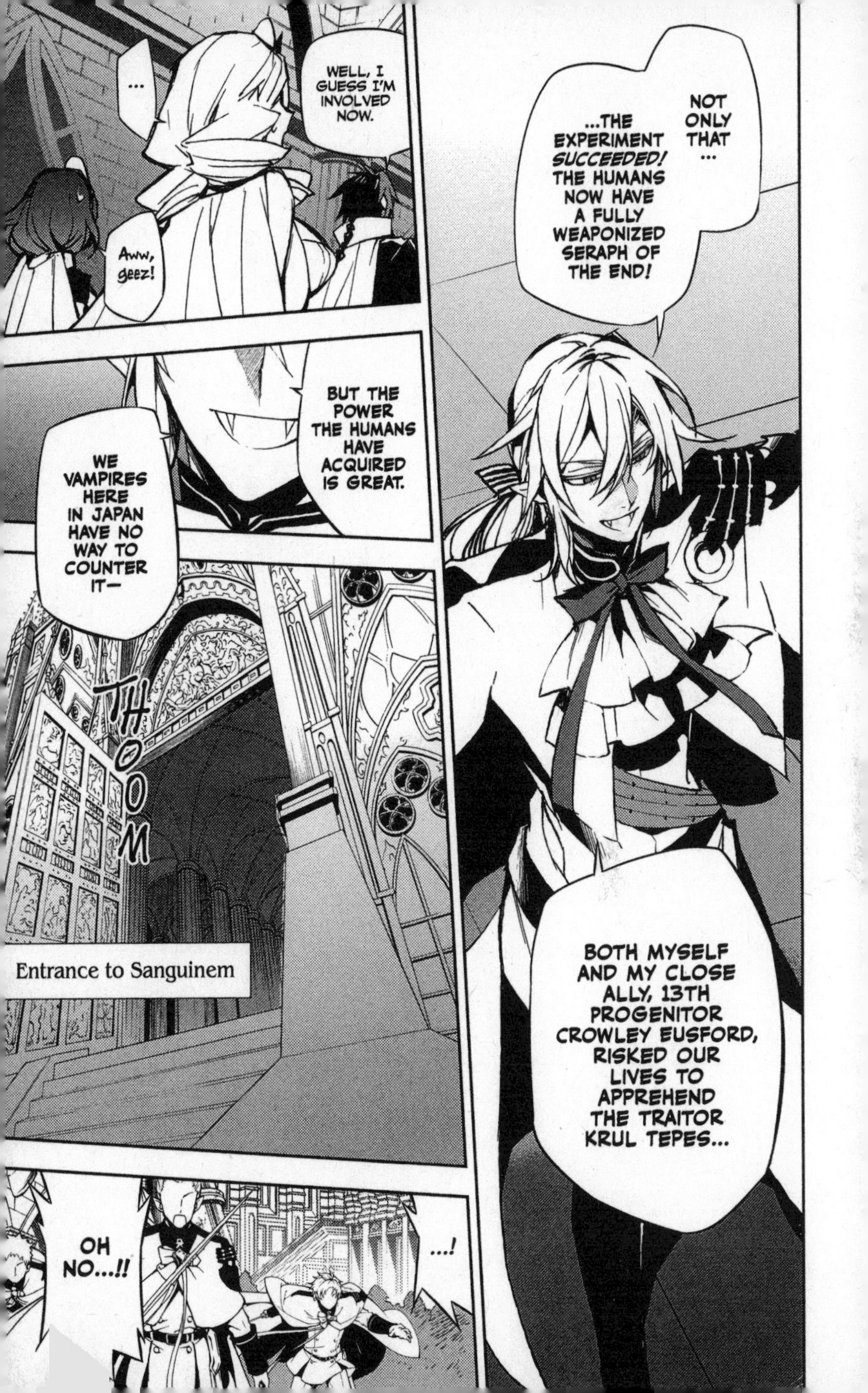
NOT ONLY THAT...
...THE EXPERIMENT *SUCCEEDED!* THE HUMANS NOW HAVE A FULLY WEAPONIZED SERAPH OF THE END!
BOTH MYSELF AND MY CLOSE ALLY, 13TH PROGENITOR CROWLEY EUSFORD, RISKED OUR LIVES TO APPREHEND THE TRAITOR KRUL TEPES...
WELL, I GUESS I'M INVOLVED NOW.
...
Aww, geez!
BUT THE POWER THE HUMANS HAVE ACQUIRED IS GREAT.
WE VAMPIRES HERE IN JAPAN HAVE NO WAY TO COUNTER IT—
THOOOM
Entrance to Sanguinem
...!
OH NO...!!

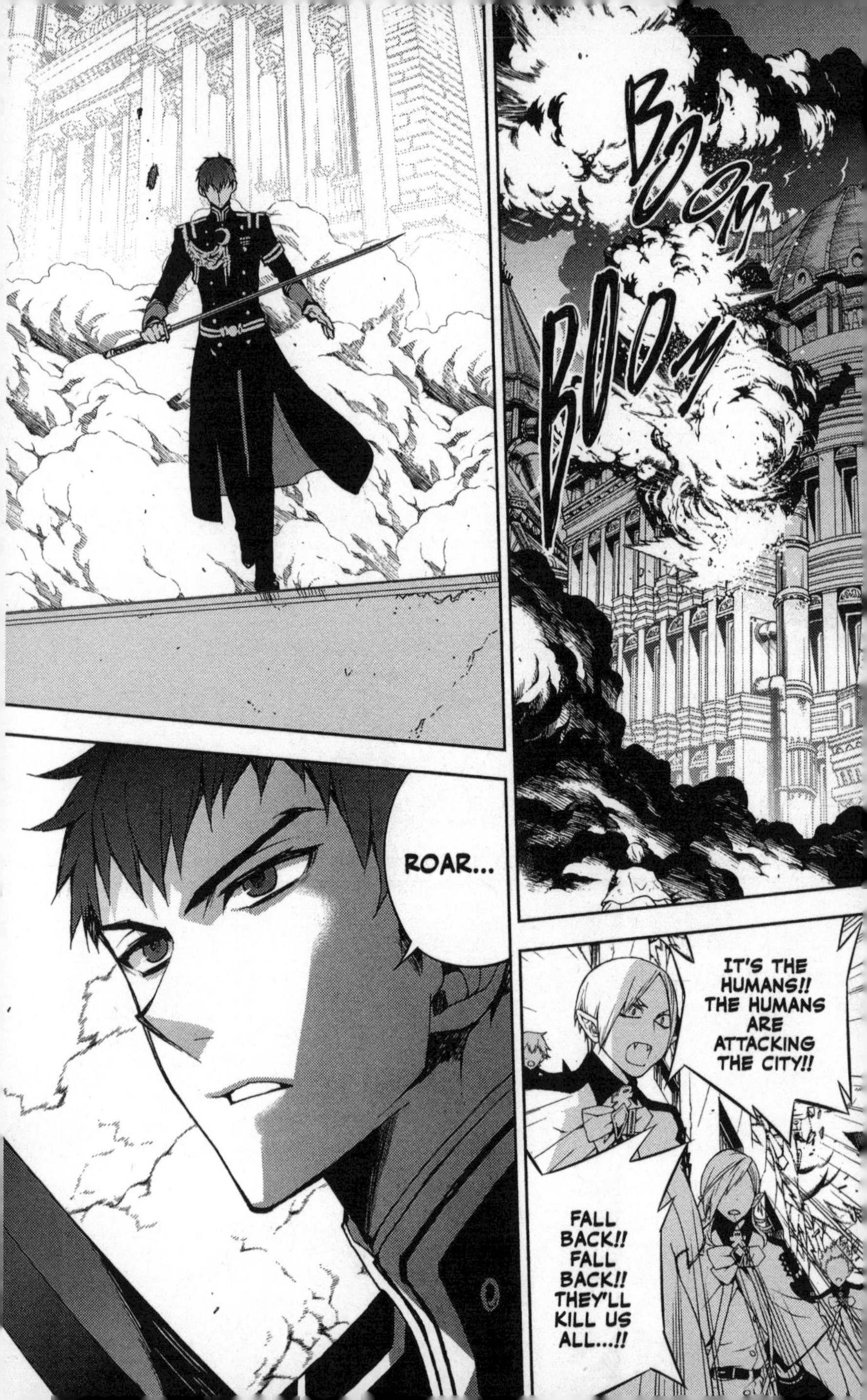
BOOM
BOOM
ROAR...
IT'S THE HUMANS!! THE HUMANS ARE ATTACKING THE CITY!!
FALL BACK!! FALL BACK!! THEY'LL KILL US ALL...!!

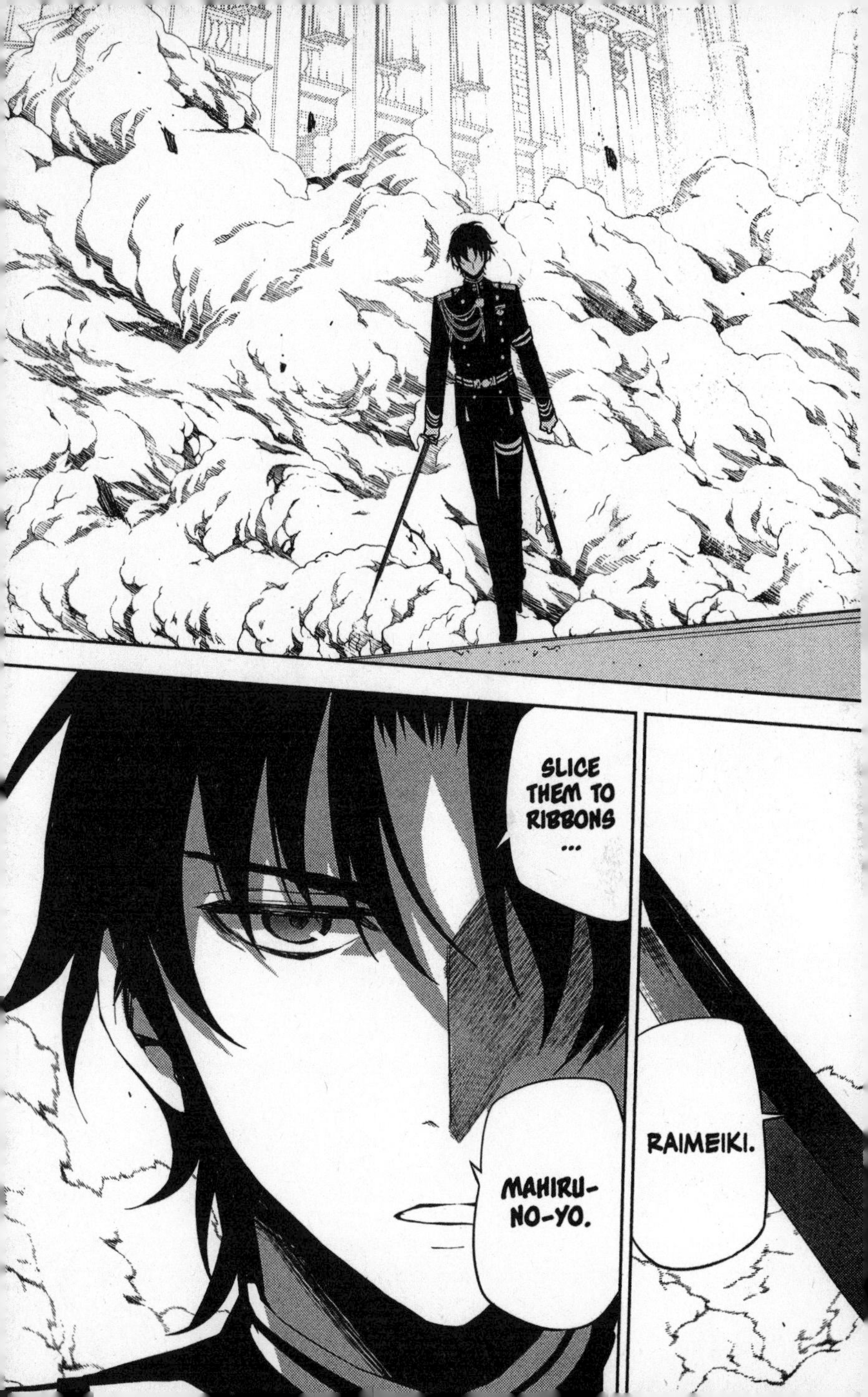
RAIMEIKI.
SLICE THEM TO RIBBONS...
MAHIRU-NO-YO.

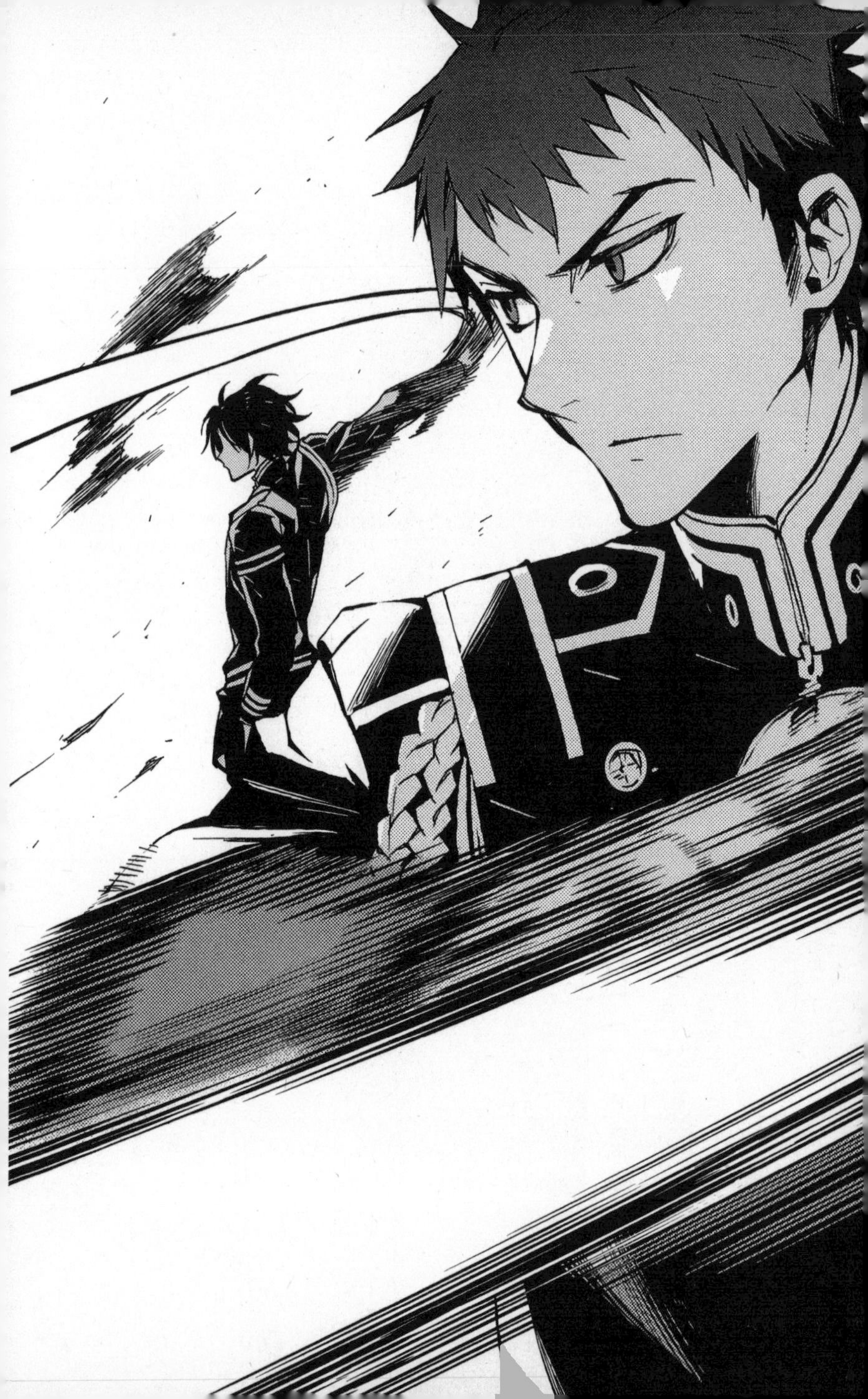

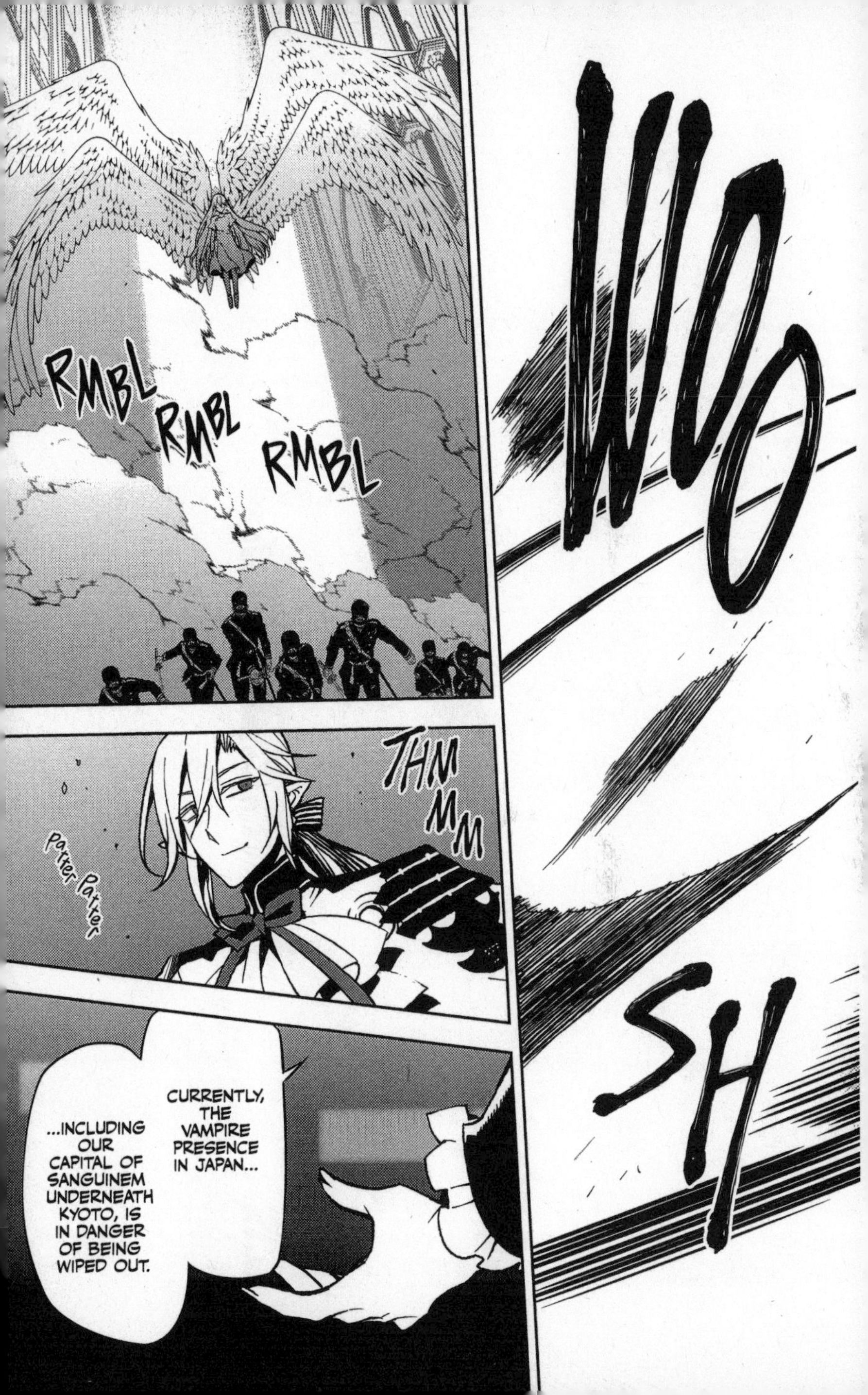

WHO
SH
RMBL
RMBL
RMBL
THMMM
Patter Patter
CURRENTLY, THE VAMPIRE PRESENCE IN JAPAN...
...INCLUDING OUR CAPITAL OF SANGUINEM UNDERNEATH KYOTO, IS IN DANGER OF BEING WIPED OUT.

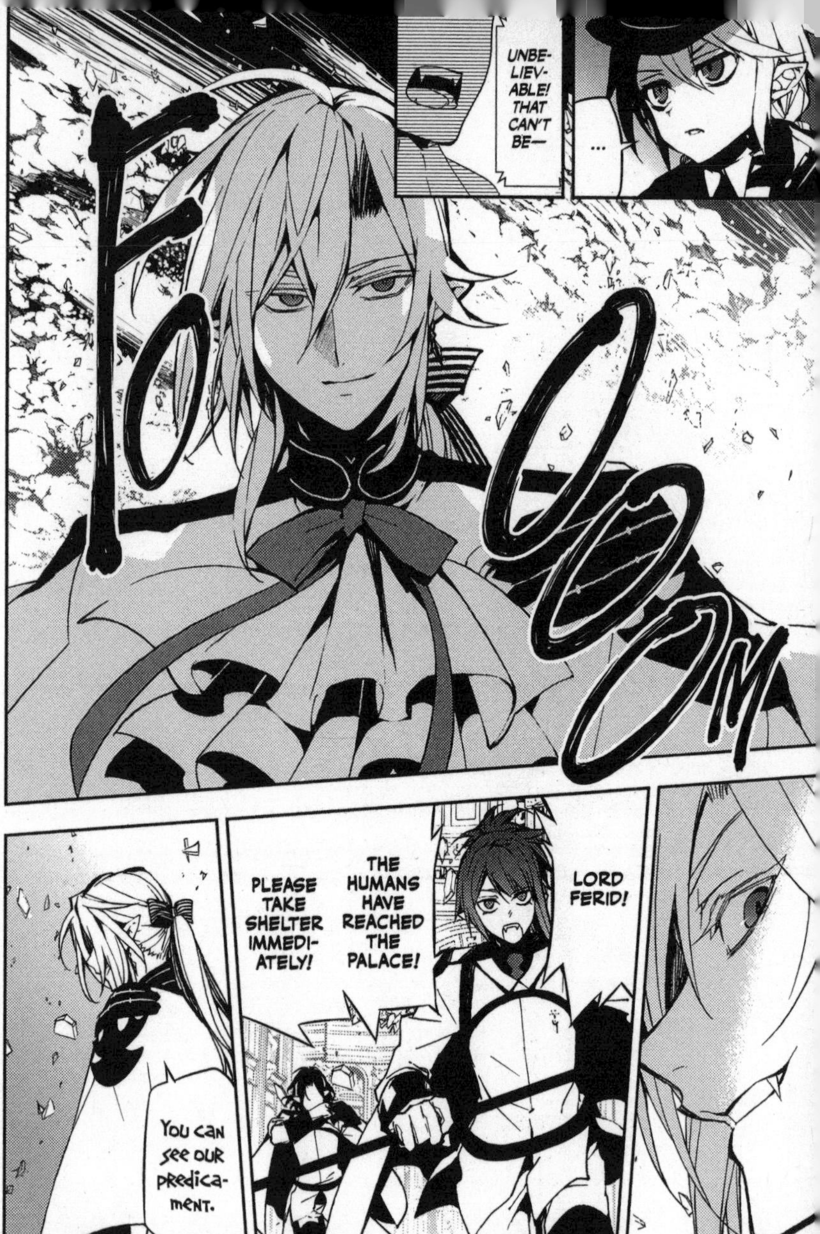
...
UNBE-LIEV-ABLE! THAT CAN'T BE—
FOOOOM
LORD FERID!
THE HUMANS HAVE REACHED THE PALACE!
PLEASE TAKE SHELTER IMMEDI-ATELY!
You can see our predica-ment.

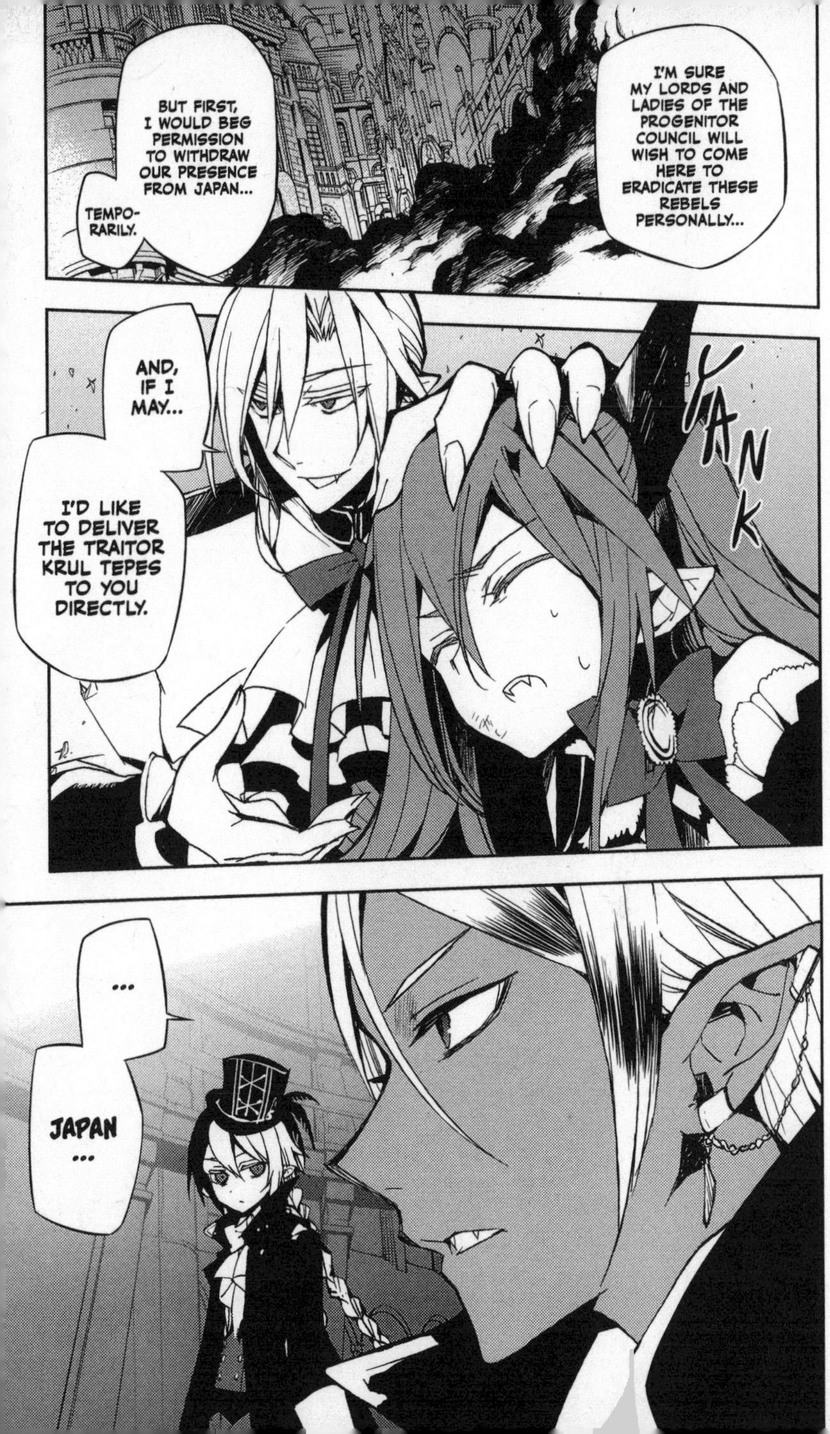
I'M SURE MY LORDS AND LADIES OF THE PROGENITOR COUNCIL WILL WISH TO COME HERE TO ERADICATE THESE REBELS PERSONALLY...
BUT FIRST, I WOULD BEG PERMISSION TO WITHDRAW OUR PRESENCE FROM JAPAN...
TEMPO-RARILY.
YANK
AND, IF I MAY...
I'D LIKE TO DELIVER THE TRAITOR KRUL TEPES TO YOU DIRECTLY.
...
JAPAN ...

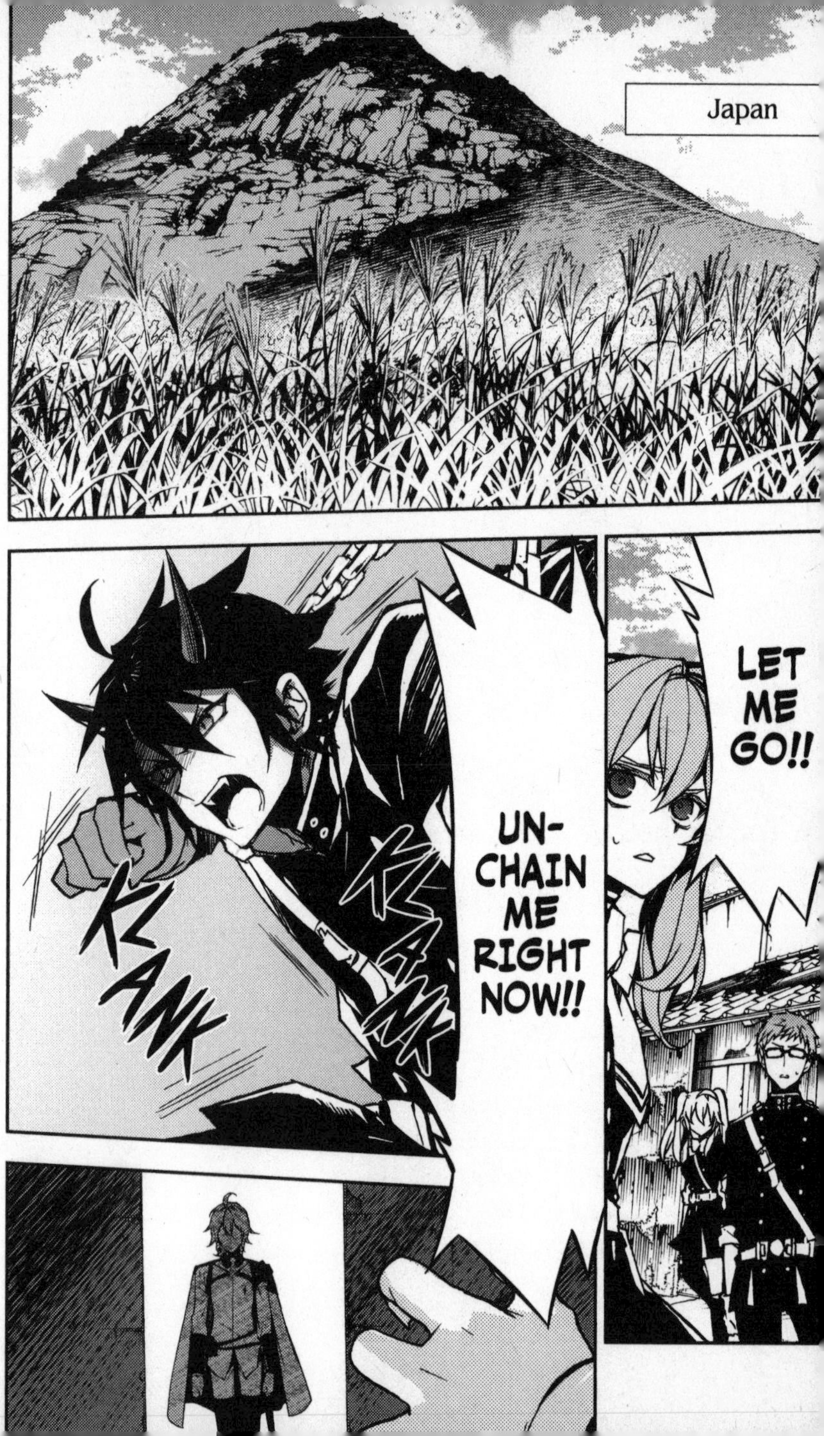
Japan
LET ME GO!!
UN-CHAIN ME RIGHT NOW!!
KLANK
KLANK

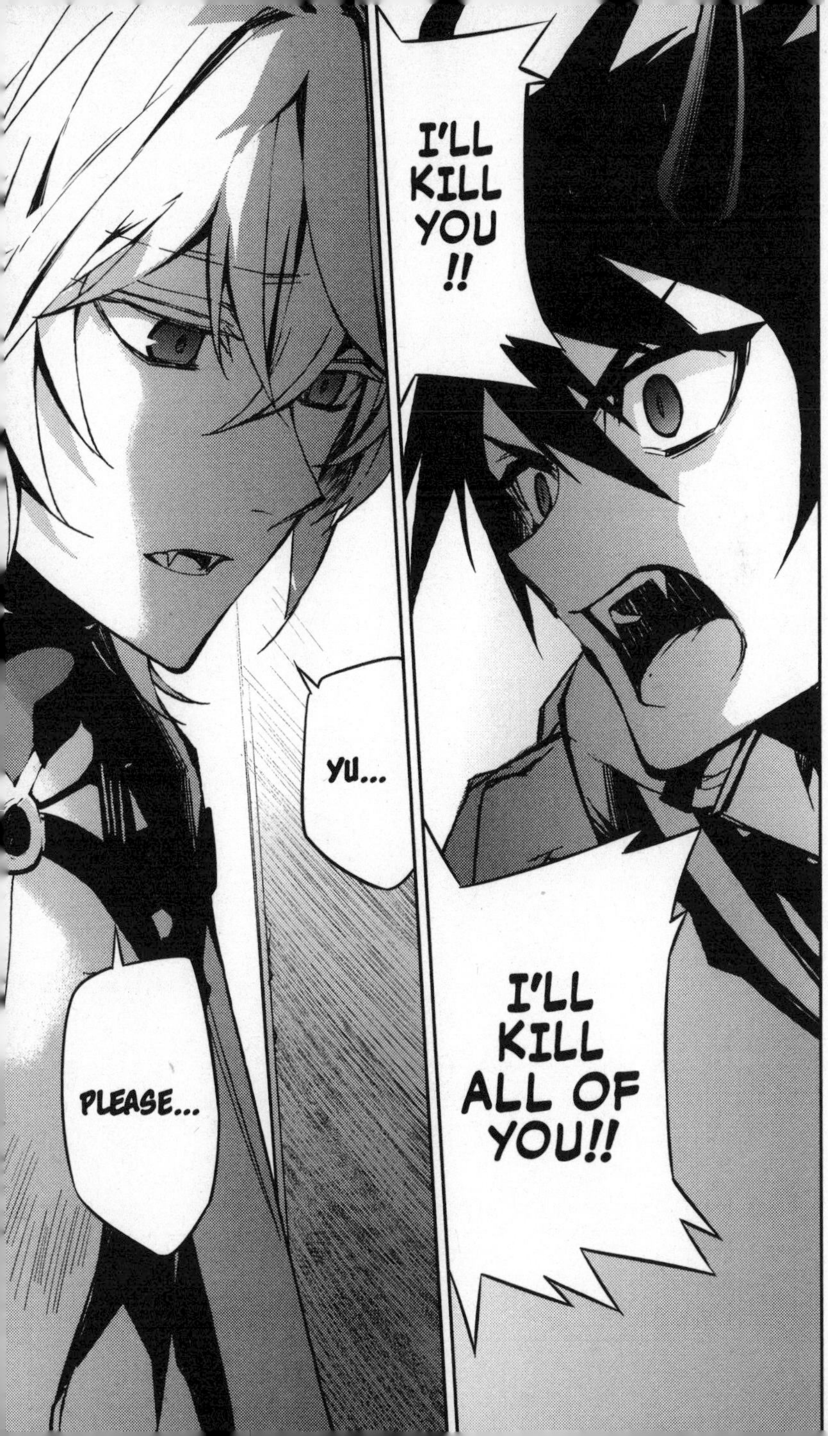
I'LL KILL YOU!!
YU...
I'LL KILL ALL OF YOU!!
PLEASE...

Seraph of the End

—VAMPIRE REIGN—

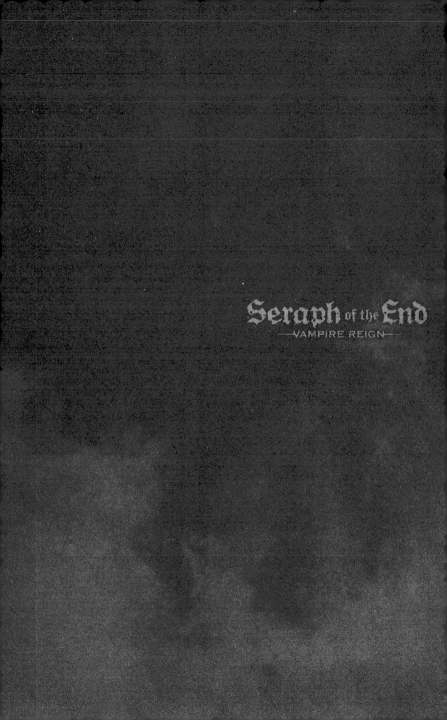

CHAPTER 43 Where It All Begins

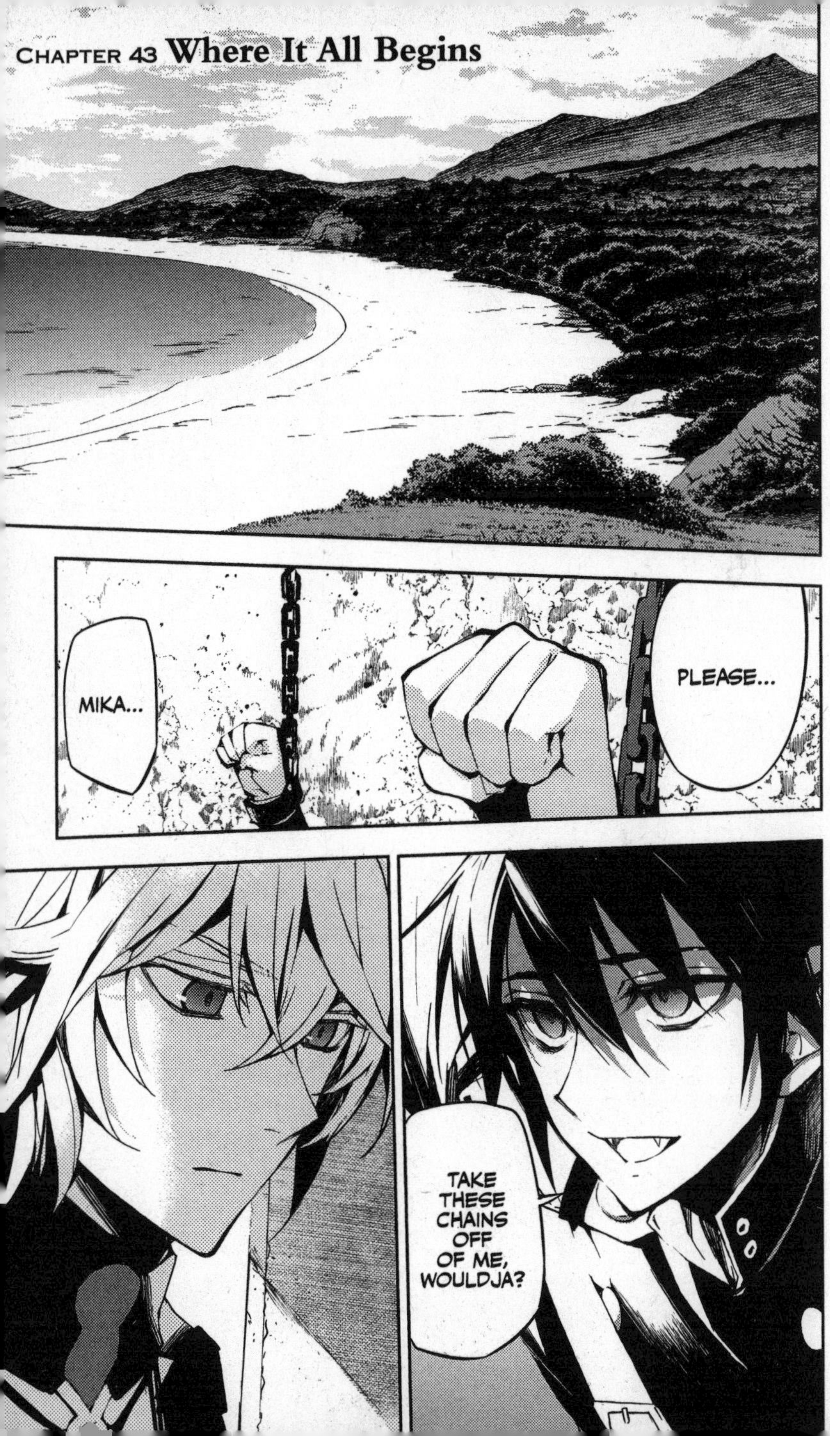
PLEASE...
MIKA...
TAKE THESE CHAINS OFF OF ME, WOULDJA?

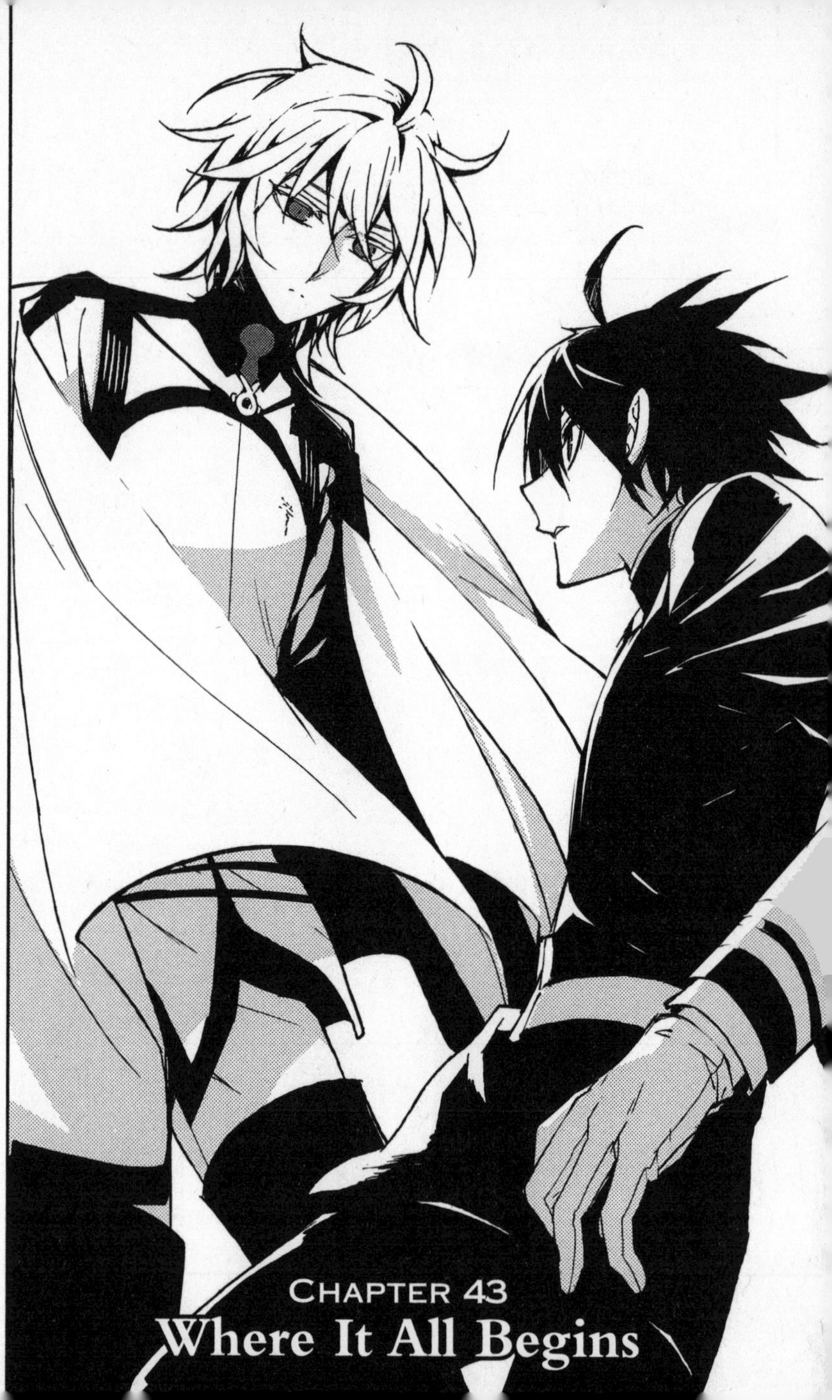

Chapter 43
Where It All Begins

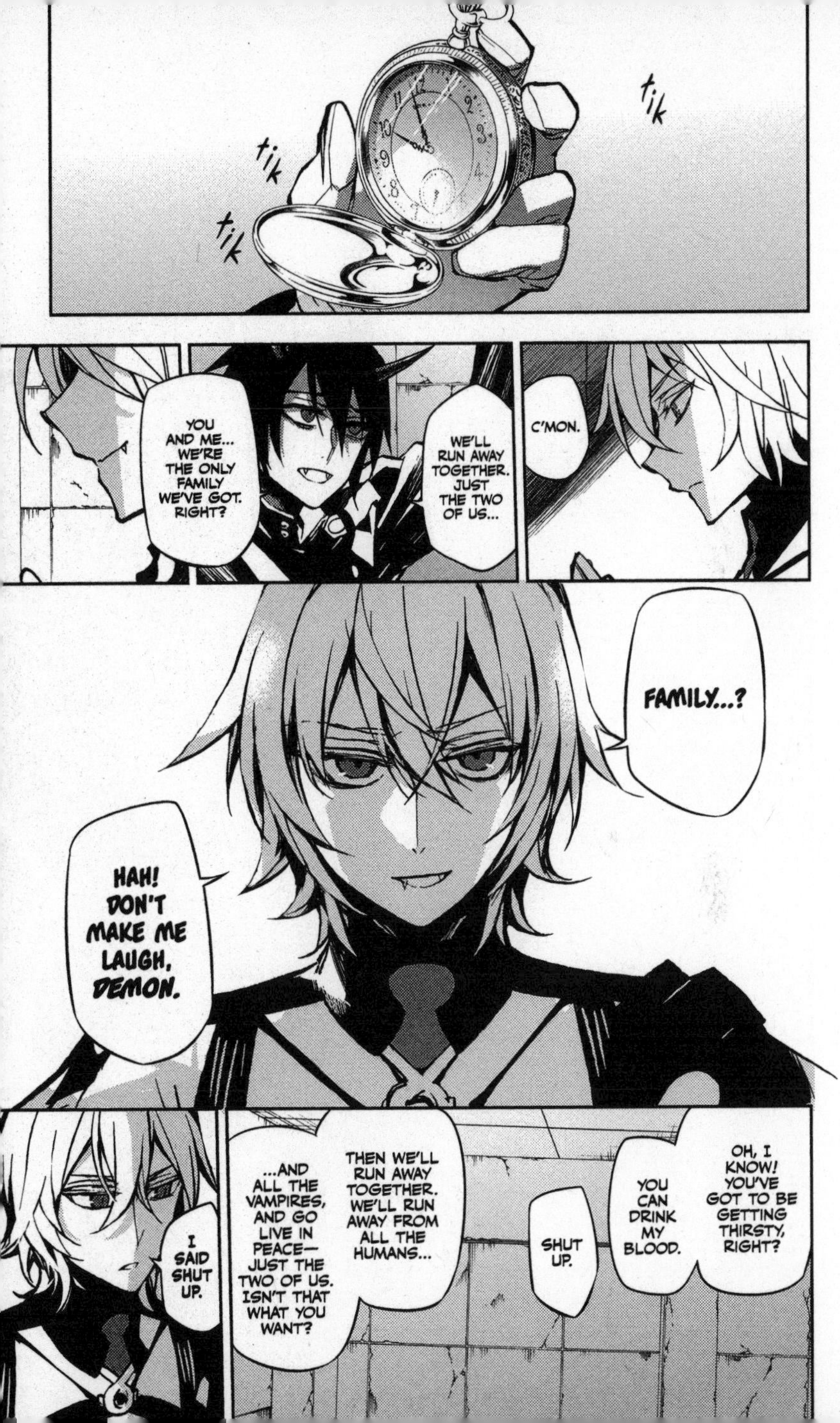
tik
tik
tik
C'MON.
WE'LL RUN AWAY TOGETHER. JUST THE TWO OF US...
YOU AND ME... WE'RE THE ONLY FAMILY WE'VE GOT. RIGHT?
FAMILY...?
HAH! DON'T MAKE ME LAUGH, DEMON.
OH, I KNOW! YOU'VE GOT TO BE GETTING THIRSTY, RIGHT?
YOU CAN DRINK MY BLOOD.
SHUT UP.
THEN WE'LL RUN AWAY TOGETHER. WE'LL RUN AWAY FROM ALL THE HUMANS...
...AND ALL THE VAMPIRES, AND GO LIVE IN PEACE—JUST THE TWO OF US. ISN'T THAT WHAT YOU WANT?
I SAID SHUT UP.

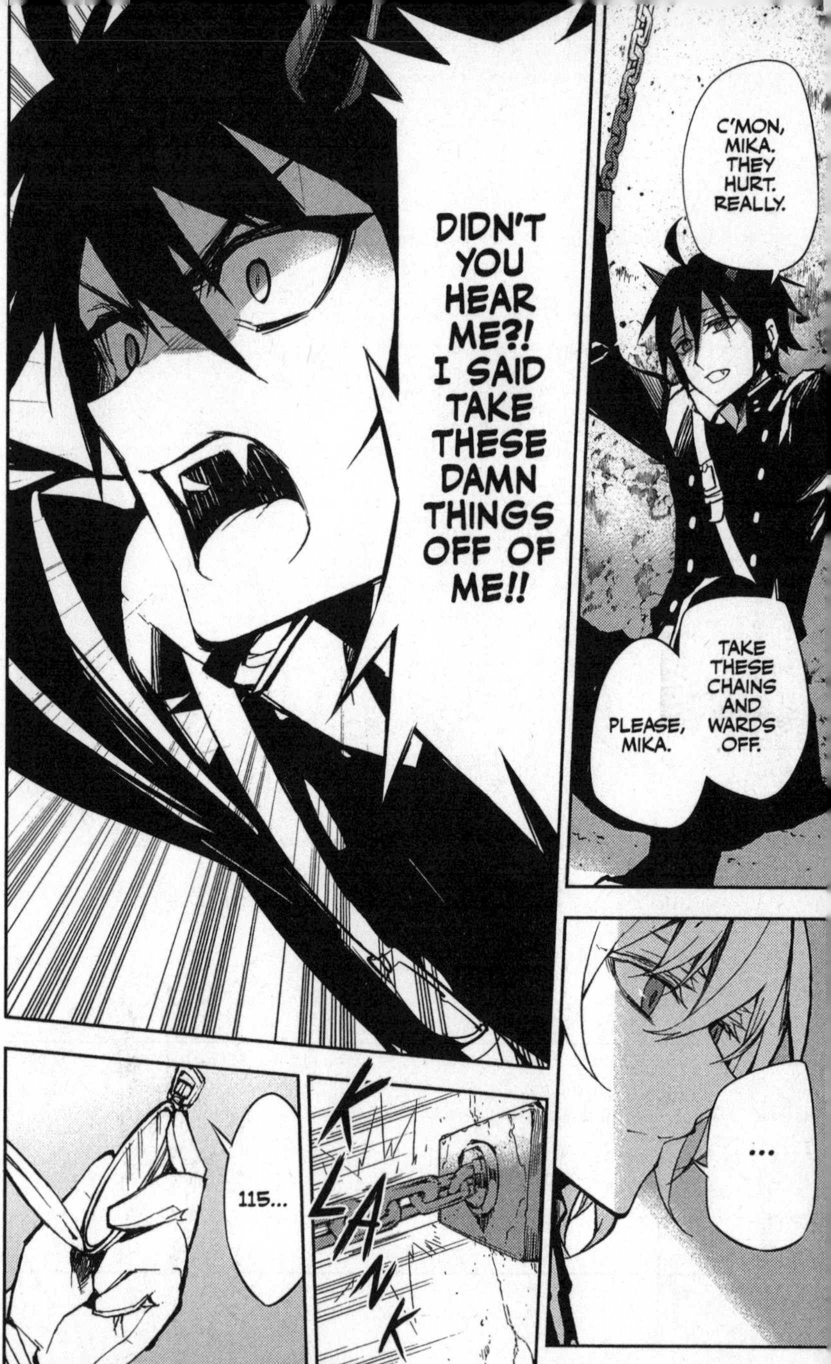
C'MON, MIKA. THEY HURT. REALLY.
TAKE THESE CHAINS AND WARDS OFF.
PLEASE, MIKA.
DIDN'T YOU HEAR ME?! I SAID TAKE THESE DAMN THINGS OFF OF ME!!
...
KLANK
115...

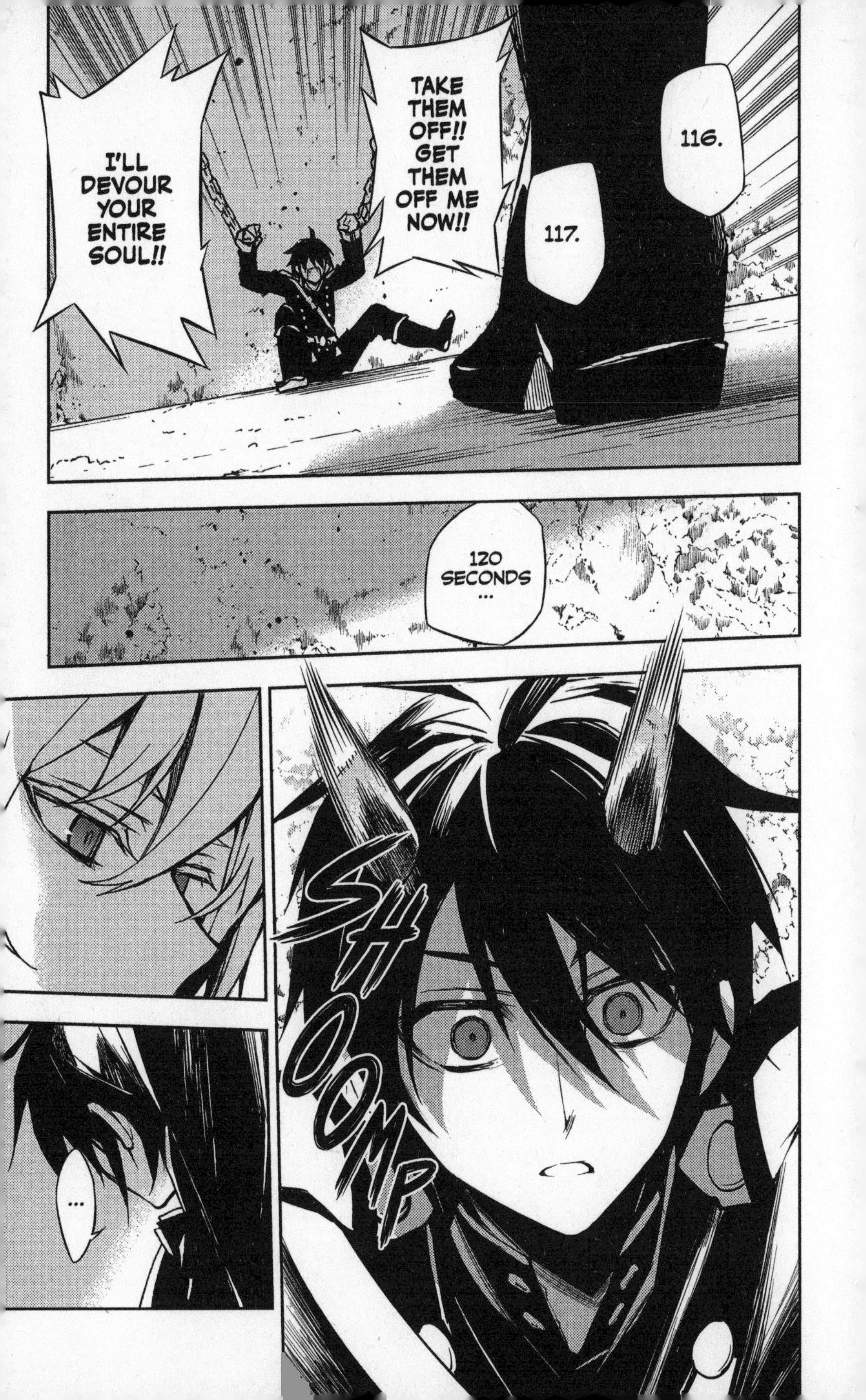
116.
117.
TAKE THEM OFF!! GET THEM OFF ME NOW!!
I'LL DEVOUR YOUR ENTIRE SOUL!!
120 SECONDS ...
SHOOOMP
...

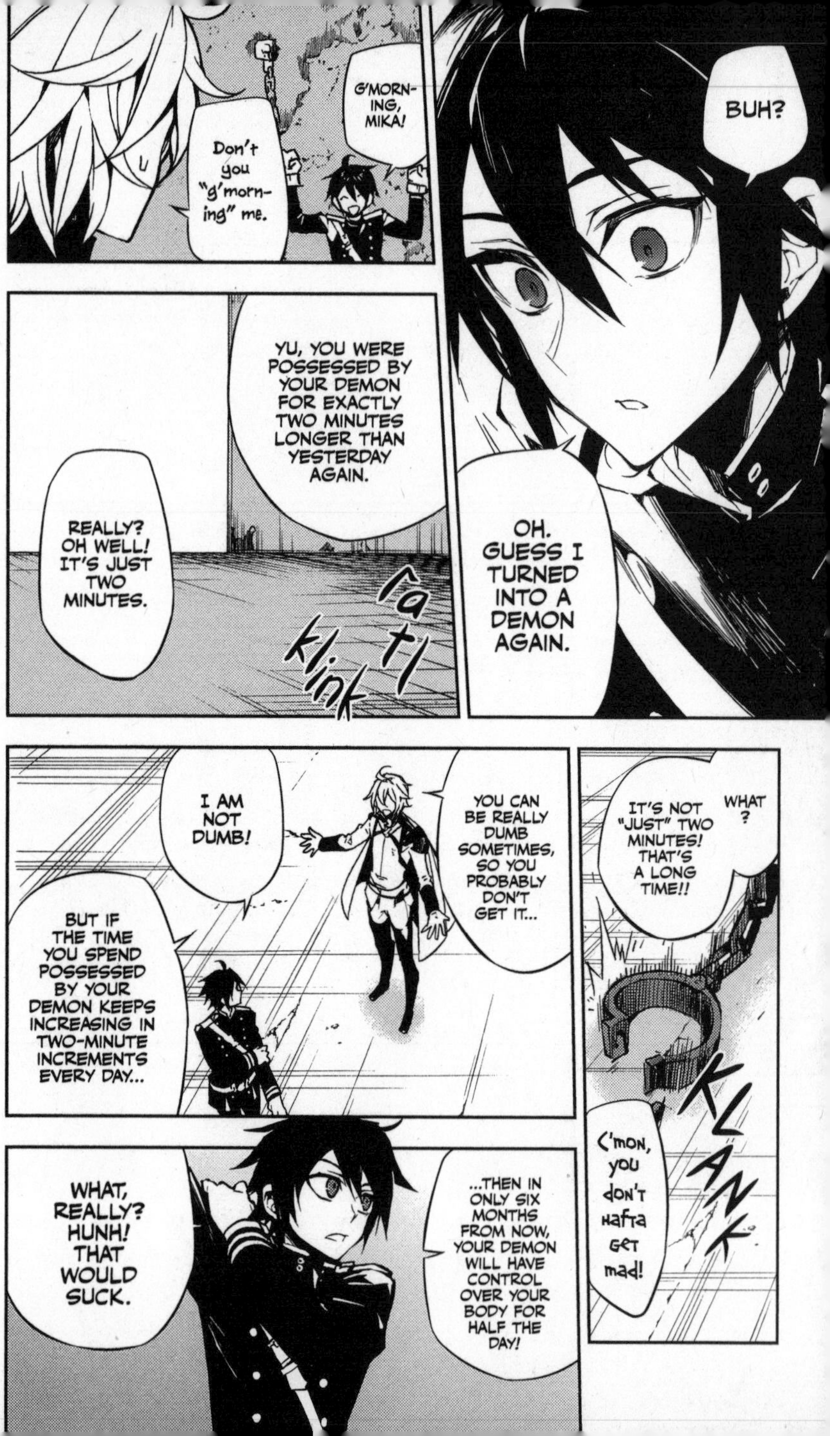
BUH?
OH. GUESS I TURNED INTO A DEMON AGAIN.
G'MORNING, MIKA!
Don't you "g'morning" me.
YU, YOU WERE POSSESSED BY YOUR DEMON FOR EXACTLY TWO MINUTES LONGER THAN YESTERDAY AGAIN.
REALLY? OH WELL! IT'S JUST TWO MINUTES.
ratl klink
WHAT?
IT'S NOT "JUST" TWO MINUTES! THAT'S A LONG TIME!!
KLANK
C'mon, you don't hafta get mad!
YOU CAN BE REALLY DUMB SOMETIMES, SO YOU PROBABLY DON'T GET IT...
I AM NOT DUMB!
BUT IF THE TIME YOU SPEND POSSESSED BY YOUR DEMON KEEPS INCREASING IN TWO-MINUTE INCREMENTS EVERY DAY...
...THEN IN ONLY SIX MONTHS FROM NOW, YOUR DEMON WILL HAVE CONTROL OVER YOUR BODY FOR HALF THE DAY!
WHAT, REALLY? HUNH! THAT WOULD SUCK.

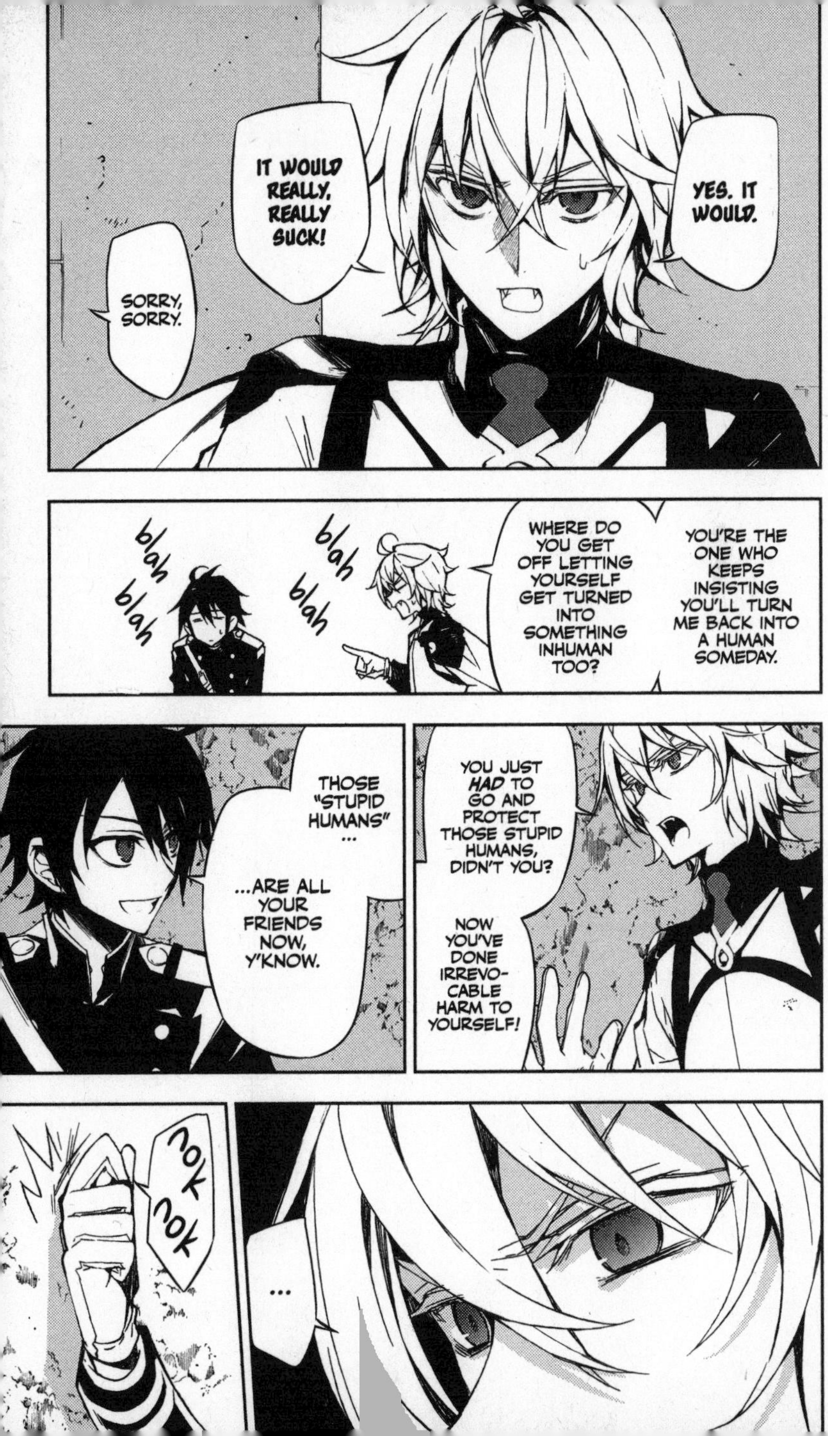
YES. IT WOULD.
IT WOULD REALLY, REALLY SUCK!
SORRY, SORRY.
YOU'RE THE ONE WHO KEEPS INSISTING YOU'LL TURN ME BACK INTO A HUMAN SOMEDAY.
WHERE DO YOU GET OFF LETTING YOURSELF GET TURNED INTO SOMETHING INHUMAN TOO?
blah blah
blah blah
YOU JUST *HAD* TO GO AND PROTECT THOSE STUPID HUMANS, DIDN'T YOU?
NOW YOU'VE DONE IRREVOCABLE HARM TO YOURSELF!
THOSE "STUPID HUMANS"...
...ARE ALL YOUR FRIENDS NOW, Y'KNOW.
...
nok nok

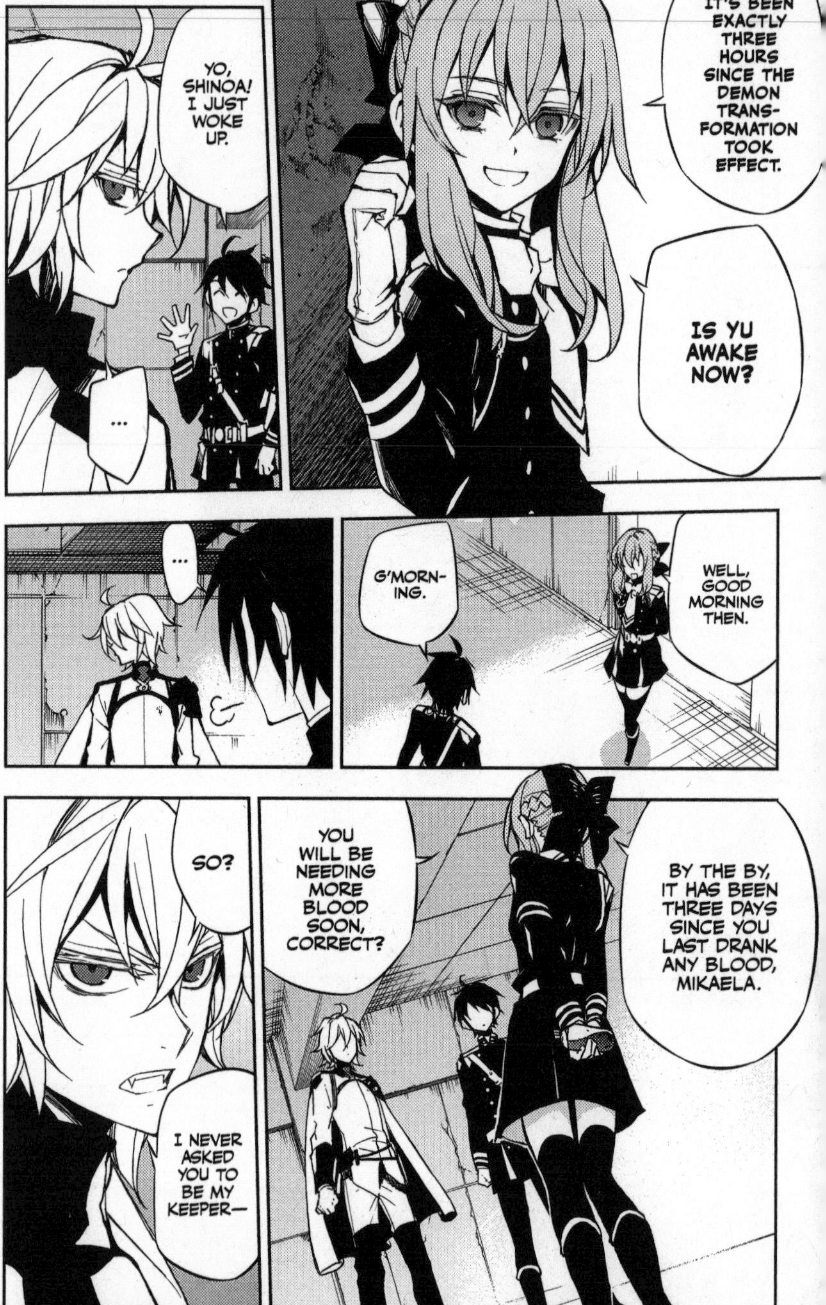
IT'S BEEN EXACTLY THREE HOURS SINCE THE DEMON TRANS-FORMATION TOOK EFFECT.
IS YU AWAKE NOW?
YO, SHINOA! I JUST WOKE UP.
...
WELL, GOOD MORNING THEN.
G'MORN-ING.
...
BY THE BY, IT HAS BEEN THREE DAYS SINCE YOU LAST DRANK ANY BLOOD, MIKAELA.
YOU WILL BE NEEDING MORE BLOOD SOON, CORRECT?
SO?
I NEVER ASKED YOU TO BE MY KEEPER—

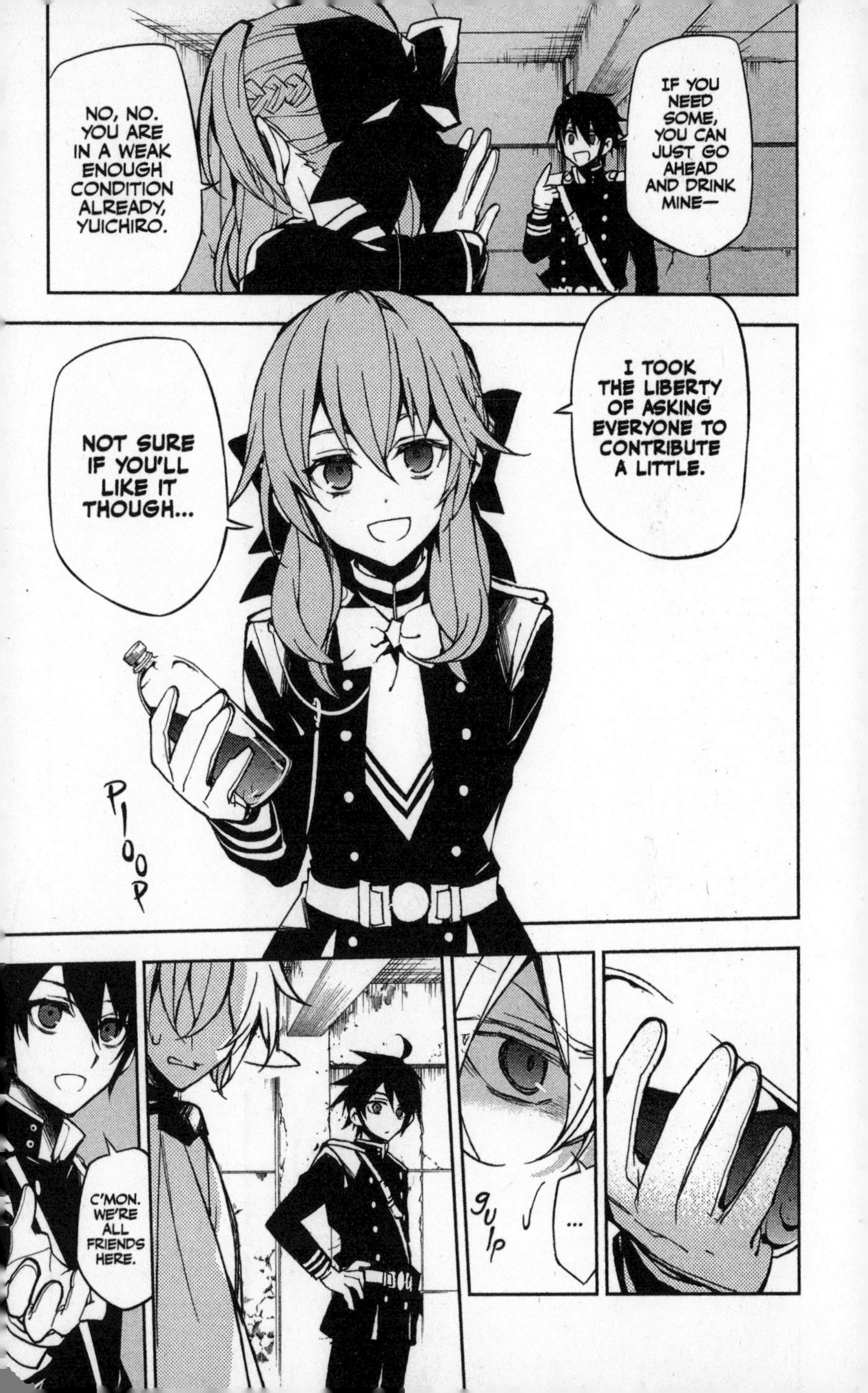
IF YOU NEED SOME, YOU CAN JUST GO AHEAD AND DRINK MINE—
NO, NO. YOU ARE IN A WEAK ENOUGH CONDITION ALREADY, YUICHIRO.
I TOOK THE LIBERTY OF ASKING EVERYONE TO CONTRIBUTE A LITTLE.
NOT SURE IF YOU'LL LIKE IT THOUGH...
PLOOP
...
GULP
C'MON. WE'RE ALL FRIENDS HERE.

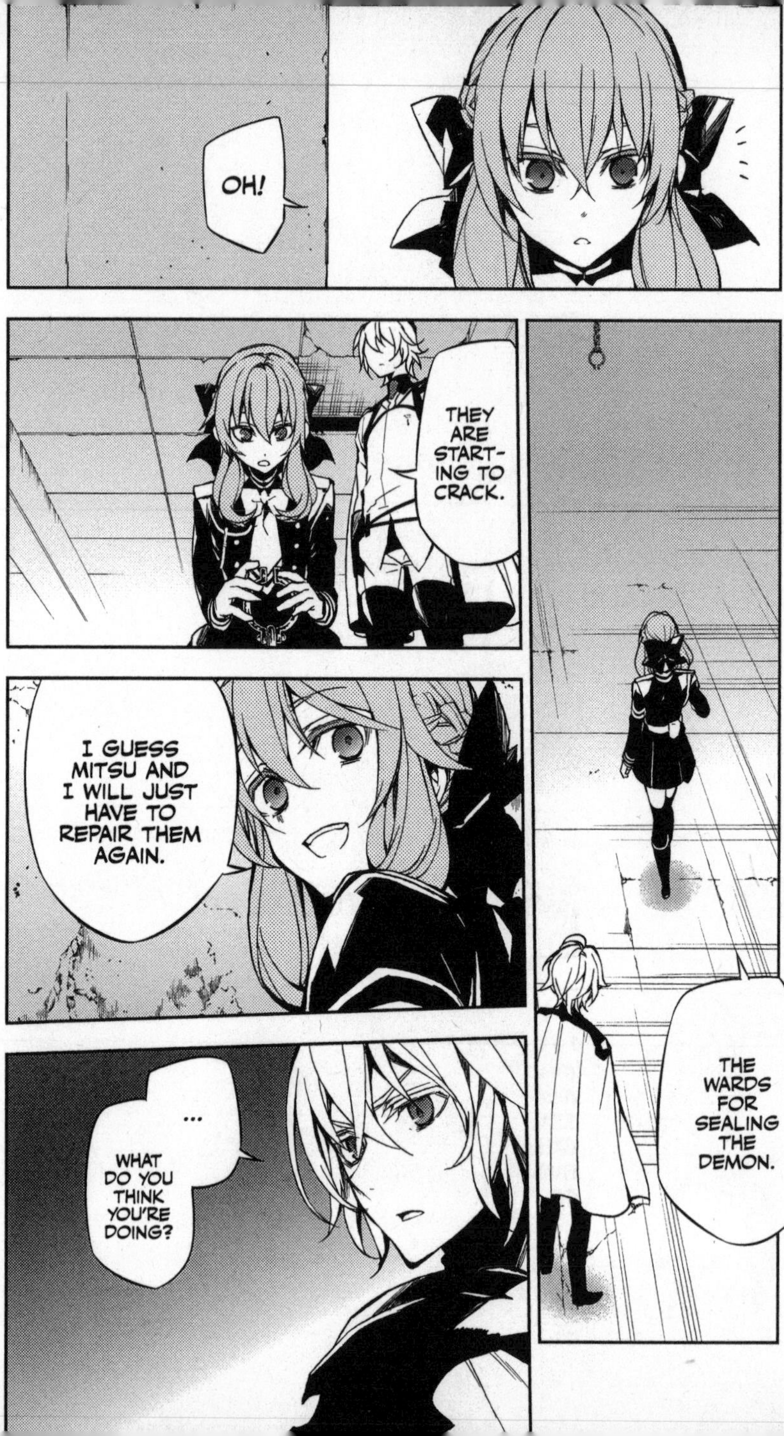
OH!
THE WARDS FOR SEALING THE DEMON.
THEY ARE STARTING TO CRACK.
I GUESS MITSU AND I WILL JUST HAVE TO REPAIR THEM AGAIN.
...
WHAT DO YOU THINK YOU'RE DOING?

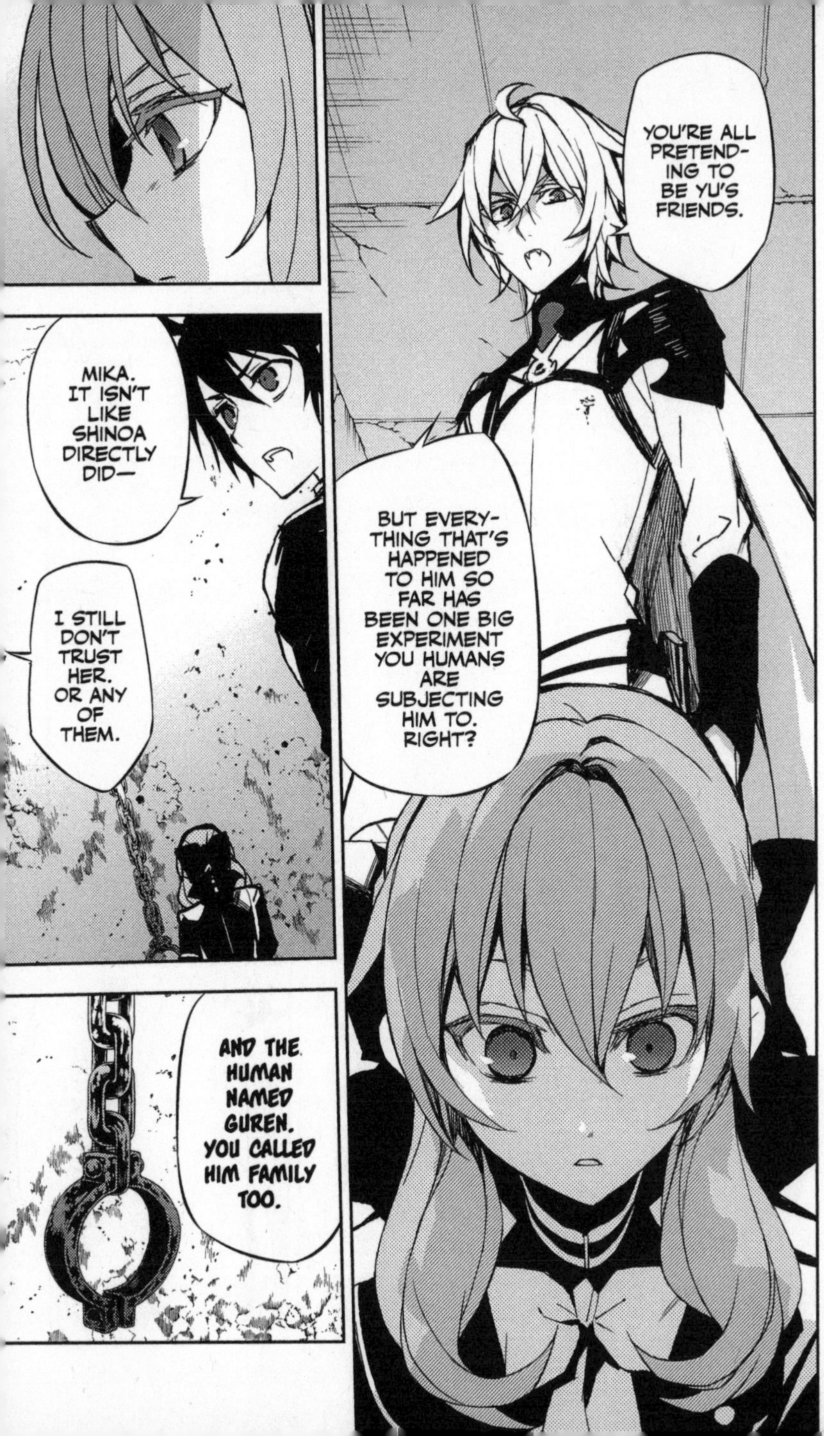
YOU'RE ALL PRETEND-ING TO BE YU'S FRIENDS.
BUT EVERY-THING THAT'S HAPPENED TO HIM SO FAR HAS BEEN ONE BIG EXPERIMENT YOU HUMANS ARE SUBJECTING HIM TO. RIGHT?
MIKA. IT ISN'T LIKE SHINOA DIRECTLY DID—
I STILL DON'T TRUST HER. OR ANY OF THEM.
AND THE HUMAN NAMED GUREN. YOU CALLED HIM FAMILY TOO.

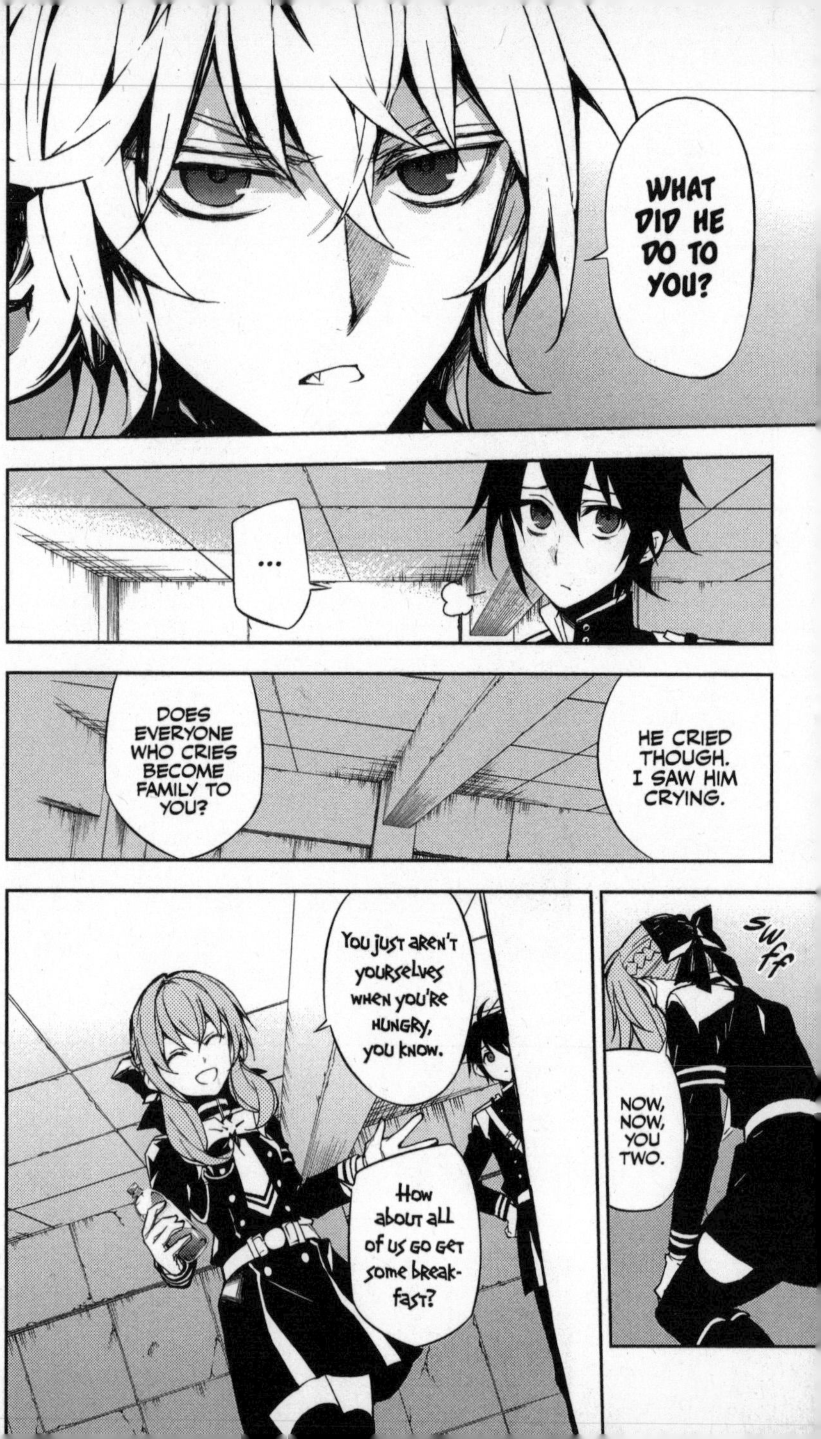
WHAT DID HE DO TO YOU?
...
HE CRIED THOUGH. I SAW HIM CRYING.
DOES EVERYONE WHO CRIES BECOME FAMILY TO YOU?
SWFF
NOW, NOW, YOU TWO.
You just aren't yourselves when you're hungry, you know.
How about all of us go get some breakfast?

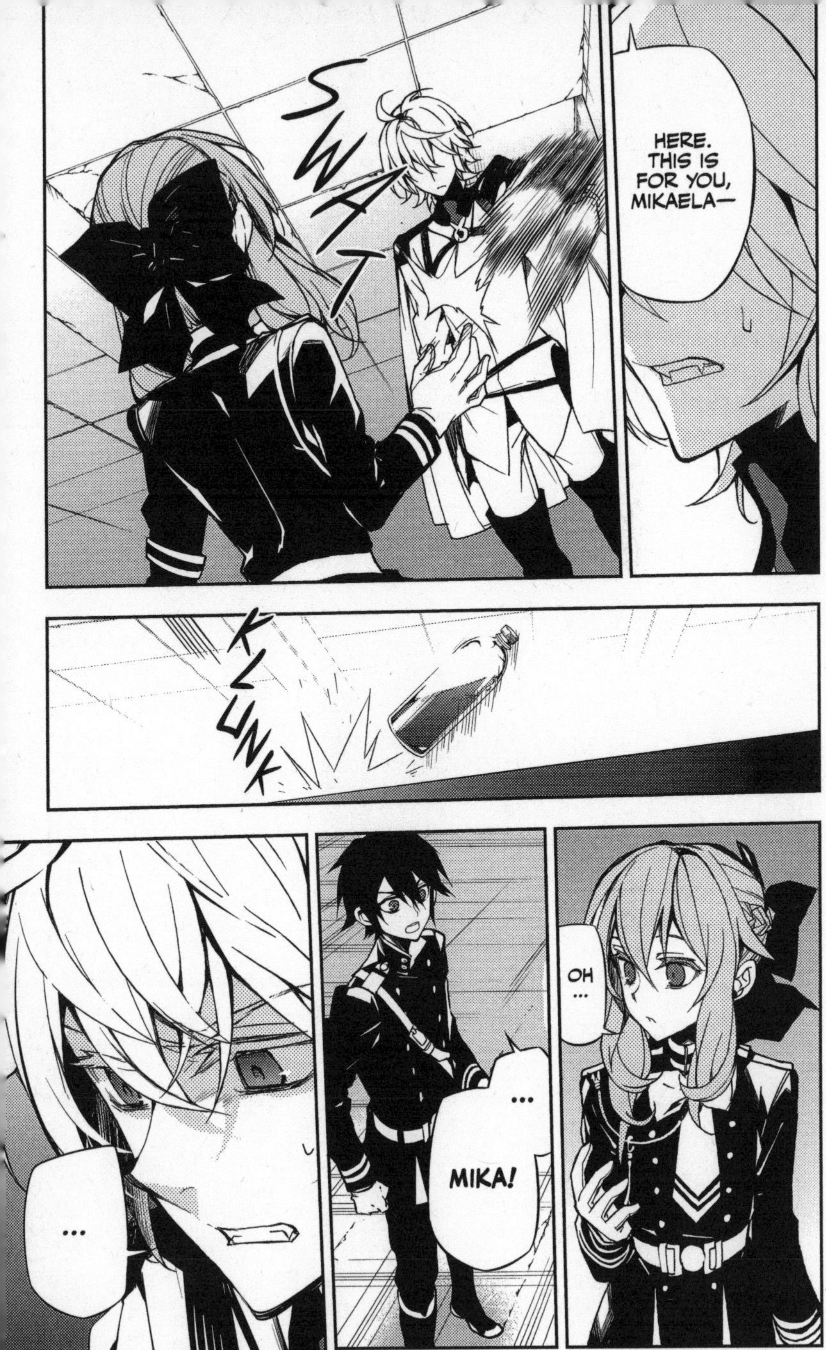
HERE. THIS IS FOR YOU, MIKAELA—
SWAT
KLUNK
OH ...
... MIKA!
...

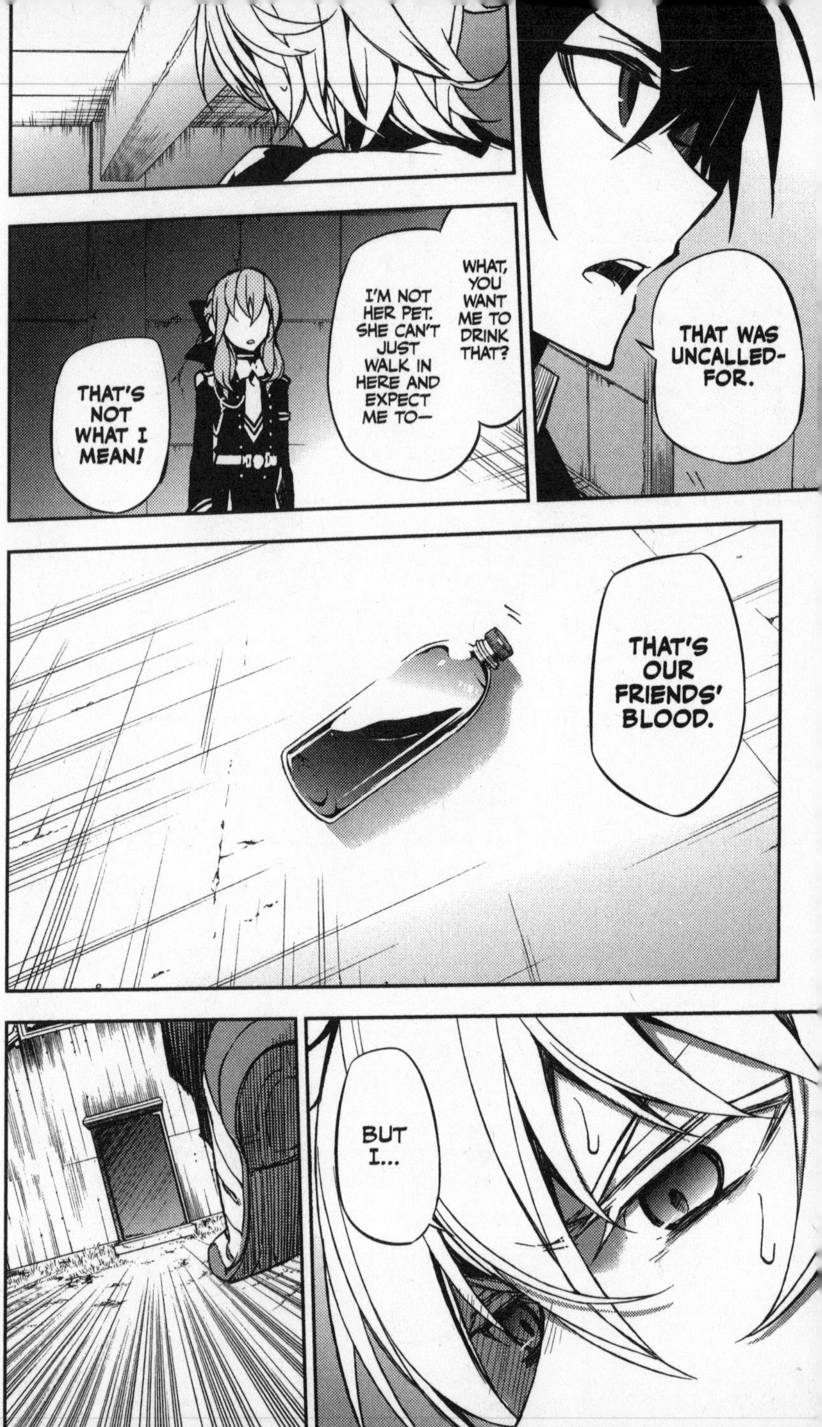
THAT WAS UNCALLED-FOR.
WHAT, YOU WANT ME TO DRINK THAT?
I'M NOT HER PET. SHE CAN'T JUST WALK IN HERE AND EXPECT ME TO—
THAT'S NOT WHAT I MEAN!
THAT'S OUR FRIENDS' BLOOD.
BUT I...

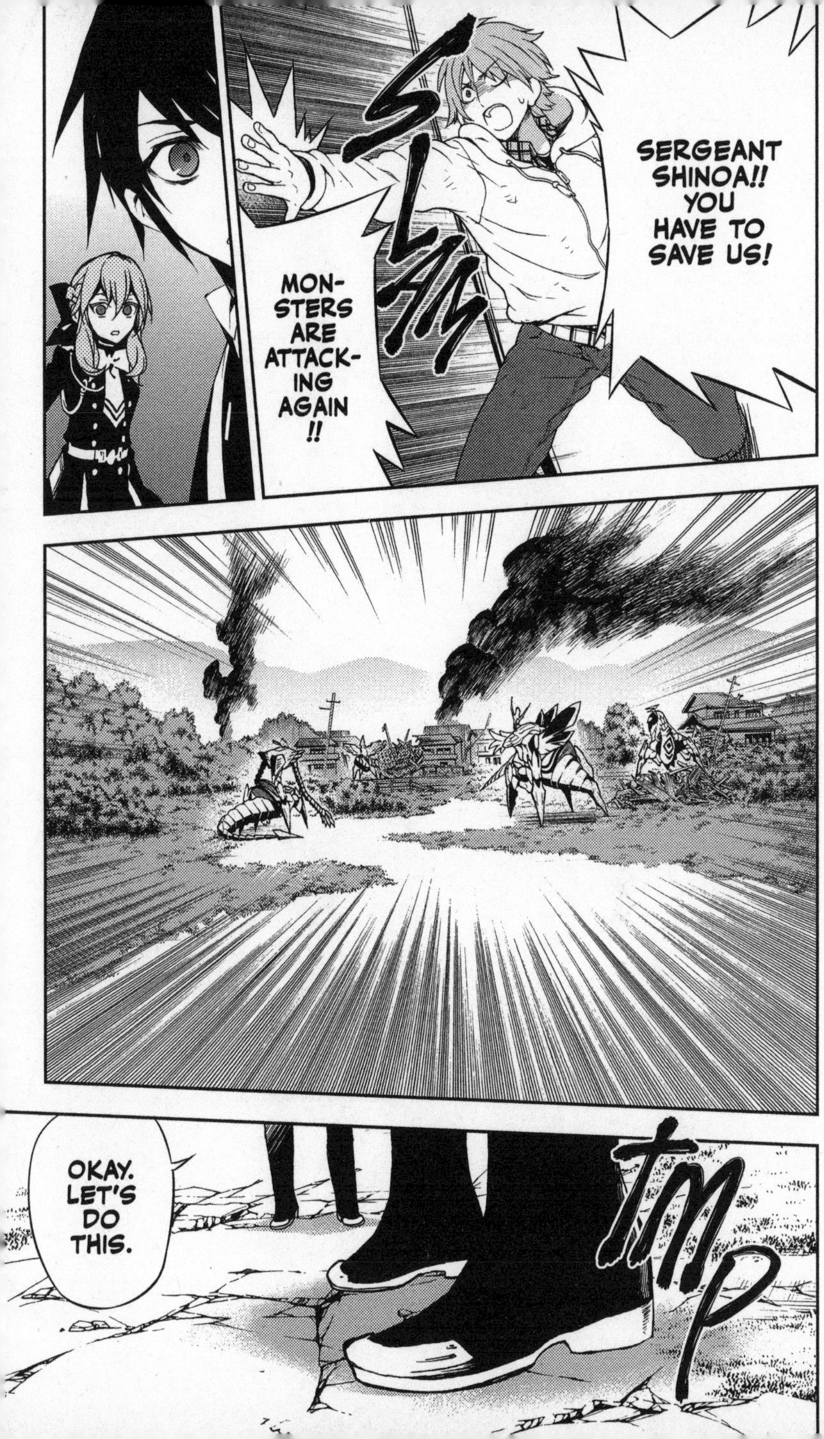
SERGEANT SHINOA!! YOU HAVE TO SAVE US!
SLAM
MON-STERS ARE ATTACK-ING AGAIN!!
tmp
OKAY. LET'S DO THIS.

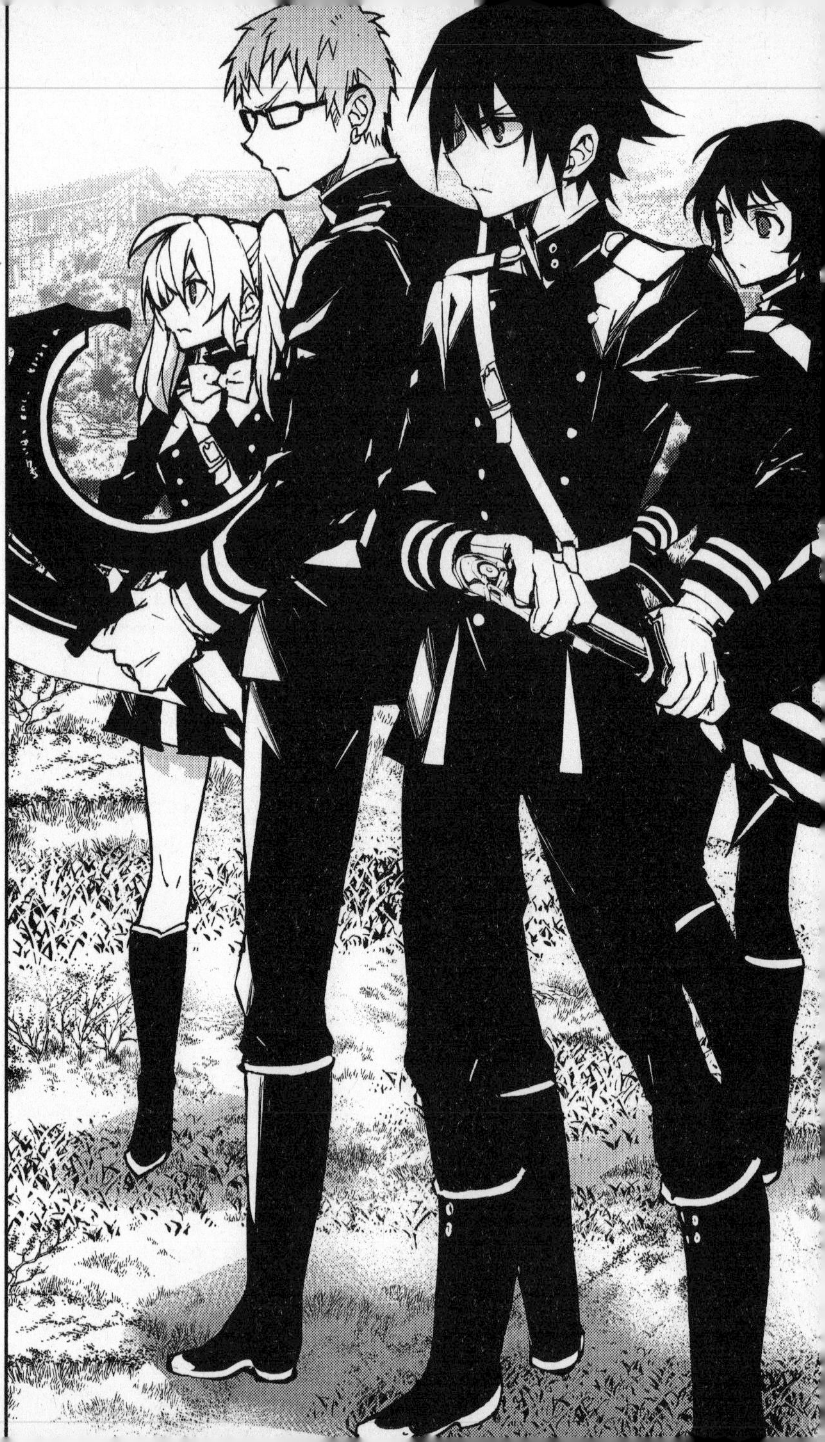

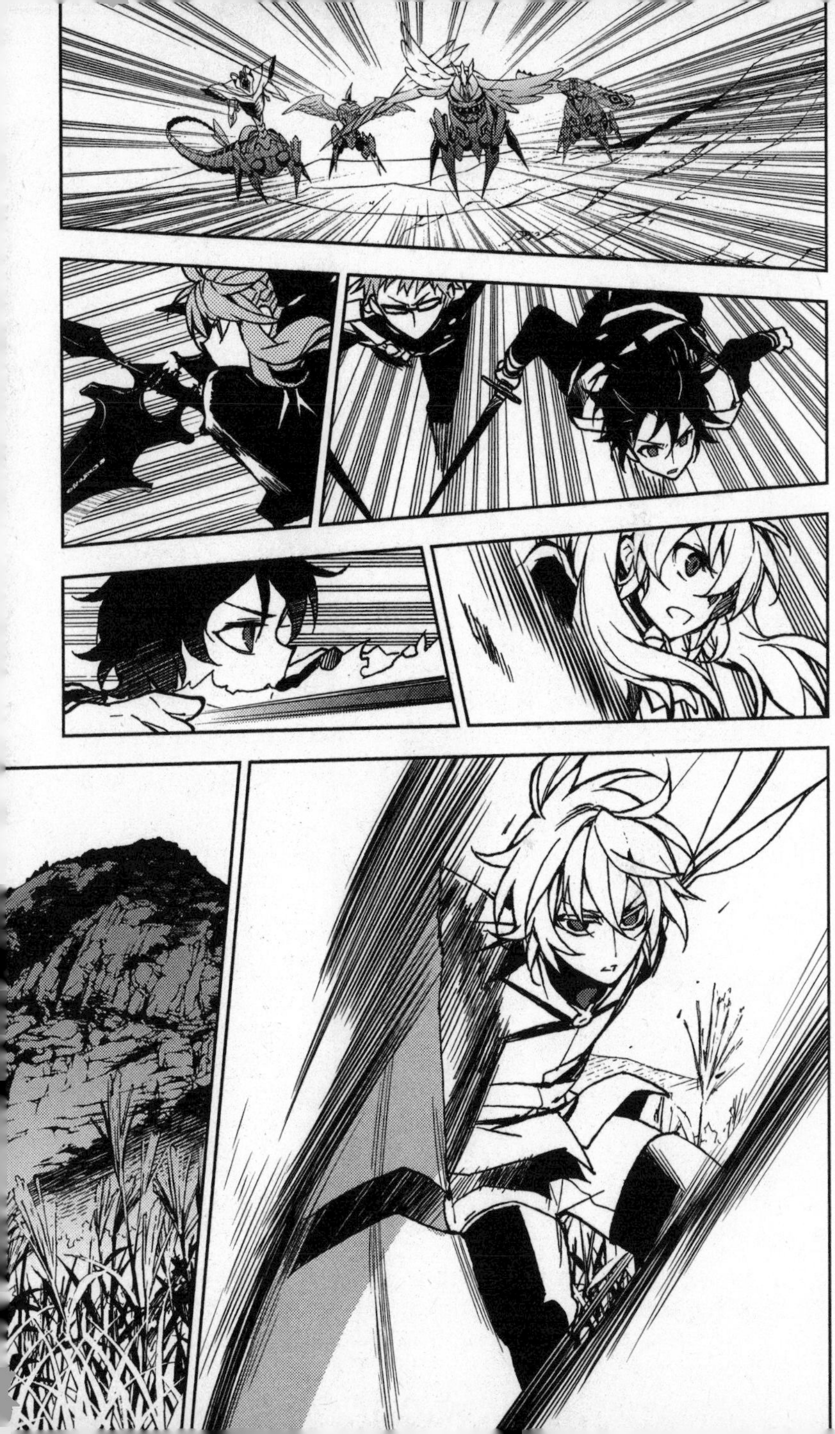

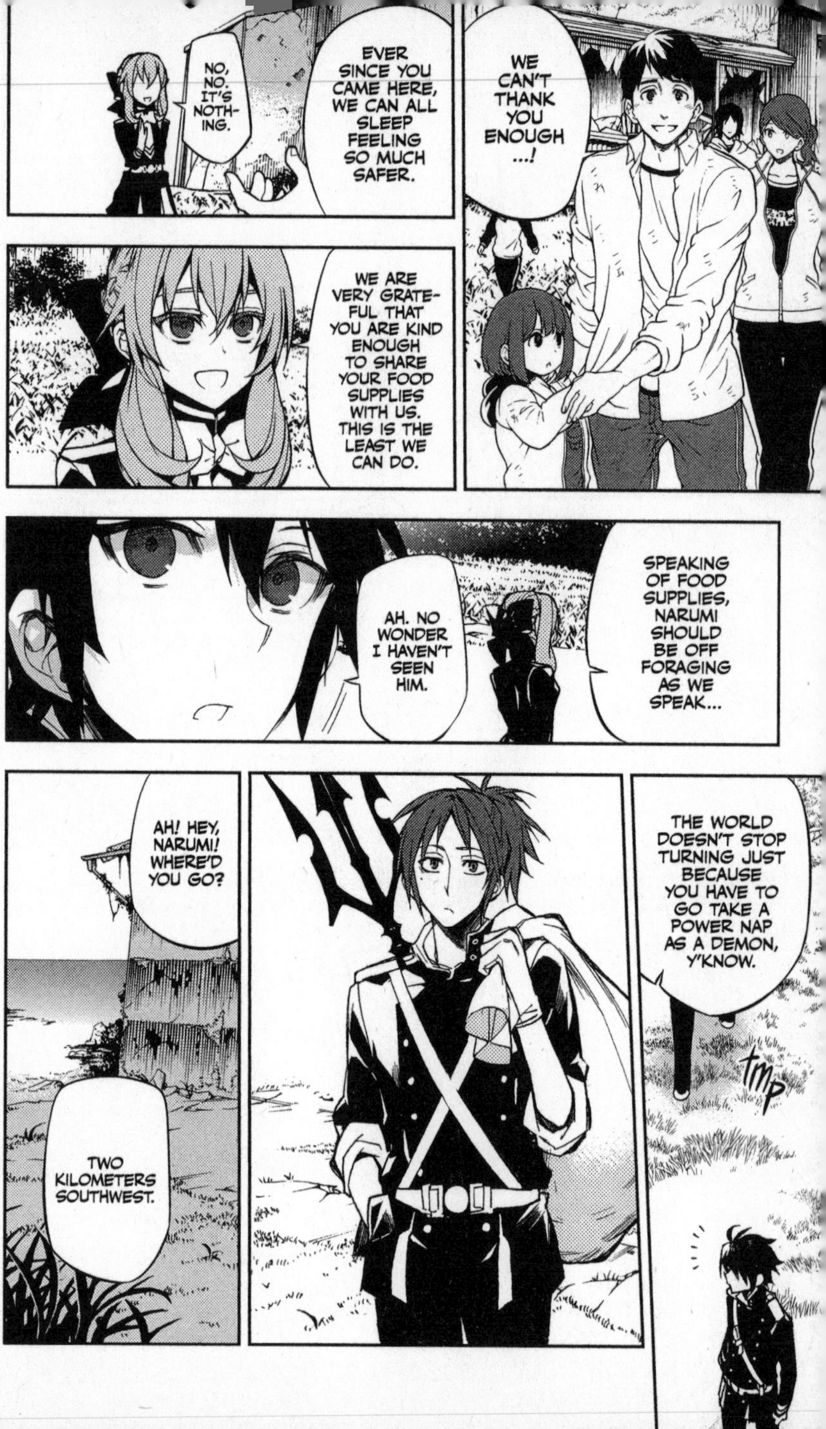
WE CAN'T THANK YOU ENOUGH ...!
EVER SINCE YOU CAME HERE, WE CAN ALL SLEEP FEELING SO MUCH SAFER.
NO, NO. IT'S NOTHING.
WE ARE VERY GRATEFUL THAT YOU ARE KIND ENOUGH TO SHARE YOUR FOOD SUPPLIES WITH US. THIS IS THE LEAST WE CAN DO.
SPEAKING OF FOOD SUPPLIES, NARUMI SHOULD BE OFF FORAGING AS WE SPEAK...
AH. NO WONDER I HAVEN'T SEEN HIM.
THE WORLD DOESN'T STOP TURNING JUST BECAUSE YOU HAVE TO GO TAKE A POWER NAP AS A DEMON, Y'KNOW.
tmp
AH! HEY, NARUMI! WHERE'D YOU GO?
TWO KILOMETERS SOUTHWEST.

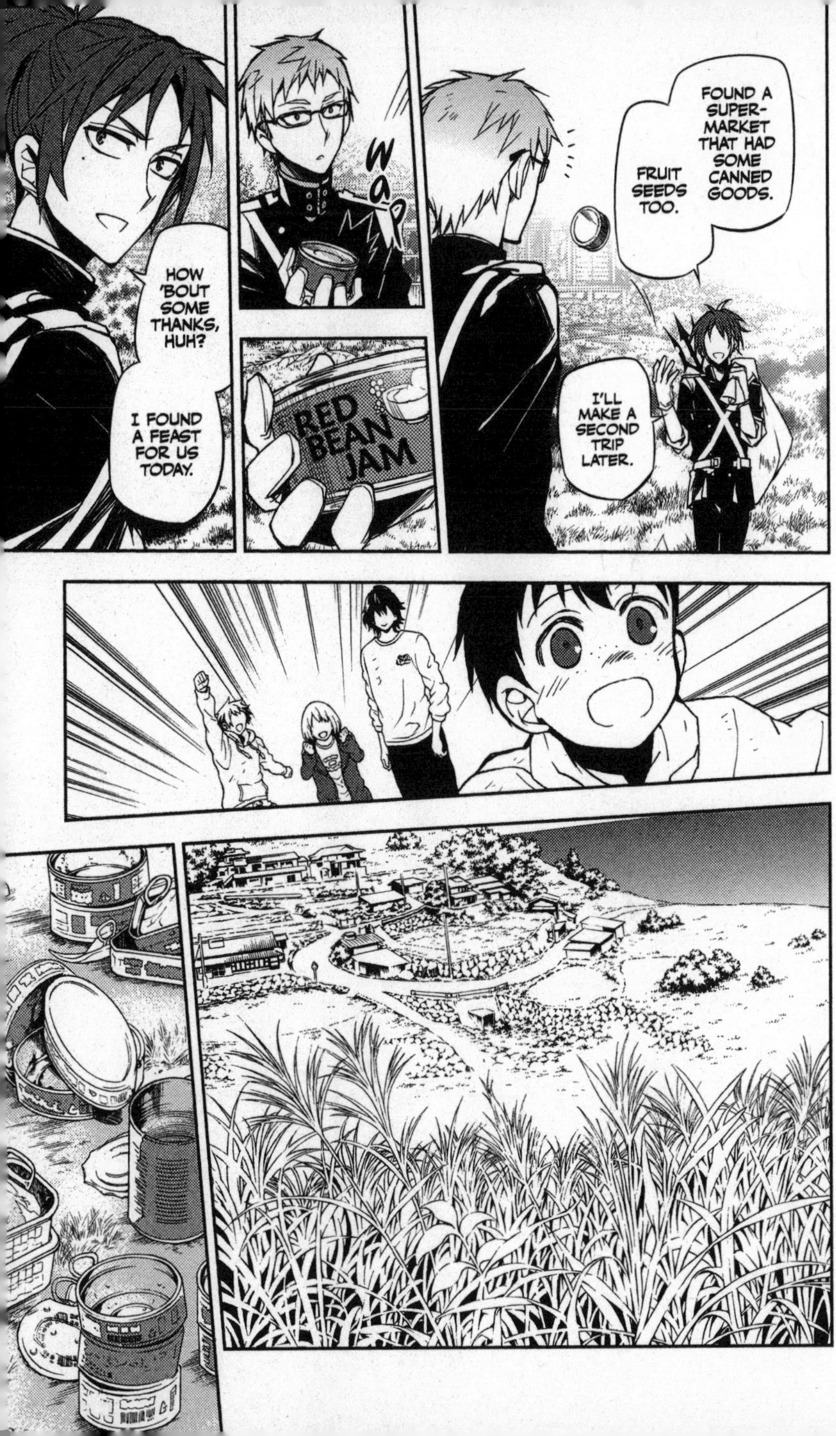
FOUND A SUPER-MARKET THAT HAD SOME CANNED GOODS.
FRUIT SEEDS TOO.
I'LL MAKE A SECOND TRIP LATER.
WAP
RED BEAN JAM
HOW 'BOUT SOME THANKS, HUH?
I FOUND A FEAST FOR US TODAY.

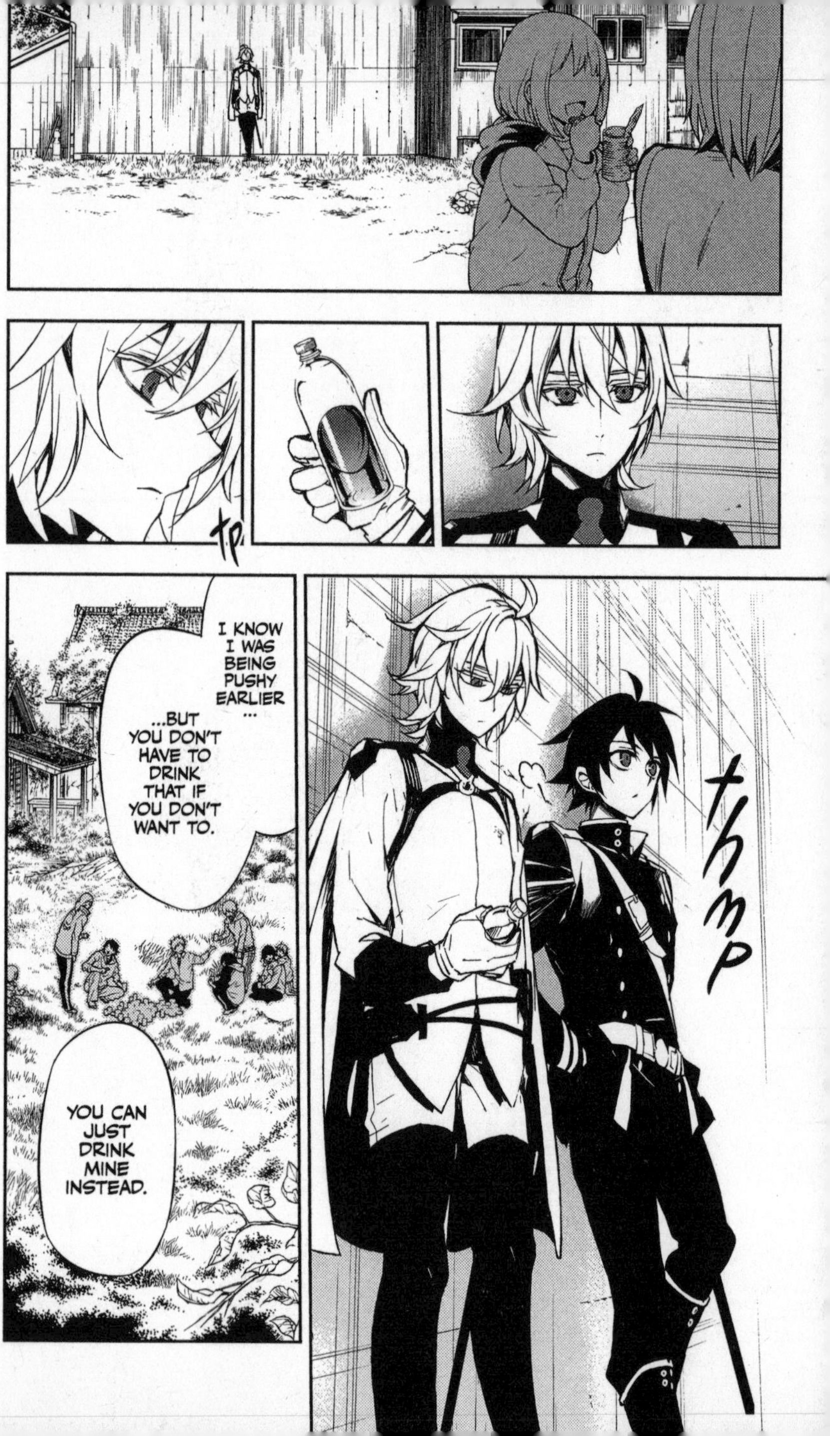
TP.
THMP
I KNOW I WAS BEING PUSHY EARLIER ...
...BUT YOU DON'T HAVE TO DRINK THAT IF YOU DON'T WANT TO.
YOU CAN JUST DRINK MINE INSTEAD.

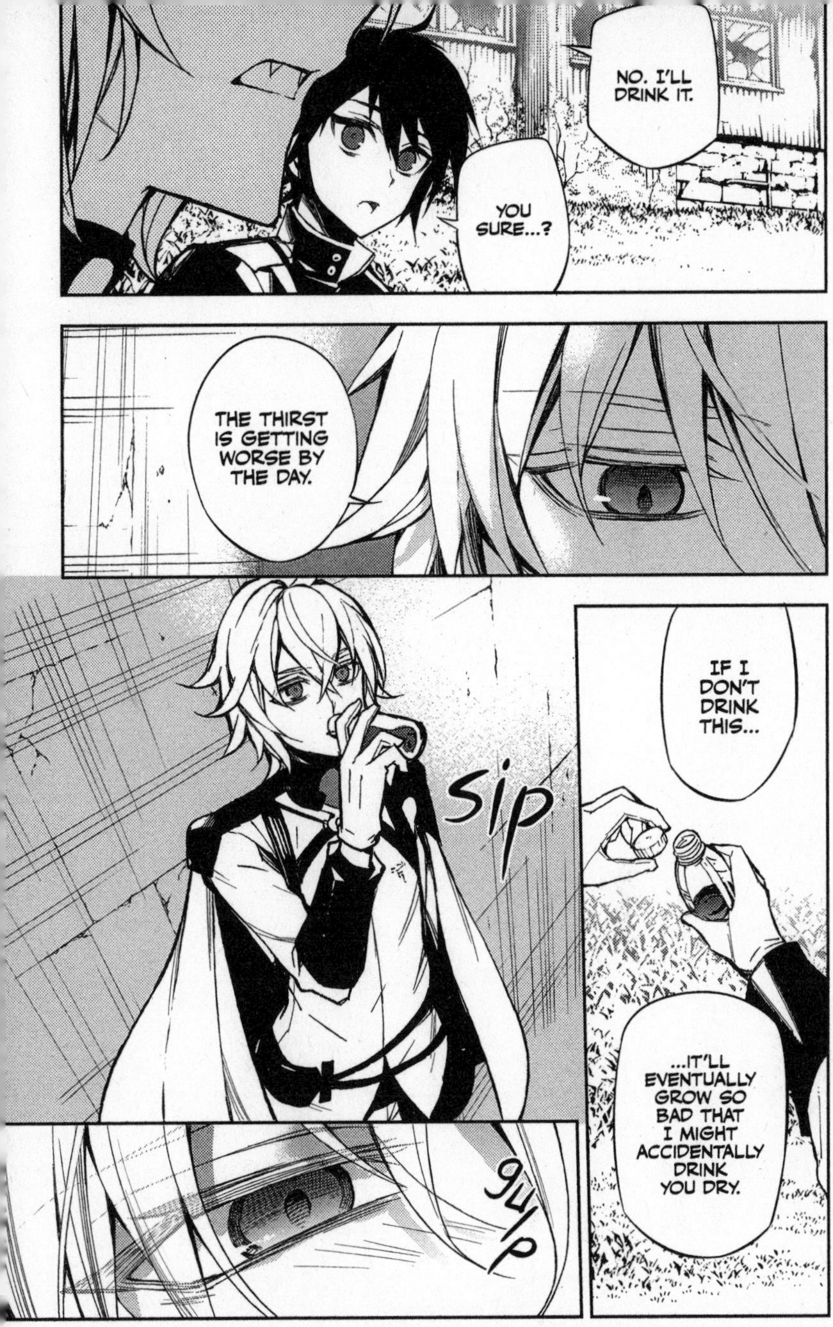
NO. I'LL DRINK IT.
YOU SURE...?
THE THIRST IS GETTING WORSE BY THE DAY.
IF I DON'T DRINK THIS...
SIP
...IT'LL EVENTUALLY GROW SO BAD THAT I MIGHT ACCIDENTALLY DRINK YOU DRY.
GULP

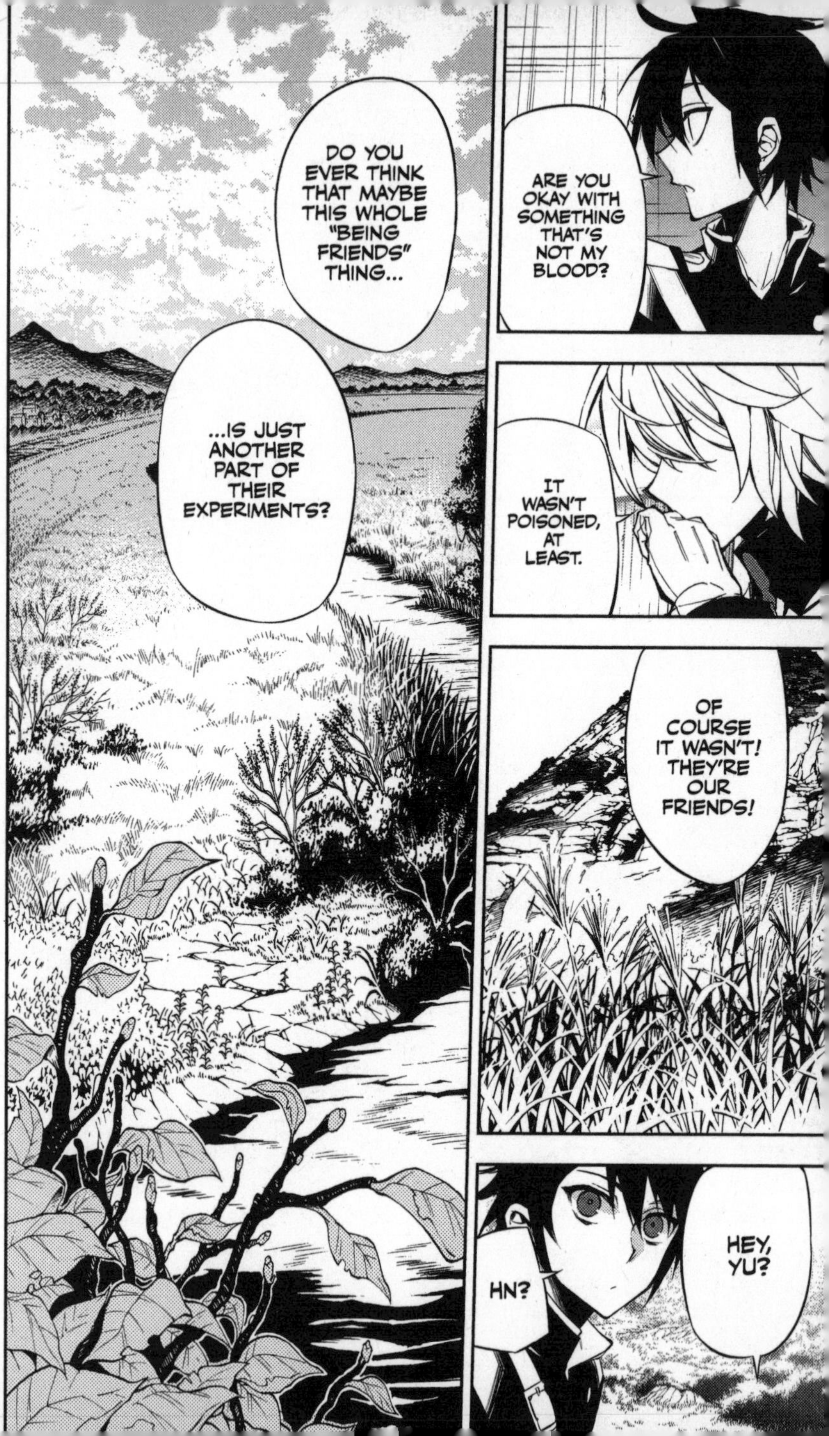
ARE YOU OKAY WITH SOMETHING THAT'S NOT MY BLOOD?
IT WASN'T POISONED, AT LEAST.
OF COURSE IT WASN'T! THEY'RE OUR FRIENDS!
HEY, YU?
HN?
DO YOU EVER THINK THAT MAYBE THIS WHOLE "BEING FRIENDS" THING...
...IS JUST ANOTHER PART OF THEIR EXPERIMENTS?

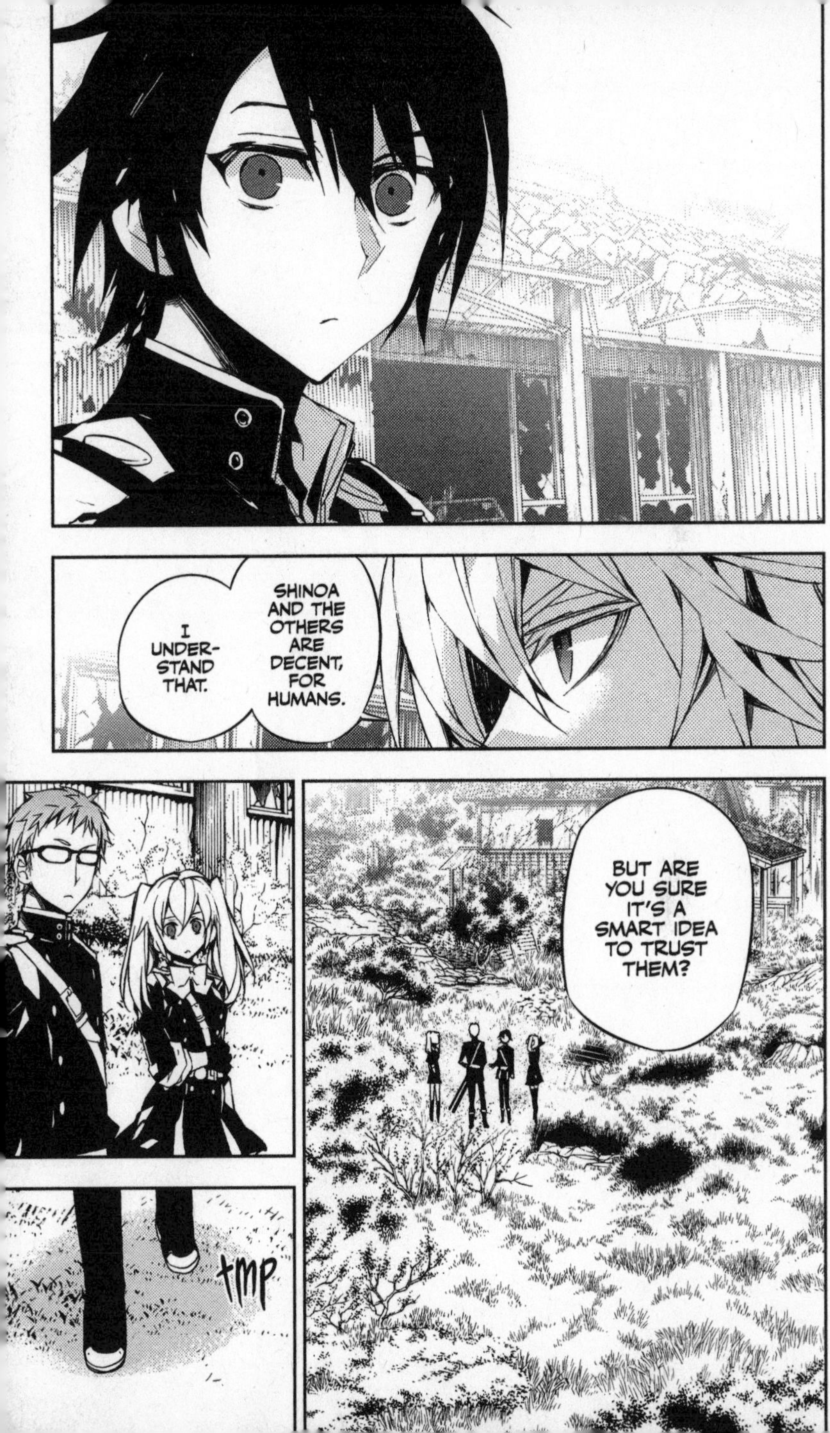
SHINOA AND THE OTHERS ARE DECENT, FOR HUMANS.
I UNDER-STAND THAT.
BUT ARE YOU SURE IT'S A SMART IDEA TO TRUST THEM?
tmp

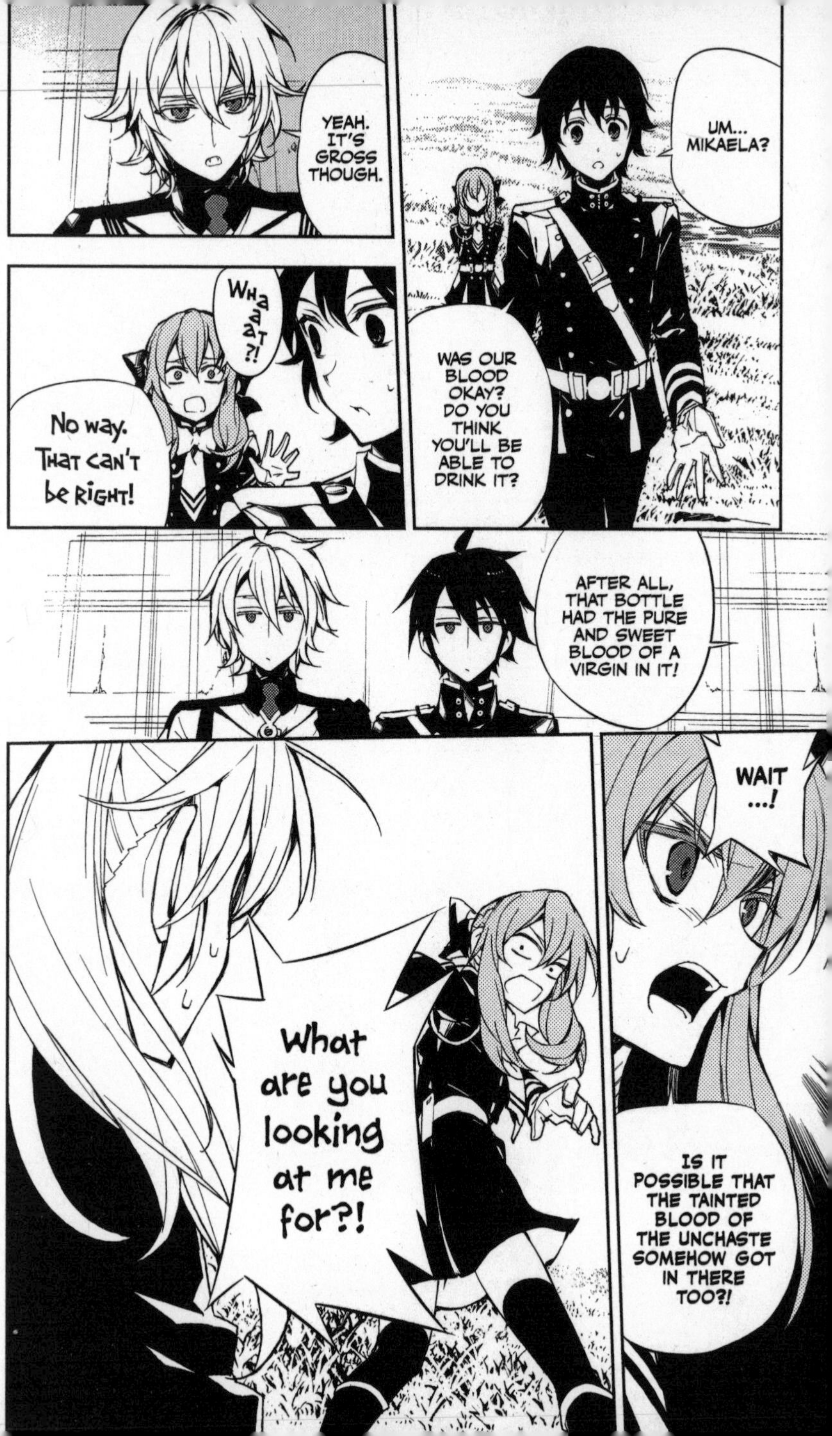
UM... MIKAELA?
WAS OUR BLOOD OKAY? DO YOU THINK YOU'LL BE ABLE TO DRINK IT?
YEAH. IT'S GROSS THOUGH.
Whaaat?!
No way. That can't be right!
AFTER ALL, THAT BOTTLE HAD THE PURE AND SWEET BLOOD OF A VIRGIN IN IT!
WAIT ...!
IS IT POSSIBLE THAT THE TAINTED BLOOD OF THE UNCHASTE SOMEHOW GOT IN THERE TOO?!
What are you looking at me for?!

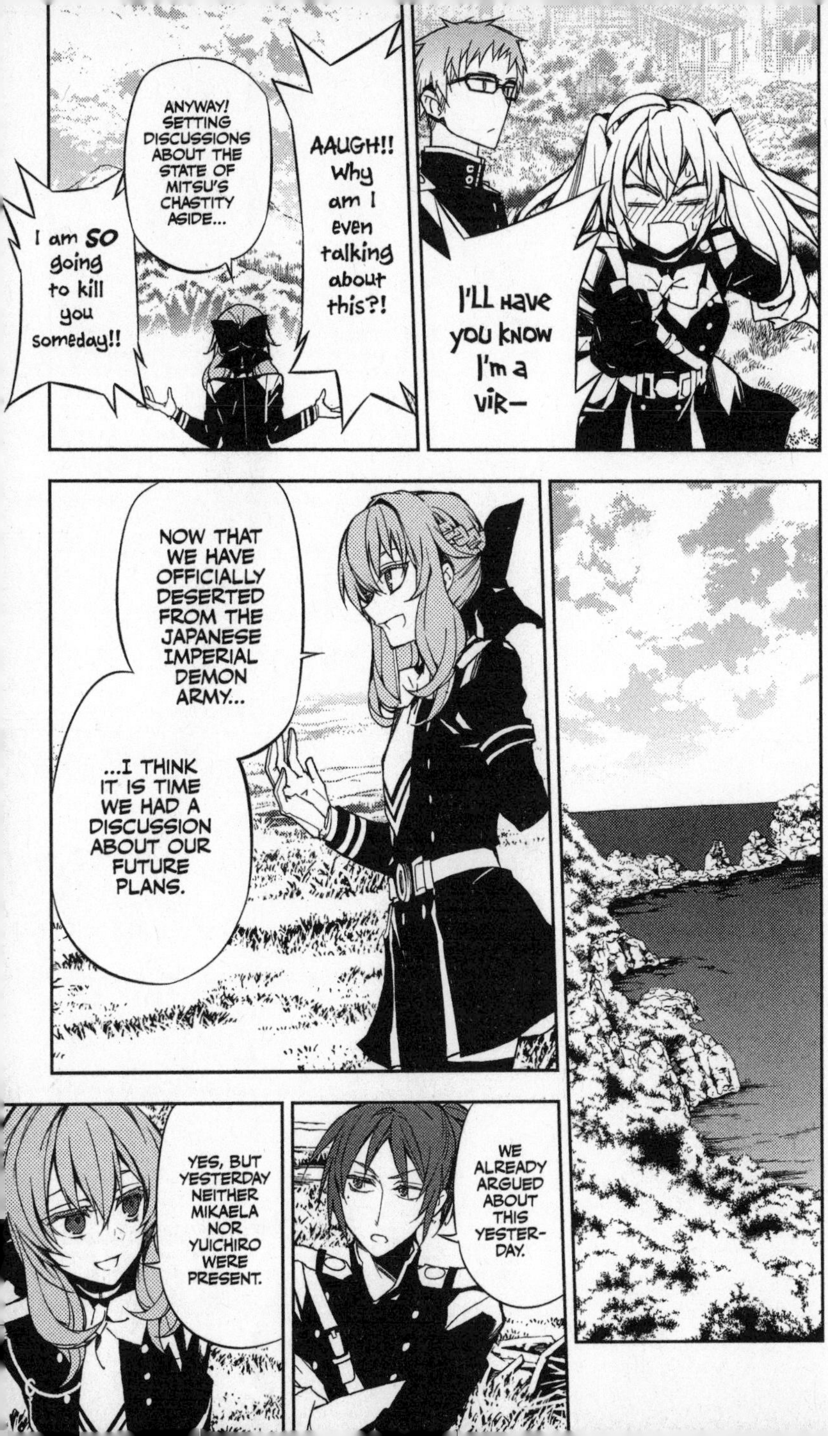
I'LL have you know I'm a vir—
AAUGH!! Why am I even talking about this?!
ANYWAY! SETTING DISCUSSIONS ABOUT THE STATE OF MITSU'S CHASTITY ASIDE...
I am SO going to kill you someday!!
NOW THAT WE HAVE OFFICIALLY DESERTED FROM THE JAPANESE IMPERIAL DEMON ARMY...
...I THINK IT IS TIME WE HAD A DISCUSSION ABOUT OUR FUTURE PLANS.
WE ALREADY ARGUED ABOUT THIS YESTER-DAY.
YES, BUT YESTERDAY NEITHER MIKAELA NOR YUICHIRO WERE PRESENT.

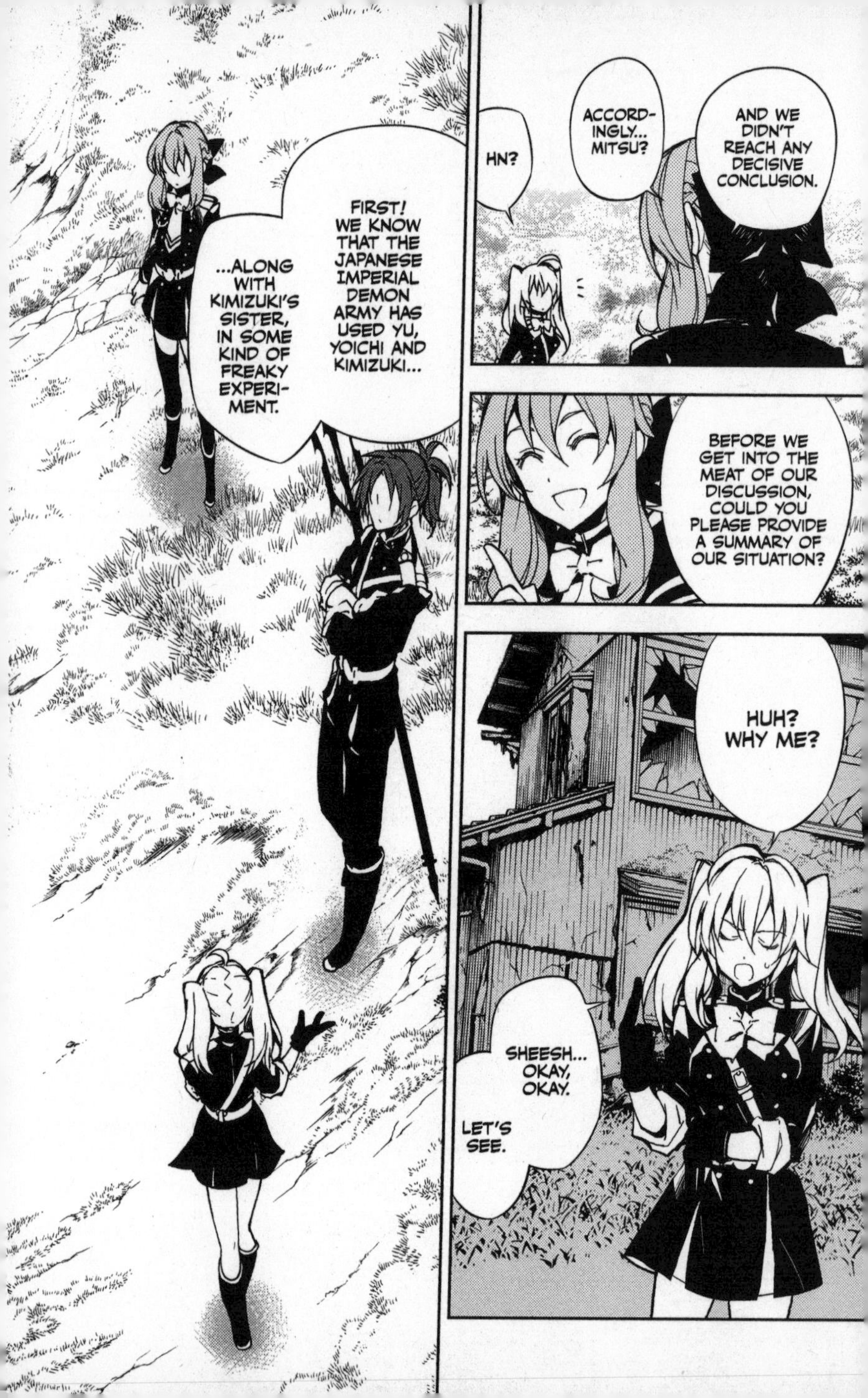
AND WE DIDN'T REACH ANY DECISIVE CONCLUSION.
ACCORD-INGLY... MITSU?
HN?
BEFORE WE GET INTO THE MEAT OF OUR DISCUSSION, COULD YOU PLEASE PROVIDE A SUMMARY OF OUR SITUATION?
HUH? WHY ME?
SHEESH... OKAY, OKAY.
LET'S SEE.
FIRST! WE KNOW THAT THE JAPANESE IMPERIAL DEMON ARMY HAS USED YU, YOICHI AND KIMIZUKI...
...ALONG WITH KIMIZUKI'S SISTER, IN SOME KIND OF FREAKY EXPERI-MENT.

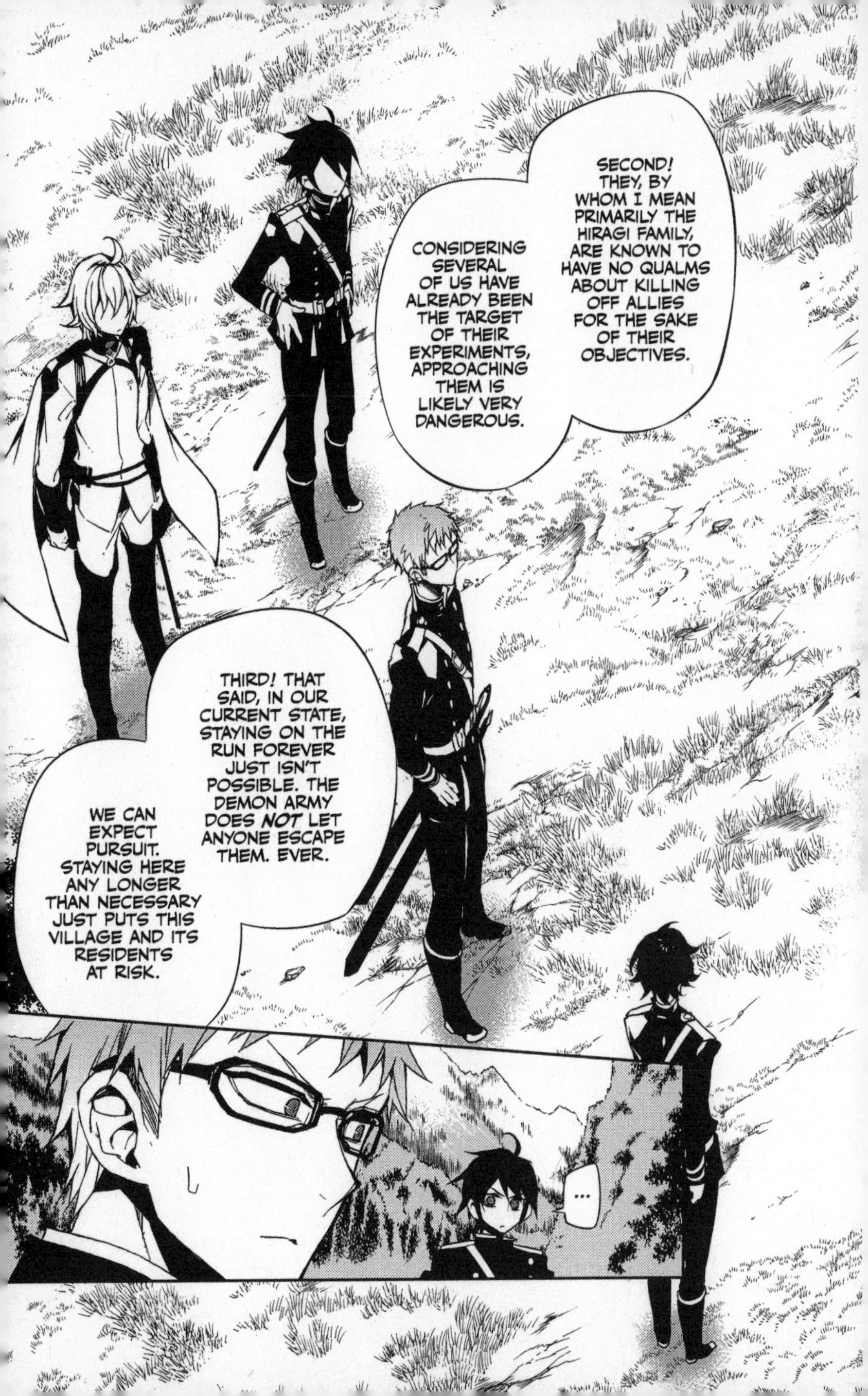
SECOND! THEY, BY WHOM I MEAN PRIMARILY THE HIRAGI FAMILY, ARE KNOWN TO HAVE NO QUALMS ABOUT KILLING OFF ALLIES FOR THE SAKE OF THEIR OBJECTIVES.
CONSIDERING SEVERAL OF US HAVE ALREADY BEEN THE TARGET OF THEIR EXPERIMENTS, APPROACHING THEM IS LIKELY VERY DANGEROUS.
THIRD! THAT SAID, IN OUR CURRENT STATE, STAYING ON THE RUN FOREVER JUST ISN'T POSSIBLE. THE DEMON ARMY DOES *NOT* LET ANYONE ESCAPE THEM. EVER.
WE CAN EXPECT PURSUIT. STAYING HERE ANY LONGER THAN NECESSARY JUST PUTS THIS VILLAGE AND ITS RESIDENTS AT RISK.
...

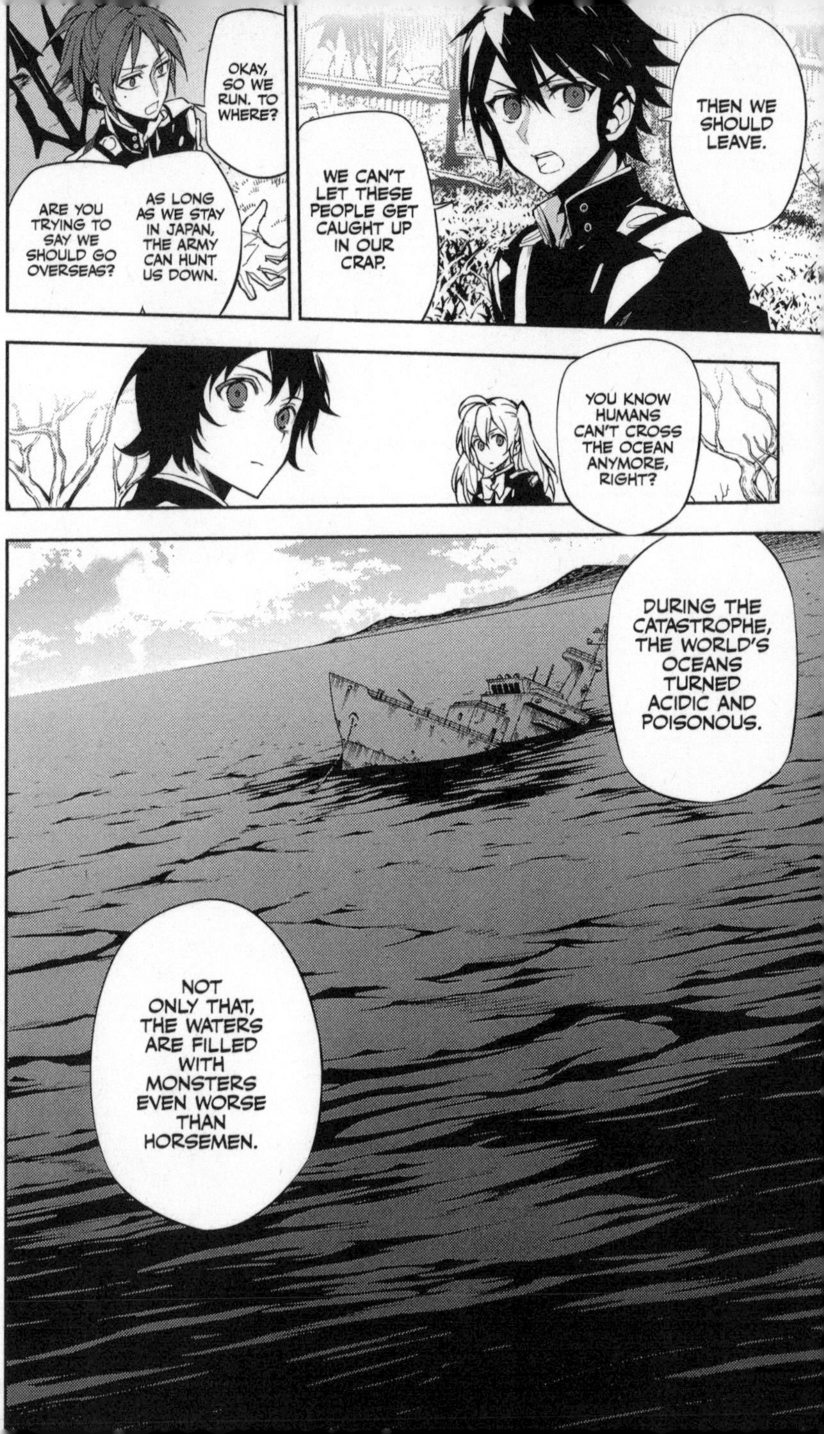
THEN WE SHOULD LEAVE.
WE CAN'T LET THESE PEOPLE GET CAUGHT UP IN OUR CRAP.
OKAY, SO WE RUN. TO WHERE?
AS LONG AS WE STAY IN JAPAN, THE ARMY CAN HUNT US DOWN.
ARE YOU TRYING TO SAY WE SHOULD GO OVERSEAS?
YOU KNOW HUMANS CAN'T CROSS THE OCEAN ANYMORE, RIGHT?
DURING THE CATASTROPHE, THE WORLD'S OCEANS TURNED ACIDIC AND POISONOUS.
NOT ONLY THAT, THE WATERS ARE FILLED WITH MONSTERS EVEN WORSE THAN HORSEMEN.

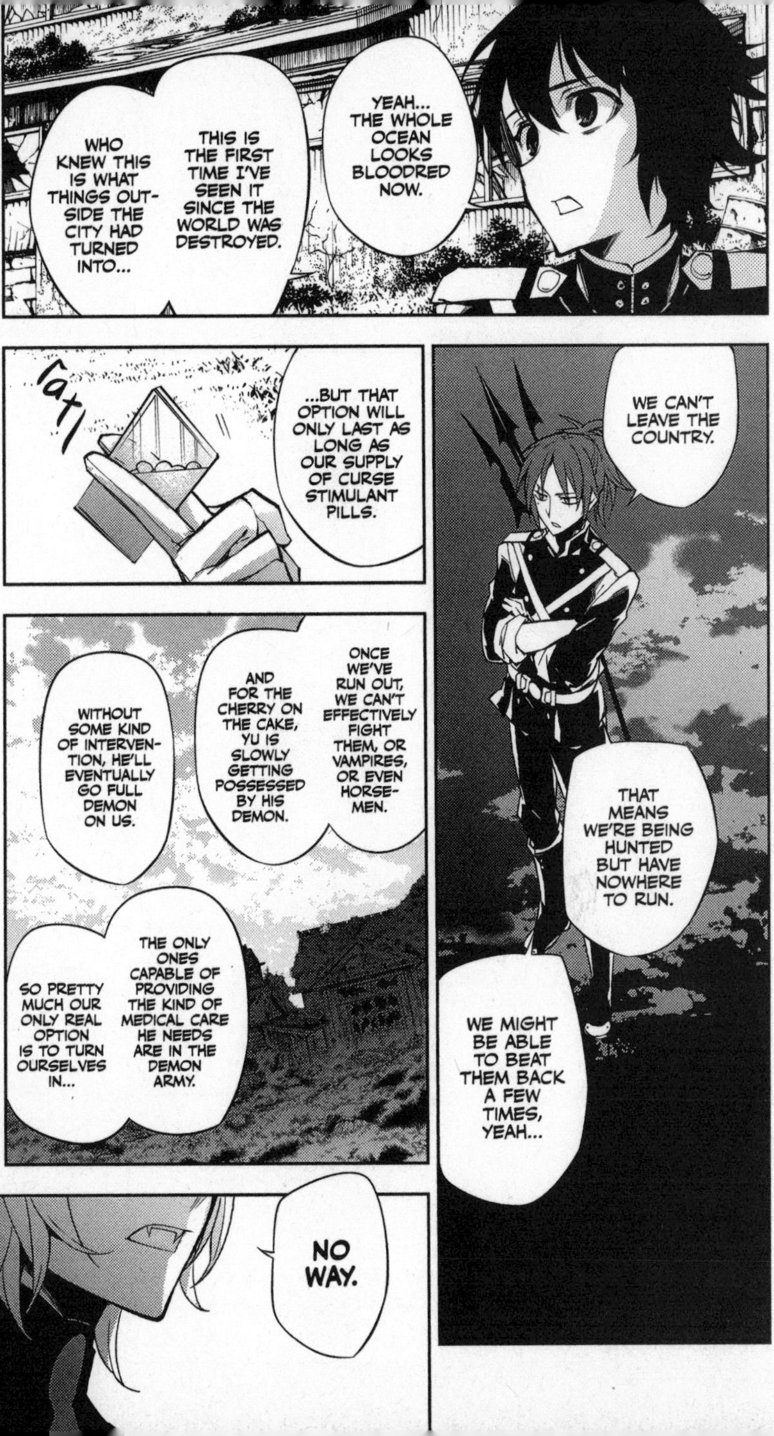
YEAH... THE WHOLE OCEAN LOOKS BLOODRED NOW.
THIS IS THE FIRST TIME I'VE SEEN IT SINCE THE WORLD WAS DESTROYED.
WHO KNEW THIS IS WHAT THINGS OUT-SIDE THE CITY HAD TURNED INTO...
WE CAN'T LEAVE THE COUNTRY.
THAT MEANS WE'RE BEING HUNTED BUT HAVE NOWHERE TO RUN.
WE MIGHT BE ABLE TO BEAT THEM BACK A FEW TIMES, YEAH...
...BUT THAT OPTION WILL ONLY LAST AS LONG AS OUR SUPPLY OF CURSE STIMULANT PILLS.
ONCE WE'VE RUN OUT, WE CAN'T EFFECTIVELY FIGHT THEM, OR VAMPIRES, OR EVEN HORSE-MEN.
AND FOR THE CHERRY ON THE CAKE, YU IS SLOWLY GETTING POSSESSED BY HIS DEMON.
WITHOUT SOME KIND OF INTERVEN-TION, HE'LL EVENTUALLY GO FULL DEMON ON US.
THE ONLY ONES CAPABLE OF PROVIDING THE KIND OF MEDICAL CARE HE NEEDS ARE IN THE DEMON ARMY.
SO PRETTY MUCH OUR ONLY REAL OPTION IS TO TURN OURSELVES IN...
NO WAY.

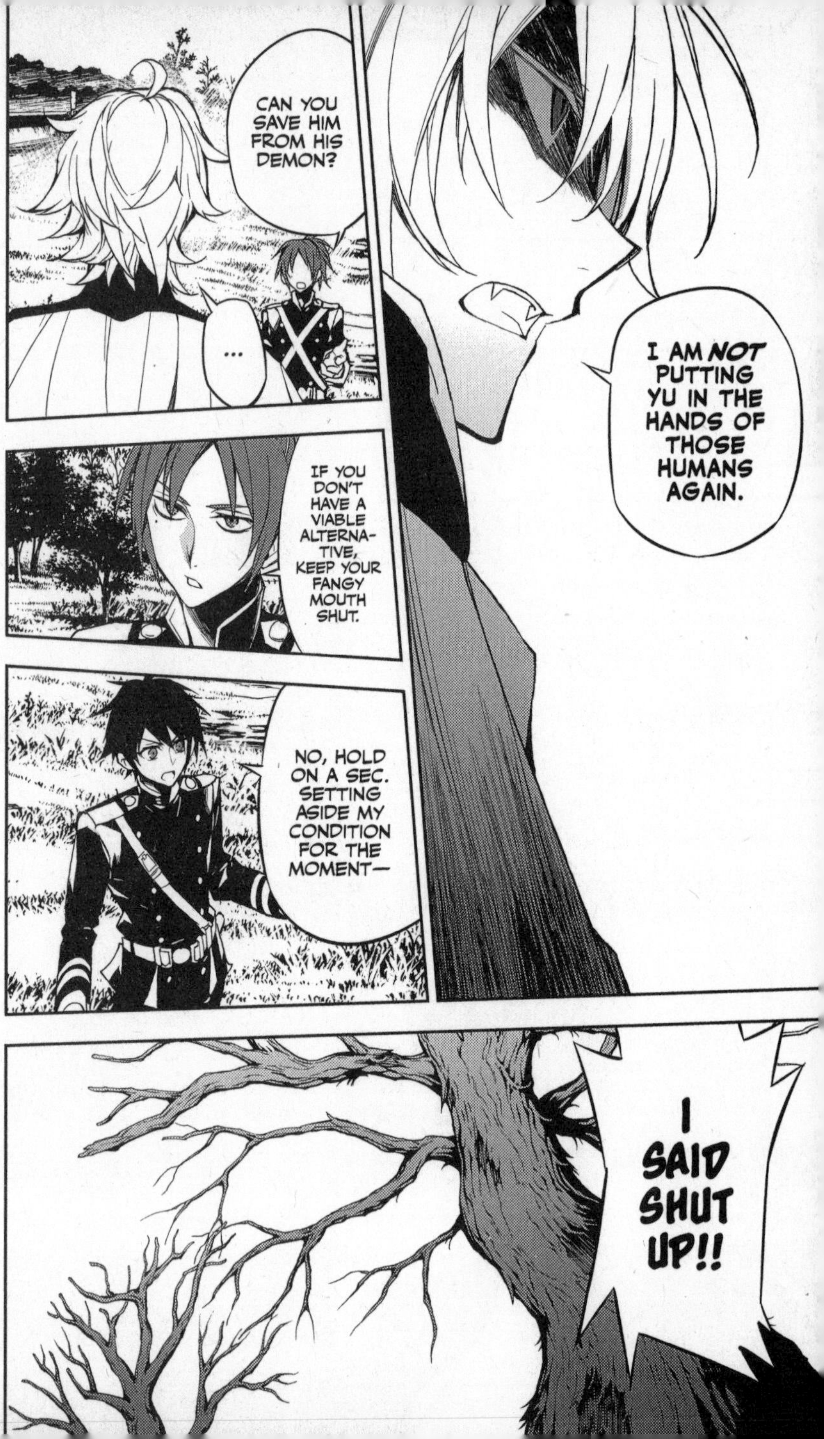
I AM *NOT* PUTTING YU IN THE HANDS OF THOSE HUMANS AGAIN.
CAN YOU SAVE HIM FROM HIS DEMON?
...
IF YOU DON'T HAVE A VIABLE ALTERNA-TIVE, KEEP YOUR FANGY MOUTH SHUT.
NO, HOLD ON A SEC. SETTING ASIDE MY CONDITION FOR THE MOMENT—
I SAID SHUT UP!!

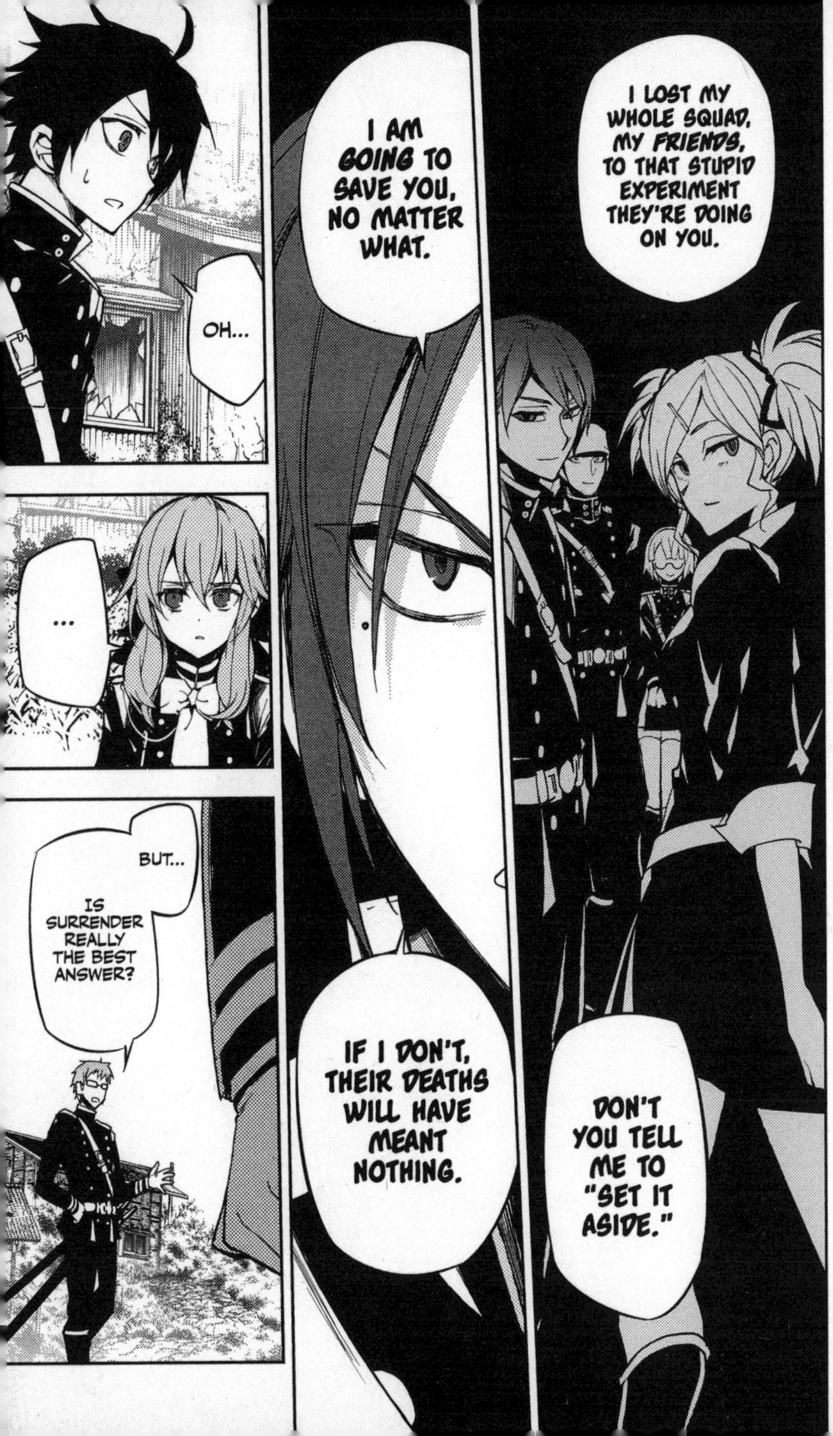
I LOST MY WHOLE SQUAD, MY FRIENDS, TO THAT STUPID EXPERIMENT THEY'RE DOING ON YOU.
DON'T YOU TELL ME TO "SET IT ASIDE."
I AM GOING TO SAVE YOU, NO MATTER WHAT.
IF I DON'T, THEIR DEATHS WILL HAVE MEANT NOTHING.
OH...
...
BUT...
IS SURRENDER REALLY THE BEST ANSWER?

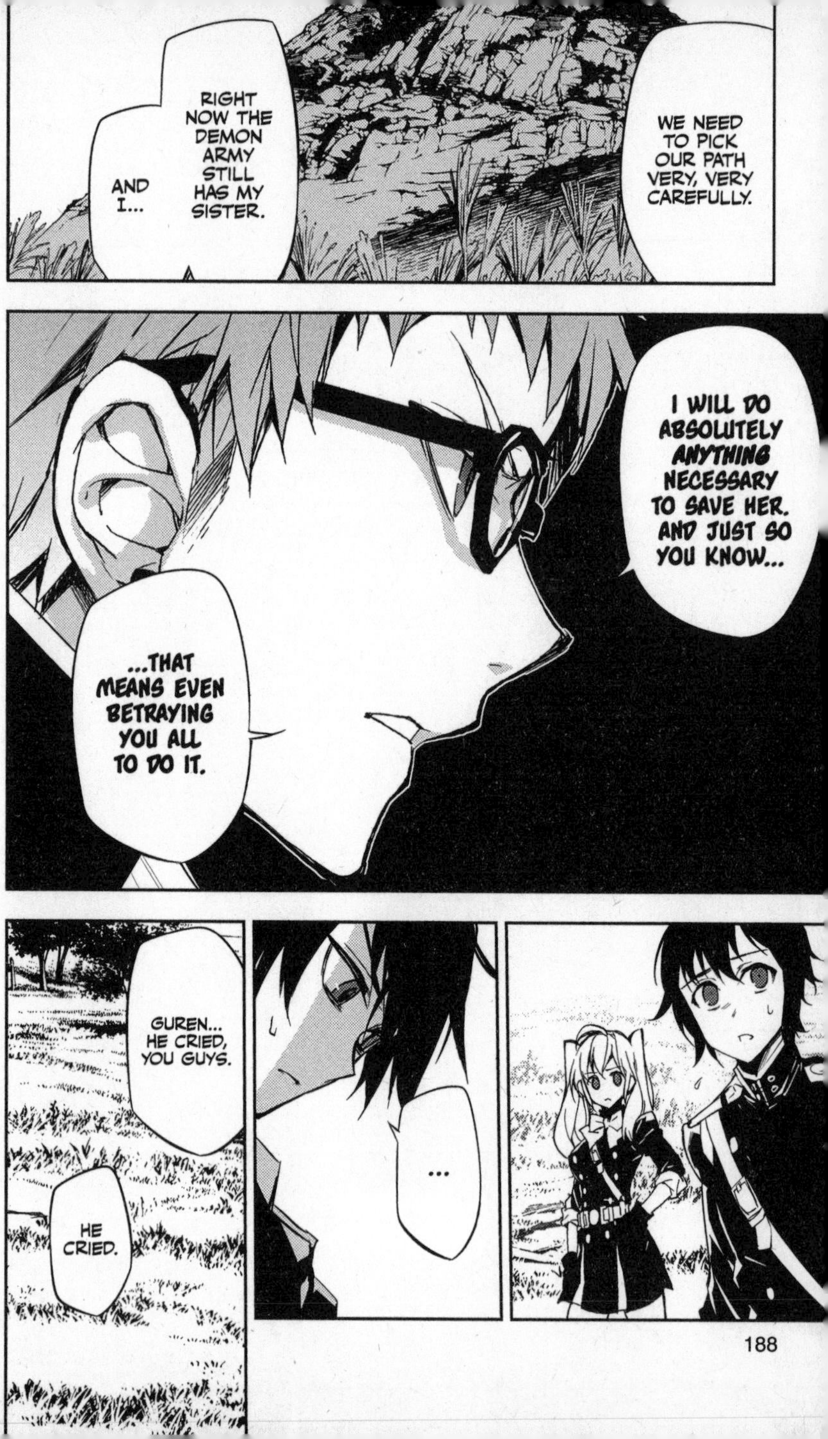
WE NEED TO PICK OUR PATH VERY, VERY CAREFULLY.
RIGHT NOW THE DEMON ARMY STILL HAS MY SISTER.
AND I...
I WILL DO ABSOLUTELY ANYTHING NECESSARY TO SAVE HER. AND JUST SO YOU KNOW...
...THAT MEANS EVEN BETRAYING YOU ALL TO DO IT.
...
GUREN... HE CRIED, YOU GUYS.
HE CRIED.

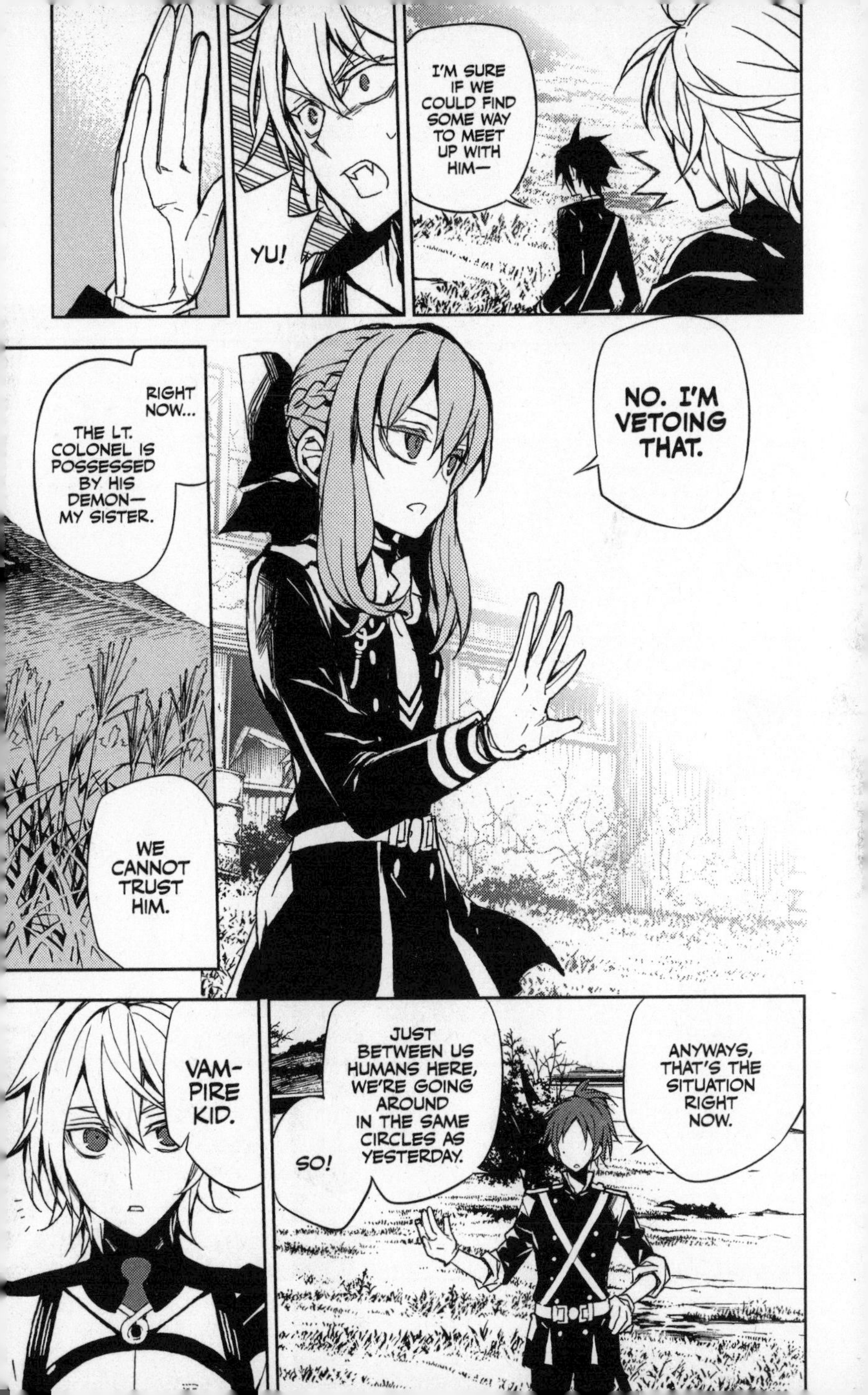
I'M SURE IF WE COULD FIND SOME WAY TO MEET UP WITH HIM—
YU!
NO. I'M VETOING THAT.
RIGHT NOW...
THE LT. COLONEL IS POSSESSED BY HIS DEMON— MY SISTER.
WE CANNOT TRUST HIM.
ANYWAYS, THAT'S THE SITUATION RIGHT NOW.
JUST BETWEEN US HUMANS HERE, WE'RE GOING AROUND IN THE SAME CIRCLES AS YESTERDAY.
SO!
VAM-PIRE KID.

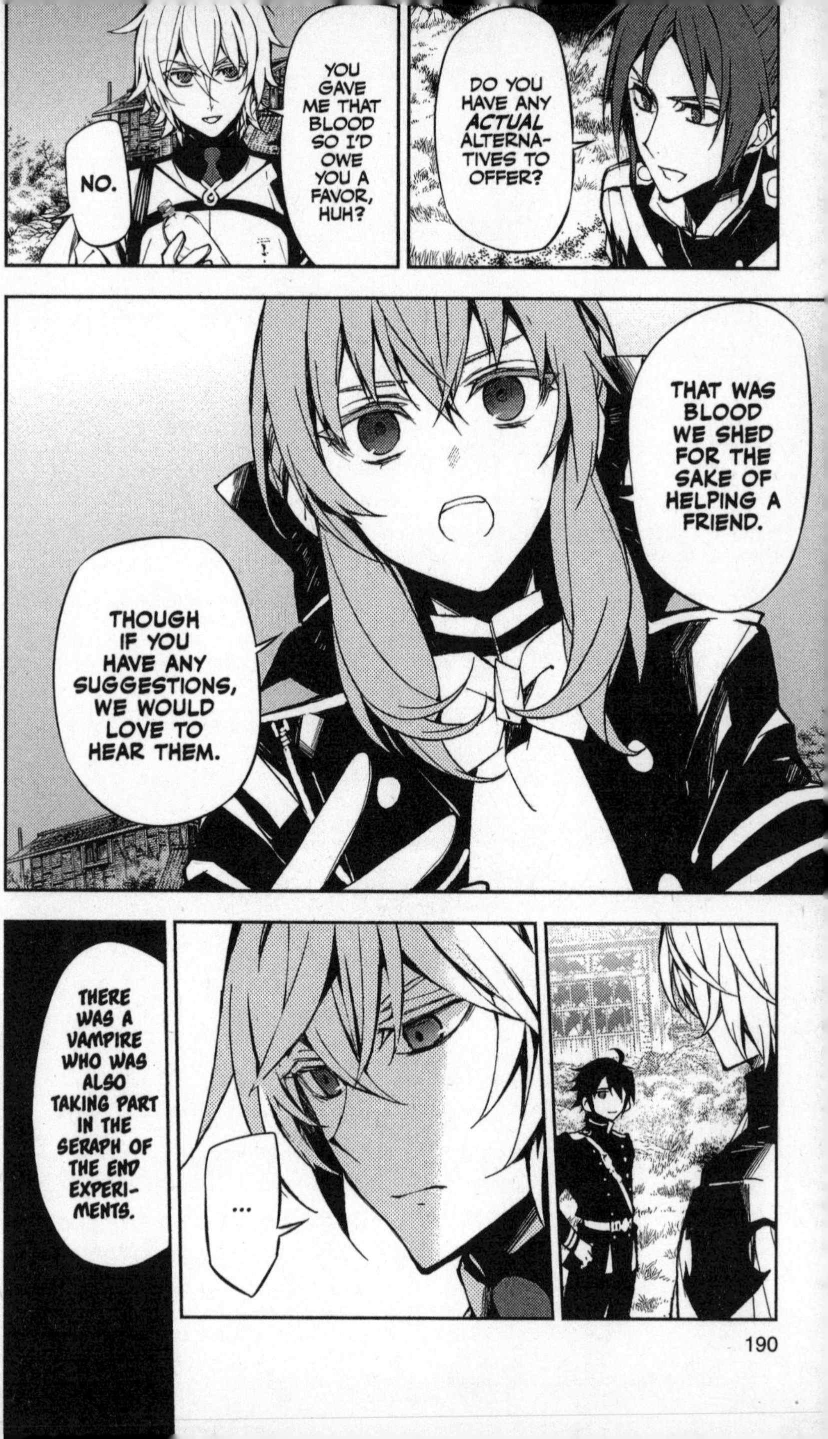
DO YOU HAVE ANY ACTUAL ALTERNATIVES TO OFFER?
YOU GAVE ME THAT BLOOD SO I'D OWE YOU A FAVOR, HUH?
NO.
THAT WAS BLOOD WE SHED FOR THE SAKE OF HELPING A FRIEND.
THOUGH IF YOU HAVE ANY SUGGESTIONS, WE WOULD LOVE TO HEAR THEM.
...
THERE WAS A VAMPIRE WHO WAS ALSO TAKING PART IN THE SERAPH OF THE END EXPERIMENTS.

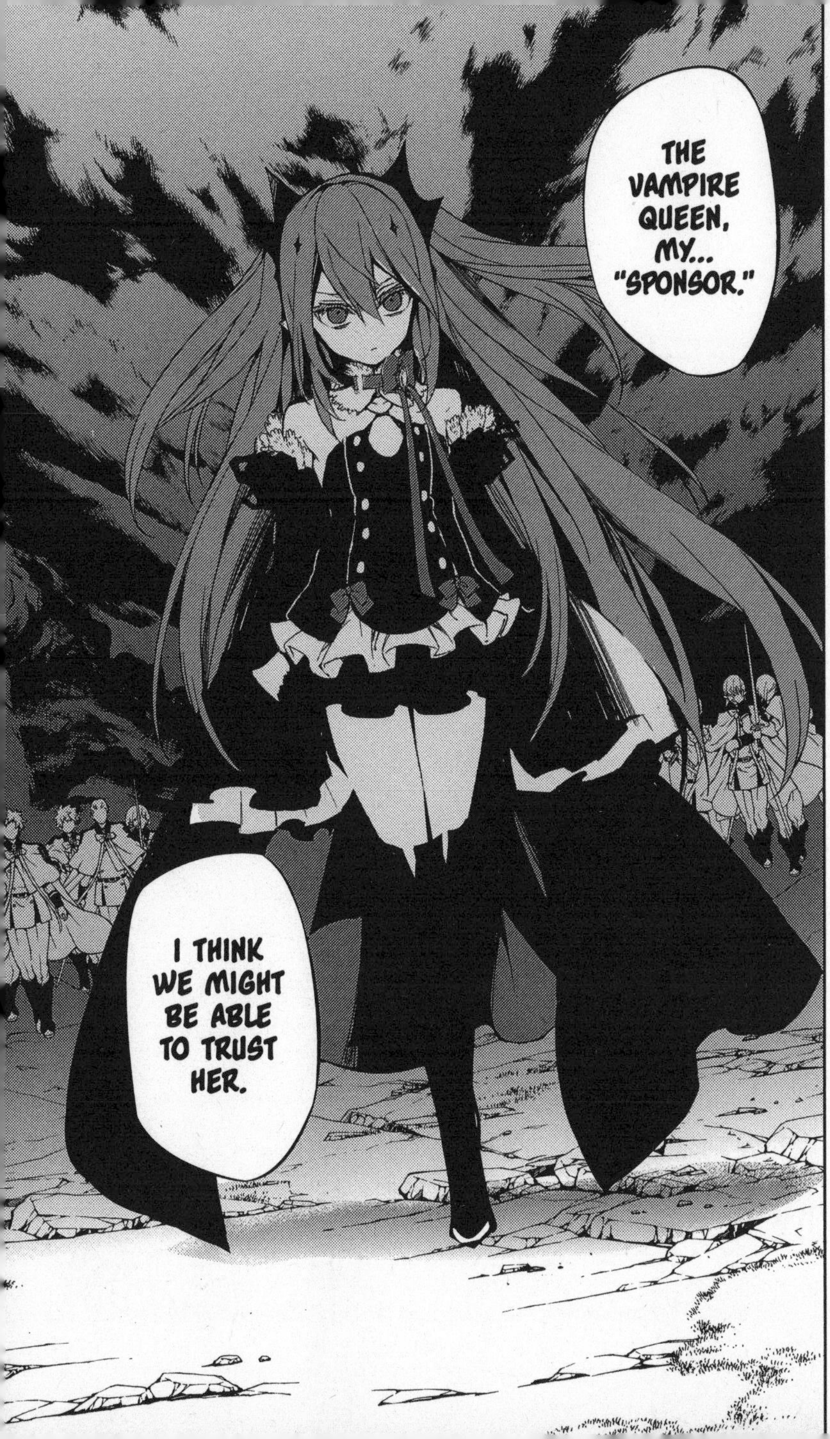
THE VAMPIRE QUEEN, MY... "SPONSOR."
I THINK WE MIGHT BE ABLE TO TRUST HER.

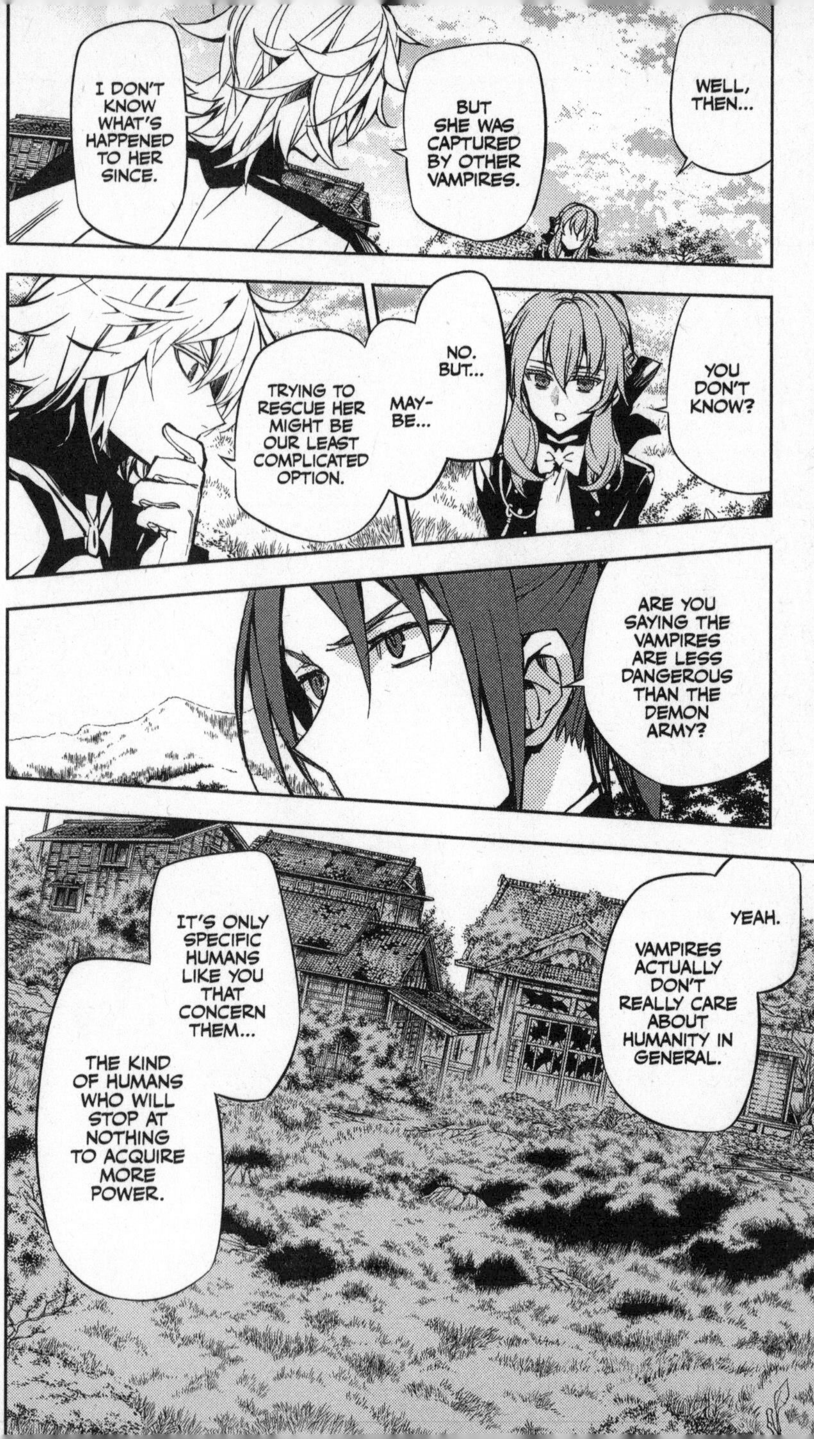
WELL, THEN...
BUT SHE WAS CAPTURED BY OTHER VAMPIRES.
I DON'T KNOW WHAT'S HAPPENED TO HER SINCE.
YOU DON'T KNOW?
NO. BUT...
MAY-BE...
TRYING TO RESCUE HER MIGHT BE OUR LEAST COMPLICATED OPTION.
ARE YOU SAYING THE VAMPIRES ARE LESS DANGEROUS THAN THE DEMON ARMY?
YEAH.
VAMPIRES ACTUALLY DON'T REALLY CARE ABOUT HUMANITY IN GENERAL.
IT'S ONLY SPECIFIC HUMANS LIKE YOU THAT CONCERN THEM...
THE KIND OF HUMANS WHO WILL STOP AT NOTHING TO ACQUIRE MORE POWER.

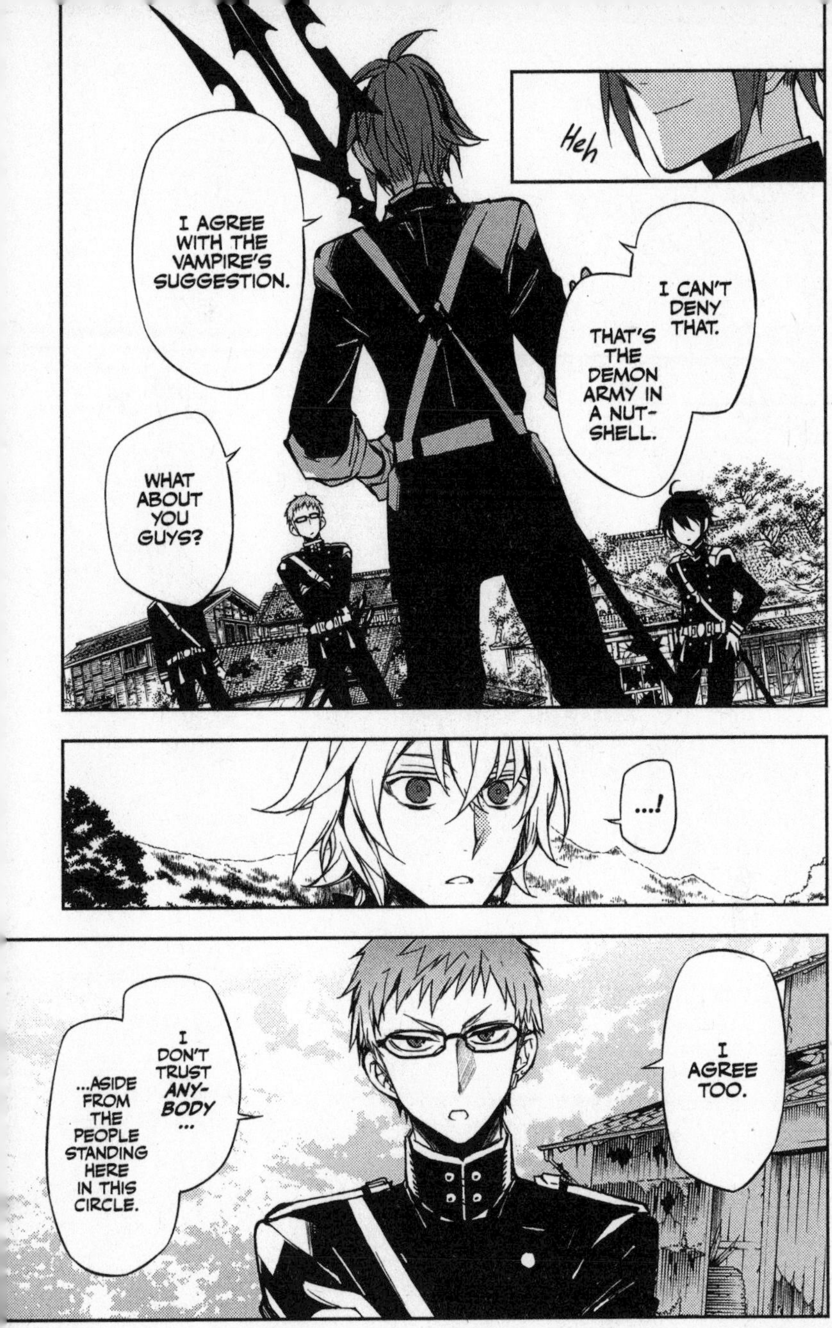
Heh
I CAN'T DENY THAT.
THAT'S THE DEMON ARMY IN A NUT-SHELL.
I AGREE WITH THE VAMPIRE'S SUGGESTION.
WHAT ABOUT YOU GUYS?
...!
I AGREE TOO.
I DON'T TRUST *ANYBODY*...
...ASIDE FROM THE PEOPLE STANDING HERE IN THIS CIRCLE.

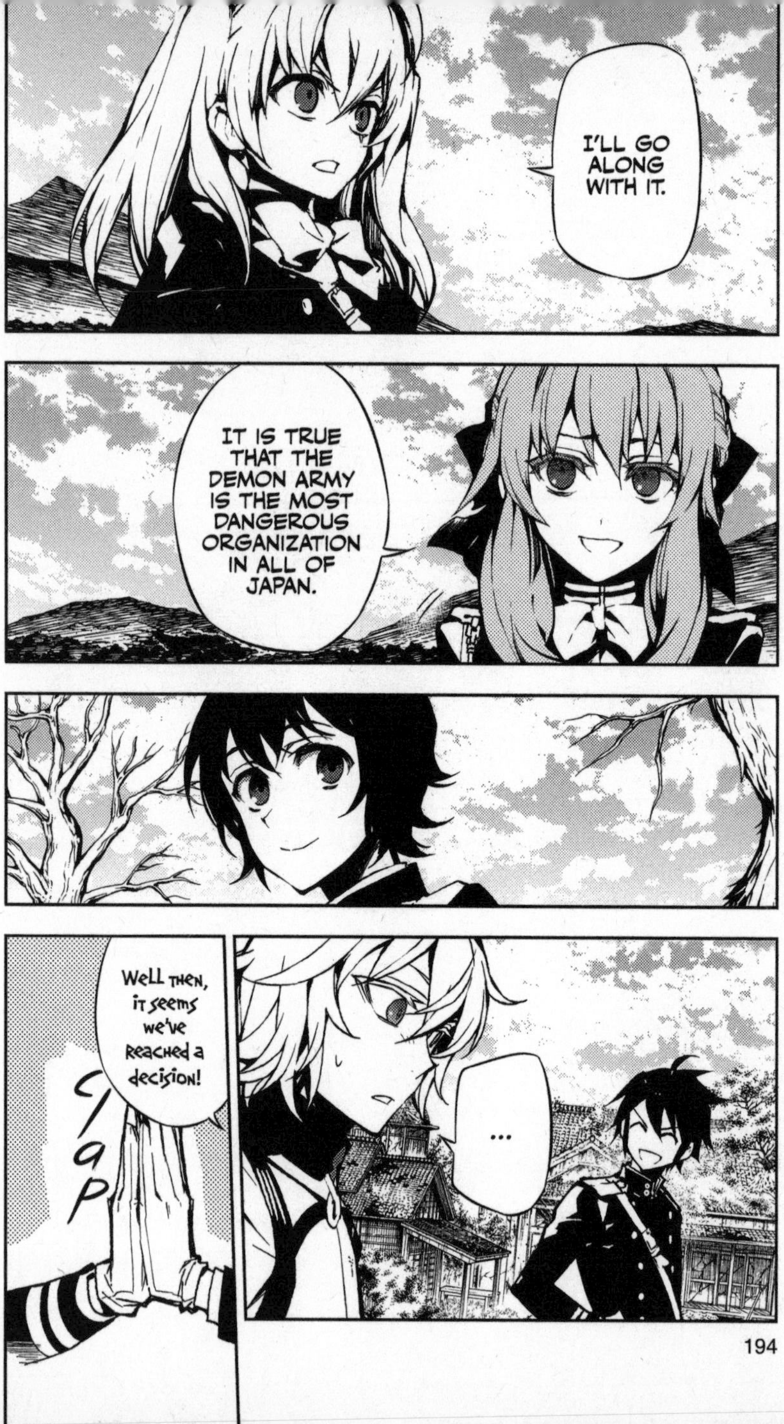
I'LL GO ALONG WITH IT.
IT IS TRUE THAT THE DEMON ARMY IS THE MOST DANGEROUS ORGANIZATION IN ALL OF JAPAN.
...
Well then, it seems we've reached a decision!
CLAP

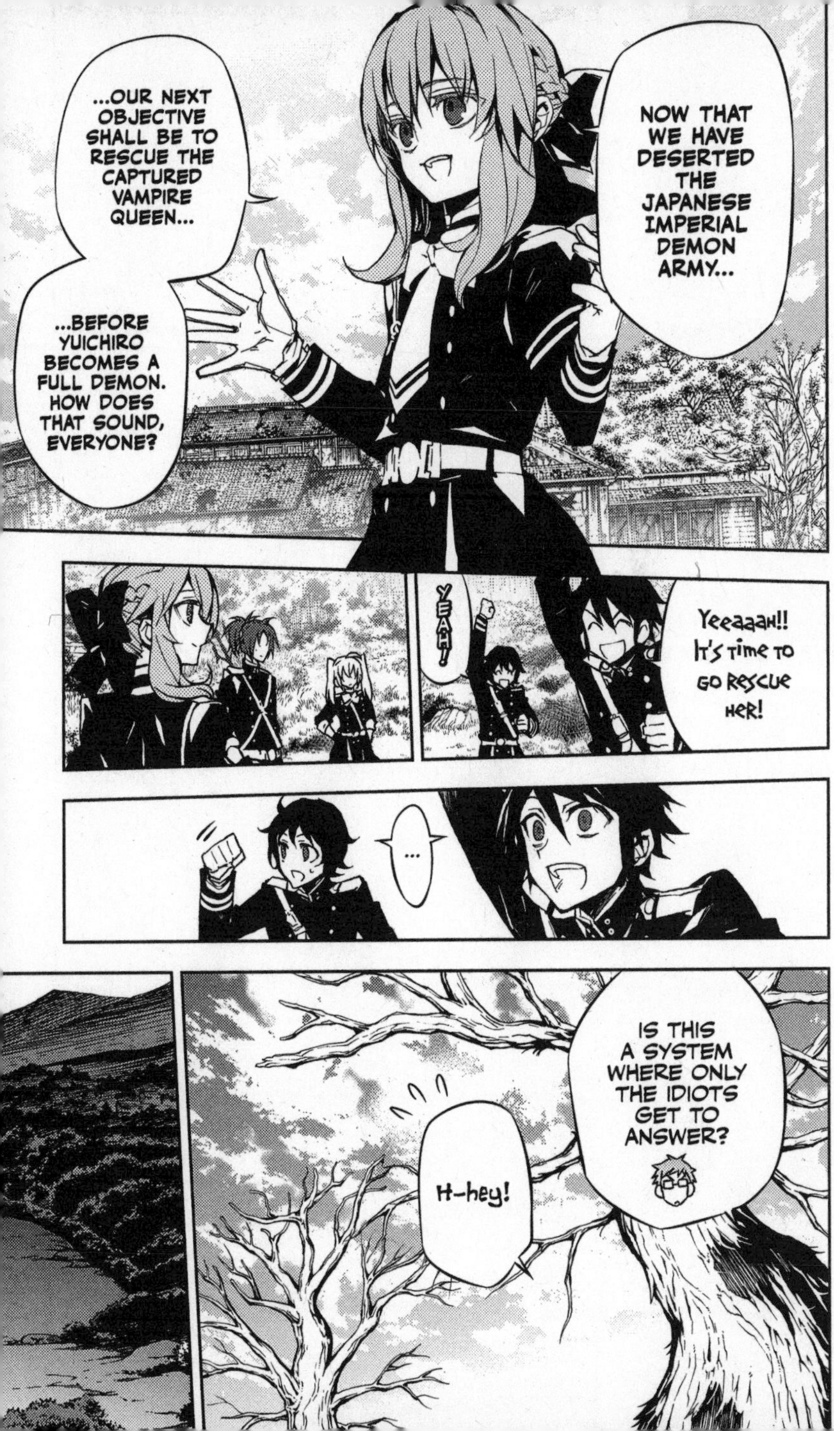
NOW THAT WE HAVE DESERTED THE JAPANESE IMPERIAL DEMON ARMY...
...OUR NEXT OBJECTIVE SHALL BE TO RESCUE THE CAPTURED VAMPIRE QUEEN...
...BEFORE YUICHIRO BECOMES A FULL DEMON. HOW DOES THAT SOUND, EVERYONE?
Yeeaaah!! It's time to go rescue her!
YEAH!
...
IS THIS A SYSTEM WHERE ONLY THE IDIOTS GET TO ANSWER?
H-hey!

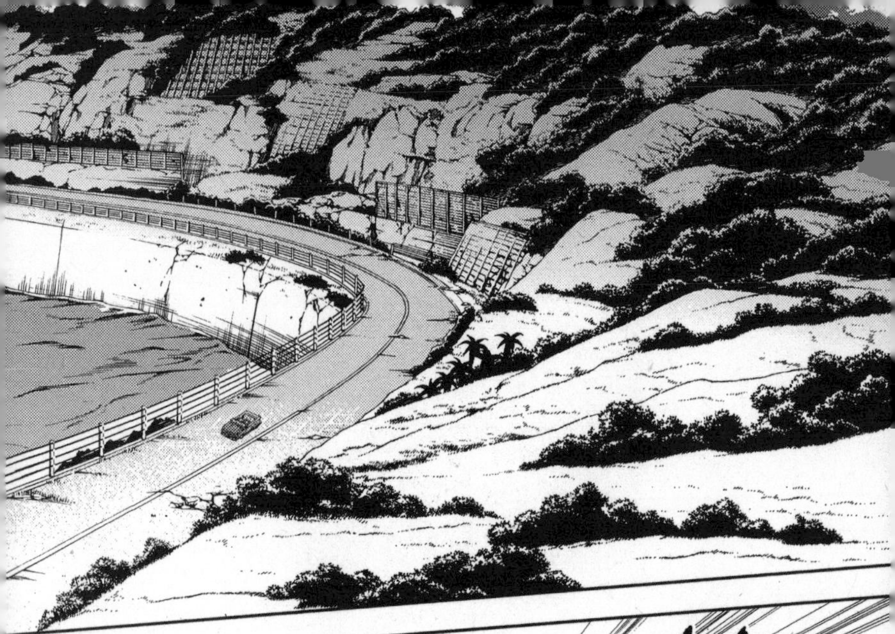
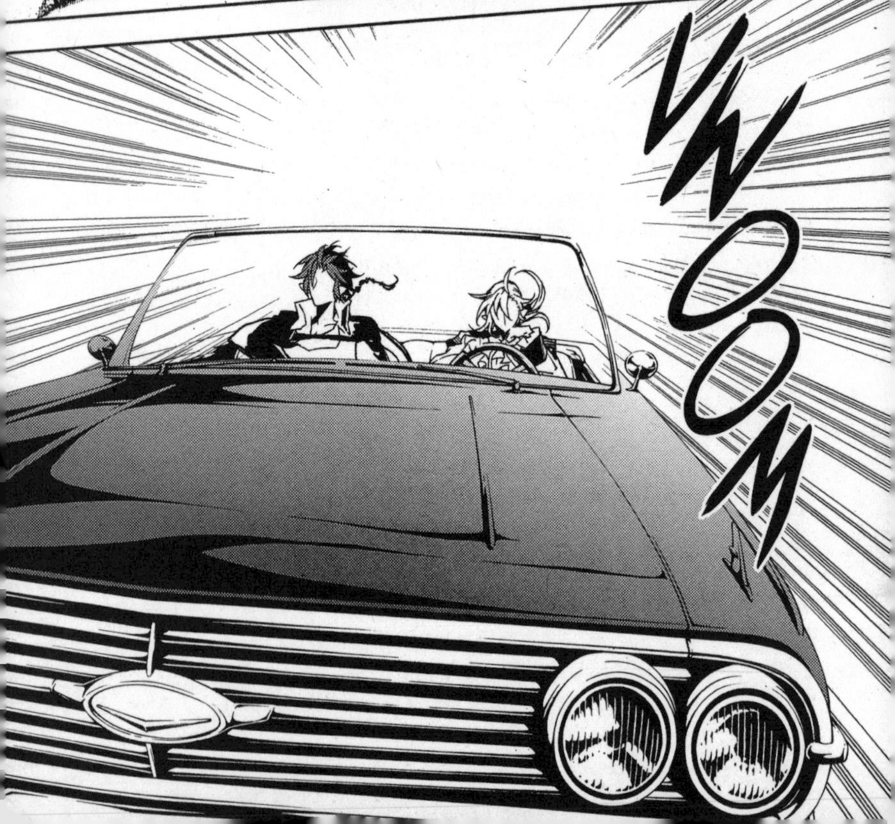
VWOOM

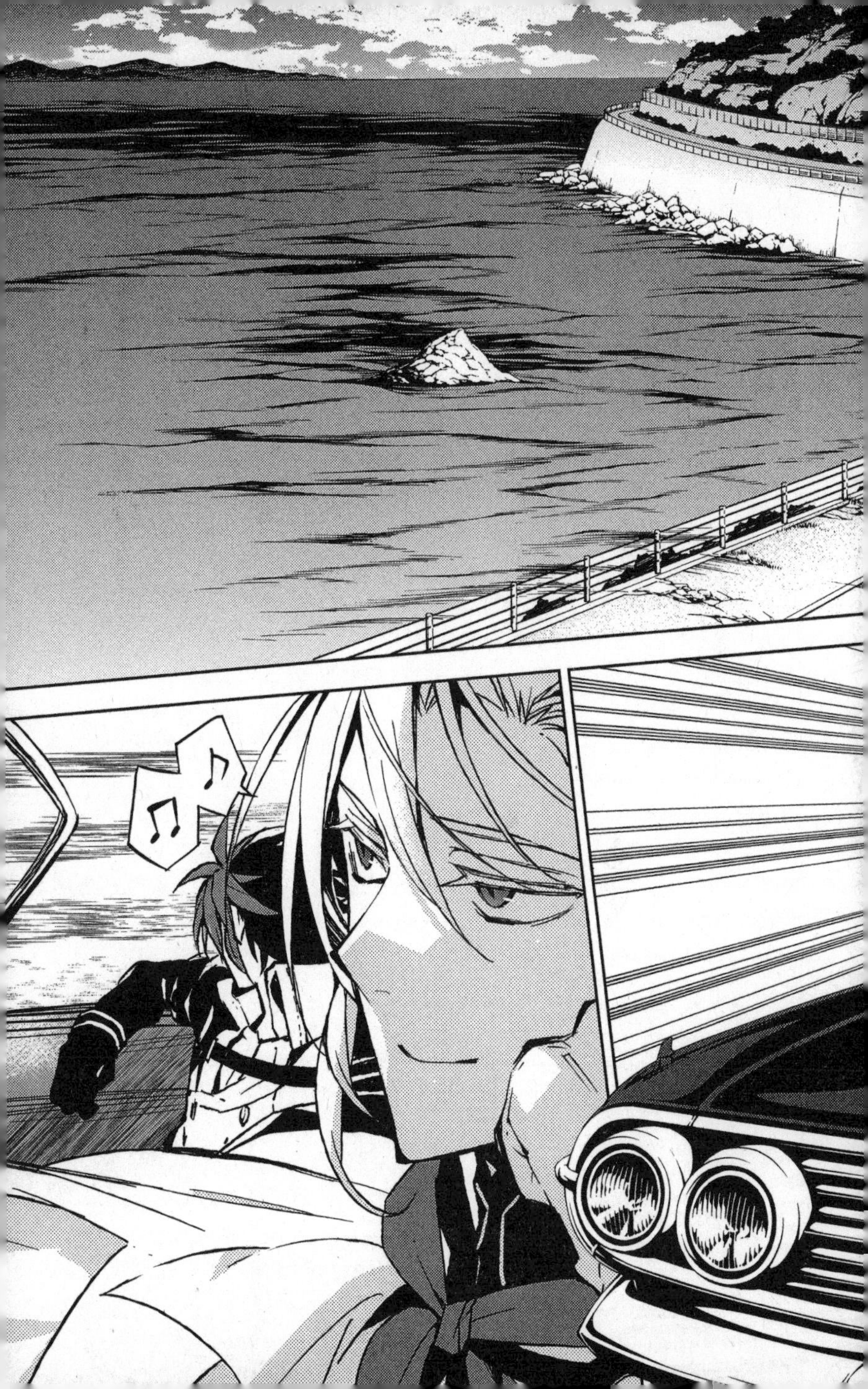

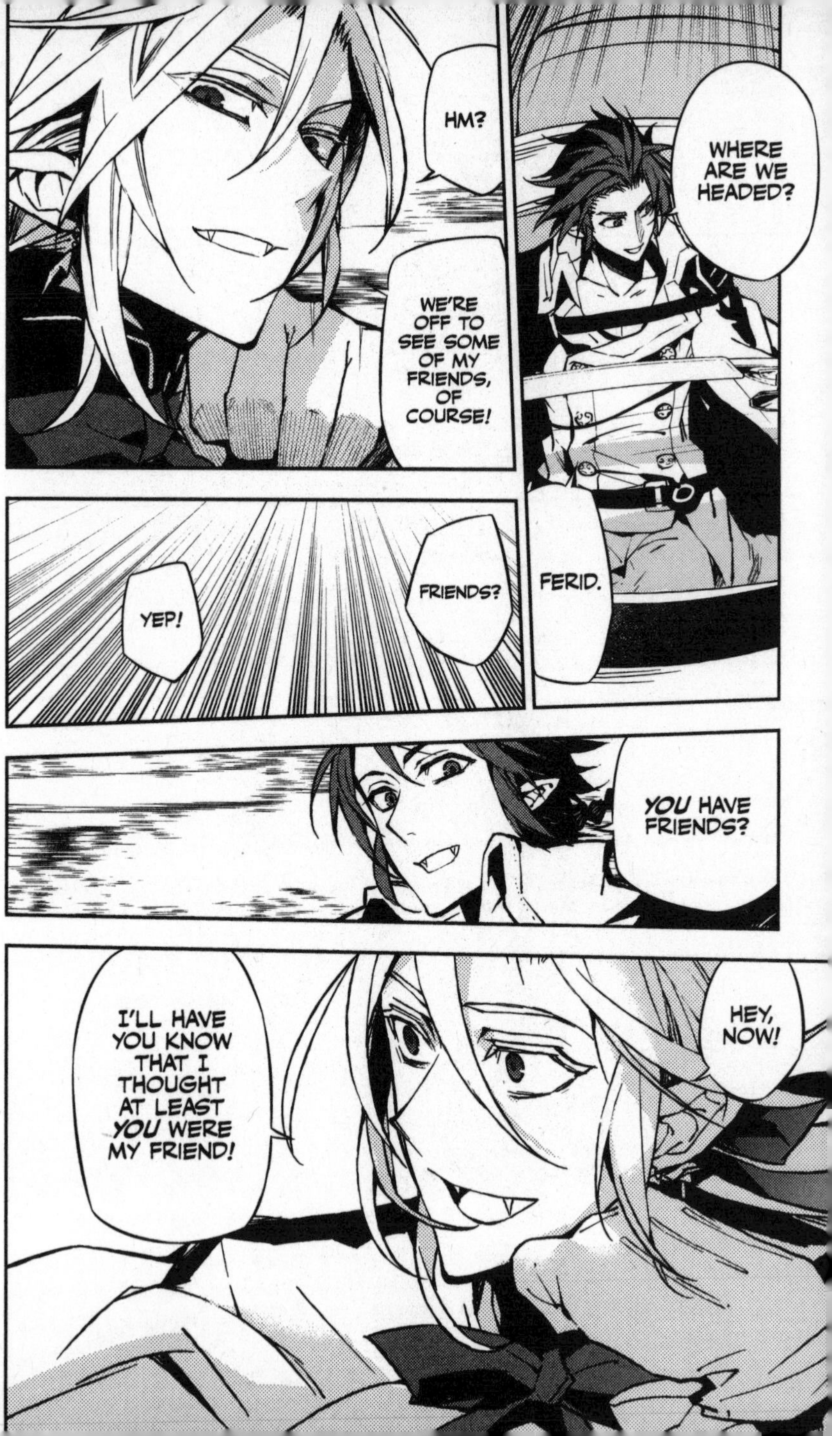
WHERE ARE WE HEADED?
FERID.
HM?
WE'RE OFF TO SEE SOME OF MY FRIENDS, OF COURSE!
FRIENDS?
YEP!
YOU HAVE FRIENDS?
HEY, NOW!
I'LL HAVE YOU KNOW THAT I THOUGHT AT LEAST *YOU* WERE MY FRIEND!

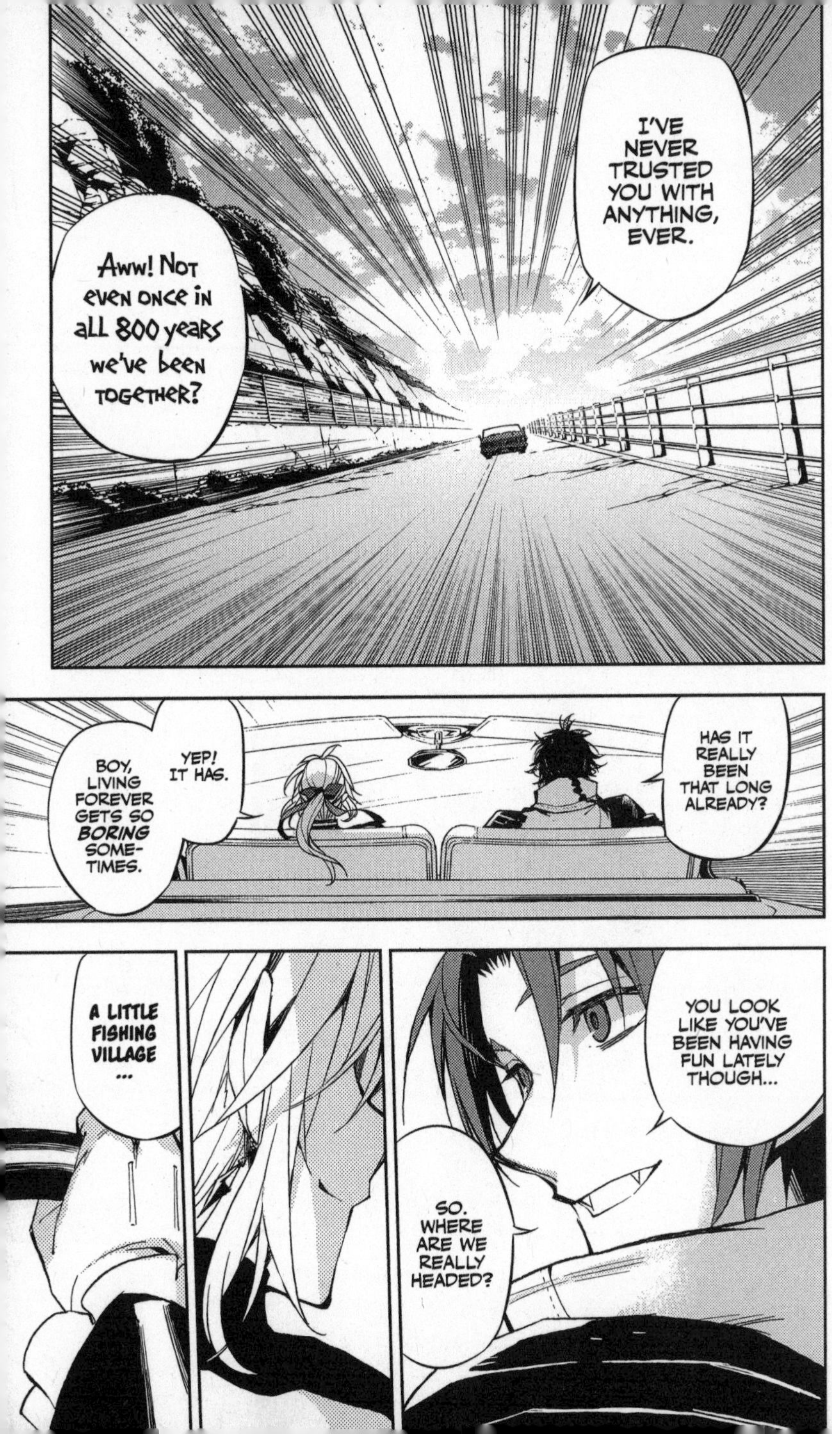
I'VE NEVER TRUSTED YOU WITH ANYTHING, EVER.
Aww! Not even once in all 800 years we've been together?
HAS IT REALLY BEEN THAT LONG ALREADY?
YEP! IT HAS.
BOY, LIVING FOREVER GETS SO *BORING* SOMETIMES.
YOU LOOK LIKE YOU'VE BEEN HAVING FUN LATELY THOUGH...
SO. WHERE ARE WE REALLY HEADED?
A LITTLE FISHING VILLAGE ...

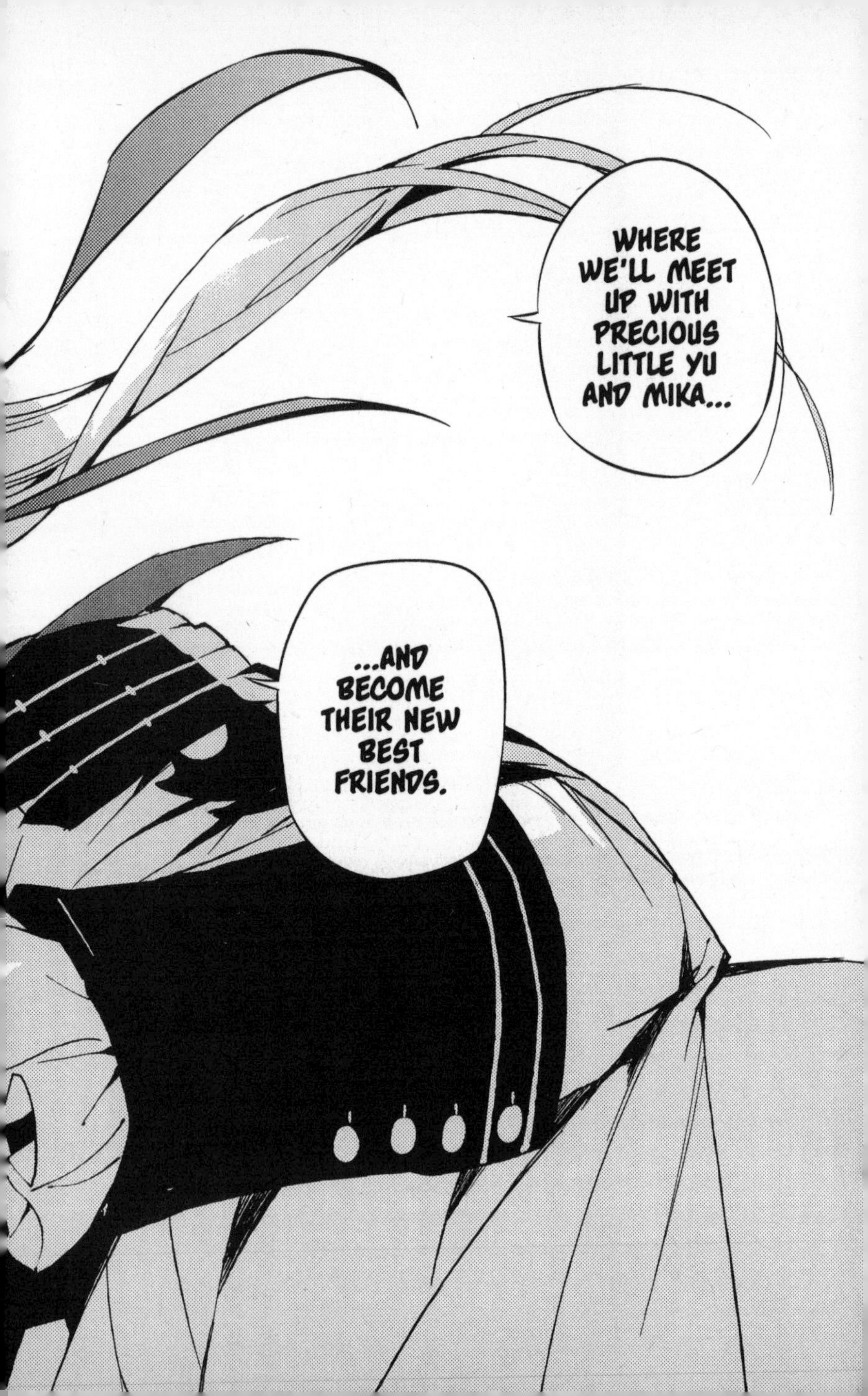
WHERE WE'LL MEET UP WITH PRECIOUS LITTLE YU AND MIKA...
...AND BECOME THEIR NEW BEST FRIENDS.

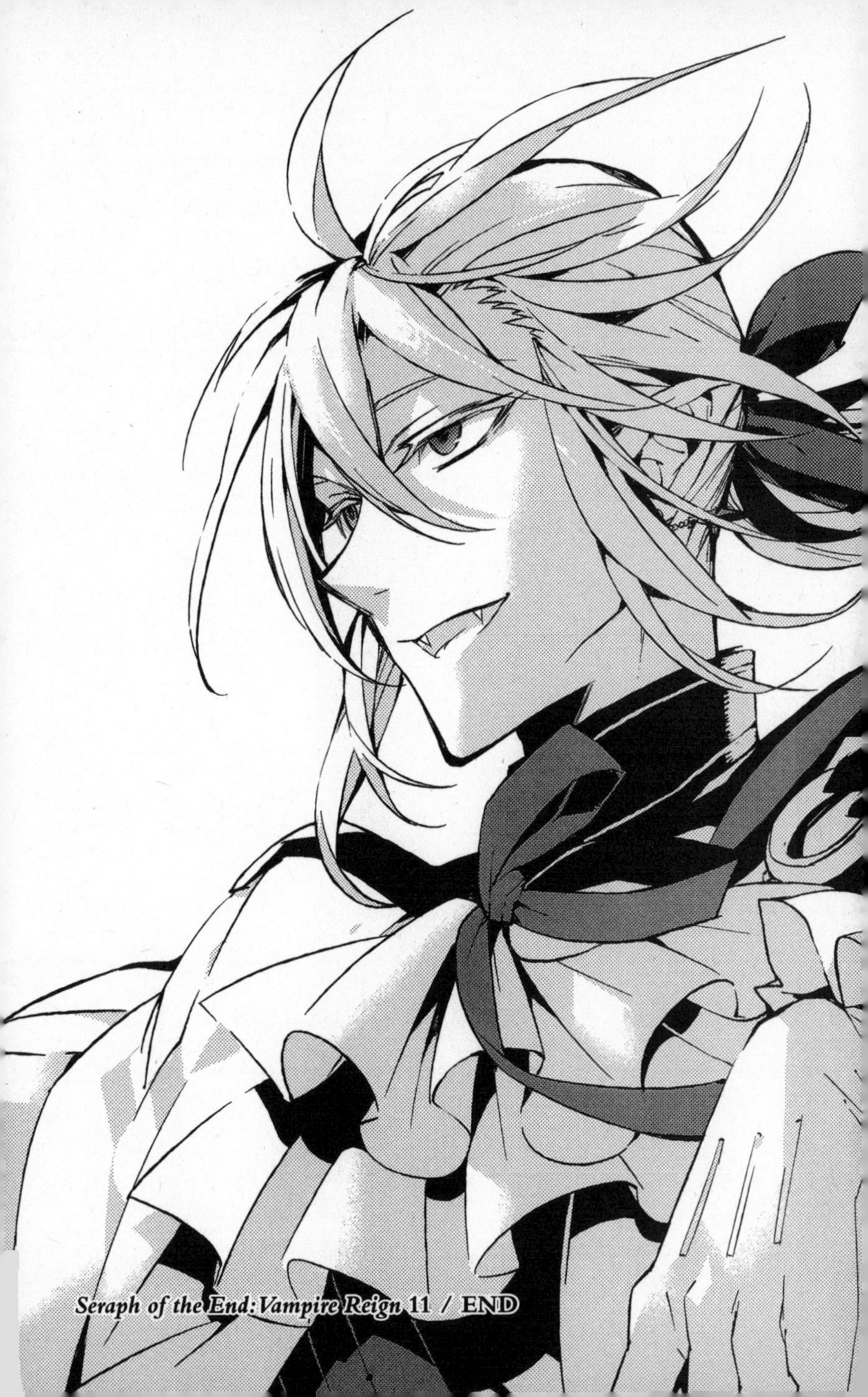
Seraph of the End: Vampire Reign 11 / END

Seraph of the End
VAMPIRE REIGN

Character Materials Collection and Afterword by Takaya Kagami

SEISHIRO HIRAGI

SEISHIRO:

"YOU'VE GOTTA BE KIDDING ME!! WHAT THE HELL IS THIS?! HOW COME I'M THE ONLY ONE TREATED LIKE A FREAKING *FOOTNOTE* IN THE AFTERWORD, GETTING CRAMMED INTO THIS TEENY SPACE?!"

Seishiro Hiragi, a pure-blooded son of the Hiragi Family, is an elite. He's a very powerful and skilled person. Really. He is. But with Kureto and Mahiru for half-siblings, along with Shinya as an adopted brother, the poor guy tends to get overshadowed and lost in the shuffle.

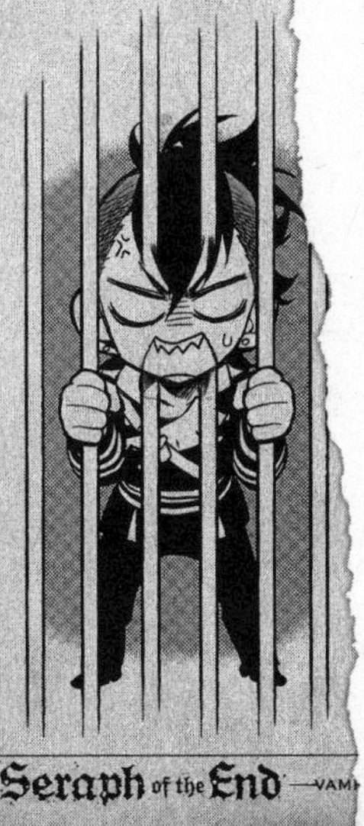

SINCE THERE ARE A WHOPPING FIVE CHAPTERS IN THIS VOLUME, WE ONLY GET THIS ONE PAGE FOR THE AFTERWORD. WITH THIS VOLUME, WE'VE FINALLY REACHED THE TITULAR "SERAPH OF THE END" ARC OF THE STORY! HAVE SOME OF YOU STARTED TO GUESS WHERE THE STORY IS GOING? FROM HERE ON OUT, I INTEND TO START BRINGING ALL THE VARIOUS STORY THREADS TOGETHER TO BUILD TOWARD A GRAND CRESCENDO. ALL THE SECRETS THAT HAVE BEEN HINTED AT SINCE VOLUME 1 WILL START SEEING THE LIGHT OF DAY. I HOPE YOU'RE LOOKING FORWARD TO IT!

ALSO, THE NOVEL *SERAPH OF THE END: GUREN ICHINOSE: CATASTROPHE AT 16* HAS FINALLY REACHED THE DAY OF THE CATASTROPHE! THIS STORY ALSO IS ABOUT TO GET REALLY INTENSE REALLY FAST. I'M EVEN SURPRISING MYSELF WITH WHERE IT WENT TO THE POINT WHERE I'M LIKE, "WAIT, THIS IS WHAT LEADS INTO THE MANGA CONTENT?" I HOPE YOU'RE AS EXCITED FOR IT AS I AM!

OH! OH! AND THEN THERE'S THE *VAMPIRE MIKAELA'S STORY* NOVEL, WHICH WILL GO EVEN FURTHER BACK, ACROSS 1,300 YEARS OF VAMPIRE HISTORY, TO TOUCH ON THE ORIGINS OF A CHARACTER WHO FINALLY STARTED TO STEP OUT ONTO CENTER STAGE AT THE END OF THIS VOLUME—FERID BATHORY. IT WILL ALSO COVER WHAT MIKAELA WAS UP TO AFTER HE WAS TURNED AND BEFORE HE REUNITED WITH YU.

ALL THREE STORIES AND THEIR MYSTERIES WILL BEGIN TO BOUNCE OFF ONE ANOTHER, PICKING UP A TON OF SPEED ALONG THE WAY. I HOPE ALL OF YOU WILL STICK AROUND FOR THE RIDE!

—TAKAYA KAGAMI

A brilliant sketch of Yuichiro by the author!

TAKAYA KAGAMI is a prolific light novelist whose works include the action and fantasy series *The Legend of the Legendary Heroes*, which has been adapted into manga, anime and a video game. His previous series, *A Dark Rabbit Has Seven Lives*, also spawned a manga and anime series.

66 I got a bad case of food poisoning and was taken by ambulance to the hospital. I drifted in and out of consciousness for hours, but I still finished *Mikaela's Story* volume 2 on time! How about that, huh?! I'm the epitome of a perfect and diligent author, write? (Really?) Anyways! The manga is entering a brand new arc. I hope you like it! 99

YAMATO YAMAMOTO, born 1983, is an artist and illustrator whose works include the *Kure-nai* manga and the light novels *Kure-nai*, *9S -Nine S-* and *Denpa Teki na Kanojo*. Both *Denpa Teki na Kanojo* and *Kure-nai* have been adapted into anime.

66 Volume 11 is the beginning of a brand new arc. I'm going to give it my all with renewed enthusiasm. I hope you all enjoy it!! 99

DAISUKE FURUYA previously assisted Yamato Yamamoto with storyboards for *Kure-nai*.

Seraph of the End
—VAMPIRE REIGN—

VOLUME 11
SHONEN JUMP ADVANCED MANGA EDITION

STORY BY **TAKAYA KAGAMI**
ART BY **YAMATO YAMAMOTO**
STORYBOARDS BY **DAISUKE FURUYA**

TRANSLATION **Adrienne Beck**
TOUCH-UP ART & LETTERING **Sabrina Heep**
DESIGN **Shawn Carrico**
EDITOR **Marlene First**

OWARI NO SERAPH © 2012 by Takaya Kagami,
Yamato Yamamoto, Daisuke Furuya
All rights reserved. First published in Japan in 2012 by SHUEISHA Inc., Tokyo.
English translation rights arranged by SHUEISHA Inc.

Printed in the U.S.A.

Published by VIZ Media, LLC
P.O. Box 77010
San Francisco, CA 94107

10 9 8 7 6 5 4 3 2 1
First printing, January 2017

PARENTAL ADVISORY
SERAPH OF THE END is rated T+ for Teen and
is recommended for ages 16 and up. This
volume contains violence and some adult themes.
ratings.viz.com

RATED **T+** FOR OLDER TEEN

www.viz.com   www.shonenjump.com

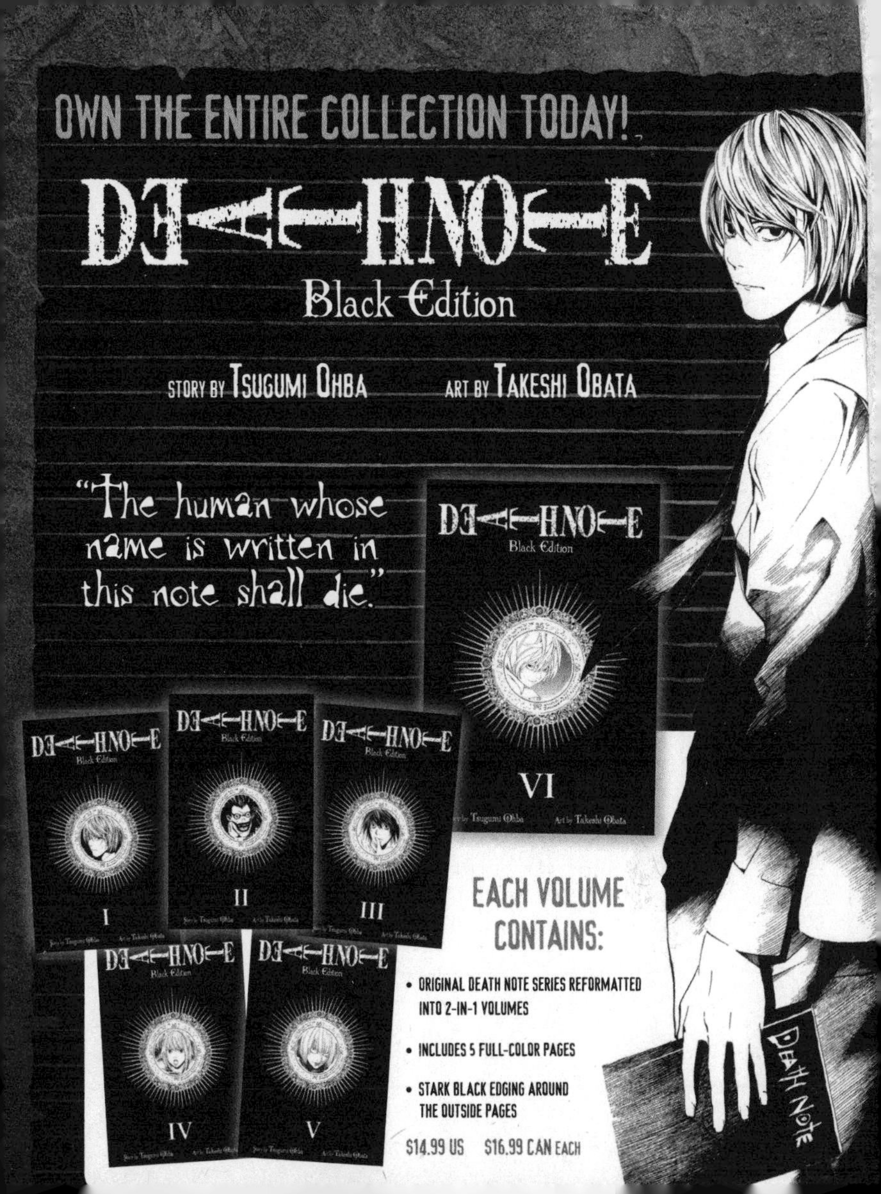
OWN THE ENTIRE COLLECTION TODAY!
DEATH NOTE
Black Edition
STORY BY TSUGUMI OHBA
ART BY TAKESHI OBATA
"The human whose name is written in this note shall die."
I
II
III
IV
V
VI
EACH VOLUME CONTAINS:
• ORIGINAL DEATH NOTE SERIES REFORMATTED INTO 2-IN-1 VOLUMES
• INCLUDES 5 FULL-COLOR PAGES
• STARK BLACK EDGING AROUND THE OUTSIDE PAGES
$14.99 US $16.99 CAN EACH
DEATH NOTE

YOU'RE READING THE
WRONG
WAY!

SERAPH OF THE END reads from right to left, starting in the upper-right corner. Japanese is read from right to left, meaning that action, sound effects, and word-balloon order are completely reversed from English order.

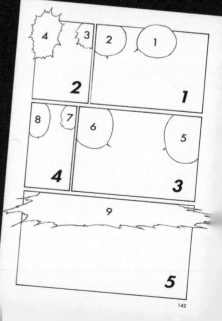